Praise for Tom

'Harper effortlessly draws the reader into an unfamiliar time, bringing alive the characters and their motivations.'
Publisher's Weekly on *Knights of the Cross*

'Tom Harper has been writing elaborate thrillers that marry ironclad narrative skills with some of the most elegantly understated writing in the field; he's the thinking person's Dan Brown.'
Barry Forshaw, author of *The Rough Guide to Crime Writing*

'Pacy, sharp and beautifully described, it's one of those books for which the cliché "hard to put down" is happily true.'
SFX on *Zodiac Station*

'A thrilling, chilling rollercoaster ride – Tom Harper's *Zodiac Station* is a breakneck read but also the kind of novel that sticks in the memory long after you put it down. Highly recommended!'
William Ryan, author of *The Holy Thief*

'As one would expect from a Tom Harper thriller, the plot is deliciously clever and is as twisty as you could wish for...'
For Winter Nights on *Zodiac Station*

'Harper is a master storyteller. This story reminded me deliciously of Hammond Innes at his very peak.'
Peter James, author of *Perfect People*

Also by Tom Harper

Lost Temple
The Book of Secrets
The Lazarus Vault
Secrets of the Dead
The Orpheus Descent
Zodiac Station

The Crusade Series
The Mosaic of Shadows
Knights of the Cross
Siege of Heaven

TOM HARPER

BLACK RIVER

HODDER

First published in Great Britain in 2015 by Hodder & Stoughton
An Hachette UK company

First published in paperback in 2016

1

Copyright © Tom Harper 2015

A CIP catalogue record for this title is available from the British Library

ISBN 978 1 444 73147 7

Typeset in Plantin Light by Palimpsest Book Production Limited,
Falkirk, Stirlingshire

Printed and bound by Clays Ltd, St Ives plc

Hodder & Stoughton policy is to use papers that are natural, renewable and recyclable products and made from wood grown in sustainable forests. The logging and manufacturing processes are expected to conform to the environmental regulations of the country of origin.

Hodder & Stoughton Ltd
Carmelite House
50 Victoria Embankment
London EC4Y 0DZ

www.hodder.co.uk

For Robin and OJ Burns,
who taught me to travel in the realms of gold

Disclaimer

Place names and geographical features have been altered: no one should attempt to replicate the journey described in this narrative.

Names have been changed to protect the reputations of the living, and the memory of the dead.

Someone's going to die out here.

I'd thought it so often, that last fortnight, you'd think I'd have been ready when it actually happened. It could have been any one of us, a dozen times a day – a badly aimed machete swing, a snakebite, a nasty fall. But that was abstract. If you'd pinned me down and asked who my money was on, whose pulseless wrist I'd have to lift, it would have seemed absurd. Not Fabio, so reassuringly solid even as the food ran out; not Tillman, who charged through the jungle like a boar. Definitely not Anton, or Drew, or Zia. Not even Howie.

I suppose that leaves me. And why not? I didn't know what I was doing; should never have been there. But in our own minds, we all think we're immortal.

The night we met, Anton told me, 'The jungle's not so dangerous as people say. You take a bigger risk walking to the store back home.' He was right about that, like a lot of the surprising things he said. Strip away the snakes and the croco- diles (overrated, he said, and he was right about that too), the biting ants and the howling monkeys; forget the jaguars (I never saw one) and the piranhas, and all the plants that could cut or crush or poison you. The real danger – like anywhere in the world – is the people around you.

But one thing I found out about Anton – afterwards, when it was too late – is he never told you the whole story. The Amazon might be safer than your local high street, but there are some significant differences. At home, when things go wrong, you call the police, get an ambulance. You go to your house and lock the door and pour a glass of wine and say thank God that's over.

In the jungle, there's no escape. You've got the most vibrant life on the planet, but life has to feed, and once you're there you're fair game. *Survival of the fittest*. The soil's so thin, you can't even bury the dead.

But right up until that morning, I still thought we'd make it.

There's a place in the Andes where the Amazon begins. I've seen it in a photo: a glacier on top of a mountain like a scoop of ice cream. Meltwater seeps down, and eventually spits out of a hole in the rock to make a stream. Six thousand kilometres later, it reaches the sea, by which point it's carrying enough water every second to float the *Titanic*.

But that's an artificial beginning. A geographer's fiction. The truth is, every single drop of rain that falls between the Andes and the Atlantic, they all end up in the river. Each is its own beginning, no more one than another, and who's to map the paths that bring them together?

But if my story has a beginning, a moment where the droplets make a stream and spurt out into daylight and I can plant my sign that says THIS IS IT, then it has to be that day in Mexico. A day I really did think I might die.

The day I met Anton.

One

Mayaland

'You're going the wrong way.'

Cate, in the passenger seat, looked up from the map. Outside, a dull landscape of scrub and dust passed by the window. It hadn't changed in the last two hours.

'This map's no good.'

The map was the freebie that came with the car, a glossy piece of promotion designed on the principle that all tourists are short-sighted. I should have taken the GPS option, but that had cost forty dollars extra, and I'd already felt ripped off by the car hire price. Never book through a hotel.

'You should have taken the GPS.'

'I don't believe in GPS. Anyway, we're having an adventure.' I tried to make a joke of it, but the time for jokes had passed about fifty kilometres back.

'Can we go home?' Peggy asked from the back seat. She'd been fractious since the iPad battery died. Apparently, that was my fault too.

'Daddy's going to turn around in a minute,' Cate promised her.

'What's that?' I jammed on the brakes. A cloud of dust billowed through the open windows and got in my mouth. I craned my head back to see the building we'd just passed. A mint-green breezeblock shack, with two hens and a Coca-Cola sign out the front. The sign on the wall said Montezuma Bar Café.

'Montezuma Bar. That's the one.' A dirt track split off the main road behind the bar, heading up towards a clutch of trees on a low hill. I turned on to it.

'How much longer?' said the little voice from the back.

'Five minutes,' Cate said grimly.

We'd been in Mexico six days. Long enough for the jetlag to wear off, long enough to get properly fed up. Cate hated the heat. Peggy hated the food. I hated the crowds, the feeling I'd been dropped on a conveyor belt whose sole purpose was to extract cash, while speeding me past the sights in a superficial blur. Tourism on rails. That was why I'd hired the car that afternoon – to get off the tourist trail, to *experience* something rather than just be shown it. No air-conditioned busses and itineraries and cultural programmes and vendors swarming like ants the moment you stopped to draw breath. I was thirty-eight, with a wife (adored), a mortgage (hefty) and a six-year-old daughter (cross, because her *Octonauts* had been cut off). But I wasn't ready to give up on adventures just yet.

I should have taken the extra damage insurance on the car. Potholes bounced us around; loose stones rattled off the paintwork. The catch on the glove compartment shook loose, spilling paperwork all over Cate's legs.

'*One minute*,' said Cate, in the voice she uses when Peggy won't put her shoes on for school.

I drove as fast as I dared, flinching each time a rock pinged the car. 'I feel sick,' came the inevitable complaint from the back.

'Look straight ahead.'

We crested the ridge and reached the trees. Greener than anything else in that parched landscape, a genuine oasis.

'This must be it.' I stopped the car and checked the webpage

I'd bookmarked on my phone. '"*Cenote de los Muertos*. The Well of the Dead."'

'Sounds fab.'

'"A hidden gem deep in the Yucatán countryside, claimed to be the origin of the Fountain of Youth myth . . ."'

'Funny name for the Fountain of Youth.'

'"If you go, chances are you'll have it to yourself."'

'Chances are we won't.' Cate pointed through the dust settling around us. Another car was parked there, half hidden by the trees.

I started to swear, but Cate caught me with a look.

The moment I stepped out, a hundred mosquitoes descended on me. Monsters, B-52s compared to the ones we have at home. I slapped at them ineffectually. Peggy squealed. Cate got some Deet out of her handbag and sprayed it on Peggy's arms.

I looked at the other car. Even for Mexico, it was a strange one. A Volkswagen Beetle (a real one, not the modern estate-agent version), whose paint had been stripped back to the metal, then reapplied by a consortium of tie-dyers and graffiti artists. A riot of colours.

I couldn't resist peering in the window. Some kind of extravagant folk-art charm dangled from the mirror; paper cups and food wrappers littered the floor. A polka-dotted bra lay draped across the back seat.

'This way,' I said, leading them away from the car before Cate saw. We went along a narrow path – well trodden, for a hidden gem – until we arrived in a clearing.

'Here we are.'

Three holes yawned from a bulge in the ground, two small and one about five metres across. You could definitely imagine it as a pair of eye sockets and a mouth – even without the skull drawn on a wooden sign lying on the ground. *Cenote de los Muertos*, it said; underneath, *Entrada $20*. A tattered folding chair sat next to the sign, though I saw no sign of the attendant. No sign of the owner of the polka-dot bra, either. A knotted rope hung down into the hole.

'Do real explorers pay an entry fee?' Cate asked.

I ignored her. I could see sapphire-blue water sparkling underground, and I wanted to be in it. I peeled off my sweat-soaked clothes and got my swimming trunks out of the bag.

Cate frowned. 'Modesty?'

'There's no one to see. Aren't you coming?'

I knew she was wearing her swimming costume under her skirt. I'd seen her put it on at the hotel. But she stayed back, holding Peggy against her legs.

'C'mon.'

'Someone has to stay with Peggy.' She peered into the cenote. 'You're not just going to jump in, are you? You could break your leg.'

'The website says it's fine.'

'And what about getting out?'

I kicked the rope. 'This.'

'And if it breaks?'

'It won't.'

I could feel myself getting hot, and I didn't want to start a fight. It was supposed to be my adventure. I turned, held my breath and jumped in feet first.

It was further down than I thought. I had time to wonder, in mid-air, *Is this a good idea?* Then I smacked the water. It rushed up my nose; I felt myself sinking. Too deep, too fast. *You'll break your leg.* I flailed and kicked.

My head broke the surface. I gasped down a breath and took half a gallon of water with it. I expected to gag, but the water was fresh: sweet and clear and so cold it made my heart freeze.

It was the best, purest moment of the holiday. Sunlight shone through the hole and made a perfect halo. Treading water, looking down, I could see tiny fish scurrying about my toes; the dappled limestone walls sinking into darkness. The black mouth of a tunnel in the side wall yawned open. A flaking metal sign bolted to the rock above said, in English and Spanish, 'Experienced Divers Only'. From Wikipedia, I knew the system ran for miles, an underground labyrinth of fresh water caverns riddling the peninsula.

Cate's face appeared at the edge of the hole. A long way up.

'Are you OK?'

'You should come down here,' I shouted. The moment I spoke, the cave filled with an echo like giant laughter.

'Is there anyone else there?'

I shook my head. 'It's perfect. Come on in.'

She looked as if she was considering it. Ten years ago, she'd have been in there like a shot, even without a swimsuit. But now—

'I'd better stay with Peggy.' At least she sounded as if she regretted it. Small victory.

I lay on my back and kicked around for a few minutes, basking in the sunlight coming through the roof. When that got too hot, I duck-dived underwater, chasing the fish and skimming along the rock walls like an eel. All around the cave, my own private paradise.

But there was one place I kept coming back to. The tunnel mouth, dark and tempting. I felt around it with my hands; I braced myself against the walls and peered in, trying to make anything out. I thought I could see light at the far end.

I knew what the website said. *Most spectacularly, a ten-metre swim down a side tunnel brings you to a Mayan ritual site, where the bones of sacrificial victims still lie in a hidden cave.*

Of course, Cate would point out, that wasn't all. *This should only be attempted by properly certified cave divers with the correct equipment and precautions.* But that was just to cover themselves. You can't buy a coffee these days without a health and safety briefing. And I'm a decent swimmer. Ten metres underwater shouldn't have been a problem.

This is my adventure.

I resurfaced, and saw Cate looking down again.

'Are you coming out soon?'

'In a minute.'

'The mosquitoes are eating Peggy alive. I'm taking her back to the car.'

I waited until she disappeared. Then I took a deep breath.

I swam for what felt like a long way, kicking myself forward while my hands traced the tunnel wall. I couldn't shake the phrase *underwater labyrinth* from my head – but this was only ten metres. I must have gone far enough. I gave another couple of kicks, just to be sure, then let myself float towards the surface. My lungs were beginning to feel the strain.

My head bumped rock. But I was still underwater: I must have come up too soon. Holding my breath was getting more painful. I lunged forward, feeling ahead for an opening.

Did the website say the Mayan cave had air in it? Suddenly, I wasn't at all sure. Had I imagined that? Did you need scuba gear to go down there?

The bones of sacrificial victims still lie in a hidden cave. All I could see was skeletons, my own bones sinking to the sandy floor of the cave. And the look on Cate's face.

I had to go back. I opened my eyes. Dim light illuminated the water, but I couldn't tell which way it was coming from. I twisted around, turning somersaults this way and that, looking for the source. It seemed to be coming from everywhere. And now I'd lost any sense of direction – didn't know which way was up.

I couldn't hold my breath any more. I let go, but of course there was nothing to breathe but water. My lungs felt as if they'd pop; my head was spinning. I knew it was crazy. I couldn't have come far. I ought to be able to get back. I fought it. But my movements were slow and limp, as if the water was fighting back. Lava-lamp spots danced in front of my eyes. My mind turned in on itself.

Underwater labyrinth underwater labyrinth underwater labyrinth.

I've sent so many people under in my life, I knew exactly what was happening. Phase one: a mild state of euphoria, similar to drunkenness, according to the textbook (I've experienced both: drunkenness is much better). Phase two, where you no longer respond to commands until finally you wouldn't even feel a knife sliding into your guts. Phase three.

The black blurs were coalescing into a shape, a human figure swimming out of the void. That's when I started to believe I was dying. Was this how it ended? Was this what those patients had seen, the ones who didn't come out? I'd always wondered. He'd come so close he filled the crystal water with his darkness. He reached out and took my arm. For an angel, he had a surprisingly strong grip. Long fair hair fanned around him; I could see the wings bulging out behind his shoulder, but something hid his face.

He forced something into my mouth. I would have resisted, but I was well towards phase three. With some primal infant instinct, I bit down on the regulator (which is what it was) and sucked in. Old, rubbery air that probably tasted like a bicycle tyre, but to me it was like sucking on pure ether.

The angel tapped my shoulder and made a 'slow down'

gesture. I nodded, and tried to control my breathing. My vision was clearing. He wasn't an angel – he was a diver. The wings on his back were an oxygen cylinder. Wide blue eyes watched me from behind his mask.

He borrowed back the regulator for a quick breath, then took my wrist and pulled me down the tunnel. Not far – maybe four or five metres. I remember thinking at the time, *That's the difference between life and death.* Later, of course, I learned they're a whole lot closer.

We surfaced in a small, domed cave. Air – real air – and light from a diver's torch placed on a ledge. I breathed in, grinning like an idiot and not caring. A stone idol with enormous square ears screamed warnings at me from a niche in the wall.

That was how I met Anton.

2

Anton (the diver) pulled off his face mask. He had a wild mane of dirty blond hair, a sun-beaten face, and pale blue eyes like portals to another dimension. He wore his oxygen tank without a wetsuit; between the straps, I could see a fat scar slashed across his ribcage, and a black shark's tooth on a leather cord around his neck. I wondered if the two were related.

We weren't alone. There was a girl, treading water. Maybe it was lack of oxygen, or the hormone rush that came from my escape, but I couldn't take my eyes off her. She was in her mid-twenties, lithe skin immaculately tanned, dark hair slicked back down her neck as if she'd just stepped out of the shower. She wore a white bikini, too thin for the icy water. I wondered if she owned a polka-dotted bra. She looked about the right size.

She lifted a hand out of the water and waved. 'These tunnels can be pretty dangerous, huh?'

Our legs brushed as we all trod water in that tight space. A shiver went through me. I started to say something formulaic about saving my life, but Anton wasn't interested. He took the torch from the ledge and shone it straight down.

'I guess this is what you came for.'

I almost jumped out of the water. On the sandy bottom, right under my feet, the torchlight picked out a pile of bones. Arms and legs and ribs; femurs, tibias, thoraces, the works. Worst were the skulls, staring up at me with empty eyes, angry at being disturbed from their rest. Several had been broken open like eggs, jagged holes where no holes should be.

'The Mayans clubbed them to death,' Anton said. 'And have you seen Momma?'

He'd turned the torch towards an alcove in the wall, to the left of the screaming idol. Another nasty surprise: more bones, a whole skeleton laid out on the rock shelf, with a fracture in the skull just behind the ear. Water seeping down over the centuries had covered the bones in a glossy calcium case, so you couldn't tell if the figure was being born out of the rock, or sucked into it. Straight out of *King Solomon's Mines*.

'Momma,' said Anton.

I shuddered. 'Why do you call her that?'

'It was the conquistadors,' said the girl. 'They told the Mayans it was the bones of the Virgin Mary, so they'd treat it like a holy place.'

'Usual crock of Catholic shit,' said Anton.

If I were a religious man, I'd have crossed myself. But I was superstitious enough to avert my eyes – straight at the girl. She wasn't wearing an air tank, or a mask. Had she swum through the passage unassisted?

She caught me looking, and gave me a warm smile. I returned it with interest.

'You come alone?' Anton asked.

I blinked. Since he'd rescued me, I hadn't had time to think of Cate. She didn't know where I'd gone, only that I'd disappeared from the cenote. She must be frantic. Had she called the police?

'My wife's outside. And my daughter. They didn't want to come.'

'You should tell them you're OK,' said the girl earnestly.

'Right.'

I didn't want to go. Now that I'd caught my breath, and got over the shock, I could feel the dark magic in that place. Reflected light rippled over the ceiling, while the yellow torch-beam turned the sand at the bottom gold. Even the bones didn't frighten me any more.

'Did anyone ever find any treasure in here?'

Anton laughed. 'If they did, they didn't leave any behind.'

I took a last look around. Three months later, in another cave with another family of bones, I remembered that moment. Sacrificial victims.

With a light and a guide and an air supply, taking turns with Anton's cylinder, the journey back took no time. We came out in the main chamber and swam for the dangling rope. We must have been longer than I'd realised. The sun had moved on. The golden cave had gone grey.

'Where the *hell* have you been?'

Cate had stripped down to her swimming costume and was halfway down the rope.

'Are you coming in?'

She glared down at me – like an avenging god descending in some Greek play. 'I was coming to rescue you.'

'It's OK,' Anton called. 'We already rescued him for you.'

The echoes in the cave made conversation almost impossible. The overlapping sounds throbbed uncomfortably in my ears. Cate wanted to say something but it was futile. She turned her back, pulled herself up the rope and disappeared out over the edge. Pretty quick. She'd kept herself in reasonable shape, even after Peggy was born.

I glanced at my rescuer. If he was embarrassed by us, he didn't show it. Later, when I'd worked him out a bit more, I understood he was immune to embarrassment – and a few other things too. Doubt; hesitation; danger. Totally bulletproof.

'I'm Kel, by the way,' I introduced myself.

'Anton. And she's Drew.' He nodded to the girl. *Girlfriend?* The way he said her name, there was definitely something possessive in it: a sense of intimacy, or ownership.

It's amazing how easy it is to feel jealous of the man who saved your life.

'I owe you,' I said with a big smile.

'Next time, bring an air tank. Nothing's dangerous with the right preparation.'

'Seriously.' I lowered my voice so Cate wouldn't hear, though the echoes made it gibberish anyway. 'I could have died in there.'

He shrugged it off. But I *was* grateful, maybe profoundly, and I wanted to make him understand it. Perhaps I had other reasons, too.

'Let me buy you dinner.'

3

I heard them arrive before I saw them. Anton's psychedelic VW made a noise like a jackhammer ripping up the hotel car park. Two minutes later, he came through the door of the restaurant, scanning the room like a predator. He'd changed into jeans and a white linen shirt, sleeves rolled up and buttons undone to the sternum. His dirty-blond hair sprang out in every direction like a lion's mane. Cowboy boots would have completed the outfit. Instead, he was wearing flip-flops.

I stood up and waved my margarita glass. Drew wasn't with him.

'I didn't recognise you with your clothes on,' he said as the maître d' led him over.

'Likewise,' I joked, though it wasn't true. He had a presence you'd know anywhere, like a piece of iron knows a magnet. And those eyes. If they were all you could see, you'd still recognise him at once.

'Is Drew coming?' I asked, offhand.

'Freshening up. She likes the running water here.' He took the seat opposite me. 'How about your wife?'

'Just putting our daughter to bed.'

He looked around. Not a casual glance, but a deep searching gaze, as if he'd never seen a restaurant before.

'You like this place?'

His tone put me on the defensive. I felt I had to justify myself.

'Well, there's a lot of space for Peggy to run around. And you can't beat the location.'

I pointed through the trees that lined the hotel compound. Spotlit behind them, the steps of Chichen Itza, the Observatory pyramid, climbed towards the night sky.

'You don't get a ruined Mayan city next door at the Hilton. We wanted to beat the tourists.'

'Mayaland.' He chewed the word over like a piece of bubblegum. 'Don't you think it sounds like Disneyland?'

'Maybe that's the point. I mean, you know what Chichen Itza's like . . .'

He shook his head. 'Never been.'

I stared at him. 'Never?'

'Too touristy.'

I couldn't argue with that. The hotel had a private entrance to the site, but even that was limited value. The moment you crossed the threshold, you were fair game for the vendors. Hundreds of them, some not much older than Peggy; a cacophony of 'one dollar, one dollar' and 'special price for you' that almost drowned out the guide. And once the tour buses arrived . . .

'It's enough to make you believe in human sacrifice,' I said. 'That's why I went to the cenote. I wanted . . .'

Anton had stopped listening to me. He'd turned around, and was beckoning Drew, who was threading her way between the tables.

I stood, slightly awkwardly, and tried not to stare – though I wouldn't have been the only one. She'd looked good in a bikini; she looked stunning now, in a simple white jersey dress that clung so tight there couldn't have been room for much underneath.

She flashed me a smile. I leaned in and gave her a gallant kiss on the cheek. Her perfume smelled of some sweet flower I couldn't name.

'Sorry I'm late,' she said.

'Not at all.'

She sat down next to Anton. He put his hand on her arm. He wore a lot of rings, I noticed: fat steel and silver. Drew had none.

'This hotel is the best,' she enthused. She nestled against Anton's shoulder. 'Why can't we stay someplace like this?'

'Where are you staying?' I asked. I had to look her firmly in the eye, to avoid any hint of my gaze drifting down the V of her dress.

'Anton's got us camping out in the sticks. In hammocks,

not even a tent, would you believe? Only a campfire to cook on, and no running water.'

'There's a stream,' said Anton.

'There's a stream *bed*.'

'It sounds great,' I said, and I meant it. The hotel's decor – 'hacienda style', the website called it – was starting to embarrass me.

'Where are you from?' Anton asked.

'Scotland. But I live in London now. You?'

'Kind of all over.'

'You make it sound so *romantic*,' said Drew. Her eyes met mine and she said in a stage whisper, 'He's really from Tampico, Illinois.'

'Birthplace of Ronald Reagan,' said Anton.

He scraped back his chair. Cate had arrived. She looked nice, in a Boden catalogue sort of way: a pretty flower print T-shirt with ruched sleeves, a denim skirt several inches longer than the ones she used to wear when we met.

'Sorry,' she apologised. 'Peggy wouldn't stay down.'

Anton kissed her on both cheeks, Continental-style. I made the introductions. With Anton and Drew having to sort out their dive equipment, and Cate desperate to get Peggy back for her tea, there hadn't been an opportunity at the cenote. I caught her giving Drew a shrewd look. Perhaps it was a sex thing, two females of the species sizing up the competition.

'So you're the man I have to blame for saving my husband,' she said, as we took our seats.

I hadn't meant to tell her what happened in the tunnel. I didn't want to worry her. But she'd worked it out of me, over an excruciating hour on the drive back.

'It's an amazing place,' Drew volunteered. 'Next time, we'll bring enough equipment for everyone. Your daughter, too.'

The waiter arrived and took our drinks order before Cate could say what she thought of that idea.

'Anything you want,' I said. 'My treat.'

Drew took a daiquiri. Anton ordered tequila – 'blue agave, neat' – and I asked for another margarita.

'Maybe a pitcher?' the waiter suggested.

'Sure.'

'And I'll have a glass of wine,' said Cate.

The waiter left. No one moved to pick up the conversation. Cate's arrival seemed to have broken the flow.

'So I guess you're here on vacation?' said Drew. If all else fails, talk about your holidays.

'Just a week for half-term,' said Cate. 'Kel's always fancied himself as Indiana Jones. You too?'

'Some downtime.' Anton stretched back his arms, looping one over the back of Drew's chair. 'We've got a big project coming up, so it's good to chill out. And I need to get Drew used to roughing it.'

'What do you do?' Cate asked.

'I'm a treasure hunter.'

I didn't know what to say, so I laughed. Cate thought he was making fun of her.

'Come on.'

'Seriously.'

'Is that an actual job?'

It came out sounding harsher than she probably meant. Anton didn't take offence.

'Better than working some office job to get a gold watch after forty years.'

'I don't think they give out gold watches any more,' I said.

'There you go.'

The waiter had brought the drinks. I took a big gulp of my margarita, and topped it up from the pitcher. Cate shot me a warning look. I added a bit more.

'It sounds great,' I said. 'Out in the sun all day, digging and diving. Real adventure. Not like what I do.'

Anton shook his head. 'Everyone gets the wrong idea. Treasure hunting's like gambling. Anyone can try it out, and maybe they'll get lucky. Maybe very lucky. But that's one in ten million. To make a career, you have to know your shit. Put in the hours, connect the dots. I probably sit a hundred hours in the library for every hour I'm in the field.'

It was hard to imagine Anton in a library.

'Are you connected to a university?' said Cate.

The question irritated me more than it should have. Here was this amazing person, and she was trying to place him in a bourgeois box, as if she was a matriarch in a Jane Austen novel and he was her prospective son-in-law.

I tried to make a joke of it. 'I don't think they offer degrees in treasure hunting.'

'College is a waste of time,' said Anton, confirming every one of Cate's suspicions. 'Look at those people in England, the ones who found the king. The hunchback guy.'

'Richard III,' said Drew.

'Right. I saw them on the History Channel. You know who they were? One was a screenwriter, and one was an author. The proof had been sitting there for five hundred years, but all the college types were too "educated" to see it. There was this story that the body had got thrown in a river, lost for ever, and because it was written in a book everyone believed it. So you know what the screenwriter did? She went back to the sources and found there was another story, an *earlier* story, that said Richard was buried in this church and that they knew where it was. And she said, "Hey, what if the guys who wrote the first story were telling the truth?" First day of digging, she found the skeleton.'

He drained his tequila and bit hard on the lime.

'First day,' he repeated. 'Same thing with Machu Picchu. Bingham wasn't trained. He read his sources and he backed his judgement. Or Troy. Everyone knew where it was, but no one believed it except Schliemann. All you have to do is respect history, take it seriously. Truth is, no academic ever found anything worth a damn, because their whole careers depend on not taking risks. It's the explorers and adventurers and treasure hunters who make the big-time discoveries. If you work in the university, what's the biggest prize you dream of? A piece of paper, right? But what I do . . .'

He pulled out a faded brown wallet and flipped it open. Something round bulged inside the leather. He slid it out.

It was a coin – about the size of a ten-pence piece, but thicker. Quartered by a cross, with lions and castles nestled between the arms.

'You know what this is?'

He spun it on the table. The silver glittered like a flame.

'A *peso de ocho*. A piece of eight.'

I wasn't sure if I should believe him.

'It's for real.' He tossed it to me across the table. 'You see the writing?'

It was heavier than I'd expected, the weight of age and vanished worlds. Time had tanned the silver deep grey. I couldn't believe he kept it in his wallet like a condom.

'Where—?'

'I got it in Panama,' he said. As casual as if he'd found it down the back of the sofa. 'Spaniards used to bring their treasure over the isthmus on mule trains. Road was bad, mules slipped, some treasure ended up in a ravine a thousand feet deep. I took a team up there a couple of years ago and found some.'

He held out his hand for the coin. I didn't want to let it go. Who knew what this coin had witnessed? Desperate conquistadors stumbling out of the jungle; galleons in full sail; blood-soaked pirates. And now I had it in my grasp. I could feel the history prickling my skin like an electric charge.

He was still waiting. Reluctantly, I dropped it in his hand. He slid it back into his wallet.

The waiter arrived for our food order.

'I'm afraid it might be a bit bland,' I warned them when he'd gone. 'They worry about setting the tourists on fire.'

Anton nodded. 'If you want to eat Mexican food, you got to get it where the locals eat.'

'There's an amazing shack near where we're camping,' Drew added. 'Salsa like you never taste back home, and burritos to die for.'

'Blows off your head like a shotgun.' Anton snapped a tortilla in two and scooped up some of the dipping salsa on the table. 'This shit's like ketchup.'

'So where's next?' I asked. 'Spanish galleons? Treasure islands?' I couldn't shake the image of that silver coin. 'Or is it a big secret?'

Anton crunched his tortilla and stared into the darkness. Over the wall, I could hear the music from the son et lumière show beginning, a low bass rumble from the mists of time (according to the blurb in the guidebook). A dribble of salsa ran down Anton's chin.

'You ever hear of a place called Paititi?' he said suddenly. I shook my head. 'How about El Dorado?'

'The lost city of gold.'

'Right. Well, kind of. Technically, El Dorado was a man, the "golden one". Indian king who got a rub-down in gold dust every day. But time passed, stories got mixed up, and now most people think it means the city of gold. So, Paititi *is* El Dorado. And that's where I'm going.'

'I thought El Dorado was a myth,' said Cate.

'*El Dorado*'s a myth. Paititi's real.'

'Real as in really real?'

'It's in Peru. Five hundred years ago, when the Spanish conquered Peru, the last Incas retreated to the jungle. First

they went to the fortress of Vilcabamba, where they held out
for like seventy years or something.'

'Seventy-six,' said Drew.

'When the Spaniards conquered that, Incas fled to the
rainforest. They took their greatest treasures – everything
they managed to hide from the Spaniards since the invasion.
The great golden disc from the Temple of the Sun in Cuzco,
six feet across. The mummies of the fourteen Inca emperors.
The chain of the emperor Huascar, a thousand feet long and
every link made of three-inch thick solid gold. They escaped
down the Andes and vanished into the rainforest.'

He waved his empty glass at the waiter.

'Some time after 1600, a Jesuit in Peru, Andrea Lopez,
reported to the Vatican that he'd spoken to a group of
Christianised Indians. They'd travelled down from the mountains and found a city in the jungle, every wall covered in
gold. Lopez went to find it himself . . .'

'. . . And was never heard of again?' Cate laughed. Anton
looked put out. 'Isn't that always the way?'

'It sounds amazing,' I said. Kicking Cate's foot under the
table. 'And you're really going to look for it?'

'We're going to *find* it.'

Something changed. His blue eyes held mine, overpowering
me with their certainty. Irresistible images of jungles, stone
temples and golden idols danced in front of me. I wanted to
go there. I *had* to go there.

'I wish I could come with you,' I said.

'Everyone says that.'

He looked away. The moment his eyes let me go, I felt
myself drop about thirty storeys. For a moment, we'd seemed
to share something. Now his voice said that I was nothing
special, no different from all the other wannabes and play-
actors. Nothing personal.

Cate was pulling her long-suffering wife face, like when

we need to leave a party to get back for the babysitter. Only Drew looked as if she believed in me.

'I mean it,' I insisted. A couple of notches too loud. The margaritas had made my cheeks flush. 'You said yourself you don't have to be an expert.'

'I said you have to know your shit.'

'I've always been interested in this sort of thing,'

'He means he's played a lot of *Tomb Raider*,' said Cate. I couldn't believe she'd taken Anton's side. After all, I wasn't seriously asking to go. I just wanted them to accept that it wasn't as crazy as they all seemed to think. That *I* wasn't as crazy.

'I'm just saying it sounds amazing.'

'Yeah,' said Anton, 'but I've got a full crew and I don't take passengers. You go in the jungle and you don't know what you're doing, you don't come out.'

Drew gave me a sympathetic smile. 'And the mosquitoes eat you alive.'

'Are you going?'

Anton answered for her. 'Drew's our lucky charm. Goddam expert. PhD from Yale.'

'You're an archaeologist?'

A grain of salt from the margarita glass had got stuck on her lip. She wiped it away. 'History, actually. But I did some Arch. and Anth. courses for my major.'

'More than just a pretty face,' said Anton, rubbing her cheek. 'When we find Paititi—'

'*If*,' said Drew.

'She'll be the one who got us there.'

I refilled Drew's drink, and then my own. I raised the glass. 'Good luck to you both.'

I hoped I didn't sound too bitter.

We talked and we ate. Anton could have kept a conversation going in an empty room. If he ever flagged, Drew was always ready to smooth the gaps. They were so comfortable in each other's company, so confident in themselves, I couldn't help feeling envious. Especially with Cate bristling and prickling beside me. Anton didn't mention Paititi again – even he had picked up on Cate's hostility.

I don't suppose I was great company, either. As I said, I was realistic enough to know that Paititi was out of the question. But I hated the idea that the adventures were over, that I'd crossed some threshold into middle age and even thinking it was out of bounds. Cate would say I was overgeneralising.

As soon as we'd finished the puddings, Cate started wrapping things up.

'I'm just going to the loo,' she said, in the voice that means, '. . . and then we're going.'

'You have a great wife,' said Anton, when she'd gone.

Across the room, I saw the concierge heading for our table. I knew what that meant.

'*Perdone*, Dr MacDonald,' he said to me, 'the listening service has asked me to say that your daughter is awake.'

'I'll be right there.'

I picked up my drink to finish it. Over the salt-smeared rim, I saw Anton staring at me as if I'd suddenly become very interesting.

'What?'

'You're a doctor?'

It sounds silly, but we'd never talked about what Cate and I did back home. I'd actually been embarrassed to bring it up – it sounded pathetic, in front of a treasure hunter. And Anton had done most of the talking.

I glanced at the door. No sign of Cate yet. We couldn't leave Peggy long.

Anton leaned his elbows on the table, as if he was about to launch himself off. 'I need a doctor for the expedition.

The guy who was supposed to come with me, he dropped out.' He jabbed his fork at me. 'This is perfect.'

Perhaps it was the margaritas, but I couldn't quite process what had happened. Half an hour ago, I'd been begging Anton to let me go along (even if it was only in principle). Now he was putting the squeeze on me.

It was a crazy, misguided idea, and I should have stopped it right there. But Cate came back then. She didn't sit down.

'Peggy's awake,' I told her.

'Then why didn't you go?'

'I was waiting for you.'

Cate bit back whatever she wanted to say and turned to the others. 'It's been really lovely meeting you. But it's been a big day – and if Peggy's not settled it'll be a long night.'

She looked at me expectantly. She nodded, not so subtly, to the door.

'I'll just stay for one more drink.' The margarita jug was empty. 'Unless Anton . . .'

He stretched his arms. 'Whatever.'

'Another drink sounds great,' said Drew.

'You'll pay for it in the morning,' said Cate. Lightly, with a smile, but I knew she wasn't talking about hangovers.

I kissed her goodnight and watched her leave.

'You think she'll let you go?' said Anton.

Drew made a face at him. 'Don't let Anton bounce you into going.' To Anton: 'You don't even know what kind of doctor he is.'

They both looked at me expectantly.

'An anaesthetist.' I'd drunk so much, I could hardly pronounce the word. 'But I did A&E as part of my training.'

'The jungle's no place for people who don't know what they're doing,' Drew reminded Anton.

'It's not as dangerous as you think.' Anton had a politician's ability to forget anything he'd said more than thirty seconds ago. Even now, I can't decide if it was calculated, or just the way he went at life. Headlong, never looking back. 'It's stories, mostly, that guys tell to make themselves look big.'

'He has a kid,' said Drew protectively.

'Yeah. But this is the adventure of a lifetime.' Anton turned to me. 'If we make it, you'll be *the guy who found El Dorado.*'

After that, things get hazy. The margaritas short-circuited my memory. I seem to remember we ended up crowded round a small table in the bar, jostling elbows and rubbing knees. Anton did most of the talking, while Drew and I listened – stories about shipwrecks and maps and buried treasure, like Robert Louis Stevenson editing *National Geographic*. I think at some point I started giving what Cate calls my modern-life-is-rubbish lament – *any thought we think, any sight we see, someone's already posted it on Facebook and got fifteen Likes* – and I remember Anton and Drew nodding as if it was the wisest thing they'd ever heard. And all that time, I know, the thought was growing inside me like a ball of shining light, radiating possibility through my veins. Real treasure. Real adventure. A real city of gold.

I knew I shouldn't go. The same way I knew that however often my leg brushed Drew's or our eyes met, however often I found my gaze drooping to the V of her dress (alcohol makes you terribly uninhibited), nothing would happen. It was a warm night with new friends, at the end of a holiday, and I was drunk. A time to crack open the door of your life and peer at the sunshine outside – just looking – before reality slams it shut again.

I don't remember going back to the room. But I must have done, because the next thing I knew I was waking up from a dream with my heart racing a hundred miles a minute, and the telephone on the bedside table ringing to wake the dead.

4

'Are you coming?'

Drew's voice cut through my hangover like icy water. I couldn't see a thing in the darkness. I reached across the bed.

Cate was next to me. I felt her bare shoulder where she'd thrown off the sheet in her sleep. From the bed in the corner, I heard Peggy's snuffly snores. The phone hadn't woken her.

'Um, what?'

'We're in the lobby.' She sounded impossibly bright given how much she'd drunk last night. This night? It was still dark outside.

'Right.'

'Ek' Balam?'

I wondered if I was still drunk (in retrospect, the answer was 'yes'). But it registered somewhere in the alcoholic haze of my brain. Tequila shots, and toasts, and Anton telling me that no one should leave the Yucatán without seeing the sun rise over the pyramids.

There was something else he'd told me, but I couldn't remember what it was.

Drew was getting tired of waiting for me to catch up.

'We have to leave now if we're going to make it.'

'I'll be right there.'

I leaned over and battered the bedside table until I found the phone cradle. When I turned back, Cate was sitting up in bed.

'Who was that?'

'Anton.'

'It's half past four.'

Christ. I was pretty sure I remembered being awake at two.

'He wants me to see the sunrise. Some Mayan temple you can climb up. He said it was amazing.' I saw the look on her face. 'You're invited too.'

I took Peggy to the car park while Cate finished getting dressed. Anton was there, leaning on his car and smoking a cigarette.

'Why's he here?' Peggy demanded.

'He's going to the Amazon.'

Peggy looked him up and down. 'Will you see a capybara?'

I laughed, embarrassed. 'I don't know what she's talking about.'

'No, she's right.' Anton knelt down so he could look Peggy in the eye. If Cate had been there, she'd have freaked out at Peggy being so close to a cigarette. 'You want to come with me, kid?'

Peggy nodded solemnly. 'Will you find treasure?'

'Definitely.'

'How did you know about the capybara?' I asked. Embarrassed at being shown up by my six-year-old daughter.

'I saw them on the *Octonauts*.'

I saw Cate coming down the path. I murmured in Anton's ear, 'This whole Amazon thing – I haven't had a chance to mention it to Cate yet. Please don't bring it up.'

'Right.'

Cate took one look at Anton's VW (from an age before seat belts), then one look at me, and announced that she would drive. We still had the hire car from the day before. Anton sat up front; I went in the back, squashed between Drew and Peggy. Drew stared out of the window, and Peggy dozed in her car seat; I needed to sleep, but every time I started to slump towards Drew, Cate's eyes in the rear-view mirror had me bolt upright again.

We drove for almost an hour. The sky got lighter. A ghost landscape of grey trees and silver leaves appeared beyond the window. The houses we passed were shuttered and dark. Peggy leaned out of her car seat and snuggled against me. It felt as if we were the only five people in the world.

Anton directed Cate through a small village and down an unpaved road. We stopped by a low chain-link fence among trees and got out. The damp air cooled my face and cleared my head. I drank in deep breaths, the smell of sagebrush and passion flowers.

'Where's the entrance?'

The fence was only chest high. Anton leaned on the top and vaulted over.

Cate stood her ground. 'What about the guards?'

'In bed. If they come, we give them ten dollars and it's no problem.'

I could see she didn't like it. I hesitated.

Anton pointed through the trees. 'You wanted to see what the other guys don't get to see? This is it.'

I didn't think she'd do it. But suddenly Cate was at the fence saying 'Give me a lift', and I was making a stirrup with my hands, and passing her Peggy, and then we were all inside and running in the deep shadows under the ceiba trees. I found Cate's hand and squeezed it.

The guidebook will tell you that Ek' Balam isn't as big as Chichen Itza. But darkness made it vast. We came out on to a baked-earth plaza; massive structures towered against the bluing sky. Anton jogged ahead. He led us to the highest pyramid and started scrambling up the steps.

At Chichen Itza, all the temples are roped off and guarded by men with guns. Here, there was nothing to stop you. I slipped on steps worn smooth by millions of feet – tourists, perhaps, but Mayans before that. I could feel the history under me, living in the stones the Maya had cut and dragged through the jungle.

The top of the pyramid was a platform, with a square stone block in its centre. Light brimmed over the horizon. We sat on the eastern edge of the pyramid and waited for the dawn. Cate and I cuddled Peggy between us; I stretched out and put my arm around both of them. It was the best moment of the holiday.

And that was before the sun came up. Picture perfect, a ball of fire rising behind the forest, as if time was rewinding and the comet that hit here sixty-five million years ago had been thrown back into the sky. It shone through the mist that shrouded the forest, so that the treetops and the pyramid became islands in a sea of blazing fog. A chorus of birds erupted into song.

'Realms of gold,' I murmured, a fragment of that old poem we learned at school. Perhaps it was the margaritas still buzzing in my bloodstream, but I felt more alive than I had since Peggy was born. I leaned across and kissed Cate's hair. She smiled, and kissed me back.

I'd left my camera at the hotel. Part of me couldn't believe I was missing these pictures; part of me was glad. Nothing to break the moment, to distract me from the experience of *now*. Nothing to become Facebook fodder for the eternal online bragging war. It could be that rarest of rare twenty-first-century treasures: something private.

Peggy had squirmed away to investigate on her own. Cate jumped up to grab her before she fell off the edge. Something about children: they always head for the most dangerous places.

Anton leaned over. 'This is amazing, right?'

'It's amazing.'

'Now imagine this isn't some Mexican tourist site where

TOM HARPER

we jumped the fence, and your hire car's parked on the street. Imagine we're in Peru, deep in the Amazon, and this is Paititi, and you're the first human being to see it for five hundred years.'

I could imagine it. Forest sweeping down from the mountains, white mist hanging in the trees, the wild cries of unknown birds and animals echoing across the landscape. And the mist parting, a stone temple, carved with ancient symbols that signposted a lost city.

'You sure you won't come on my adventure?'

Two

Wild West

5

I was in the cloud. Grey fog all around, now clumped together like cotton balls, now spun out so thin I could glimpse the sky behind. Light and dark swirled in the air. Rain droplets beaded on the window.

My thoughts were a mess. I hadn't slept in twenty-four hours – and the night before had been a frantic scrum of packing and last-minute panic. I'd spent weeks dismissing the dangers. That last night, they ganged up on me in an all-out assault that kept me awake hour after hour, almost in tears. I even found myself checking my email at 4 a.m., hoping I'd find something from Anton to say the whole thing was off. Then it was the airport, hugging Peggy so tight I might have cracked a rib, kissing Cate and promising her I'd be back soon. Not wanting to let go, but at the same time impatient for the adventure to begin. Amsterdam, Panama City, Lima. Eight hours in Lima Airport, dozing off on plastic seats. I had a sleeping pill in my pocket, but I didn't dare take it in case someone stole my bag while I slept. Finally, a small prop plane to Puerto Maldonado to meet Anton. That sunrise in Mexico seemed a lifetime away. In fact, it was only five weeks.

The plane bounced like a pebble skimming off a pond. I checked my seat belt, though I hadn't unfastened it since take-off. I stared at the clouds. Fragments of a conversation with Cate played through my head: a single conversation, sprawled across weeks, that began that morning in Mexico and didn't finish until she waved me off at the airport yesterday morning.

'How do you know you can trust Anton?'

'He saved my life.'

'Only because you were stupid enough to nearly drown yourself.'

Touché. 'I'll be careful.'

'I've Googled him ten times. There's almost nothing. If he's done all the things he says he has, why didn't anyone report it?'

That wasn't entirely fair. We'd found various references to Anton, various websites, just none of them exactly BBC News. Turns out there's a fair-sized treasure-hunting tribe on the web, with their own sites and blogs and forums and whatnot. Anton didn't participate, but people spoke about him the way guitar enthusiasts talk about Joe Satriani.

There was some stuff about Drew online, too, but I didn't tell Cate I'd been looking at that.

'That's exactly my point,' I argued. 'He's not living some fake life online. He's out in the world, doing it for real. You can't update your status in the jungle.'

'Has he asked you for money?'

'*No.*' Getting exasperated. 'I have to get myself out there. After that, it's all taken care of.'

'So who's paying?'

'He got a grant.'

'From *whom?*'

'I don't know.' In fact, I suspected that at one stage the funding (wherever it came from) had almost fallen through. I'd been emailing Anton almost constantly since we got back, but there'd been two weeks when I'd heard virtually nothing. The one email I did get in that period was so negative I spent three days wondering if I'd offended him, or done something to make him think I wasn't up to it. I nearly cancelled the sabbatical I'd twisted so many arms to get from work. But then he was back full throttle, more positive than ever. He'd hired a boat. He'd arranged permits. He was in Peru, just making final preparations. Couldn't wait for me to join him. In a month, we'd be in Paititi.

By then Cate had a new line of attack.

'Look at this.' Brandishing the iPad under my nose. Wikipedia's page on Paititi, subheading *Expeditions*. '"1971. Three explorers disappeared, presumed killed by wild Indians."'

'That was before I was born.'

'"1997. Lars Hafskjold set out from Puerto Maldonado in Peru and disappeared somewhere in the unexplored parts of Bolivia." This is the twenty-first century. I didn't know there were "unexplored parts" of *anywhere*.'

'We're not going to Bolivia.'

'You're starting from the same town. And this one's from this year.' She tabbed to a page from one of the news sites. '"Still no trace of the Menendez expedition, which vanished in the Peruvian Amazon while conducting a public health campaign." That was *six months ago*.'

I reached over and hugged her against me. 'We'll probably poke around the jungle for a couple of weeks, give up and come back. No harm done. We'll never find anything.'

The plane shuddered again and dropped a couple of metres. I heard cries and murmurs from the other passengers. The woman next to me – a stout Peruvian, in a stripy shawl and a bowler hat – crossed herself. I remembered the last words Cate said to me, whispered fiercely in my ear:

'Make sure you come back.'

We slid below the clouds. Light flooded in. I stared at my

first view of the Amazon. Endless green from one horizon to the other, swallowing us up as the plane descended.

The airport was more than a tin shack in the jungle – but not much more. There was a baggage carousel, but it never moved. Our bags came on a trolley and were dumped unceremoniously on the floor by a pair of unsmiling porters. Sharp-toothed Alsatians sniffed around, straining at their leads. A pair of giant staring eyes watched from a poster on the wall, above the slogan *No a la Droga*. Sweat prickled down my back. If they opened my suitcase, I'd have a lot of questions to answer.

There were no barriers. People who'd come to meet passengers just waited by the door. I scanned the faces, looking for Anton. Or Drew. I seemed to be the only gringo in the entire airport.

'Doctor MacDonald?'

He was Peruvian, a handsome young guy with tousled dark hair and a serious look in his eyes, holding out his hand. I liked him at once.

'I am Nolberto,' he introduced himself. 'Anton send me.'

'Is Anton here?'

He grabbed my bag. '*Sí, sí*. In Puerto Tordoya. We go to him.'

He took me out the front, past half a dozen motorcycle taxis, to an army-surplus jeep with the top off. I liked that, too. It was probably older than me, but it seemed solid and right, just the sort of thing a well-equipped expedition would use. First impressions were good.

Nolberto threw my bag in the back and turned on to the highway. After thirty-three hours in aeroplanes and airports, the warm breeze in my face was a gift. I felt the travel tension blowing away down the road, possibilities opening up ahead. Nolberto put in a tape (a tape!) and Dire Straits came on.

Sultans of Swing. So cheesy, so perfect for that moment, I laughed out loud.

'I haven't heard this song since 1989,' I said. Probably the last time I played a tape, too.

Nolberto smiled. 'You come from England?'

'Scotland.'

That always gets foreigners. 'Rangers? Whisky? Sean Connery?'

The smile got wider. 'Ah, *sí*. Enya.'

Never mind. 'So what's your role in this madness?'

He looked puzzled.

'Your job.' I was too jetlagged to risk my Spanish just yet. I pointed to myself. 'Me, I am the doctor. You?'

'Ah.' He smiled. 'I am the cook.'

'Have you worked with Anton before?'

He shook his head. 'Is first time.'

'Me too.'

Nolberto said it would take three hours to Puerto Tordoya. I settled back to enjoy the ride. For an hour or so we travelled on a good road, the fresh blacktop of the Trans-Oceanic Highway. Fruit farms and cattle fields lined the way; the jungle was a green smear on the horizon. We passed a flatbed lorry carrying what looked like giant cable drums. It was only when we were alongside that I realised it was a tree trunk, cut into sections and loaded crossways. Four sections, each one thicker than I was tall.

We turned off the highway, on to a blink-and-you-miss-it farm track. I checked my watch: only an hour down.

'This is road to Puerto Tordoya,' said Nolberto.

We'd gone from First World to Third World in seconds. And soon the road got worse. We forded streams, crossed gullies on bridges that weren't more than two planks laid across. I realised I was beaming like a little boy. 'I feel like Indiana Jones already.'

The jungle closed in as we went on. The fields got thinner, the stands of trees between them longer. Black stumps pocked the grass like gravestones. I had the sense we were being funnelled into something. I smelled burning in the air. Flecks of soot blew against my face and up my nose. One got in my eye. The jungle that had crowded the road suddenly leapt back. In its place was open ground, cinder grey. Ash filled the air and blocked the sun.

'They are clearing,' said Nolberto.

Of course I'd read about deforestation. But to see it here – one moment, riotous forest; the next, a valley of ashes – brought it home, in a way earnest chuggers outside Waitrose never could.

'I didn't think it would be so fragile.'

Nolberto gave me a sideways look. 'All life is fragile.'

We passed an old sign pointing down a track, rusting and riddled with bullet holes. The word – what remained of it – looked like 'Aeropuerto'.

'Puerto Tordoya has its own airport?'

'There was. But *narcotraficantes* uses it. One day, the army comes in helicopters, many guns and bombs. They destroy the runway, kill many people.'

'How long ago was that?'

He thought for a moment. 'Since 1990.'

'And no one's fixed it since?'

'Maybe next year.'

I couldn't believe they hadn't repaired the airport in twenty-five years. Then we reached Puerto Tordoya, and I couldn't believe it had ever had an airport at all. Forget Third World: this was full-on nineteenth century, a gold-rush town straight from the Wild West. Four-square wooden buildings lining mud streets, rough-sawn planks and tin-roofed porches. All they needed was saloon doors and a horse-hitch. A cowboy or a forty-niner would have felt right at home – until he got run over by a motorbike, or one of the tuk-tuk taxis that roared through the crowded streets twenty-four-seven.

Strong nerves and the horn got us through to the waterfront. With a name like Puerto Tordoya, I'd expected a thriving river port. Instead, the town gave up ten metres from the Rio Santa Maria, leaving an empty strip of dirt and then a drop to the water. There was one building on the bank, cut off halfway in a tangle of concrete and steel bars trailing down the slope to the river.

'Police station,' said Nolberto.

'Is there anything in this town which isn't broken?'

He stopped the jeep outside a breezeblock hostel. A fat woman watched us from a plastic chair in the open lobby. I got out and walked to the river. Plastic sandbags shored up the embankment. At the bottom, a hollow palm trunk made a Heath Robinson gangplank-cum-jetty where three open boats had moored. A pickup truck had backed up to the water's edge, where a gang of men loaded freshly sawn planks from a barge. All FSC-certified, no doubt.

'When does our boat get here?'

'Is there.' Nolberto pointed to the largest of the three boats I'd seen. It looked like a pleasure boat, the sort of thing tourists might use for an hour's sightseeing. No cabins, not even walls: just a canvas awning stretched over a wooden frame to shade the low deck. The name painted in faded letters across the stern was *Sierra Madre*.

'Where do we sleep?'

'Tonight we are in the hostel.' Nolberto carried my bag over. The fat woman gave him a key, and led us up a flight of stairs, along a concrete balcony and into an airless room. There was a bed, a fan and a mosquito net with holes the size of fifty-pence pieces.

'Toilet is downstairs.' The landlady left; Nolberto made to follow.

'Aren't you staying?'

'I go to the market.'

'*Hasta luego*,' I said. He smiled and disappeared.

I wasn't going to stay in that room. I went downstairs, across the dirt street and down to the water. I picked my way along the palm trunk to the *Sierra Madre*. I rapped on the hull and stuck my head under the awning.

Two men sat on deck playing cards on a plastic tub. They were talking animatedly in a language I couldn't understand, but they both shut up when they saw me arrive. Both looked like locals: one stocky and barrel chested, the other tall and gangly.

'Is Anton here?' I asked in Spanish.

They glanced at each other. The stocky one shook his head.

'No.'

'I'm Kel,' I introduced myself. 'The doctor. Did Anton tell you I'd be coming?'

No answer.

'Where is Anton?'

They exchanged a private look.

'He went up the river.'

'He had some shit to do,' said the gangly one.

I left them to their game and went back up to the hostel. I flopped in a plastic chair outside and got out my phone. Even here, on the edge of the world, I could get a signal. I was slightly disappointed.

Arrived safely. All well. Very hot. Miss u lots. Give Peggy a big hug.

I stared at the phone, willing it to buzz with a reply from Cate. A little way downriver, naked children jumped into the water from a half-sunk boat.

The hostel owner saw me looking. 'Hospital ship,' she said. 'The Dr Menendez clinic.'

The name sounded familiar, though I couldn't think why. The kids were leaping off the ship's roof with no thought for what sharp-edged traps might be waiting underwater. They tussled and laughed, pushing each other in and then hauling themselves back up the rusting superstructure. The hospital ship had become a death trap.

'How come it sank?'

The woman shrugged. 'Explosion.'

I watched the children playing on the shipwreck, terrified that one of them would hurt himself and I'd have to dive in to the rescue. I closed my eyes and tried to doze, though the flies made it impossible to sleep. Motorcycle taxis puttered by; the children laughed and screamed.

Shouts opened my eyes. A woman in a green tank top and New York Yankees baseball cap was standing on the riverbank, berating the children in a stream of angry Spanish. Had one of them fallen in? I sat up for a closer look. No one looked very worried. The children stood on the deck, pretending to ignore her.

Eventually, the children got bored of being harangued. They swam to the shore and trooped off somewhere else. The woman didn't stop for breath until they were out of sight.

'*Bueno*,' I called to her, as she walked past the hostel. '*Es muy peligroso.*'

She looked at me. The cap hid her face in deep tropical shadow.

'Do I know you?'

'I doubt it.'

'Then fuck you,' she said, in perfectly accented English, and walked away.

I had a headache coming on. My clothes were soaked through with sweat, and I hadn't had a drink since I landed. I bought a bottle of water from a street vendor and drank it back in my plastic chair. A half-naked blonde pouted over her shoulder at me from a petrol company calendar. On the opposite wall, another calendar showed happy schoolchildren beaming at their desks under the slogan '*Educación en la Amazonia: Misioneros Dominicos*'. Dominican missionaries? It sounded like something from Anton's conquistador stories.

I felt as if the two calendars were competing for my soul. Between them, someone had pinned a huge map of the Amazon basin. I traced the rivers with my eyes, wondering which one led to the lost city. There were so many – thin tendrils stretching in every direction, gradually joining and braiding into the great trunk river that flowed past where I sat. It reminded me of brain scans I'd seen in medical school, networks of unfathomable complexity, as if the rivers were the seat of some fierce intelligence in the body of the jungle. Perhaps even a soul.

A car pulled up, one of the heavy 4x4's I'd seen shuttling back and forth along the road from the airport. A door slammed on the far side; someone got out. Anton? I got out of my chair.

The 4x4 roared away, leaving a cloud of dust and a single passenger standing in the middle of the street. Not Anton, or Drew, but a gringo, with neatly combed fair hair and a polo shirt buttoned to the neck. Two bulging duffel bags lay at his feet. He was speaking rapidly on his mobile, darting quick glances all around him as if he expected to be mugged.

He was out in the sun; I was in shade under the hostel's veranda. He hadn't seen me. I stepped out of the shadow. 'Are you here for Anton?'

He looked round like a burglar surprised in the act. For a moment, that clean-shaven face seemed to snarl like an animal.

Or perhaps it was a trick of the sun. When I blinked, there was nothing but an amiable grin.

'Hey there.' American accent. He put the phone in his pocket and stuck out his hand. 'Howie. How you doing?'

'Kel.'

'You been here long?'

'Just got here an hour or so ago. Let me help you with those.' I grabbed one of the bags: it weighed a ton. I felt something hard and angular inside, lots of corners and edges bulging against the fabric. Strong padlocks fastened the zips.

'Did you bring a sack of bricks?' I joked.

'Leave that,' he said – and he meant it. I caught another flash of that anger. Then back to the grin.

'Only trying to help.'

He lugged the bags to his room. I enjoyed seeing him struggle with the weight. When he came out, he was covered in sweat and carrying two cans of Diet Coke. He offered me one.

'I found the vending machine.'

What I really wanted was a beer, but I wasn't picky. We cracked open the cans, and Howie took a chair.

'How did you get involved with all this?' he asked.

'I met Anton on holiday. He saved my life, and then he persuaded me to join his crew.'

I admit, it was a line I'd rehearsed. And I was pleased with the effect. A big, admiring smile.

'Sounds like a great story. You'll have to tell me some time.'

'And you?'

'I work for the Foundation.' He looked at me expectantly. 'The Linguistic Frontier Foundation?'

I shook my head. He seemed put out.

'We put up a chunk of change to pay for this trip.'

One question was answered. 'How come?'

'We're going someplace no white man's ever been, right? So there's a high likelihood of uncontacted tribes. Wild Indians.'

I remembered Cate's Wikipedia research. *Three explorers, presumed killed by Indians.*

'The Foundation's job is to map the world's languages. We're pretty excited about the possibility of discovering a whole new tribe, a new language with no outside influences. It would answer a lot of questions about universal grammar and how languages develop. So we teamed up with Anton.'

I squinted at him. 'You're a linguist?'

He adopted an English-accented robot voice. 'I am fluent in over three million forms of communication.'

'I hope you know the Indian words for "Don't shoot!"'

'Right.'

'Have you done many expeditions with Anton?'

'First time.'

'Me too.' And Nolberto. I'd imagined Anton would have a team, a tight-knit group of people he could rely on. Perhaps they were coming later.

We drank our Cokes and chatted. He came from California. He was twenty-six (he looked impressed when I told him I was thirty-eight, in a slightly depressing, not-bad-for-an-old-man sort of way). He had three degrees in linguistics, and spoke six or seven languages fluently. He'd never travelled in the jungle before.

'You really think it's out there?' he asked me. We'd been talking longer than I'd thought. The sun had come down below the clouds; the river reflected a blood-red sky. The town had started to wake up. Groups of people wandered along the waterfront, laughing and talking. A military helicopter buzzed low over the water like something from *Apocalypse Now*. Still no sign of the rest of the crew.

I looked up the river. Puerto Tordoya barely made a dent in the jungle. Not far from the hostel, the trees reclaimed the riverbank, an unbroken wall curving out of sight. An immense nothingness.

'There must be something out there,' I said. Ignoring the Wikipedia hall-of-shame list of those who'd died and failed. 'Anton seems confident.'

'I think Anton's always confident.'

A powerful engine roared down the street. The jeep had come back, Nolberto at the wheel. I didn't see Anton, but there was Drew: sunglasses and tank top, hair in a ponytail through the back of her cap, cool as a cigarette ad.

She gave me a big smile. She looked as good as I remembered. 'You made it.'

'Couldn't miss another near-death experience with Anton.'

A man came around from the passenger seat. Someone else I didn't recognise. A gringo, thickset and bull necked, with a puffy face and dirty red hair in short dreadlocks. He wore combat trousers, and a T-shirt that said, 'Kill 'Em All (Let God Sort Them Out)'.

The two Peruvians appeared from the boat. Suddenly, we were a crowd.

'Are you Howie?' said the redhead. Another American, definitely short on charm. I shook my head and pointed out Howie.

'Anton said you're bringing the cash,' said the redhead.

'That's right.'

'You got it here?'

I could see Howie didn't like his tone. Stiffly, he went off to his room. He came back with a small black backpack.

'How much?'

'Five thousand dollars.'

'Then let's go,' said the redhead. He looked at me. 'Who the fuck are you?'

'Kel. I'm the doctor. I—'

'You come too. We're going shopping.'

The back of the jeep was piled with sacks and cardboard boxes. The two Peruvians had started unloading, tossing them down to the boat. Rice, flour, potatoes. Enough to feed an army.

'Where are we going?'

'To see El Dorado.'

'El Dorado?'

He gave an evil grin. 'Didn't Anton tell you? He's right here in town.'

6

The redhead was called Tillman. He drove, with Drew in the passenger seat. Howie, Nolberto and I crammed in the back. We got plenty of attention from the locals. Men in combat fatigues patrolled what felt like every street corner, submachine guns cradled in their arms. One of them tracked us with his gun. Probably bored.

'Has there been some kind of a coup?' said Howie.

'They're police,' said Drew. 'Puerto Tordoya's a big stop on the cocaine trail.'

Anton hadn't mentioned that. 'I thought coca grew in the mountains.'

Drew shrugged. 'It has to go somewhere, I guess.'

'And where are *we* going?' said Howie. If Puerto Tordoya had a centre, we were heading well away from it. The houses got smaller, then gave way to a neighbourhood of shacks. Women sat knitting on plastic beer crates; crippled men offered strings of lottery tickets. Probably the only hope in town.

It was very nearly dark, but Tillman didn't slow down – except to slam on the brakes to avoid an oncoming 4×4 or moto-taxi, then roar off again in a cloud of dust. I gripped the side of the jeep so I wouldn't get bounced out. With no walls or roof or even a seat belt, I felt horribly exposed.

We skidded up to a junction, paused, then made a turn so tight we almost flipped the jeep.

'For Christ's sake,' I shouted. 'There are kids about.' I could see them in the road, shadows darting out of our way at the last possible minute, flitting at the edge of our headlight beams like moths.

Tillman stopped the car. We'd arrived, though I couldn't guess where. I saw a breezeblock wall topped with barbed wire. Behind it rose the corrugated-iron roof of some kind of warehouse.

Then Tillman cut off the headlights and I couldn't even see that.

'Everybody out,' he ordered. He sounded wired. He jumped down from the driver's seat and started rattling the gate. 'Anybody home?'

'Is this a good idea?' moaned Howie.

'*Quién es?*' said a voice from inside the gate. Though it was hard to tell in the dark, something in his tone made me think he was talking down the barrel of a gun.

'*Qué pasa, amigo?*' Tillman said. He spoke Spanish as if he'd learned it from taco adverts. 'Is Lorenzo here?' And then, when there was no reply, 'Anton sent me.'

Voices conferred inside. The gate creaked open.

'After you,' said Tillman.

The moment we stepped in, floodlights snapped on as if we'd tried to cross the Berlin Wall. I shielded my eyes. Through my fingers, I saw a wooden warehouse, like a barn, with a lorry backed up to it. A faded, giant Inca Kola logo was painted on the warehouse wall, and crates of glass bottles were stacked against the walls.

'Did we come here to buy soda?' said Howie, incredulous.

Trees rustled beyond the fence. We must have come right to the edge of town. A man stepped out of the warehouse and came towards us. A baseball cap hid his face.

'Lorenzo,' said Tillman. And then, aside, 'They call him El Dorado.'

'Why?'

'Because he gets all the gold. All the wildcatters and prospectors running barges in the jungle, they all bring it back to him.'

The man in the baseball cap stopped a little distance away, silhouetted by the security lights. He hadn't come alone. Half a dozen men in overalls leaned against the wall behind him, arms folded.

The baseball cap moved from side to side, examining us.

'Did you bring what I need?'

'We've got it,' Tillman said.

Lorenzo said something under his breath I didn't quite get. I thought I caught 'Anton', and also *'policia'*. The men around him laughed. The whole situation was so surreal, it was only afterwards I wondered if I should have been frightened.

'Come into my office.'

In Peru (I found out that night), no one ever gets straight to the point. It's bad manners. You pretend you've just come for a visit, you chat and eat and drink, and maybe after half an hour you get round to what you really want. Even gun runners, apparently. Lorenzo took us through the warehouse, piled with crates of the fizzy yellow drink, and into an office at the back. Mosquitoes buzzed around a naked fluorescent bulb in the ceiling. A square steel safe stood against the wall – so obvious, I wondered if it was just for show.

Tillman, Lorenzo and Drew sat around his desk, sipping Inca Kola from bottles. The rest of us crowded around awkwardly. I almost expected someone to break out a guitar.

'So you are going into the jungle to look for Paititi,' said Lorenzo. 'The golden city.'

I exchanged a nervous glance with Howie. So much for Anton's secrecy.

'You want to find gold in the jungle, you come and work for me.' There was a set of fine jeweller's scales on his desk, the weights lined up like soldiers. He tapped the pan, so that it seesawed up and down. 'I pay you ten dollars per gram.'

Tillman sucked his cola in silence.

Lorenzo suddenly looked up – straight at me. 'You like Peru?'

'I only got here this afternoon.'

'Your first time?'

I nodded.

'You should go to Cuzco. Nazca Lines, Machu Picchu, touristic excursion. I think this is the only lost city you will find here.'

'I've always wanted to see Machu Picchu.'

Lorenzo opened a small brown envelope and tipped it out on to the scales. A fine tawny powder, surprisingly dull. More like ground cinnamon than the stuff of dreams – except for a few gleams winking in the light.

'This is the only real gold in the jungle. Paititi, the lost cities, it is stories and legends.'

Tillman drained his drink, banged the bottle on the table and said, 'Enough with the social crap. Let's just get this done.'

Lorenzo's face tightened. For a horrible moment, I thought Tillman had gone too far. For all the hospitality and fizzy pop, there was no mistaking Lorenzo for anything other than a dangerous man.

'OK.'

He nodded to his men. Four of them went out into the warehouse. When we followed, two steel boxes had appeared in front of the stacked Inca Kola crates.

Tillman snapped open one of the lids and lifted out a long

black gun gleaming with oil. At that point, I'd never held a gun in my life, but I knew it was a shotgun because I'd seen them on TV. A second one lay in the box.

Part of me – the part that turns down the radio when the news comes on in case Peggy hears something she shouldn't – cringed at the sight of those squat black guns. But another part, the eternal ten-year-old boy, thought this might be the coolest moment of my life. I'd wanted adventure – and here we were in a warehouse, in the dead of night, buying real guns from a real arms dealer.

Tillman squinted down the barrel, then put it to his shoulder and jerked it up at the rafters. The hammer clicked as he pulled the trigger.

'Looks OK,' he said. He opened the other box. Two more guns – rifles (I can tell you now), in mint condition.

'Direct from the factory,' said Lorenzo. 'I give you very good price.'

I glanced around. Drew's face was unreadable. Our two Peruvians looked bored. 'What do we need these for?' I asked.

'Hunting,' said Tillman. 'Gotta eat.'

'The jungle is very dangerous,' said Lorenzo. '*Indios bravos.*' He made a tube with his hands and pretended to blow through it. 'They find you in their land, they kill you before you see them.' He grinned. 'Maybe they cut off your head and tie it on their pants.'

For some reason, he looked straight at me while he spoke. I tried to look nonchalant, and thanked God Cate wasn't there to hear it.

Tillman insisted on checking all four guns. 'And the ammo?'

Lorenzo lifted the lid of a cardboard box on top of a crate of Inca Kola. I saw rows of red shells packed inside. Tillman snapped open the shotgun and made to take one. Lorenzo put out his hand.

'First, you pay.'

Tillman scowled. He pulled a wad of notes from his pocket. Lorenzo counted them.

'This is three thousand dollars. With Anton, I agreed five.'

Tillman shrugged. 'He told me three thousand.'

I couldn't believe he was willing to haggle. The baseball cap hid Lorenzo's face, but I could guess what he thought of it. His guards had gone rigid.

'Three thousand dollars, is not worth it to me.'

'It's what we got. Take it or leave it.'

'You shoot monkeys, caiman, Indians, is OK. But if you shoot *narcos*, and they find out who sold you these guns, then for me it is a big problem. I need insurance.'

Tillman shrugged.

'Maybe you want to go without the guns?' said Lorenzo.

'Nope.' Tillman snapped the barrel of the shotgun in place and swung it around, straight at Lorenzo. 'I want to pay you three thousand dollars for them.'

Lorenzo stared Tillman down. All his men around us looked ready to pounce. Two had their hands in their jackets.

'You have no ammunition in your gun.'

'Don't I?' Tillman's eyes were wide, his nostrils flared. 'Check the ammo box. One missing, right?'

It sounds crazy now, but even at that point the ten-year-old inside me was still there. A Mexican stand-off – how *cool*. It was like a movie. Better – like being *in* a movie.

Why wasn't I thinking about Peggy and Cate? Why wasn't I thinking about *me*, and the chances I might not make it out of there alive? Part of me was: absolutely terrified. But as a species, we crave excitement above everything else, and it's a sweet hit when you get it. That's what gets us into trouble.

All eyes switched to the box of ammunition. All except Tillman's. Sure enough, a gap had opened in the factory-packed rows of shells.

'Should've paid attention while you were counting your money.'

Lorenzo stuck his hands in his pockets. Tillman twitched the gun. Suddenly, everything felt less exciting and much more real.

'You want to negotiate? You owe me eighty thousand dollars already. Maybe I call in my debts now?'

'You know Anton's good for it.' Tillman took a half-step back.

Lorenzo spat on the floor. 'I give you the guns for four thousand,' he said. 'And five hundred for the ammunition.'

'*Hasta la vista*,' said Tillman.

7

The guns didn't leave much space for passengers in the back of the jeep. I squeezed in the front seat between Tillman and Drew, while the others bounced around and hung on in the back. Tillman was exultant, mashing the gears and spinning the wheel like a rally driver.

'How awesome was that?' he crowed. 'Did you see the look on his face? I thought he'd shit his pants.'

I nodded. With no seat belt, I felt I might fly out of the jeep on every bump or corner. I felt nauseous, but that had nothing to do with Tillman's driving. Excitement's a drug like any other. After the high, the withdrawal hurts like hell.

'You were lucky he didn't shoot us all and keep the money,' said Drew, staring straight ahead. 'That was a dumb stunt to pull.'

'I knew what I was doing,' said Tillman. He blasted the horn at a three-wheeled motorcycle taxi. 'These guys, they respect power. You gotta earn it. It's a macho thing.'

'Macho bullshit,' said Drew.

'Tell me,' I said. 'Was the gun really loaded?'

Tillman took his hand off the wheel and pulled a red shell out of his pocket.

'I palmed it when he wasn't looking.'

'You're insane,' I told him. He took it as a compliment.

'Did we get the guns or did we get the guns?'

'We were lucky.'

'That's right. Lucky you were with me.'

Tillman jabbed a tape into the cassette deck and turned the volume high. Guns N' Roses, *Appetite for Destruction*. An avalanche of angry guitars buried any further discussion.

We drove past the fountain in the central square and back to the waterfront. The two Peruvians grabbed the first box and carried it down the gangplank. There seemed to be an unspoken understanding that if there was lifting or carrying to be done, the locals were first in line. I wasn't entirely comfortable with that, so I went round the back of the jeep and started pulling off the second box. Tillman came with me.

'Listen,' he said, as we hoisted the box on to the ground. 'Anton doesn't have to know I got a deal on the guns. If he asks, tell him I paid the whole five thousand.'

He was looking over his shoulder as he said it, so he didn't see the look on my face. He'd almost got us shot for *five hundred dollars*? Not to brag, but I can earn that in an afternoon. I could have got it out of a cashpoint for him.

'Great story to tell your wife when you get back, huh?'

I didn't have anything to say to that. Except: 'Was he serious about the Indians? Attacking us?'

'Sales pitch,' said Tillman. 'Arms dealer, he wants to scare the pants off you so you buy more shit.' He gave me a playful punch on the shoulder, hard enough to bruise. 'Did he get you?'

'He sounded serious.'

'He lives in the city. He doesn't have a fucking clue what it's like in the jungle. Point is, we got the guns now. If the Indians come at us, it's yippee-kay-ay motherfuckers.'

We lifted the box and started carrying it to the boat.

'What did he say about Anton owing him money?'

Tillman smirked, as if I'd discovered a dirty secret. 'Lorenzo gave us an advance on the expedition.'

'I thought Howie's outfit was paying.'

'Yeah, well . . . They—'

The roar of an engine cut him off. Dazzling headlights swept around the corner. I waited for the car to pass, but the lights only got brighter. Coming straight for us. No way the driver hadn't seen us: we were pinned like rabbits.

I dropped my end of the box and jumped behind the jeep. The car rolled towards us and stopped ten feet away. The engine cut out, but the lights stayed on. A door opened, then slammed shut. Two men got out.

'You trying to kill us?' demanded Tillman.

I stayed quiet. Now that I could see again, I could read the blue block writing across the car's bonnet. *Policia*.

The two men stepped into the light. Both wore white shirts and peaked caps, and blue polyester jackets that looked far too warm for that evening. Both were stocky, barrel-chested men in the Peruvian mould. One had a moustache.

'*Buenas noches*,' said the man with the moustache. He spoke calmly and precisely. He fished in his pocket and produced a badge. 'Comandante Lupo. My colleague is Teniente Chávez.'

He tapped our steel box with the toe of a spit-polished boot. 'Can you open this please.'

'You got a warrant?' Tillman said in English.

The *comandante* took out a cigarette. His lieutenant lit it for him. In the lighter's flare, I saw a pair of bright eyes under the peak of his cap, lined and wizened by experience.

'We have a tip-off.'

'Fucking Lorenzo,' Tillman muttered under his breath.

'You have identification?' said the lieutenant. '*Pasaporte?*'

Tillman unzipped the cargo pocket on his shorts and pulled out a battered blue passport. He handed it to the lieutenant. Somewhere in transit, three of Howie's hundred-dollar bills had got tangled up in it.

The lieutenant handed it to his boss. The *comandante* studied the passport. He didn't touch the money.

'You are *estadounidense*,' he said. 'In Peru, it is illegal to bribe a police officer.'

'Right,' said Tillman, smirking again.

'So I ask you again. Please open this box.'

The *comandante* stared at Tillman. Tillman stared back, the pig-headed superiority of an American abroad who thinks he's untouchable. And I realised he didn't have a clue.

I stepped between them.

'*Hola*,' I said, a thousand times more cheerful than I felt. Both policemen looked at me.

'*Soy médico.*' I showed him my passport – still in my pocket from when I got off the plane. Then I got out my wallet and gave him my hospital ID. He studied it carefully. Policemen love credentials.

'You are Kelvin MacDonald?'

'That's me.'

'You are a doctor?'

'Yes.'

'Why does your ID say "Mister".'

'I'm a consultant. In England, consultants are "Mister".'

'And these boxes belong to you?'

'They are medicines,' I told him in Spanish. 'Important medicines.'

I was babbling. If they opened the boxes and saw the guns, my lies would only make it worse. We'd surely go to prison

– and I'd be Accomplice Number One. How would I explain *that* to Cate?

'We are taking antibiotics to the Indian villages up the river.' The same Indians who were apparently going to cut off my head. 'For the children. If you open the box, you spoil the medicines and they are no good. Maybe people will die.'

Lupo stared at me. I felt his shrewd eyes examining me from under the shadow of his cap.

'You have proof? Paperwork?'

'At the airport in Puerto Maldonado.' I offered him my phone. 'You can call them if you want.'

'They are closed.'

I tried not to let my relief show. It had been an educated guess: small airport, 9 p.m. and Latin American working hours. But still only a guess.

He thought for a moment. 'I will take them to the police station. In the morning, you will show me the paperwork.'

'No,' I said.

He scratched his moustache. 'No?'

'Chain of custody is very important with these medicines. If I cannot guarantee how they have been stored, I cannot certify them. If I cannot certify them, I cannot use them.'

Another long stare. But I was getting used to it.

'If you want, you can come also.' He smiled. 'We have some very safe rooms in the police station.'

'OK.' I shrugged, and prayed he was bluffing. 'Let me get my bag.'

A radio squawked from inside the police car. The lieutenant ran back and stuck his head in the door. I stayed where I was.

'*Comandante*,' he called. '*Importante.*'

For a few seconds, Lupo didn't move. Neither did I. I felt like I do sometimes at work, watching the bleeps to see whether the patient lives or dies. Out of my hands – I've done all I can.

Lupo spat out his cigarette butt and ground it out in the dust with his shoe.

'I come back tomorrow,' he said. 'For now, be careful, *Mister* MacDonald. Puerto Tordoya is a dangerous town.'

The police car disappeared around the corner, blue lights flashing. I stood there, perfectly still, until the siren had faded into the background roar of Puerto Tordoya.

Only then did I become aware of the others. Howie, still in the back of the jeep, and Tillman standing behind me. Drew and the Peruvians watching from the deck of the boat.

I leaned against the jeep so I wouldn't collapse under my own weight.

'Pretty fly, for the new guy,' said Tillman grudgingly. 'You didn't say you spoke Spanish.'

I could smell the smoke from Lupo's cigarette, and I badly wanted one myself. Bad idea. I felt sick; the headache was flooding back.

Howie and Nolberto carried the boxes down the gangplank and stowed them in the front of the boat.

'Let's get some beers,' said Tillman.

8

Nellie's Bar (said Tillman) was the only place to drink in Puerto Tordoya. I don't know if he meant it was the best, or literally the only bar, but it certainly pulled a crowd. We found it a block away from the main square, a big room, open at the front, people spilling out over the pavement. Lights flashed; women danced to the music thumping from the back. I felt overdressed.

Tillman took a wad of Howie's money and came back

from the bar with a bucket full of beer bottles, and a tall glass filled with a frothy white drink. I drank the beer quickly, enjoying the cold spike down my throat. Drew sucked the white drink through a straw.

'What is that?' I had to shout in her ear to make myself heard.

'Pisco Sour.' She offered it to me and I took a sip. It tasted good. 'What's in it?'

'Pisco. It's the Peruvian national spirit. And lemon juice and egg white.'

'Can you believe this country?' said Tillman. 'No electricity or running water, and the national drink has raw egg in it. Fucked up.'

'That's why they need Kel's medicines.' Drew's eyes danced with mischief. 'To fight a Pisco Sour poisoning epidemic upriver.'

'I'll try that line next time.'

I felt dangerously relaxed. Drunk, exhausted and elated. It was probably the maddest day of my life, but I'd come through and I felt good. And the trip had hardly started.

'How come you speak such good Spanish?' Drew said. I had to stoop close to hear her.

'I did an elective in the Philippines, helping out in a clinic for street kids.'

'That must have been tough.'

I nodded. The truth is, it felt like it had happened to someone else, a lifetime ago.

She put her hand on my arm. 'I'm glad Anton found you.'

'When will he get here?'

'Tomorrow, I think.'

We drank and talked. Drew went on the dancefloor (she looked good, dancing). Tillman rolled a spliff, which he didn't offer to share. Howie nursed a Diet Coke. Time slipped by, and I started wondering about getting back to the hostel. Maybe after the next drink.

At the bar, I found myself standing next to another Westerner. He wore a pressed white polo shirt tucked into khaki slacks; with his trim haircut, he looked like an accountant on a golfing weekend. He caught my eye.

'You must be the new guy.'

'Sorry?'

'Not many gringos in P-T. I figured you must be new.'

'I arrived from the UK this afternoon.'

'That's a long day,' he sympathised.

'You have no idea.'

'You on vacation?'

'I'm going upriver with some friends. Exploring the jungle.' I didn't want to go into details, so I added quickly, 'How about you?'

'I'm with the UAV programme.'

With a couple of drinks on top of no sleep, I must have looked as confused as I felt. 'What's that?'

'Flying the friendly skies, taking out bad guys.' He made an imaginary pistol with his thumb and forefinger, fired an imaginary shot and blew imaginary smoke off the top of his finger.

I was still two steps behind. 'You're American?'

'Right.'

'A pilot?'

'Yeah. Well, kind of. A joystick jockey. You know the Predator?'

I was struggling. 'The Arnie film?'

'No. I mean, yeah, why not? If it bleeds, we most definitely can kill it, yo. But these Predators, they fly around at twenty thousand feet. Death from above.'

The penny rolled around my empty head, and finally dropped. 'Drones.'

'UAVs. *Unmannned Aerial Vehicles.*' He pronounced the 'H' in 'vehicles'.

I slid on to a bar stool. 'So you're military?'

'Jesus, no. Civilian contractor.'

'And why are you flying your drones in Peru?'

'Counterterrorism. Well, actually it's counter-narcotics, but if we tell Congress it's counter-terror then we get more money to buy toys. You know *Sendero Luminoso*? Shining Path?'

'The guerrillas.' They'd definitely come up during Cate's propaganda campaign. 'I thought they were defeated in the nineties.'

'They're back in business. Once you get out of the jungle, the other side of those mountains is V-R-A-E. Valley del Rios Apurimac and Ene. What Thailand is for mail-order brides, that place is for cocaine. Ground zero. That's where the Shining Path are getting their shit together, and that's why we're here. Unofficially, of course. On the QT.'

I wondered why he was telling me this. He didn't look drunk.

'Any time they send a plane over the Andes loaded with the bad stuff, we zap it.'

'How can you tell?'

He grinned. 'We can't. That's why we don't take any chances. You flew in from Lima?' I nodded. 'That take longer than usual?'

'Two and a half hours.'

'It should be one and a half, but they have to route you around our no-fly zone. Any aircraft that strays in, boom.'

He banged his beer bottle down on the counter. 'You been in the jungle before?'

I shook my head.

'You be careful out there. Lot of bad guys. Indians, *narcos*, Sendero Luminoso. Total bandit country. I hope you came prepared.'

I reached in my pocket and pulled out a rounded lump of yellow plastic. About the size of a baby monitor – which is what Cate had called it, when I unwrapped it in London. Her going away present to me.

'It's a Personal Locator Beacon,' I said. 'If anything goes wrong, satellites can pick up the signal anywhere on Earth and launch a rescue.'

'But how are they going to reach you?' He spun a beer mat on the bar. 'Some of the drones we got now, they don't even need a human operator. If their sensors catch something breaking that no-fly zone, they'll hit the button without thinking. I think we toasted a couple of condors last week.'

'OK.' I rubbed the sweat from my forehead. I'd had too much beer and not nearly enough sleep. The music had pounded its way into my head and was pogoing on my brain. I needed my bed.

I stepped away from the bar. The room spun. Disco lights flashed in my eyes.

'It was nice meeting you,' said the American. He stuck out a hand. 'Travel safe.'

I looked for the others. Tillman was at the back, chatting up a girl. She looked like the woman who'd shouted at the kids playing on the sunken boat. I couldn't find Drew or Howie. I pushed my way out on my own, glad to get away from the sweat and the noise. The river was only a couple of streets from the main square. I thought I remembered the way.

'Doctor Kel?'

I'd forgotten Nolberto. He'd followed me out.

'I'm going back to the hostel.'

He nodded, and fell in beside me. I was glad of the company. At that time of night, the streets weren't busy enough to feel safe, but not empty enough to feel alone, either. The soldiers I'd seen patrolling earlier had gone away. I wasn't sure if that made it safer or not.

'Crazy day,' said Nolberto, shaking his head.

'You can say that again.' I liked Nolberto. He was the only one who seemed to have noticed how bizarre the whole set-up was.

Something Lorenzo had said was bothering me. 'Nolberto, why is Anton not here?' I said in Spanish.

He smiled. He always smiled. 'I am just the cook.'

'Lorenzo mentioned the police.'

'For a man like him, there is always police.'

'I promised my wife and daughter I wouldn't do anything stupid.'

'Anton is good man,' said Nolberto earnestly.

'What about the guns?'

'For hunting.'

'Really?'

'*Sí, sí.*' The smile he gave me was utterly genuine. 'In the jungle, we must hunt to eat.'

We were crossing the main square. Even that late, there were still people hanging out in the glow of its single street light. Couples held hands or kissed by doorways. A group of teenagers sat around the central fountain, laughing and joking. For the first time, I started to feel comfortable in Puerto Tordoya.

'You have a wife and children in Scotland?' said Nolberto.

I was about to say we live in London now, and stopped myself. Plenty of time for the finer points of British geography on the boat. 'Yes.'

'You have pictures?'

I stopped by the empty fountain and pulled out my phone, flipping back through the last few photos. The weekend before I left, we'd gone to Kensington Gardens so that Peggy could play in the Peter Pan playground. A tourist had taken a photo of the three of us – one of those spontaneous shots that comes out better than you could ever have staged it. Peggy peering over the rim of her ice cream, Cate looking radiant, all three of us beaming in the English summer sunshine. A complete family, wanting for nothing.

It hurt to realise how much I missed them. And I'd barely been gone a day.

I held the phone out so Nolberto could see it and say something nice.

The square had gone very quiet. The couples had gone home to their parents or their beds. The teenagers who'd been here, by the fountain, had disappeared. Was there a curfew?

Suddenly, I didn't feel so comfortable.

A motorcycle roared around the corner. Not one of the rickety three-wheeler taxis; a powerful racing bike, black nose bulging like a cruise missile.

The driver hunched low and jumped the concrete kerb. Behind him, the passenger riding pillion stretched out an arm, pointing us out as if to warn the driver.

He wasn't warning the driver. He was holding a pistol.

Someone shouted, '*Cuidado!*' Look out!

Then I went down.

9

I know I shut my eyes, because otherwise the flashes would have blinded me. I heard the bangs, though, even above the motorcycle engine. A double thunderclap, and then a ringing in my ears like a car alarm. I didn't feel the pain at that stage, but I did feel the debris, sharp stone flakes raining down on me. I covered my face with my hand. The motorcycle engine faded into the distance.

I finally opened my eyes. A man hovered over me, far too high up. His arms were stretched out, and an amber halo shone behind his head. His face looked like Jesus. Had I died?

I was lying in the empty fountain in the middle of the square. The figure above me *was* Jesus; it was the statue. His sodium halo came from the street lamp, still flickering as if nothing had happened.

How did I get there? Did the bike hit me? I patted myself down, checking for blood or worse. My hip hurt like hell where I'd landed on something hard, and a rock splinter had cut my cheek. Otherwise, I seemed to be in one piece.

Was it a miracle? I looked up at Jesus, but he wasn't telling. I wanted to look around, to know what was out there, but I also wanted – badly – to not get hurt again..

I rubbed my sore hip and felt something hard. Cate's present, the emergency beacon. I pulled it out and stared at it dumbly, the bright yellow plastic unharmed by the impact.

Should I activate it? Was this an emergency?

The ringing in my ears had dialled down the volume. I could hear a siren wailing in the distance; and, a lot closer, the sound of someone swearing in pain. Nothing else. The plaza – perhaps the whole town – seemed to have been shocked into silence.

I scrabbled for the rim of the fountain and pulled my head above the parapet. My whole body was screaming to get down, to curl up in the concrete basin and wait for the police. But I had to see what was out there.

Nolberto lay on the ground just outside the fountain. He must have pushed me in. He probably saved my life.

He'd paid for it. His whole right side was a mangled mess of flesh and blood and torn clothes. Blood welled from a hole in his chest. *Was that a bullet hole?* A minute ago, he'd been looking at pictures of Cate and Peggy.

I had nothing to staunch the bleeding except my T-shirt. I pulled it off and did the best I could until I managed to wave down a passing moto-taxi. We loaded Nolberto in the back seat, not gently; I had to squat on the baggage rack and cling on.

As we pulled away from the square, I looked back. The solitary street light still shone. In its light, I saw the strangest thing of all. People had come back. Couples walked, old men gossiped, and a group of teenagers entertained each other with skateboard tricks. The police still hadn't showed up.

As if it had never happened.

Hospitals are sinister places at the best of times. Endless corridors and endless waiting. Information withheld. A sense of utter powerlessness. People come and people go; there seems to be a system, but you never see the people in charge. You start to doubt your own existence. I should know: I spend my life in those places.

But a Third World hospital, after midnight, sleep-deprived and suffering from shock: even Kafka would be lost for words. Dead-eyed souls haunted the corridors, waiting for their number to come up. There were no seats, so they sat on the floors and the stairs, blocking doors and exits. Every so often, a nurse came and shouted at them, or some orderlies tried to force a stretcher through. Then the crowds would shuffle back against the walls, like muscles contracting, until a path opened. Thirty seconds later it had closed again.

In a British hospital, I might have been able to do something. Here, I was helpless. Doctors took Nolberto away – quickly, thank God. After that, all I could do was wait. I couldn't even call Cate. Nolberto had been holding my phone. If the bike hadn't crushed it, it would certainly be gone from the square by now.

Some time around 3 a.m., the surgeon came out. He had the grey skin and haggard eyes that come from a life lived under fluorescent lights.

'Señor Rodríguez is your friend?' he asked.

63

I rubbed my eyes. *My friend?* I'd met Nolberto that afternoon. I'd had two conversations with him. Didn't know where he came from, if he had a family. Until I looked in his wallet when they admitted him to hospital, I didn't even know his surname.

'Is he OK?' I said in Spanish.

The surgeon gave me a measured look. 'The bullets perforated his stomach and punctured the gall bladder. Also, the impact of the motorbike broke his leg, his arm and three ribs. And he has lost two fingers. But I think he will live.'

He handed me a prescription scrip. 'You must take this to the pharmacy for the medicines he needs. Also, needles. Can you contact his family?'

'I'll try.' I didn't know where to begin. I thought I should tell the others on the boat, but I had no way to contact them. Didn't even know what part of town I was in.

The surgeon gave me a quick, appraising look. 'You need something for pain? For shock?'

'I'll be OK.'

It took me half an hour to find the hospital dispensary. Another half-hour to wait in the queue at the little window. When I got to the front, all they gave me was a stamp on my prescription, and directions to yet another queue. Repeat. I remember thinking, *Anyone who criticises the NHS . . .*

At last I got my hands on a little bag filled with medicines and sterile needles. Then I had to get back to Intensive Care. I was so busy trying to find my way, I barely noticed the police officers coming towards me. One of them held the door. I mumbled some thanks, and was about to go through when he suddenly stepped out and blocked my way. I looked up.

For the second time that night, I was looking into the lined face of Comandante Lupo. Lieutenant Chávez loitered in the corridor behind him.

'*Mister* MacDonald,' Lupo said. Lingering on the *Mister*, as if it was a private joke between us. He eyed my blood-soaked T-shirt. I'd had to put it back on when the ambulance arrived: I didn't have anything else.

'I think we must stop meeting so often.'

I was too far gone for small talk. 'The attack. Nolberto Rodríguez. Did you find the person who did it?'

'We have taken witness statements.'

Witnesses? I remembered how eerily empty the square had been the moment before it went off. As if everyone had known.

'You were with Nolberto Rodríguez?' he asked.

'Yes.'

'Did you see who was driving the motorcycle?'

'They were both wearing helmets.'

'You know any motive they might have?'

I felt like I was drowning. 'I don't know why anyone would want to kill Nolberto.' I didn't dare mention Lorenzo. Could it be payback for Tillman's stupid stunt with the shotgun?

A long pause while those dark eyes searched me for something. 'Perhaps they did not want to kill Nolberto Rodríguez.'

'What—?'

'Perhaps the gun was aimed for you.'

I almost laughed, it was so ludicrous. 'I've only been in Peru twelve hours.'

'Then you have made enemies quickly. Or you have dangerous friends.'

I remembered the American in the bar. 'Could it have been terrorists? *Sendero Luminoso?*'

He studied me, until I started to feel that simply knowing the name made me guilty of something. 'We investigate all possibilities.'

'Or drug traffickers?'

'We investigate,' he repeated. 'You will come to the police station in the morning and we make a formal statement.'

Was fatigue making me paranoid, hearing a threat in that invitation? 'And after that,' he told me, 'you go home to England. In Peru there is only trouble for you.'

I still had the drugs to deliver. I found Nolberto on a ward behind a moth-eaten curtain, trussed up like a mummy. Blood had soaked through the bandages, and a couple of enterprising mosquitoes were lapping it up. They left bright red streaks down the walls when I swatted them.

At least he looked stable. I put the drugs on the bedside table and was about to go, when Nolberto's unbandaged eye opened. He stared at me dreamily, pupil dilated and blurred.

'You saved my life,' I told him. I felt ashamed. How do you face a man with those injuries and tell him you were worth it?

His lips moved. I leaned closer, trying to hear. He was straining every muscle, so much that I could see fresh blood welling into the bandages. I tried to push him back down but he grabbed me with his good arm and dragged my head against his.

The words came out in harsh breaths, like steam hissing through a pipe. Two words that nearly killed him.

'*Black water.*'

'What do you mean?'

His eye closed. His head sank into the pillow. Whatever he had to tell me, I wouldn't get it that night.

There was light in the sky when I got back to the hostel; a cock had started to crow. I pounded on the locked door, but no one answered. In the end, I stumbled down to the boat and curled up in the bow. I felt cold. I was probably still in shock.

And I couldn't sleep. Tired as I was, the moment I shut my eyes my mind started running a million miles a minute.

The motorbike. Nolberto's mangled body. Faces from the hospital. Lorenzo's men with guns.

I couldn't go another day with no sleep. Not with a police interview to get through, so many explanations, and God knows what else. I still had the sleeping pill from the flight in my pocket. I swallowed it dry.

I'd done a lot of stupid and dangerous things that day – starting, you might say, with stepping off the aeroplane. But in terms of consequences, that might have been the worst decision of the lot.

Three

Black Water

10

I felt worse when I woke up than before I went to sleep. My head throbbed, my neck ached, and my clothes were soaked with sweat. The tropical sun shone off the varnish straight into my eyes. I was dying for a drink of water.

I pushed myself up and almost fell over. The deck wobbled. I didn't know where my sunglasses were. I grabbed on to the side.

The first thing I noticed was the trees. The sandbagged riverbank had vanished. So had the collapsed police station, the sunken hospital ship and the motorcycles. The whole town.

We were in the middle of the river.

We were moving.

I looked around – a three hundred and sixty degree sweep. All I saw was trees and water and sky. A small wooden skiff, tethered on a rope, rocked in the dirty brown wake we churned behind us.

'Big night last night?'

A woman looked down at me. She wore a bloody apron, and her arms were covered in blood up to the elbows. She looked familiar, in a dream-logic sort of way, though with the sun and the shock and the pill still clogging my brain, I couldn't place her.

'I'm Zia,' she said.

She was slim and dark, with black hair tied back in a short

ponytail. Under her apron, she wore a green tank top and baggy black shorts. She had a tattoo on her chest, just above the left breast. Some kind of snake, coiled around a stick and baring its fangs.

The woman from the riverbank. That's where I'd seen her, shouting at the children who'd been playing on the sunken boat. And again in the bar, with Tillman.

I pinched my forehead. I couldn't breathe in that heat. 'Why are you here?'

'I'm the cook,' she said. On top of a cool box in front of her, a dead fish spilled its guts out on a chopping board. That explained the blood.

'Nolberto's the cook.'

'He didn't make it. I'm his replacement.'

He didn't make it.

I ran to the back of the boat, clambering over the stacks of baggage. Tillman was there with the two Peruvians I'd seen playing cards the day before. He had a bag of pretzels in his hand. He grunted when he saw me.

'Can't handle your drink?'

'Where are we going?'

'Anton called. Told us to get our butts in gear. Plus, no sense waiting for the cops to come back and take another look at our guns.'

The police. I'd told Lupo I'd go to the police station that morning and make a statement. He must be waiting for me right now.

'What about Nolberto?' I said.

'Didn't show. I couldn't raise him on his cell this morning, and I wasn't going to sit on my ass in Puerto Tordoya waiting.' He shrugged. 'You snooze, you lose. Anyhow, we found a replacement.'

I couldn't believe him. 'Do you think that's what really matters here?'

He tossed a pretzel in his mouth. 'Gotta eat.'

I wanted to snatch the bag out of his hand. 'We have to go back.'

'The fuck are you talking about?'

'Don't you know what happened last night?'

He leaned back. He noticed the blood on my shirt and smirked. 'Did you get in a *fight*, Doc?'

I told him what had happened, as quickly as I could. We were still motoring upriver, away from Puerto Tordoya. Every minute took me further away, made me look more guilty.

'Shit.' Tillman scowled. 'What a clusterfuck. Anton's gonna be seriously pissed.'

'We need to go back right now. Before the police come after me.'

Tillman rolled his eyes. 'They got better things to do with their time. Trust me.'

'And we have to check on Nolberto.'

'No one's doing anything until we've talked to Anton.'

'We're not far off,' said Drew. She'd come up while I was talking and heard most of the story. She handed me a hunk of bread. 'You look like you could use some breakfast.'

'And change your shirt so you don't look like fucking Charles Manson,' added Tillman.

At least someone had thought to fetch my bag from the hostel. I found it in the front of the boat and got a fresh shirt. I had a well-stocked medicine kit, but I resisted the temptation to pop a sedative. An adrenalin shot to the heart would have been more appropriate. I settled for caffeine, and made my way back to Zia's makeshift galley.

'Any chance of a cup of coffee?'

She opened a plastic tub and banged a jar of Nescafé down in front of me. No spoon.

'Stove's right there.' A camping stove, bolted to the bench. I turned on the gas.

'Any water?'

By way of an answer, she grabbed a pan, leaned over the side and scooped up a litre or so of brown river water. She banged it on the stove with a look that said I was an idiot. Words like 'giardia' and 'cryptosporidium' conjured themselves in my mind. I hoped the little stove's flame was up to the job.

I realised I was staring at Zia. Not leering or aggressive, just too tired to move my eyes. I couldn't place her. With her colouring, she could have passed as Peruvian, or any Latin American. Her English was perfect, with a generic Americanised accent you can pick up anywhere in the world.

'You took Nolberto's place.' Even saying his name was like sticking my finger in a socket, flashing lights and smoke in my memory.

She stared me down. 'He got hit by a motorcycle. It happens.'

A motorcyclist shooting a gun at him. We'd just met; I wasn't ready to go into that.

'I can't believe you just came on this expedition at a moment's notice.'

'I didn't have anything to keep me in Puerto Tordoya.'

The way she said it, you could tell there was a story. 'Broken heart?' I guessed.

The knife severed the fish's head. Two drops of blood flew off and landed on my clean shirt. Not a conversationalist.

'Thanks for the coffee.'

I ducked out to the front of the boat. We were coming round a bend in the river: there was a break in the trees, a small landing and a motorboat drawn up on a muddy beach. Further back, I saw the outline of a machine, with half-naked men working around it. Most of them ignored us, but one broke away and came down to the beach. He waved.

It was Anton.

11

We tied up the *Sierra Madre* on the mud beach beside the other boat. Tillman and Drew splashed ashore and hugged Anton. I hesitated. I was still wearing the shoes I'd worn on the flight – pathetically flimsy. I thought about taking them off, and then I remembered the bilharzia worms that live in mud and burrow into your feet.

I jumped over the edge. Mud sucked at my feet. By the time I'd waded on to dry land, the shoes were ruined.

Anton clapped me on the shoulder. 'You made it.' He had to shout. Behind him, the machine rattled and hissed as if it was about to explode, while the generator that powered it roared away. It was a strange contraption, a series of rubber belts on stalk-like legs, perched on the edge of a huge crater like a praying mantis. A high-pressure hose squirted out a mix of water, sand and gravel, which churned over the belts until the residue finally dropped into a box at the back. Water dripped through a wire mesh under the belts and landed on the filthiest carpet you've ever seen. Except, in a few places, where tiny flakes of gold sparkled in the mud.

The filthy men who tended it wore nothing except floppy hats. They looked like trolls, and ignored us completely.

'And this is Fabio. Our guide.'

He nodded to the man standing next to him: a stocky Peruvian, handsome, wearing an olive-green T-shirt and combat trousers. A gold chain gleamed around his neck.

We shook hands. 'I need to talk to you,' I shouted in Anton's ear. But Anton didn't hear me. He was staring at the *Sierra Madre* as if he'd never seen it in his life.

'What the hell is she doing here?' he said, so loud that even the machine seemed to stall and take notice.

Zia had come out on the front of the *Sierra Madre* with a bag of vegetables. She turned them out on the chopping board – then, feeling Anton's gaze, looked up. Their eyes clashed.

'That's what I have to talk to you about,' I started to say. Tillman cut me off.

'Nolberto had an accident. We had to skip town and she was available.'

'It wasn't an accident,' I said. Anton wasn't listening.

'She's *Menendez's fucking girlfriend*.'

'Who's Menendez?' I said.

The others obviously knew. Drew frowned; Tillman went bright red. He muttered something I didn't catch over the din from the machine.

Deliberately, Zia turned her back and disappeared under the boat's awning. The day had gone dark. Anton looked around.

'What happened?'

I started to tell him, but he waved me to shut up. 'I can't hear myself think.'

We walked a little way up the shore, on to a bluff where the trees muffled the noise. I scanned the undergrowth nervously, though the miners must have frightened off all the snakes and jaguars for fifty miles.

I told Anton about the men on the motorbike. He paced around the bluff – he never could stand still – watching the river go by. Down below, the trailing skiff strained against the rope that held it to the *Sierra Madre*; the *Sierra Madre* pulled against the tree we'd tied it to, and it seemed the whole world was trying to rush us back downstream. I should have taken the hint.

'So what do you want to do about it?' Anton said when I'd finished.

'We have to go back.' I wasn't sure I meant it; I said it to see how it would sound. I wasn't exactly relishing another encounter with Lupo.

Anton picked up a rock from the ground. He ran his eye over it for gold, as if he were checking out a hot woman. Total instinct.

'You're upset because someone shot at you. I know. First time I had a gun pointed at me, it freaked me out.'

The first time.

'If we were back home, a shooting in a public place would be big news, right? Prime-time. But this place is different. Shit happens.'

A warm wind stirred the air, the first breath of a storm. The clouds were coming down like a metal press.

'That's the best you can do? Nolberto's in hospital with a perforated stomach, a hole in his gall bladder and two fingers missing, and you say "shit happens"?'

'You want me to say something that makes it better?'

'I want you to *do* something.'

Anton tossed the rock into the river. It hardly made a splash.

'You're a doctor, yes?'

I nodded.

'You ever have a patient die on you?'

'Of course. But—'

'And when he died, did you quit your job and cry about it? Or did you get back to work?'

'That's different. It's . . . work.'

'And Paititi is my work. The big one, the one I've waited my whole life to find. And you want me to quit because the cook had an accident?'

'He was fucking well shot.'

74

'In Peru, that counts as an accident.'

For a moment, his blue eyes held mine, cold as the sea. Then he looked away.

'It's OK if you don't want to come. Go back to your wife and kid. This kind of thing, not everyone has the balls for it. But think about it. You can't help Nolberto any more. But if we're in the jungle a month from now and someone's hurt and they need a doctor, that's where you can make a difference.'

'What about Nolberto?'

'He's got family in Puerto Tordoya. When we get back, we'll pay him his full wages as if he came on the trip. We find Paititi, he gets a big fat bonus to set him up for life.'

He spoke quickly, saying things he knew I wanted to hear. That didn't necessarily make them untrue. He shouldered his kitbag and started towards the beach.

'I better go and talk to Zia. You're welcome if you want to come, but no one's forcing you. You want to quit, we'll get you on the next boat home and you'll be in Puerto Tordoya by tonight.'

I stood there after he'd gone, watching the river flow by, listening to the machine suck gold out of the earth. I didn't have long. I could feel the rain coming.

Knowing Nolberto had family in Puerto Tordoya made a difference. It lifted him out of my hands, absolved me, and that was a relief. You can judge me for that, if you like, but I'd only met him the day before. What more could I do?

Then there was pride. I hadn't been backward about telling people at home where I was going. If I'm honest, I enjoyed the kudos – casually letting slip I was off on a treasure-hunting expedition to the Amazon. Could I really go back after two days and tell them I wimped out? When the others found the city, had their photos plastered over every website and newspaper in the world? Front cover of *National Geographic*.

Or if they didn't, if something went wrong and I wasn't there to help them?

The truth is, I was never going to walk away. Anything else was just finessing my conscience.

12

The *Sierra Madre* had a table you could lower from the ceiling on ropes. By the time I got back to the boat, the table was down and the others were sitting round it. Anton, Drew, Tillman, Howie and Fabio. Pedro and Pablo tended the engine; Zia sat in the front, chopping her vegetables. Whatever problem Anton had with her, they seemed to have resolved it.

The rain had started. Hard and heavy, it drummed on the roof and the rails, splashing us where we sat. The river boiled; the air smelled dank and ripe. I felt as if we were in a cave, hiding from the world.

Drew smiled at me and squeezed along to make room. Anton spread a map on the table. Again, I marvelled at the tangle of rivers, flowing in down the Andes' eastern flanks. He took a hunting knife out of his pocket and tapped the tip at a bend in the main river, the Santa Maria.

'This is us.' He traced a course up to where a thin tributary came in. 'And this is the Rio Pachacamac.'

'What's that?' I pointed to a black dotted line that outlined a large rectangle on the map. Where it crossed the main river, a green dot showed 'Control'.

'A few years ago, the government declared this whole area an Indian reserve. Something like four million acres.'

'Are we allowed in?'

'We got a permit.'

The knife resumed its journey up the Rio Pachacamac.

The land around, featureless until then, suddenly began to bubble up in contours as it rose into the foothills of the Andes. The river narrowed, then stopped altogether.

'The front gate. This is where we leave the boat.'

'And then?' said Howie. He slapped at a mosquito that was sucking on his arm, though it didn't make much difference. For some reason, they swarmed to him more than anyone.

'We walk.' Anton's knife drew a line west. So sharp it slit the paper. Here, there was nothing on the map except a few vague lines that looked like cartographers trying to fill space. I remembered a phrase from Cate's Wikipedia campaign. *The unexplored parts.* Was it really feasible that no one – no white man – had ever walked there?

White man. I couldn't believe the words had even come into my head. The whole concept was barbaric and Victorian.

'And here . . .' Anton lifted the knife, then stabbed it into the centre of the white space on the map. He loved a dramatic gesture. It stood, quivering, in the table. Anton took a felt-tip pen and drew a red circle round it.

'Paydirt.'

'Unless your source is bullshit,' Tillman said, through the cigarette in his lips. Seeing him and Anton together for the first time made me think of two brothers: Anton the older one, all confidence and golden charm; Tillman the black sheep, sullen and resentful and desperate for approval.

I'm an older brother myself. I admit I might be biased.

Anton leaned back. 'Drew?'

She held up a yellow piece of paper in a plastic wallet. 'Anton's probably told you, or you've seen on the Internet, about Andrea Lopez. He's the Jesuit who reported the story of the Indians who went to Paititi. His narrative was lost in the Vatican archives—'

'Or hidden,' Anton interrupted.

'—And only discovered in 2001. Lopez says the Indians found the city ten days' march from the borders of Peru. But we don't know where the borders were, and we don't know which direction they went. So not a big help. The best we can say about Lopez is that he definitely places Paititi somewhere in this neck of the woods.' She swept her hand over the map. 'But there's a lot of woods in this neck of the woods.'

Anton picked up again. 'Eighteen months ago, a friend of mine was working in the *Archivo General de Indias*, in Seville. Amazing place. Nine kilometres of shelving, eighty million pages of documents. Mostly account books and trial records. Stuff so boring it hadn't been looked at in five hundred years.'

The rain pounded harder on the roof. A tree floated past in the stream. Its roots waved in the air as if it was drowning.

'By complete dumb luck, she found something else. One in a million; one in *eighty* million. A piece of paper that got misfiled. It comes from diplomatic correspondence between the Spanish and the Portuguese governments about a fugitive named Diego Alvarado. He fled Peru in 1592, and turned up nine months later at the mouth of the Amazon in Brazil.'

Drew passed me the paper to look at. I slid it out of the plastic wallet. It felt much thicker than modern paper, yellow and spotted with age.

'Is this a copy?'

'Can't beat the real thing.'

I dropped it as if it was electrified. 'This is the original sixteenth-century manuscript?'

'From the library. We borrowed it.' Anton laughed at the look on my face. 'Don't worry about the overdue fines. We'll pay them when we get the treasure.'

I put it back in the wallet before the rain got on it. Through the cloudy plastic, I could see tiny writing swooping and curling across the page.

'Alvarado's story was that he'd been having an affair with a married woman. Her husband caught them at it; they fought and Alvarado killed him. Now, the husband had a lot of brothers, and Alvarado knew they'd come for him. Conquistadors could be pretty creative when it came to inflicting pain. So he fled into the jungle. He got lost, went way too far, and eventually he realised the only way out was to follow the rivers until he reached a settlement.'

Drew passed around a sheaf of photocopies. For a surreal second, it was like being in a Professional Development seminar at home, fumbling with the papers to make sure everyone got one.

'Bottom line: he made it. Reached a Dominican monastery near the mouth of the Amazon. While he was recovering, he wrote down his story. Drew made a translation.'

The True and Authentic Narrative of Diego Alvarado
Given under his own hand in the Year of Our Lord Fifteen Hundred and Ninety Three

After these events, I journeyed some days down the treacherous river. The Lord alone knows what torments I suffered, for though I burned with hunger, yet my belly also was on fire with some pestilence, and if ever I found the least morsel of food, my stomach rebelled and would not accept it. And I grew so weak I thought I must surely die, for there was no path in that forest, and the trees grew so thick I could scarce move. Nor could I trust my fate to the waters, for the river in those parts is shallow and treacherous, broken by many rocks and cascades which would have killed me more swiftly even than hunger.

Then there came a time where my strength left me. I lay down by the river and wept, and prayed the Lord to grant me death or deliverance, for I could not bear to live one hour longer in this wise. And the merciful Lord heard my prayer, for a tribe of Indians found me. And though they have no love for the Spanish, on account of the cruelties perpetrated upon them, they recognised I was no danger and treated me kindly, after their own savage ways. They bound my wounds, and fed me with a particular plant they have, which has purple flowers and a taste as sweet as honey. And so I regained some of my former strength.

When I could walk again – this took some days – they led me by secret paths through the forest to their city. The marvels of that city, and the wonders I saw, I shall not dwell on, for I do not wish to tire the patience of My Lord King. If he desires to know more, he has only to command me and I will answer any question. Yet I will say a little.

The city is not so large as our fair Seville or Toledo, but it occupies an impregnable situation, for it sits on an island where two rivers meet. The only entrance is by a bridge across the river gorge, which they defend day and night.

And I do not think it was built in recent times, nor by the savages who inhabit it now, for it seemed to me the stones were of such age and manufacture that they could not have been built by those Indians, who are poor in the use of tools. Yet even now it is rich in treasures: much gold, worked in the fashion of the mountain Indians, and also silver and richly embroidered cloths. To their high temple, they would not admit me, but I guessed from their private words that it held the most sacred and valuable treasures of their ancestors.

Many times, I asked them what city this was, but either they did not understand me or they would not reveal their secrets. Yet these idolaters showed great interest in the silver cross I wore, and I explained by what words and signs I could that this was the mark of Our Lord Jesus Christ, by which we are all redeemed and made whole, and by Whose Grace I had been delivered from death in the jungle. And they implored me to return with men who could instruct them in the ways of the True Faith, for they saw how God had favoured me and were greatly desirous of knowing His Grace. And I promised I would return with many men of God who could teach them all they desired. And on this oath they allowed me to depart.

The river at that city, as I have said, was treacherous and boiling with rapids. The Indians do not navigate it, for they say it will crush any vessel like a serpent. But I learned of another, larger river to the east, by which I might descend from the accursed forest and return to the realm of Christians. The Indians implored me not to go that way, saying there was no path; but I trusted in the Lord and was not afraid. And though the forest beset me from every side with thorns like daggers, yet it seemed to me that the way I walked must once have been a road, for the forest was less thick, and the way often ran straight, as with the roads I have seen in the mountains of Peru, wrought in the days before the Spanish came. And oftentimes I found stones carved with strange faces, that gave me to think they must be markers as we in Spain use milestones. And though these signs frightened me (for I conceived they must be the Indians' demon gods), and I daily prayed almighty God to deliver me from evil, yet I was also heartened that this road must in the end lead me to my salvation.

I walked for thirteen days, always following the sunrise, until by the grace of God on the fourteenth day there came to my ears the sound of tumbling water. Hastening my pace, I came at length upon the most blessed sight imaginable. A torrent of water falling over a cliff, and at its foot a serene open river whose waters were black as night.

I fell to my knees and thanked Almighty God, for I saw at once that this river might carry my weary body to safety, and so find redemption from the cruelties of that savage forest. And so it proved.

The adventures I suffered, and the hardships I endured thereafter, I will relate in another place. But in time, by the river and the grace of Almighty God, who alone is the author and guarantor of our fates, I came to the settlement of the Dominicans, at Belem do Para. There the brothers clothed me and fed me, and have treated me with all Christian Charity.

And if it pleases his Holy Majesty King Philip to pardon his servant Diego, then he undertakes to equip, at his own expense, an expedition, to return up that black river and to effect the capture of that miraculous city, and to claim its wealth and lands for the Crown of Spain. And he is certain he will find it again, for beside the waterfall where he gained the river, there are carved symbols in the heathen language of the Indians, which – though he could not comprehend them – he held in his memory and sets down here.

So concludes the narrative of Diego Alvarado, given this twentieth day of October, in the Year of Our Lord Fifteen Hundred and Ninety-Three.

'So he walked east for thirteen days,' said Howie. 'And he got to a river with a waterfall. There must be about a million waterfalls round here.'

Anton squawked like a buzzer and made an X with his arms. 'Ix-nay. You forgot the most important clue.'

'Alvarado described rock carvings by the waterfall. More than that, he actually copied them down.' Drew leaned over the table and pointed to the bottom of the original sheet of paper. 'Here.'

We all craned forward. Howie smoothed the plastic flat. Underneath, I saw a row of compact shapes, like doodles at the bottom of the page. There was a spiral that could have been a snake, and a circle with a dot in the centre, and wavy lines that might represent water. If you squinted, some looked like birds or animals, or stick figures with alien, heart-shaped faces. And some didn't look like much of anything.

'You know where these are?'

Drew nodded. 'In 1913, a German rubber tapper called Franz Meier paddled up the Rio Pachacamac as far as he could go. The first recorded ascent of the river. When he got back to civilisation, he reported seeing strange symbols carved on a cliff by a waterfall. He told it to a priest, who wrote it down, and it found its way into a very dusty, very hard-to-find treatise on Peruvian petroglyphs. I tracked it down in Arequipa.'

Anton beamed and slapped her bottom. 'I told you she was good.'

'Did you "borrow" that one too?' I asked.

'Just a photocopy.'

She put another piece of paper on the table. Half of it was a badly reproduced photograph, so murky it obscured all detail. Underneath was a block of line drawings similar to Alvarado's doodles.

'Are you sure these are the same?' I said. 'I mean, they're similar . . .'

'Alvarado drew them from memory, months after he saw them,' said Anton smoothly. 'He was probably fucked up with malaria and malnutrition. It makes sense he didn't copy them one hundred per cent.'

There wasn't much to say to that. I looked around the table to see if anyone else thought that trusting the five-hundred-year-old memory of a diseased, half-starved conquistador was a bad idea.

'Even if the carvings are there . . .' said Fabio. He followed the route with his finger, from the headwaters of the Pachacamac to Anton's red circle. 'Alvarado says thirteen days to walk this.'

'I think we can do it faster,' said Anton.

'Alvarado says the path was good for him. Maybe now not so good. To cut through the jungle, making a path, is not so easy.'

'I know that.'

'Then we have to find the city. How long for that? Two weeks? Three?'

'I'm more optimistic than that.'

'We can carry food for four weeks from when we leave the boat,' put in Zia. 'That includes the trip back.'

'So we are in the jungle at least a month. But now is the dry season: every day, the river drops. If we leave the boat at the waterfall, it will not float again until Christmas.'

'Relax,' said Anton. 'Your job is getting us to the city. I'll take care of getting us out.' He picked up the map and folded it away.

'Now we just have to get there.'

13

Dear Cate and Peggy,

I'm writing this from our boat, the *Sierra Madre*. It's named after a film where some men find treasure. It's funny being a treasure hunter. Sometimes I feel like a pirate, sailing on our adventure looking for gold. Yesterday I saw a scarlet macaw. I might try to train one as a parrot.

I wish I could call you, but my phone broke. There isn't any reception here, anyway. We have the satellite phone, but we can only use it for emergencies to save the batteries.

But I'm having a good time. We've been travelling up the river for three days now. It takes a long time because the current against us is so strong. In another four days, we should get to the end of the river. Then we'll start hiking overland. Anton says we might not be able to use the satellite phone then – the forest canopy is so thick the signal can't get through.

I miss you both very much, but the people I'm with are nice, and I'm in good hands.

I love you,

Kel

PS – Peggy: I haven't seen a capybara yet. But I'm keeping my eyes open.

I looked over what I'd written and tried not to feel guilty about the lies. Mostly lies of omission: the arms dealer, the motorcyclist, Nolberto, the police . . . I never like keeping secrets. But there was nothing Cate or Peggy could do, and I didn't want to worry them. The one thing worse than lying would be telling the truth.

I clicked 'send' and waited for the message to go. The satellite connection took so long, I might have been faster sticking the message in a bottle and throwing it in the river. I drummed my fingers and watched the riverbanks slide by. Three days. I'd never imagined how quickly wild adventure can become monotonous.

The truth is, I could have called them from Anton's Globalstar phone. The boat had a generator, so batteries weren't a problem (yet), though calls cost a fortune. But I could handle the separation: what I couldn't handle was breaking it. Bringing Cate and Peggy into the Amazon, hearing their voices on the boat, would bridge two worlds that belonged apart. I knew it would make me miserable.

The deck creaked as Anton came forward. I closed the email quickly, and switched to Google Earth. Anton had already made a couple of pointed comments about how expensive the satellite uplink was.

'I was looking for the rivers you mentioned,' I said. 'The ones that are supposed to meet at Paititi. If we can locate those, we'd have a position to aim for.'

'You find anything?' He gave me a crooked grin, as if he already knew the answer.

'The photos aren't very high resolution. I can't even work out where we are.'

I leaned back to give him a better view. There wasn't much to see except wall-to-wall forest. It didn't even look like a photograph — more like a single block print repeated over and over.

'You won't find those rivers. Someone's doctored the maps.'

Even by Anton's standards, that sounded as mad as a box of frogs.

'Don't you think you're being a little paranoid?'

'Don't you think the first thing I did, when I got hold of Alvarado's story, was to look for those rivers? I've seen these pictures a hundred times. I'm telling you, it's been fixed.'

'How on earth could anyone doctor satellite pictures?'

'Easy. If they're the guys who own the satellite.'

He tapped the bottom of the screen. *Data: SIO, NOAA, US Navy.*

'I looked these guys up. NOAA is part of the US Department of Commerce. SIO belongs to the Pentagon. US Navy, that's self-explanatory. One way or another, all these pictures come from Uncle Sam.'

'Even so . . .'

'You don't believe it?' Anton rummaged in his bag and got out the GPS unit. He held it out over the side of the boat to get a reading, then moved the cursor on the laptop until the coordinates on screen matched the coordinates on the GPS. He zoomed in as far as he could go.

Over the rail, the mud-brown river stretched a quarter of a mile either side of the boat. No way you could miss it, even

86

from space. On screen, the gunsight hovered over an unbroken sea of green.

'You see?' He snapped his fingers. 'They made us disappear *like that*.'

He seemed quite comfortable with the idea. I looked up at the sky, half expecting to see a black helicopter buzzing over us, or one of those drones the man in the bar told me about. *Predators*. If anything was watching us, the clouds hid it.

'Cheer up.' He slapped me on the back. 'It's a good thing.'

'Really?'

'Why would they change it if they didn't have something to hide?'

Later, the email I'd written replayed itself in my head. *The people I'm with are nice* . . . To a point. Before I came, I imagined a ship full of Antons, *Boys' Own* adventurers yarning round the campfire and swapping jungle lore over bottles of beer. Camaraderie and good times. The only bit I got right was the beer. For the rest of them, we'd spent three days on this tiny boat and I still didn't know them at all. Anton, Drew, Tillman, Howie, Fabio and Zia – plus the boat's crew, Pedro and Pablo.

Pedro and Pablo never said a word, except to each other. Zia wasn't much more forthcoming. I hadn't found out what Anton had against her: he'd let her stay, but he obviously wasn't happy. She mostly kept to herself in the kitchen area, reading a book or staring off the bow. That suited me fine. I still couldn't quite credit how quickly she'd stepped into Nolberto's shoes. I kept my distance, and watched her carefully.

Tillman was more talkative, but not in a good way. The second morning, he'd found me shaving at the back of the boat.

'You ever hear of MRSA?'

More than I ever wanted. 'Methicillin-Resistant Staphylococcus Aureus. The superbug.' There was an outbreak at the hospital where I work a few years ago. Several people lost their jobs over it – not to mention the patients who died.

'I knew a guy out here who caught it. Got it in a shaving cut, next thing his goddam face nearly melted off. He made it home with about six hours to live.'

He sauntered off, smirking. I finished shaving, to make a point, but the next day I started letting my beard grow.

Howie wasn't much better company. He complained about the heat; he complained about the bugs; he complained about the food . . . it was like travelling with Peggy. 'Just wait until we're in the jungle,' said Tillman. He sounded as if he was looking forward to it.

Fabio was a cool guy, almost the opposite of Howie. Totally self-contained: he could spend hours scanning the river in silence. Personal questions got minimal answers that left me none the wiser; he never asked me about myself. He seemed competent, which made me feel better; I was glad we had him with us.

And then there was Drew.

I didn't mean to flirt with her. I'd promised myself (and, implicitly, Cate) I'd be on my best behaviour. But – we hit it off. She laughed at my jokes and looked me in the eye. She teased me. She was smart, funny and quick. She made me think; she made me feel interesting, which I hadn't felt in a long time.

I know, in the caveman logic of these things, she belonged to Anton. But someone, maybe Scott Fitzgerald, said that the test of intelligence is being able to hold two contradictory ideas and still function. I knew I was walking a tightrope: that was part of the buzz. You don't stay married for eight years without knowing the rules. *Here*, but no further. As long as I didn't fall, it was fine.

Sometimes, when we were joking, I caught Tillman glaring at us. I wondered if he fancied her, too. The last thing we needed was a bizarre love triangle developing in the middle of a jungle.

So we were an odd assortment – like the first days of uni, when you make friends indiscriminately and spend the rest of term stuck with your choices. The only one who'd worked with Anton before was Tillman, who struck me as the last person you'd want to bring back on your team.

'I thought you'd have a crew you used regularly,' I said to Anton one afternoon, while we were washing up the lunch dishes. Our turn on the rota.

'Different strokes, different folks. Guys I worked with before, some only do diving jobs, some couldn't make it this time. Some hated my guts.' He grinned. 'Most folks aren't in this for the long haul.'

He handed me a stack of plates to dry.

'To be honest, I wouldn't trade any of you. Fabio knows the jungle. Howie can speak to the Indians like a native. Drew's got a PhD from Yale; Zia's a tasty cook . . .'

'I thought you didn't want Zia to come.' I remembered his reaction when he saw her on the boat. I wanted to know more about her inconvenient boyfriend.

'Yeah, well . . .' Before he could go on, something caught his eye. He pointed to the shore. 'You see that?'

I looked. Among the trees, a red and white billboard broadcast some official message in stern block letters. Branches dangled in front of it, obscuring the message, but I felt certain it was a warning. In the bottom corner, I saw the silhouette figure of an archer with a bent bow.

'What does it say?'

'Stay away from the wild Indians,' said Anton. 'This is the edge of the reservation. Sometimes they come down here and loose a few arrows if anyone gets too close.'

He glanced at the opposite shore. 'Killed a guy, last year.'

I scanned the jungle. If the Indians were watching, they kept themselves well hidden.

'If this is the edge of the park, shouldn't there be a ranger station or something? The map said there was a control point.'

'Indians burned it down two years ago. But our permits are all in order.' He put the pile of clean plates back in the plastic tub where they lived. 'Anyhow, like I was saying. Drew, Fabio, Zia, Howie – all experts in their fields. You're a hotshot doctor from London. We're like the Magnificent Seven.'

'You forgot Tillman.'

Anton laughed. 'That's easy. He's Charles Bronson.'

The next day, the river started to break up. Like a rope unravelling, the main course split into channels, twisting between islands and sandbanks. Pedro steered unerringly, without once looking at a chart or the GPS. Some of the channels he chose were so narrow a fallen tree could have blocked them; some so shallow, I could almost feel the hull shiver. I wondered how we'd ever find the junction with the Pachacamac.

I sat in the shade and read my book. In the background, I could hear the rasp of Fabio sharpening his knife, Zia chopping vegetables for supper and Howie complaining about something or other.

A big fist yanked the book out of my hands. Anton grinned down at me.

'Whatcha reading?'

'*Heart of Darkness*. It's about some people going up a river in a boat.'

He studied the cover. 'Yeah, I read it.'

I tried not to look surprised.

'I liked the movie better.'

'The movie?'

'You know. Brando. *I love the smell of napalm in the morning.* All that crazy Doors shit at the end. *Dah da daah dah, dah da daaah dah* . . .' He hummed a few bars of *Ride of the Valkyries.*

'*Apocalypse Now.*'

'The guy who wrote the book, he just seemed kind of naive.'

I didn't think anyone had ever accused Joseph Conrad of that. 'It's pretty depressing. He called it *Heart of Darkness,* after all.'

'But then the bad guy dies in the end. In the real heart of darkness, you don't get that kind of hope.'

He said it with such intensity, I had to wonder whether he'd ever suffered from depression. It would make sense. All that manic energy, the crazy ideas; a career (if you can call it that) built on ludicrous hopes and inevitable disappointment. I could imagine he suffered some pretty black moods.

He dropped the book back in my lap. I found my place.

'"We live, as we die, alone,"' I read aloud.

'Told you,' said Anton. 'An optimist.'

He hunched his shoulders, screwed up his face and croaked in a sinister voice, '*The horror. The horror.*'

He straightened up. 'You ever wonder how the hell they did it?' he said, to no one in particular.

He often asked questions like that. It meant he wanted us to listen.

'Do what?' said Drew.

'I was thinking of the old times. Diego Alvarado, those early conquistadors – what they must have thought when they saw this for the first time.'

He waved at the jungle sliding by.

'They probably shat themselves,' said Tillman.

'Most of them came from a place called Extremadura. You ever been, Kel?'

'The only place I've been in Spain is Barcelona. And that was for a stag do, so we didn't see much.'

'Extremadura's nothing like that. It's a bitch of a place: mountains round the edge and a dustbowl in the middle. Like the Old West; these guys who came out of it were tough as nails. You know what Extremadura means? "Beyond Hard".'

'That'll be me after four weeks in the jungle,' said Tillman.

'Unless we find some Amazon queen who likes white dick.'

'Or if you get lucky with Zia.'

I glanced back, embarrassed on Zia's behalf. She had her back to us.

'My point,' said Anton, 'is it must have blown their minds. Piloting their boats down these rivers, nothing but sandbanks, marshes, forests and savages. Diseases. Humidity so thick it could rust your armour from the inside.'

'They must have died like flies,' said Drew.

'Look there.'

Fabio had put down his knife and was pointing out at the river. A little way off our bow, a tree floated towards us, a big balsa trunk. I couldn't see anything special about it.

Anton grabbed his binoculars and aimed them at the tree.

'My God,' he said, and the awe in his voice made us all sit up. 'I've read about this. Never thought I'd see it.'

We leaned over the edge, lined up like sightseers on a cruise ship. Anton passed along the binoculars. The trunk was enormous, easily six feet across, low in the water like a breaching whale.

And riding on its summit, like some Amazonian Ahab, a human body.

'Some of the remote Indian tribes, they don't bury their dead because the soil's too thin,' said Anton. 'They lash the corpse to a log and send it out into the river. Eventually the log sinks, and the body gets absorbed back into nature.'

'Fish shit,' said Tillman.

'See how low the tree is riding,' said Fabio. 'It came a long way.'

I stared at the body on the tree with a car-crash sort of fascination. Beside me, Drew tugged my arm, impatient for her turn. The ragged body lay flat against the mighty tree, clinging on like moss. Nothing holding it: the ropes must have come undone or rotted off.

'I'm amazed he's stayed on,' I said. I knew what the river could do. Just that morning, I'd seen two trees smashed together so hard they shattered.

'That's like a piece of history,' said Anton. 'A fossil. The exact same thing Alvarado could have seen five hundred years ago.'

I lowered the binoculars to give them to Drew. Then snatched them back.

The body had moved. The log must have hit a wave; the body rolled up on to its side. I watched, hypnotised, waiting for it to roll into the water. I could see its face staring at me, burned almost black by exposure. Tattered clothes and a ragged beard. I felt ill.

A floppy arm extended into the air. I waited for it to fall, but it hung there, defying gravity. It waved in the breeze like a snapped twig.

Through the binoculars, I saw two eyes blink open in the burnt face.

'*He's alive.*'

14

We nearly lost him. We didn't have space to turn the *Sierra Madre*, and the tree had already slipped past. Chaos ensued, as Anton and Tillman and Fabio struggled to get into the skiff. Pedro had to keep moving to maintain steerage way, and all the time the river was taking the tree further behind us.

'Come on.' Anton grabbed me and almost threw me in the skiff – a thin wooden canoe, with an outboard motor bolted to one end. It almost capsized when I landed on it, and almost tipped over again as he jerked the starter cord. It felt like balancing on a hamster wheel. No lifejackets.

The current swung us downstream the moment we cast off, pushing us after the tree. Fabio squatted in the stern to steer, while Anton crouched in the bow with a rope. I huddled in the middle with Tillman. Water splashed over the low sides, soaking my trousers. The engine hammered out every other noise.

We overhauled the tree. The river had funnelled into a fast, narrow channel between two islands, racing us along. Fabio guided us alongside. Up close, I could see how massive the tree was – as big as a bus. One bump from it could have tipped us all in the river, or flattened us, but Fabio kept us inches away, reading every eddy and change in the river.

Anton stood. He swung the rope and hooked an outcropping branch first time. His body swayed with the current but his head stayed still, all his focus locked on the target.

He jumped. The boat rocked over and I grabbed the side. When I looked up, I saw the hulking tree, towering above me, and Anton on top of it silhouetted against the clouds. He picked his way through the dead branches like a cat on a fence. Totally focused, totally at ease. I'll never forget the sight.

Fabio was shouting something at me, but I couldn't hear with the engine. He waved at the rope, which was slipping into the water. I grabbed it just before it went over the side, holding us close while Fabio edged us forward

Racing down that river, with a tree that could have killed me so close I could touch it: I don't think I'd ever felt more alive. Not my wedding day, not when Peggy was born, not my first day as a junior doctor, when the surgeon turned to me in theatre and it suddenly hit me I'd been granted the power of life and death. Never.

We'd come level with the top of the tree, where the not-dead body was lying. That turned out to be the easy part. Tillman gripped the tree, while Fabio and I stood in the bow and Anton lowered him down. The man was emaciated, a sack of bones, but it was all dead weight and I had to keep my balance on a floating cigar tube. Holding him wasn't nice. He stank of decay. Cuts and sores covered his legs, covered in blood that had bled, dried and cracked apart again. Pus oozed out of the open wounds. Ants the size of a ten-pence piece crawled over him. When one of them scuttled on to my arm, I nearly dropped the body in the river.

We got him down. Anton slithered off the log and almost sank us as he landed in the boat. Tillman pushed off, and Fabio gunned the engine.

I looked down at the man we'd rescued – gaunt, infected, broken. A corpse that refused to accept it was dead. A chill went through me like a premonition – probably the adrenalin draining out.

'So who is he?'

We got him aboard the *Sierra Madre* and laid him out on the table. Zia boiled a pan of water; I cut away his clothes with Anton's bush knife. The injuries were even worse than I'd thought; barely an inch of skin hadn't been sliced, torn or bitten to shreds. A long wound opened his calf almost from the ankle to the knee. Too straight to have been made by an animal.

'Aren't you going to do something, Doc?' said Tillman.

In the face of so much trauma, all I could do was stare. I didn't know where to begin.

Zia appeared with a pot of steaming water and handed me a cloth.

'Clean him up.'

I dipped the cloth in the water and started sponging off the dirt. His skin was so dark it didn't make much difference: all I did was expose more bruises, and a tapestry of tattoos that covered almost every inch of him. Screaming eagles with outstretched talons; a skull wreathed in fire; a gigantic anaconda wrapped around his right arm, its open jaws snapping towards his neck.

I wrung out the cloth. Zia just stood there, staring.

'Aren't you going to help?'

I started on the left arm. Black water slopped on to the deck as the dirt came away. More cuts and bruises – and another tattoo. Another snake, only a small one, wrapped around a pole.

I'd seen it before. So had Anton. He grabbed the neck of Zia's top and yanked it down, showing her bra and the black tattoo above her breast. A snake, coiled round a stick.

Side by side you couldn't doubt it. They weren't similar: they were identical.

'He's one of Menendez's guys, right? *Right?*'

Zia's face was set like stone. But she didn't deny it.

'I fucking knew it.' Anton looked at me. 'Fix him up good, Doc. We need to talk to him.'

I lifted the patient's wrist to check his pulse – and made another discovery.

'Look at this.'

I held out the arm. 'What the hell is that?' said Anton.

On the skin of his forearm, where I'd swabbed away big streaks of mud, was a series of numbers. Printed in dark ink, like the tattoos, but messy as a child's handwriting. A mass of tiny scars squirmed around it; the skin was red and inflamed.

'He must have done it to himself.'

'Or someone did it to him.'

The scars weren't old and the ink wasn't deep. I tried to imagine why this man – alone in the jungle, starving and with almost no chance of rescue – should have repeatedly punctured his skin for a series of numbers. 69241513028.

'Is it a telephone number?'

The man groaned. We all flinched back. The eyelids fluttered; his mouth moved, but no sound came out. I tipped a cup of water to his lips. A little went in; more dribbled down his beard.

His eyes opened. Dark and bloodshot and filled with panic. He writhed on the bed; he tried to sit up but I held him down.

'Where did you come from?' Anton demanded. 'Where's Menendez?'

The patient's eyes locked on to me, as if he was searching for something he couldn't live without. I wished I knew the answer.

I rummaged through the medical kit for a needle and some painkiller. Sweating, with the others crowded round me, I could hardly remember the dosage.

I handed the vial and the syringe to Zia. 'Can you prepare this? Ten milligrams.'

'Ten milligrams?' she repeated.

'What is that?' said Anton.

'Diamorphine.'

'What's that?'

'Heroin.' I swabbed his upper arm with an alcohol wipe and took the syringe from Zia. I hated doing this with an audience.

'Holy fuck,' said Tillman. 'You dealing?'

'He won't be able to tell us anything if you get him high,' complained Anton.

'He's in no condition to tell us anything anyway.'

Zia handed me the prepared syringe. I was trembling so

hard, I had to try three times before I got the needle in. Zia gave me a crooked look.

'What kind of doctor did you say you are again?'

'In hospital, you'd do this with a canula and an automated driver.' I pulled back the plunger to check for blood. Then squeezed down, and prayed I'd got the dosage right.

His eyes opened wide as the needle went in. I saw the pupils collapse in on themselves, wide with bliss or terror. The body convulsed and settled. The eyes closed.

'Is he going to live?' said Anton.

Everyone looked at me. As if I knew. I checked the pulse again and tried to gather my thoughts.

'He's in a bad way. A lot of infections, probably riddled with parasites too. I think one of his legs might be broken. How long he lasts depends on how the infections progress, and how much damage has been done already. He needs specialised care.'

Tillman snorted.

'Put it in numbers,' said Anton. 'Fifty-fifty? Sixty-forty?'

You'd be a fool to make predictions on a case like that. 'Fifty-fifty,' I hedged. 'He's survived this long, so he's obviously tough as old boots. With food and rest and medicine, there's no reason he shouldn't recover.'

Fabio studied the chart. 'There is a village, Esperanza. Not far. It says on the map they have a clinic.'

I unzipped one of the sleeping bags and spread it over the patient like a blanket.

'Now,' I said, 'is someone going to tell me what this is about?'

15

The boat chugged round a bend.

I don't know why I wrote that. The river was nothing but

bends, curving this way and that until I couldn't be sure we weren't simply going in circles, a snake eating its own tail. *Going around the bend.*

The man we'd rescued lay on the table like a body in a morgue. The rest of us (apart from Pedro and Pablo, who seemed gloriously uninterested in our new passenger) gathered in the bow and waited for Zia to give us some answers.

'His name's Roberto.' She stared down the back of the boat, avoiding eye contact. 'He was one of Felix's guides.'

'Felix?' said Howie.

'Felix Menendez. My fiancé.'

And suddenly I remembered the name. Cate, sitting up in bed reading off her iPad. *Still no trace of the Menendez expedition* . . .

'I thought Menendez was a doctor. Something about a medical mission.'

'Medical mission, yeah.' Anton shot a glance back at the patient, as if he didn't trust him not to vanish overboard. 'That was horseshit. Why else would you come right to this part of the jungle, when no one's been up here in a hundred years?'

'You're wrong,' said Zia. 'Felix's mission was to help the Indians. He thought Paititi was a fairy story, and he'd never heard of Alvarado.'

Another memory: the woman in the hostel, pointing to the sunken hospital boat. *Menendez Clinic.*

'Did he run a clinic in Puerto Tordoya?'

Zia nodded. 'I was a nurse there.'

'Point is,' said Anton, 'how come his buddy Roberto ended up drifting past our boat like the Ancient fucking Mariner? And where's Menendez?'

Anton stared at Zia. Zia stared back. Fabio stood. He pointed to the shore.

The bend had straightened. Onshore, I saw a break in the

trees, and a sandbank that merged into a muddy beach where three peque-peques and a balsa raft were pulled up. A naked child watched us from the top of the bank, long dark hair covering her face. She fled into the forest the moment our boat touched the beach.

'Let's hope we can keep him alive long enough to find out.'

Cate would laugh, but I had certain expectations of my first encounter with the Amazon Indians. Mist rising on the river, eyes blinking from the undergrowth. Painted bodies, naked except for the odd feather or bone piercing. Probably some kind of drumbeat.

I know that's a cliché, and maybe borderline racist (some of my best friends are Amazonian Indians, honest!). Even so. We beached the boat and scrambled up a muddy bank, through banana trees to a clearing. A dozen-odd huts stood on stilts, thatched roofs perched on wooden frames that were open at the front and sides. A rusting iron cross stood at the edge of the clearing, with a clutch of rotting wicker baskets at its base. Naked children played in the dirt, while grown-ups in flip-flops and T-shirts sat at the edges of their huts as if they were waiting for a bus. I doubted it would come any time soon.

One of the Indians came forward, an older man with a wispy beard. He wore an MTV T-shirt, shorts and a necklace made from teeth and bones. Ink dots speckled his cheeks and forehead.

Anton, Fabio and Howie went to meet him. Fabio put a machete on the ground in front of him and gestured for him to take it. Howie added a few words. After all the warnings I'd heard about wild Indians, it seemed odd to be giving them a weapon they could use to hack us to pieces. Though now we were here and face to face, they didn't look that wild. They looked defeated.

The headman picked up the machete and thumbed the blade. He spoke with Anton; Howie translated. It seemed to take a long time.

I started to get impatient. 'Did you explain about Roberto? Do they have a clinic?'

Howie put it to him and the headman nodded. He led us down a little path between banana plants, to a patch of cleared ground. A square block building stood on a concrete foundation, with a tin roof and slatted wooden windows. So substantial, after the mud and the huts, it seemed unreal.

I put my head in the door.

'Hello?'

No answer. I stepped inside the gloomy room. Dry leaves crunched underfoot on the tiled floor. Automatically, I put my hand to the wall for a light switch, and just as I realised how unlikely that was, I felt it. I turned it on.

Nothing happened. Out of habit, I flicked the light switch again, up and down. My eyes began to adjust. There were no beds or gurneys. No trolleys, cabinets, desks or mosquito nets. Not even a chair. Only rustling leaves blown in through the open door, and the click-clack of a switch that had never turned anything on, and never would.

'Clinic,' said the headman proudly.

'Where are the doctors? The medicines?' I said.

Howie translated. 'He says a charity paid to build the clinic, but they didn't have enough to equip it. Some kind of problem.'

The darkness in the room hollowed me out and made me feel ill. I stumbled for the door, kicking through the dry leaves.

'Nee naw, nee naw.'

Tillman and Zia came up the path, carrying our patient in a hammock between them. Tillman looked at the empty clinic.

'Where do you want him, Doc?'

That evening, the headman, Raul, sat with us around the fire. He passed around grilled fish, banana porridge and a bowl of some drink with the texture and taste of vomit that we couldn't refuse. The rest of the Indians watched from their huts like a Greek chorus. I tried not to stare at them; they weren't nearly so inhibited. They pointed and gossiped; children ran up and pulled my fair hair, then ran away giggling. I'm sure I caught a couple of the younger women making eyes at me.

Maybe they wanted me for a ticket out. I couldn't blame them. The village was dying. Of the thirteen huts, five sat empty. All the men were under ten or over fifty.

From what I understood – fragments of Spanish, and the bits Howie translated – an oil company had come up the river a few years ago. They offered the Indians money and jobs, in return for the rights to build a pipeline across their land. A man from the Ministry of Indian Affairs had calmed their concerns, promised them development and healthcare. They signed a contract. The oil company employed the Indians as labourers on the pipeline, finding paths and cutting trails.

But there were side effects. Some of the Indians – a quarter of the village – fell sick and died: whether from new diseases, or construction chemicals leaching into the groundwater, they didn't know. The forest emptied as animals fled the chainsaws and bulldozers. The Indians discovered alcohol.

'Maybe we should have run like the animals,' the headman said, gazing into the fire. The forest that had fed them for ever couldn't support them any more. They had to spend more and more of their wages on food, purchased from the oil company at extortionate prices.

'For the first time, we knew what money is. And then we knew we were poor.'

And then the pipeline was built and there was no more work. The young men in the village left for Puerto Tordoya and never came back. Some of the wild animals returned after the bulldozers left, but by now the Indians had forgotten how to hunt. They had guns, which they'd never had before, but they couldn't afford ammunition. And so the village starved, and lost its people one by one to the towns and to drink, and other forms of oblivion. They thought they were owed more money from the contract, but nobody could find it.

'That's terrible,' said Drew. She sat on the log, bare legs tucked up to her chest. Firelight shone on her skin and made it golden.

The headman was saying something more, fast and passionate. Howie could hardly keep up.

'He says, uh, the real bad guys weren't the mining companies. He says it was . . .' He hesitated, struggling over the words. 'It was the priests.'

'*Misioneros*,' said Raul.

'You mean the Spanish? Like the ones who rescued Alvarado?'

'*Norteamericanos.*'

It seemed a group from an American church had arrived a few months before the mining company, racing up the river in fast boats ('fast like the devil,' said Raul). They brought biscuits and Coca-Cola, toys for the children and necklaces for the women. Some of the tribe wanted to drive them back into the river, but they were talked out of it. The missionaries seemed kind and friendly. They didn't want anything in return for their gifts. They had medicines, too, which they used liberally. They built the clinic.

'They told us we should wear clothes because naked is bad. And they told us we should trust the oil company,' said Raul. 'They even helped write the contract. We were very grateful.' It was only later, when an NGO from Lima came to visit, that they found out more than half the oil revenues were going to the missionary church.

'They bought our souls, and we gave them the money to pay for it. And then they tell us there is not even enough to pay a doctor for our clinic.'

Anton played with the shark's tooth around his neck. 'How about Menendez?' he said. 'Did he come through here?'

The headman nodded, rocking back on his haunches. '*Sí, sí.*' He switched into his own language, which Howie translated.

'There were nine of them, travelling in two boats. They spent three days here. Set up shop in the clinic and gave the kids their shots.' The headman pointed to a woman standing at the edge of the firelight. A tiny head poked out of the blanket slung across her chest. 'Menendez delivered her baby.'

'I told you,' said Zia. Anton ignored her.

'He say anything about Paititi?'

That got a longer answer. 'They got talking about it one night. Telling tales; not much else to talk about round here. Mostly, Menendez wanted to know about the Indians upriver.'

'I bet he did,' said Anton.

'Does this tribe have any legends about Paititi?' Drew asked.

Howie put the question and got a long, involved answer. 'He says it was his ancestors who built this place. Many generations ago.'

'Does he know the way?'

Howie concentrated hard.

'He says there are four signs. First, a waterfall. Second, you pass the guardian. Third, there's river flowing through a ravine, and fourth the anaconda bridge.'

'Who's the guardian?' I wondered.

'Don't you get it?' Anton was almost hopping with excitement. He took a stick and scratched rough copies of the petroglyphs from Alvarado's narrative in the dirt. Three vertical lines. A face. Three zigzag lines and then a spiral.

'That's what this is. Waterfall, guardian, river, snake bridge.'

We all stared at the pictures, shadows in the dust. Shimmering firelight animated them: I saw the waterfall pouring over the cliff; the zigzag river flowing through the canyon; the bridge swaying in a jungle breeze. Something tugged inside me, the same pull of *possibility* I'd felt in the Mayaland hotel.

Anton turned to Raul. 'Have you been there?'

Raul gave a bashful smile. The pictures went still. '*No, no.*'

'He says Paiquiqui isn't a place you walk to. It's a spiritual place, a state of mind you get to by communing with the spirit world.' Howie frowned. 'It's amazing. These people are supposed to be Christians, but those jungle legends still persist.'

'Why does he call it Paiquiqui?' I asked.

'Paiquiqui is the Inca name,' said Anton. 'Spaniards couldn't pronounce that right, some reason, so they Spanglicised it to Paititi.'

'What about upriver?' said Tillman. 'Has he ever been up the Pachacamac? Seen this waterfall, the rock carvings?'

Raul shook his head and scowled. '*Indios bravos.* Mashco Piro.' He spoke quickly, several sentences I couldn't understand. He spat on the ground.

'He says they don't go up the Pachacamac. The tribe there are wild Indians. Bad people. He says he warned Menendez not to go, but he didn't listen. He went up the river, and never came back.'

Not for the last time, I remembered Cate's Wikipedia

research. *Presumed killed by the wild tribes of the unexplored regions.*

16

Anton, Tillman and Drew went back to sleep on the boat. Howie and Fabio took one of the empty *maloccas*, the Indian huts. Zia and I stayed with Roberto at the clinic, in case anything changed in the night. He was still out, but not quiet: tossing and turning in the hammock we'd strung for him, muttering in his restless sleep. I gave him another dose of painkillers, sticking the needle right between the jaws of the tattooed snake.

I swabbed the wound with alcohol. 'What was the tattoo all about?' I asked Zia.

She glared at me, as if she suspected me of some terrible secret motive.

'It was the symbol for the expedition. A caduceus, with an anaconda. The night before they left, we went out in Puerto Tordoya. Felix, the expedition, people from the clinic. We all got the tattoo.'

'It must have been hard for you. When he left.'

Her jaw tightened. 'Felix was supposed to be in the jungle two months. But he said it could be longer. He told me I shouldn't worry: he had a good team, lots of experience. I stayed in P-T and kept the clinic running, and after two months, no messages, I told myself he must be OK. Then three months. After four, I started to panic. I tried everyone: the police, the hospital, the municipality. Nothing. So I flew to Lima and waited at the Health Ministry until they let me in. They all said the same thing. Felix's mission was unofficial – privately funded. Not their concern.'

Her eyes blazed. 'Of course, if the project had been

successful, everyone from the minister on down would have queued up to get their photographs taken with Felix. A Peruvian success. But when he vanished . . .'

She stared out of the slatted window. 'I went back to P-T. One night, I heard a noise from the river. An explosion so loud it broke windows, shook televisions from the walls. By the time I reached the boat, it was mostly under water. The police said it must be a fuel leak, oil fumes spontaneously combusting. Maybe a cigarette. Bullshit. All Felix's papers, all his research materials and vaccines were on that ship. All lost.'

'I'm sorry.'

She blinked back tears. She looked furious – with me for asking, with herself for saying so much, with the world that had taken away her fiancé.

'Get some rest,' I told her.

She shook her head. 'You sleep. I'll sit with Roberto a while.'

Once we'd made him as comfortable as we could, I retreated to one of the empty *maloccas* near by. After three days packed in with the others on the *Sierra Madre*, I craved some space of my own.

It was my first night in the jungle, but it was hard to believe in golden cities and fabulous treasure when real people were dying in man-made squalor. I could feel the forest pressing against the circle of huts, wounded and raw but not defeated. Mosquitoes droned around my netted bed like some kind of torture; leaves rustled, trees creaked; invisible animals barked and chirped and rooted in the darkness.

It was one of those nights where bad dreams seemed to last hours, but each time I woke I'd only been asleep a few minutes. Around midnight, I put on my Crocs and went back to the clinic. Zia was still awake, sitting next to the patient, murmuring something in his ear.

'How's he doing?'

'I think the fever has broken.'

He felt cooler, and his breathing was calmer. We wiped him down, and Zia gave him another injection of antibiotics. Even when the needle went in, he barely stirred.

I was walking back to my hut – stamping my feet to scare off any snakes – when I saw a light among the trees. It moved, stopped, and moved again. Then stopped again, darting back and forth as if it was searching for something.

I watched and waited. I'd read about some of the weird and wonderful species that live in the rainforest: fireflies, bioluminescent fungi and glow-in-the-dark butterflies. But this didn't look like any of those: more like someone pointing a torch. I could see a figure silhouetted against the glow.

I forgot about the snakes. Every warning I'd ever heard screamed through my head: poachers, drug smugglers, guerrillas. I didn't know what to do. I couldn't go back to my hut and pretend to sleep – no protection there. But no way could I blunder into the jungle to confront . . . *what*?

A branch snapped behind me – *inside the village*. I spun round, heart in mouth. For the first time in my life, I wished I had a gun.

It was Howie. A sliver of moon and the dying embers of the campfire showed me that much. Only three or four feet away, keeping to the shadows around the huts as if he was trying to avoid me.

I ran over and grabbed his arm. He looked as scared of me as I'd been of him.

'There's someone over there,' I whispered. I pointed into the forest. Trees hid the figure, but the glow still showed.

'It's Fabio. He went for a dump.'

'Are you sure?'

'Who else would it be?'

I could think of a dozen answers. I craned my head around,

trying to get a look at the man in the trees to convince myself it was Fabio.

'How about you? Going somewhere?'

'Just . . . you know.' He waved in no direction in particular. He had a backpack on his shoulder. 'Couldn't sleep. You?'

'Checking on the patient.'

'Right.' He rubbed his eyes. 'How's he doing?'

'I think he's past the worst.'

'That's great.'

And without another word, he stumbled off into the darkness.

I stared after him. He crossed the clearing to one of the huts and clambered in, like a student sneaking into a dorm room. After a moment, I heard low voices.

Was he sleeping with one of the Indian girls? Hard to believe. He was so clean-cut, I'd never seen him drink anything stronger than Diet Coke. Definitely a dark horse.

The light in the forest was still there. If it was Fabio relieving himself, he was taking his time. Perhaps the local food didn't agree with him.

I wasn't brave enough to find out – and I didn't want to be outside when the chief found Howie deflowering one of his virgins and came swinging with the machete we gave him. I hurried back into my *malocca*.

But I still couldn't sleep. Mosquitoes had got in under my net, and were raising merry hell. The peeping Tom side of me was straining to hear any noises coming from Howie's hut. I couldn't see the light in the forest any more, but that only made me look for it harder.

I wondered if Drew was still up. I put on my shoes and walked down to the river. The boat swung at anchor, a few feet offshore. It was nearly 1 a.m., but I could see a cigarette end glowing under the canopy. Two – no, three. I could hear voices. I didn't think they'd heard me.

Someone finished a cigarette. The red ember arced through the air and fizzled on the water as the smoker flicked it over the side. A match flared to light another. In its light, I saw the three of them: Anton, Drew and Tillman. Tillman leaned against the side, smoking a joint, while Drew sat cross-legged with Anton's head in her lap.

They hadn't heard me coming. I was about to announce myself with a knock on the gangplank, just to make them jump, when I heard Anton say my name.

'You think Kel could be in on this?'

Sound carries easily over water, especially if you're downwind. I squatted in the shadows and listened.

'I wanna know what happened to Nolberto.' Tillman's voice. 'Kel says it was a crazy motorcyclist, but who the hell knows. He's the only one there. And next morning, Zia's on the boat ready to go.'

'Because you brought her,' Drew reminded him.

'I hadn't figured it out then. I didn't even know what happened to Nolberto.'

'Anyway, Kel's innocent,' said Drew. 'The way we met him, Mexico, it's impossible he's with Menendez.'

I liked hearing her stick up for me. It gave me a nice glow – right up until the moment Tillman said:

'You just like him because he spends his time gaping at your titties. You notice that, boss?'

'No,' said Anton shortly. 'Point is, now we've found this Roberto guy, what do we do with him?'

Mortified, I hardly heard Tillman's reply.

'Leave him here with Zia and Kel. Only way to be sure.'

'Go upriver without a cook and a doctor?' said Drew. She sat up straighter. 'Are you insane?'

'Don't want to go without your buddy Kel?'

'Shut up,' Drew told him. I cringed on her behalf. 'You're not listening to this crap, are you, Anton?'

'No,' said Anton again. Not entirely convincingly.

'Kel's a nice guy. That's probably why you don't get him.'

'I get him plenty. Better than you.'

'Will you stop it?' said Anton. 'We're talking about fucking Roberto, not Kel.'

'Give it a day, at least,' said Drew. 'If Roberto comes to, he could tell us a lot about what happened to Menendez and his team.'

'We don't have time to stick around. Water's dropping every day.'

Anton took a last hit from the joint and chucked it over the side. A good throw. It landed on the beach a few feet away from me, still glowing. I was so worried they might see me, I almost missed the last thing he said.

'Maybe he won't make it through the night. Solve all our problems.'

I clambered back up the bank and spent the night in the *malocca*. As I passed the hut Howie had gone in, I could still hear murmurs and giggles. No sign of Fabio.

Before I went to bed, I made one last check on the patient. The fever had crept up a bit; but it was too soon to give him another injection. He tossed in his hammock, muttering in his sleep. I reached inside the mosquito net and wiped some of the sweat off his forehead. It seemed to help.

That was at 2 a.m.. I know, because I checked my watch. Five hours later, he was dead.

17

We joined the Rio Pachacamac the next morning. A long, white-sand beach made a shark's-tooth point between the rivers, but there was nothing else to mark it. It could have been just another meandering dead end.

Anton scowled at the map. 'Are you sure this is it?'

'Check the GPS,' said Fabio.

'It's on the fritz.' Anton took the unit out on the open deck and tried again. 'Nada.'

'I heard that when the army's launching ops against the *narcotraficantes*, they jam the GPS signals to fuck with them,' said Tillman.

'That's reassuring,' said Howie.

We all glanced up at the sky. Nothing but cloud, and a few birds wheeling overhead.

'Has to be it,' said Anton.

Nobody asked my opinion. I slouched on the bench at the far end of the deckhouse and pretended to doze. I needed to think about Roberto.

There was no reason to think his death was suspicious. No one else seemed to suspect anything. He was more than halfway dead when we picked him up, and he'd endured enough to kill him three times over. He'd seemed to be getting better, true, but that meant nothing. It could have been any one of a dozen things. Snakebites, parasites, malaria, internal injuries . . . It could have been that the will to live that got him through those weeks in the jungle finally packed up when he was rescued. It could have been he was allergic to antibiotics.

I wished I could be sure it was any of those.

I'd found him dead that morning, so peaceful in his hammock it was only the flies on him that gave it away. The body was already cold. No marks of violence, beyond what he'd already suffered. Zia was distraught. No wonder: she'd spent half the night sleeping beside a corpse, and lost her only link to Menendez.

Anton told me I'd done my best. Drew gave me a hug,

and said he was lucky I'd been there for him. I accepted their condolences professionally. They could see I was upset; they thought I blamed myself for not doing enough. I told them that in my line of work, you know you're going to lose patients. You don't last long if you can't put it behind you.

And after that, the subject was dropped. Was it superstition, a foreboding we might have glimpsed our own future, or just so bizarre there was nothing to say? No one wanted to talk about it.

That didn't mean I stopped thinking about it. *Maybe he won't make it through the night*, Anton had said. *Solve all our problems*. I wondered what he meant by that.

You can handle this, I told myself. I had to. Where else was I going to go?

We left the body in the village. Raul, the chief, wasn't happy, but Anton gave him twenty dollars to bury him. That's what a life was worth out there.

'Check out the water,' said Anton. I gave up pretending to sleep and looked over the side. The river had changed. The brown, silty flow we'd lived with since Puerto Tordoya had become black, like very strong tea. Astonishingly clear when you looked down.

'Black water,' I murmured. My voice – but in my head I heard Nolberto's. Clutching me on the hospital bed, using his last strength to gasp those two words.

'Just like Alvarado's story,' said Drew.

'Tannins from decomposing leaves,' said Anton. 'This has to be the right way.'

Fabio grabbed my shoulder and pointed to the shore. 'Kel! You see? Capybara.'

I looked over the side. Capybara had become a standing joke between us: every ripple in the water or odd-shaped log had me tugging his elbow asking if that was it. I wanted to see one for Peggy.

He gave me his binoculars and guided my gaze to the right place. Even magnified, there wasn't much to see: a tiny head, matted fur and a small nose poking out of the water.

'It looks like a drowned rat.'

I was glad I'd seen it, but it made me miss Peggy more than ever. I thought about calling, but hearing her voice would have cracked me up. I set up the laptop with the satellite transmitter and opened the email client.

'Do you have to?' said Anton.

'I'll pay you back,' I snapped.

I tapped out the email. *I saw a capybara! I miss you lots. I love you.* I typed quickly. I could feel the tension on the boat.

I wanted to send a photo, but it would probably have crashed the satellite. Instead, I opened a search engine. The sight of the black water had got me wondering what had happened to Nolberto.

Nolberto Rodríguez Puerto Tordoya.

The results took for ever to come through. There weren't many. I clicked on what seemed to be the local newspaper and skimmed through it. He was in critical condition, but doctors were hopeful. No arrests, but no mention of a boatload of gringos who'd skipped town next morning either. All good.

'You done yet, Tolstoy?' said Anton.

Just to annoy him, I went back and clicked on another link from the search results. A blog, written by an NGO worker who lived in Puerto Tordoya. I scanned the post to see if she had any more details.

She did.

I slammed the laptop shut. Everyone looked away.

'We need to talk,' I said to Anton.

Nine people on a thirty-foot boat doesn't get you much privacy. Anton and I sat in the bow, out of the shade of the awning. The others pretended not to watch, though they could hardly help it. For the first time since I met him, he looked uncomfortable.

'Is this about the guy from the log?'

'It's about Nolberto.' I put the laptop on the bow and flipped it open. I'd kept the article on screen. I pointed to the second paragraph. 'Read that.'

Sources in Lima have hinted that Nolberto Rodríguez was an officer with the Special Intelligence Unit of DIRCOTE, the national anti-terrorism directorate, working undercover. Local police continue to refuse to comment on whether the attack could have been the work of *Sendero Luminoso* or *narcotraficantes*, possibly in retaliation for the recent escalation in US-sponsored drone strikes in the so-called Red Zone.

I closed the lid. 'Did you know that?'

'Of course not.' Anton's eyes were inches from mine, pristine and righteous blue. 'You think I'd hire a cop for a cook?'

'Then *why* was he with us?'

Anton drummed his fingers on the hull. 'The article said it was Shining Path or *narcos*, right? Maybe he hitched a ride. Cover, to see if they're operating up here.'

'Or maybe he thought we were helping them.' I held his gaze. '*Are* we?'

'No.'

TOM HARPER

'How about Lorenzo?'

'How *about* Lorenzo?'

'He didn't strike me as a legitimate businessman.'

'Lorenzo's straight enough. *Narcos* are bad for his business, same as anyone else.'

It sounded plausible. But he blinked as he said it.

'Is there a "but"?' I could see I was right. 'You dragged me into this. If there's a reason the police might be interested, you have to tell me.'

Anton stared at the river.

'When we went to get the guns, Lorenzo said you owed him money,' I prompted him.

'Yeah?'

'Eighty thousand dollars.'

Anton watched a pair of macaws fly overhead. I waited him out.

'Lorenzo paid for this,' he said at last, rapping his knuckles on the hull.

'The boat?'

'The boat, the food, the gear. Pedro and Pablo's wages. Everything.'

'Howie said his organisation put up the money.'

'They gave us eight thousand dollars, and most of that went on the guns.'

I took a swig from my water bottle while I digested that. 'So why's Lorenzo backing you?'

'He owes me a favour.' Anton saw I wasn't buying it. 'Lorenzo deals in gold. Mostly from the mines, but if an antique piece comes his way he knows how to move it. If word gets out we found Paititi, and people know Lorenzo was involved, he can sell a few pieces and tell people they came from Paititi. Good excuse to make a few bucks on fakes.'

'Why would the counter-terror police care about that?'

'Antiques is a funny business. Hard to prove what anything's

116

worth, and there are a lot of cash buyers in Puerto Tordoya, if you know what I'm saying.'

'Money laundering.'

'Listen, I don't have anything to do with that shit. But if Lorenzo does, and if the Peruvians think I'm going after stolen antiquities, maybe they put two and two together, made five, and sent Nolberto to check us out.'

I digested that. It was a lot to take in. With one very obvious question outstanding.

'What happens if we find Paititi?'

'We'll discuss that when we find Paititi.'

'If I'm here so that drug barons can buy looted artefacts, I need to know.'

'You think I'd be doing this job if I cared about money? For Christ's sakes, I'd make better pay mopping up at McDonald's. I swear, anything we find in Paititi either stays there, or goes in a museum. The only thing I'm selling is my story.'

I hesitated, and then I decided to believe him. To be honest, if Anton wanted to skim off a few artefacts for himself, I didn't mind. He was a treasure hunter; I sort of assumed he would. It was the drug dealers, guerrillas and money launderers I had a problem with.

Even with the breeze coming over the bow, I was roasting in the sun. We both streamed with sweat. I turned to get back under the awning – and found Anton blocking my way.

'There's one more thing.'

Sweat turned to ice. I knew – as surely as I knew anything – he wanted to talk about Drew. Tillman had planted the seeds – *You just like him because he spends his time gaping at your titties. You notice that, boss?* I'd done nothing wrong – but there are sins of thought as well as sins of deed. Guilt must have shone through every pore of my face.

'Roberto – the way he died. You sure it was, you know, on the level?'

I sat down hard on one of Zia's cool boxes. Hopefully he thought it was the heat making me feel faint.

'Zia said something weird, like she didn't think it was natural.'

'She didn't mention anything to me. Did she think the Indians could have . . .?'

Anton lowered his voice. 'She thinks it could be one of us.'

'Jesus.' Like an idiot, I looked back down the boat. Seven people, all pretending not to watch us. 'But why?'

'She didn't say.'

I had my own suspicions – but I wasn't ready to share them.

'She's just playing silly buggers,' I told him. 'There's no way you could tell what killed him without a full post-mortem. The state he was in, it would be more surprising if he'd lived.'

'I thought it was probably crap,' said Anton. His face brightened; his blue eyes shone with relief. 'I had to be sure. No rotten apples, you know.'

'No rotten apples,' I agreed.

18

'Can I build a hotel here?'

'You've only got three houses. You need four before you can build a hotel.'

'I thought four houses equals a hotel.'

'That's not what I said. Four houses, then a hotel.'

We were playing Monopoly. Drew had brought a battered set – *I figured we might get bored.* After supper that night, camped on a bluff, she got it out and cajoled us into playing. Anton was all over the place, buying properties everywhere but missing chances to make sets, forgetting to collect his money when he passed Go. It was only when he tried to buy

'Free Parking' that we got him to admit he'd never played before.

'Did you not have a childhood?' Drew teased him.

Anton took a green house and added it to the row he'd built up. He was a quick learner. Once we'd explained the rules, he played ferociously, trading or mortgaging properties he didn't want, consolidating those he did, building houses and hotels like Donald Trump. Never more than fifty dollars in the bank: one bad roll could have wiped him out. But somehow it never did.

'Four houses on Machu Picchu.'

The set was the American edition. When I mentioned that the streets were different in different countries, Anton had taken a pen and changed all the names. Marvin Gardens (Piccadilly) became Machu Picchu; Connecticut Avenue (Pentonville Road) was Puerto Tordoya. Boardwalk (Mayfair) had become Paititi. Drew landed on it next go. Anton had already put two houses there.

'You think one day there'll be a real hotel there?'

'Paititiland?' I looked at Anton to share the joke. He was too busy studying the board.

'That's how they'll find it,' said Zia. 'When everything is slashed and burned, the excavators will be digging foundations for an apartment block, and they'll hit the ruins of Paititi.'

'Bullshit,' said Tillman. 'We're gonna find it this month.'

'If we don't, at least we'll be pretend rich.' Howie held up a fistful of Monopoly money.

Anton looked up. 'You know who Colonel Fawcett is?'

I didn't. Some of the others might have, but they knew better than to butt in when Anton was revving up for a story.

'He was a Brit in the twenties,' Anton said. 'Explorer, real old school. Went to find El Dorado in the Brazilian jungle – called it the Lost City of Z. He never came back. Other

TOM HARPER

expeditions went looking for him, and *they* never came back. Massive media mystery, like the Lindbergh baby or that airliner that went missing last year. Never found him.'

It was my turn to roll. I waited for Anton to finish his story.

'I've been to where he disappeared. There's a major highway that runs about twenty miles from it. His bones are probably under a truck stop.'

'What about the Lost City of Z?'

'Not even close. Fawcett believed he was heading for a mountain range that just doesn't exist.'

Was that so different to looking for rivers that didn't appear on Google Earth? I rolled, and landed on the Oil Company (formerly the Electric Company).

'That's two hundred bucks,' said Anton. Playing with real malice – just like I used to do to my little brother. On my next go, I landed on Community Chest. Anton grabbed the card and read it to me.

'Someone has given you a blanket. Collect ten dollars. Unfortunately, it's infected with anthrax. You die and lose all your properties.'

'Let me see that.' I snatched the tattered card out of his hands. 'It says it's my birthday.'

Drew gave me a kiss on the cheek. 'Happy birthday.'

'That's what they used to do,' said Anton. 'Rubber tappers, gold prospectors – they'd fly low over the jungle looking for villages, then toss out bundles of infected blankets. Indians took them – why not? Three months later, no village.'

'Whatever it takes, right?' Tillman grinned. I think he meant it ironically. No one laughed.

'It's inhumane,' said Drew.

'It's very fucking humane. We're human beings – that's what we do. We see something, we want it, we take it, and God help you if you're standing in my way. Law of the jungle.'

'We're better than that,' said Howie.

'Are we?' said Anton.

While he'd been speaking, the others had taken their goes and the dice had come back to me. Bad luck.

'Paititi,' crowed Anton. 'Three hundred dollars.'

'I'm bankrupt.' I threw my last few banknotes across the table and got up.

'Don't be a sore loser,' said Anton.

'I left my toothbrush on the boat.'

I went down to the boat. I never like losing, but I didn't care that much. I didn't need my toothbrush, either. I wanted a few moments' privacy.

I tiptoed along the gangplank and clambered aboard. I wanted to find out more about Zia. She'd been in the bar just before the attack, and she'd stepped into Nolberto's shoes without breaking stride.

Nolberto, who was a government spy, lest we forget.

Then she'd been with Roberto the night he died; had helped prepare some of his injections. *She said something weird, like she didn't think it was natural.*

And she was engaged to the mysterious Dr Menendez.

We'd stowed all the luggage at the front of the boat. I picked through the food boxes and oilcans until I found Zia's bag, a green canvas duffel. No lock on the zip. I rifled through the clothes, trying not to be creepy. Not that there was much to see. Zia travelled light: a few changes of clothes, a novel and a torch. A travel medical kit that was almost as well stocked as mine. A recipe book.

Up on the bluff, I heard raised voices. The game was getting bad-tempered, the way Monopoly always does. Only a matter of time before someone stormed off, or wondered where I'd gone.

I reached down to the bottom of the bag and felt around. Flat against the bottom, I felt a slim notebook. Some kind of journal? I pulled it out, spilling clothes, and flipped it open.

I felt a small pang of vestigial conscience, but I had to know.

My conscience was safe: all the pages were blank. Perhaps she'd meant to keep a diary and not got round to it. But as I held it up, a small sheaf of loose papers slid out and fell on the deck. Newspaper clippings. I scanned the headlines as I gathered them up. They all seemed to be from the Puerto Tordoya paper.

Oil Company Donates Floating Hospital
Pioneering Health Programme for Indians
Crusading Doctor Vows to Double Vaccination Rate
Menendez Expedition Takes Healthcare to the Final
Frontier
"Progress Good": Menendez Reaches Pachacamac
Headwaters
Mysterious Accident Sinks Flagship Clinic
No Word From Menendez Expedition

The first article was dated two years ago. Front-page news, a splash headline and a big picture. Grinning dignitaries cutting the ribbon on a gleaming boat. It took me a moment to recognise it as the sunken wreck I'd seen the children playing on in Puerto Tordoya.

The Mayor of Puerto Tordoya has formally opened the new Cajamarca Clinic, a floating hospital which will bring modern healthcare to communities up and down the river, as well as in Puerto Tordoya. The Clinic has been provided by the Cajamarca Petroleum Consortium, under the conditions of their new licence to drill for oil and gas in the Amaru-Mayu field. The Director of the clinic is Dr Felix Menendez, formerly of the World Health Organisation and renowned for his work on childhood vaccination projects.

Bob Mallick, Project Leader for the Cajamarca Petroleum Consortium, said, "CPC is committed to meeting and exceeding the highest environmental and social standards for extractive industries. This hospital represents tangible proof of our commitment to be good neighbours in our new home, and to make lasting positive contributions to the communities where we operate. We are in this for the long term, and are proud to be working with a local community health pioneer like Dr Menendez."

I thought of the village at Esperanza, broken and discarded when the oil company moved on. I wondered if the villagers there knew they were enjoying the highest environmental and social standards.

There were lots more articles, all in Spanish. I couldn't read fast enough: I'd already been gone too long. I leafed through quickly, scanning headlines and photos. Most seemed to be progress reports from the clinic: smiling patients, smiling doctors, smiling children with round plasters on their upper arm, sucking lollipops.

One caught my eye. Zia, in a group of men and women surrounding Dr Menendez. She was wearing a nurse's uniform.

'Dr Menendez and staff of the Cajamarca Clinic celebrate their ten-thousandth patient,' said the caption.

Nine months ago, the articles took a new direction.

In a pioneering public health campaign, Dr Felix Menendez is to lead an expedition deep into the Mashco-Piro Indian Reservation in the headwaters of the Rio Pachacamac. The goal of this ambitious project is what Dr Menendez terms "PPP": "Pre-emptive, pre-contact protection."

Speaking to reporters, Dr Menendez said, "The idea of 'uncontacted Indians' is a false concept. Loggers, gold diggers, drug smugglers and bio-pirates are already operative deep inside the national reservation. In places the Cajamarca pipeline passes only a few kilometres from Indian land. It is inevitable there will be contact, and history shows that where there is contact, there will always be public health consequences. The goal for this project is to inoculate the wild Indians in the reserve, using specially developed vaccines and without infringing on their way of life. The difference between this programme and previous government and private-sector initiatives is this: we do not want to bring the Indians to the outside world. We want them to be ready when the outside world comes to them."

However, a doctor with a leading medical NGO cast doubt on the idea. Speaking on condition of anonymity, he said, "Dr Menendez's ambition is commendable, but serious logistical considerations remain. These are the most inaccessible, uncharted reaches of the jungle. Most importantly, how will he find the Indians, without exposing them to the very diseases he wishes to protect them from?"

After that, the articles dropped off quickly. Longer gaps, shorter stories. No more smiling children. Even the accident that sank the clinic got short shrift, furtive pieces tucked on the inside pages. Almost as if they wanted to hide it.

The last article was three months ago. A single column inch, no photo.

Public officials confirmed last night that they have received no contact from the Menendez expedition. An official statement on the Ministry of Health website said, "The expedition was well equipped and led by experienced guides. We remain hopeful that they may yet emerge from the jungle."

A branch snapped up on the bluff. The game must have finished. Someone was coming. I jammed the clippings in the notebook, stuffed it in the bag and stepped on to the gangplank just as Zia came down the embankment.

'You've been gone a long time.'

'Sore loser.' I forced a grin. *Did she see me?* 'I fancied some time alone.'

I stepped off the gangplank to let her past. She didn't move. 'I need to speak to you.'

Shit. 'OK.'

She gestured me back on to the boat. What choice did I have? I went aboard, forcing myself not to look at the duffel bag. A number of crazy scenarios played through my head on extreme fast-forward.

'What's this about?' Trying to sound natural, wondering if anyone would hear me scream.

'Roberto.'

I was almost too surprised to be relieved. 'Come again?'

'What shots did you give him?'

I tried to think. Sweat ran down the side of my nose. 'I gave him two of diamorphine, and two of the antibiotics.'

'Where?'

'The arm. Upper arms: two in the right, two in the left.'

'And that's it?'

I nodded. I didn't like where the questions were going.

'When he died, he had a fifth puncture wound. In the vein of his right forearm.'

'I had no idea.'

She studied me for a good long time. I tried to play it cool. Not easy when the bag you rifled is sitting right in front of you.

'Who else had needles?' she demanded.

'You, for one.'

'Me? You think I'd have wanted to kill him . . .' Whatever she was going to say, she changed her mind. 'We wouldn't be talking now.'

'Maybe it was an insect bite.'

'I'm a nurse. I know what needle marks look like.'

I held up my hands, all innocence. Still trying not to look at her bag.

'You think I overdosed him?'

'Don't be stupid. The amount you gave him, you couldn't have overdosed a mouse.'

'I was playing it safe.'

I was suddenly very aware of how much I stank. I needed air and space. Most of all, I needed to understand what the hell was going on.

'You know what I can't decide?' she said. 'If this is all an act, or if you really are as clueless as you make out.'

She glanced at her watch. 'We'd better go back. Before people think we're fucking.'

19

Stare at something long enough, and you start to see all kinds of things. After six days of wall-to-wall jungle, I felt I'd begun to understand it. Not like Fabio, who could pick out a monkey or a capybara in the undergrowth from the far side of the river. Not like Pedro, who steered the boat eight hours a day through a floating minefield of uprooted trees, sandbars and shifting currents, without once making a wrong turn. But enough that I could make some judgements.

Ever since we turned up the Pachacamac, the world had got wilder. The river was narrower and deeper; in places, sandbanks reared up thirty or forty feet and it was like sailing through a canyon. Fallen trees stretched out into the river like arms trying to hold us back. We saw so much wildlife, I no longer rushed for my camera every time Fabio saw something. Bright scarlet macaws, tapirs, capybara, turtles, even the black-and-yellow coils of an anaconda sunning itself on a beach. Each morning, I woke up to the screech of howler monkeys in the trees; we often saw jaguar footprints in the mud. You'd have paid a lot of money for a safari like that.

Stare at the same people long enough, and you start to see things too. Since my conversation with Zia, I'd kept a wary distance from her. Was there really a fifth puncture wound in Roberto's arm? I hadn't noticed it. It could have been an old wound, or a bite or a scratch. Or she'd made it up completely, to throw me off track.

I also kept an eye on Howie. He'd never really admitted what he'd been doing in the village that night – when I asked him, he blushed and muttered something about linguistics. After that, I didn't see him much. He'd caught some kind of stomach bug and spent a lot of time hanging over the side, or begging Anton to stop the boat so he could go and squat in the woods. He blamed the food, though no one else had got it. One more thing to complain about.

Of course, Fabio had been in the village that night too. Anton, Drew and Tillman had been up half the night, only a hundred yards away. Not to mention a village full of aggrieved Indians.

At that point, I gave up. Apart from Howie, the rest of us were healthy and making good progress. I was in one of the most remote, most spectacular places on Earth, chasing a dream of lost cities and fabulous treasure. I wasn't going to mope about it.

I tried not to think about what had happened to Menendez.

The caiman still frightened me. There were lots of them about in this stretch of the river, gliding through the water or sunning themselves on beaches, as still as logs. One night, I shone my torch out across the water and saw a dozen pairs of red eyes staring back at me, just above the waterline. They always made me think of reading *The Enormous Crocodile* to Peggy.

'Is it my imagination, or are they getting bigger?' I asked Fabio one day. We were standing lookout on the bow, watching for logs and sandbars under the black water.

He nodded. 'All the animals are bigger here. No people.'

He leaned across the rail and pointed his boathook at one of the caimans, a huge beast easily twenty feet long. 'You see him? He looks like Tillman, no?'

I borrowed his binoculars. That brought the caiman a little too close for comfort. A snub snout and two close-set eyes, powerful body tensed uncomfortably forward on his forelegs.

'You've got a point.'

'Seen something?'

Tillman had come up behind us. So predictable. I stared at the river so he wouldn't see me trying not to laugh.

'I found a caiman that looks like you,' said Fabio.

Tillman took the binoculars. 'That's one bad motherfucker,' he grunted.

He was almost out of earshot when Fabio said, to no one in particular, 'Ugly and lazy.'

Tillman heard him. He spun faster than I'd have thought possible and charged for Fabio. I was caught between them. For a moment I seriously considered jumping in the river.

Fabio aimed the boathook like a harpoon. Tillman skidded to a stop. I stood in the middle.

'You going to bite, crocodile?' said Fabio.

Tillman looked as if he'd have snapped Fabio's head off, if he could (which kind of proved Fabio's point). He grabbed for the boathook, but Fabio jerked it out of reach like a fisherman working a lure.

Everyone was on their feet now. Anton pushed his way through. He grabbed Tillman by the shoulders.

'What the hell are you doing?'

Fabio lowered the boathook. I took the opportunity to edge behind him.

'Just playing.'

'For fuck's sake. You think this is a game? You're supposed to be watching for hazards.'

Fabio looked at the river. 'It's cool.'

And then he added something in Spanish. Too fast for me to understand, but Tillman got it. He twisted free from Anton and charged forward. There was a struggle, a splash, and a clatter as the boathook dropped on the deck.

Fabio wasn't there any more. He was in the water.

'Jesus!' Anton turned and waved frantically at Pedro in the wheelhouse. '*Derecha! Derecha!*'

Pedro spun the wheel. I grabbed the boathook and leaned over the rail to try to reach Fabio. He'd already floated a long way back. We didn't have space to turn. Everyone was shouting and running. Someone threw a lifejacket, but it missed and floated away.

The whole boat shuddered. The shock went through my legs and almost tipped me over into the river. I dropped the boathook and grabbed the rail. Even Tillman was knocked off balance. The only person who stayed upright was Anton, bracing himself against the roof struts.

'Sandbar,' he said. He sounded calm, but he was breathing hard. Even I could tell something was wrong. We'd grazed a couple of sandbars coming up the Pachacamac, but always slid right off them. This time we'd stopped moving. And the engine noise had changed, high-pitched and stuttering. When Pedro cut it off, it felt like putting a wounded animal out of its misery.

Pablo dropped the anchor, which seemed redundant. Fabio hauled himself in over the stern. For a moment, I thought he and Tillman might go at it again, rip each other to shreds. They settled for swapping murderous looks.

'Check for leaks,' Anton told Fabio. 'I'll take a look at the prop.'

He changed into swimming trunks and a face mask, grabbed a waterproof torch and slipped into the black water. I scanned the river for caiman and snakes.

'It's the candiru fish you got to look out for,' said Tillman. 'Swims up your dick and sinks its teeth in.'

I winced.

Anton went under three times in all. When he finally came up, he looked relieved.

'We're grounded. But the prop looks OK, which is good.'

Under the blizzard of mosquito bites, Howie's face had gone white. 'Can we get off?'

'Sure,' said Anton. He hoisted himself out of the water. Drew handed him a towel. 'We'll offload the gear, pop right out.'

'You said the river's going down all the time.'

Anton shrugged. 'All we need is one good storm and she'll come off like a prom dress.'

We spent the rest of the day emptying the *Sierra Madre*, ferrying our supplies ashore in the skiff. Draining, sweaty work: I hadn't realised how much we'd brought. Sacks and sacks of food, oil drums, backpacks and camping gear. Inflatable rafts. A chainsaw, the two gun boxes and Howie's heavy duffel bags. I thought about peeking inside, but the zips were still padlocked.

By the time we'd finished, just before sunset, we had a small mountain of equipment on the beach. My heart sank as I looked at it, contemplating the effort of reloading it next day. And if we grounded again? The river was getting lower: we could spend weeks fetching and carrying, on and off and on again, each time we hit a sandbar.

Tillman snapped open one of the gun chests. He took out a shotgun and loaded it.

'What are you doing?' The gun made me nervous.

'Going hunting.' His eyes swept around, inviting us to challenge him.

'We agreed no hunting unless it's absolutely necessary,' Drew objected. 'We didn't come here to slaughter the wildlife.'

'I didn't come here to eat rice every meal.'

'If the Indians hear shooting, maybe they come check us out,' said Fabio.

I glanced anxiously at the trees. I'd never thought we might have company. We hadn't seen a soul since we left Esperanza.

Drew looked at Anton. 'You're not going to let him go?'

Anton hesitated. Just for a moment, the golden confidence slipped and I thought he looked tired. He didn't want to offend his girlfriend. But he hated being told what to do.

'Go ahead,' he said to Tillman. 'Take Fabio.'

'Like that's a good idea,' Howie murmured to me. Quiet, so Anton didn't hear. 'Sending those two off in the forest together with a shotgun.'

'And try not to kill any endangered species,' Anton added.

We made camp on the beach. Howie and I gathered wood, and Zia built a fire. Once or twice, I heard shots echoing out of the jungle. Each time, Drew flinched. She didn't say anything, but the tension between her and Anton affected us all. I tried not to think about it.

It was dark before the hunters returned. They'd shot a boar; they carried it into camp just the way you'd imagine, hanging from a pole by its feet, head dangling back where they'd slit its throat. They left a trail of blood through the campsite. In the firelight, with blood and smoke in the air, it was a scene a caveman would have recognised. I felt something primitive stir inside me.

Tillman was cock-a-hoop. *I shot that motherfucker,* he told anyone who'd listen. *Bam blam kapow.* Fabio skinned the animal – thankfully, the darkness hid the butchery – and Zia put it on the fire. Fat bubbled and spat. The smell was enough to make me want to grab a gun and kill something myself.

We had a party that night. Even Drew forgot her reservations about the hunting and joined in. There was still plenty of beer, and Anton said it would just weigh down the *Sierra Madre,* so we drank it up. No one said it, but we all felt it: a feeling like the last night of the holidays. It was obvious we weren't going much further. If not this bend, then the next. Anton pored over the map like a gambler with his race form, but he couldn't change geography. We were still at least forty kilometres short of the falls.

Forty kilometres doesn't sound like much. Back home, you could walk it in a day, if you had to. Drive it in twenty minutes on a clear motorway. But in a wilderness choked with trees, no paths and not a foot of open ground, distance changes.

We ate and we drank, and Fabio played his guitar, and then Tillman turned on the boom-box he'd brought. Another relic from the eighties. Drew got up and started dancing, eyes closed, twisting in the firelight. Totally unselfconscious, like that cheesy greetings card line. *Dance like nobody's watching.* Anton joined her. After a decent interval, I followed; for a few moments, she shimmied between us, three of us in our own little world.

Fabio and Zia came up, and soon we were all dancing on the sand. Music echoed over the water, Tillman threw another log on the fire, and we forgot the jungle and the river. Even the mosquitoes stayed away – scared off by the smoke, or Anton's extravagant dance moves.

Later, when the fire was burning low, I found myself lying

on the sand next to Drew. Her face shone; her cheeks were flushed.

'You dance really well,' she told me.

Pedro had turned the music up loud. She had to lean close to be heard. Her face was only a few centimetres from mine. No distance at all. Especially with a beer buzz warming me.

When you're that close, things blur. The boundaries I'd drawn in my head, so clear in daylight, weren't so certain any more. I could almost . . .

Something stung my cheek. I slapped it instinctively, thinking it was a mosquito. My cheek was wet – but not with blood. I felt another bite, then two more on the top of my head.

Drew sat up and held out her hands.

'*It's raining!*'

We all ran down to the river's edge and watched the circles spreading across the water.

'Should we go back to the boat?' Howie asked.

'It'll take a few hours to flow through,' said Anton. 'We'll get some sleep, be ready first thing.'

We spread tarpaulins over our mound of gear. Pedro and Pablo stayed on the *Sierra Madre*, in case it floated in the night. To be safe, we ran a long rope from a tree on the riverbank out to the boat, so it wouldn't drift away. Between the crew, the rope and the anchor, we thought we had it covered. 'Kind of overkill, for a boat that's stuck to the bottom,' said Howie.

I went to sleep that night to the sound of rain rattling on the canopy above me. My last thought before I drifted off was Drew's face, and that tiny gap between us.

I woke and thought I was dreaming. Thick fog covered the ground, rolling in off the river and spinning between the trees. When I got up, I could hardly see my feet. The others were still in their hammocks, slung between the trees like cocoons. The rain had stopped, but I could still hear water dripping from every leaf.

I peed behind a tree, then went down to the river to wash my hands. It seemed to have risen in the night – a good metre nearer the mound of equipment. I looked out to see if it had floated the *Sierra Madre*.

For a moment, I wondered if the fog was playing tricks. Then I wondered if I really was still dreaming. Or if I'd come to the wrong part of the beach. Then I saw the rope we'd tied to the tree, loose end trailing into the water.

The *Sierra Madre* had gone.

20

'Those treacherous, lying, goddamned mother*fuckers*.' Tillman kicked an empty beer can. It flew off the beach, landed in the river and bobbed away.

'I told you those guys were no good. I told you not to trust them.'

Anton shrugged. He'd taken it unbelievably calmly. I was probably more upset the time someone smashed my car window. 'They got us this far.'

'And then they abandoned us. Chickenshit *assholes*.'

'Makes no difference. River's getting shallow – we probably couldn't have gone more than another day. And they left us the skiff. We can fit into that, plus some supplies and enough fuel to get us to the front gate.'

My mind must have wandered. 'What are you talking about?'

'The front gate. Paititi.' He smiled. 'You don't think we give up just because they stole our boat?'

Something snapped inside me. 'Actually, I think we do.

How many hundreds of kilometres have we come? And now
the only way back is in an open boat with limited supplies?
We need to set out at once.'

'It's not the only way back.'

'We'll be carried out in body bags. If anyone ever
finds us.'

'We'll be fine.'

I looked around for some support. 'Am I the only one who
wants to stay alive?'

Nobody met my gaze. I heard Tillman say, not very quietly,
'Pussy.'

'Howie?' I tried.

He gazed at his shoes and muttered something about *come
this far.*

'Drew?'

Last night, her face had been so close to mine. Now, she
was a million miles away.

'How much fuel can we take?' said Fabio.

We all looked at the skiff. It didn't look much more than
a punt.

'We have the rafts.'

'What rafts?' said Howie.

Anton picked out a plastic roll from our pile of gear, about
the size of a log. 'Pack rafts. Inflate these babies, you can
carry a moose if you have to. We'll load those with the gear
and tow them from the skiff.'

He lobbed me the rolled-up raft. It didn't feel much heavier
than a sleeping bag.

'And if the rafts sink? Or the skiff? I don't want to end
up clinging to a tree like Roberto.'

I could see that registered, at least with Howie and Zia.
Tillman pouted: I think he was actually enjoying this, the
chance to strut his macho stuff.

'How about this?' said Anton. 'We'll go until we run out

of fuel. If we find the waterfall, and if the rock signs are there like Alvarado said, we can decide what to do. If not, we'll float back here, fill up with gas and head home. OK?'

I put my hand in my pocket, and felt the emergency beacon where I always kept it. I resisted the urge to pop it open right there.

'If it comes to it, we'll go much faster with the current behind us,' said Drew.

'I'm sure that's what Roberto thought.'

We inflated the rafts, and loaded them with hammocks, cook kit, backpacks, ponchos and boots. We decanted fuel from the oil drums into jerrycans and packed them in the skiff, with sacks of pasta, flour and rice on top. Machetes, guns and ammunition went in too. It took all morning.

'You can survive in the jungle for ever, if you have to,' Anton said. 'As long as you've got a machete. Without it, you can't even move.'

I added my medical kit to the skiff. Howie wanted to bring his duffel bags, which kicked off a furious row with Anton. I was a little way down the beach, packing up, so I missed the beginning. But we all heard it when Anton shouted, 'We're in a survival situation here. Can't you understand that?'

And Howie, louder than I'd ever heard him, 'I gave you eight thousand dollars for this expedition! You do what I tell you.'

'I'm in charge of all operational decisions.'

'You're in charge so you can take me where I need to go.'

The upshot was that one bag stayed on the beach, and one bag came with us. The skiff seemed to sink a couple of inches when he stowed it.

We ate lunch, cold boar and potatoes, and left. The skiff led the way, with the three inflatable rafts daisy-chained behind it. All the boats sat worryingly low in the water, but we'd left more than half our stuff behind, hidden in the forest beyond the beach. Spare clothes and supplies, books and games and the laptop, and huge quantities of the food that Pedro and Pablo were supposed to have lived off while they waited for us. Anton thought the animals would get to it, but we packaged it as best we could, and covered it with a tarpaulin weighted with fallen branches.

I often thought of that food mountain, in the days ahead. By the end, I was dreaming about it.

Black water glided by as the beach bent out of sight behind us. In the end, we'd packed the skiff so full there wasn't room for all of us: four of us had ended up in the rafts. Howie had complained we should redistribute some of the food to the rafts; Anton refused point-blank.

'If you get wet, you can dry off. If the food gets wet, we starve.'

Afterwards, when I knew what trekking through the jungle really involved, I understood why we persisted with the boats. At the time, I couldn't imagine a worse way to travel. The skiff's outboard motor struggled against the current, against the weight in the boat and the weight of the three inflatables dragging behind it. It fought so hard I thought we'd burn it out.

The rafts were a nightmare. Each time the skiff changed direction – which was often – the motion whiplashed through the line of boats, sending us all over the river. Then we had to paddle frantically to straighten course, so we could avoid whatever obstacle had made the skiff move in the first place.

And we had plenty to avoid. The river had narrowed; fallen trees choked it at every turn. Some were so long there was no way around. Then Tillman would go to work with the chainsaw, balancing on the skiff's bow to cut an opening, while Fabio held position against the current. Some were so thick he had to jump on top, churning splinters inches from his feet. He never slipped.

Even if Pablo and Pedro hadn't done a runner, the *Sierra Madre* wouldn't have taken us much further. That was the only consolation.

'But it would have been nice to have them waiting here for when we got back,' said Drew. It was the second day in the boats, and we were sharing a raft. An easier stretch of river, for once, straight and clear of debris. Drew sat in the bow, facing me, while I kept an eye over her shoulder on the water ahead. One sharp branch could be the end of our rubber boat.

'You don't think Anton did it on purpose? Like Cortes, burning his ships so no one got cold feet.'

I said it like a joke. I wasn't sure it was so preposterous. The idea had been nagging me since yesterday morning. Before we left, I'd retrieved the broken rope. From the length that was left, it was pretty clear it had to have been cut by someone on shore. I suppose Pedro and Pablo could have snuck ashore to steal supplies and done it then, but I hadn't noticed anything missing.

No rotten apples.

I didn't mention that to Drew. Didn't want her to think she was trapped in a raft with a paranoid lunatic.

'Anton knows what he's doing,' was all she said.

It was a clear day. Out on the river, out of the shade, the sun was scorching. Music drifted back from Tillman's boombox in the skiff ahead. Led Zeppelin, 'Good Times Bad Times'.

The boat edged sideways – some small change of course, working its way through the ropes that tied the flotilla together. I dug my paddle in the water to straighten up again.

'How did you two meet?'

'Online dating.'

'Really?'

'Didn't you know? That's how everyone meets these days.'

She laughed. 'Not really. I was doing some work for an NGO in Lima. One day, I was at the Ministry of Culture and I ran straight into Anton. Couldn't miss him.'

She laid down her paddle and leaned back. She started unbuttoning her shirt. I studied the river.

'You know how he is. Kind of sweeps you off your feet.'

'Yeah.'

She shrugged off her shirt to reveal a black bikini top underneath. Tiny straps.

'We got talking and he offered to buy me lunch. Told me all about Paititi, Alvarado, this manuscript. So earnest, so passionate – he charmed the pants off me. Of course, it was only when I woke up in his bed next morning he admitted Megan had found it.'

I tried to blank the images that she'd put into my head. 'Megan?'

'His girlfriend. But they split up.' She got a bottle of sunscreen from her shorts pocket and started applying it to her shoulders. 'It was pretty much over before we met. He couldn't get the permits he needed, and she wanted to go back to the States.'

I wondered if Megan saw it that way. 'And you think the manuscript's genuine?'

'We checked it every way we could. Palaeography, linguistic analysis. We couldn't find anything else about Alvarado, but we checked the records of the monastery where he ended up. The priest he mentions was definitely there at the right time. And then there's the petroglyphs. No way anyone could have invented that, unless they'd been up the Pachacamac.'

She sprayed sunscreen on the tops of her breasts and rubbed it in. I played with my paddle, making invisible corrections to our course.

'The thing with Anton is, even if all that analysis said it was a fake, he'd still have come. That's the way he is.'

'I suppose we'll find out soon enough.'

She handed me the sunscreen. 'Do my back?'

She twisted around. I leaned forward, trying not to over-balance the tightly packed raft.

'Are you happy?' she asked.

'Sure.'

The sunscreen was thick and viscous. No way to spread it half-heartedly. Her body moved under my hands as I rubbed it in.

'No regrets?'

'The only thing I'd have regretted is not coming.'

'That's the spirit.' She stretched forward over the front of the boat, head resting on her hands like a kitten. 'I know it's been screwed up. Nolberto; the guy on the log; Pedro and Pablo cutting us loose. You're doing well.'

I didn't reply. Too busy concentrating. In a small boat, top heavy, it would have been so easy for my hands to slip round her.

'All done.' I sat back. My shirt was plastered to my skin; sweat ran down my face from the brim of my hat. I was breathing hard.

My hand was sticky with her sunscreen. I dipped it over the side of the boat to wash it off.

'Don't do that,' said Drew sharply.

I snatched it out. 'What?'

'Put your hand in the wrong place, it might get bitten off.'

That afternoon, we moored up to a fallen tree for lunch. Crackers with cheese from a tube, and Kool-Aid mixed with river water. I could already feel the waist of my trousers loosening up.

'You know why Anton has us drinking Kool-Aid?' said Tillman. 'Because he's fucking Jim Jones.'

Anton flicked a piece of cracker at him. 'That's *Indiana* Jones, asshole.'

'He's not taking us to Paititi. We're going to Jonestown, baby.'

'Don't blame me. You drank it.'

We lapsed back into silence. Suddenly, Anton sat up. 'Listen.'

'All I hear is bugs,' said Howie.

'Not that.'

I concentrated. In the distance, I heard a soft roar, like a distant motorway.

'Wind in the trees?' I guessed.

'There's no wind.'

He reached back to the engine and flipped the choke. 'Let's check it out.'

We swallowed our crackers and took our places back in the boats. Past the log, round the next bend. The river cut a deep channel, faster and narrower; the engine noise echoed off the trees like the shrieking of a million parrots. We shortened the slack between the rafts to make it easier to steer. Everyone stared ahead.

The first sign was the light. You could see it from a distance, a blaze of brightness as if the clouds had parted to let through a shaft of sun. Except there weren't any clouds. The trees spread apart, the river opened, and suddenly it wasn't a river any more, but a broad pool circled by the forest. A high cliff rose at the far end, and over it – so loud you could hear it even over the racket of the engine – a waterfall cascaded down and made the lake boil.

'The front gate,' Drew said. Almost as if she didn't believe it. I wiped my cheek and felt cool spray instead of sweat.

Fabio guided the boat as close to the falls as he dared. We pulled the rafts in tight behind, bobbing just beyond the foaming water. Anton looked at the cliffs, like a pole-vaulter sizing up his jump. We all scanned the rock face for the petroglyphs. No one wanted to go home now.

The cliffs were in shadow, and heavily overgrown with

creepers. No chance of seeing anything from that distance. Anton jumped over the side and splashed to shore.

'This is our stop.'

21

There was no beach. The trees pressed hard against the water's edge, their open roots making tangled caves on the bank where the river had cut away the soil. One tree had overreached itself, and toppled over into the water. We tied up to it and scrambled out, balancing on the trunk like a gangplank. Fabio came last, checking the knots and adding another hitch. Perhaps he had his suspicions, too.

Anton and Tillman started cutting a path. Drew followed; I started unloading the boat. Howie showed no interest in the petroglyphs and disappeared into the jungle in the opposite direction. Probably to empty his bowels: he must have been glad to get out of those boats.

'He's been sick too long,' Zia said to me. 'Are you going to give him something?'

'If it keeps up.' I was tired of her games. Every time she asked me a question like that, I felt she was trying to catch me out. 'He seems OK.'

'Do you have any Ciprofloxacin?'

I threw her my medical bag. 'Knock yourself out. Maybe give him an enema while you're at it.'

I followed the path the others had cut through the trees. The ground rose steeply, and soon came out in a small clearing at the foot of the cliff. The others must have just got here. Anton stood in front of the cliff, swiping with his machete to clear away the moss and vines that covered it. The waterfall was only a few metres away, but the trees hid it completely.

'Are you sure this is the right place?'

'Got to start somewhere.' Anton's blade rasped over the stone, setting my nerves on edge. Trees soared above me, as high as the cliff. Anything could be hiding up there.

'Jaguars mostly hunt at night, don't they?' I said.

'Any time they smell meat,' said Tillman.

Metal rang on metal – a strange, industrial sound in that wild place. Anton dropped the machete and shook his arm. We all stared at the cliff, a bare patch of rock just above head height he'd scraped clean.

A steel ring stuck out of the rock. Spotted with rust, but still shiny, with a groove gouged out by Anton's machete.

'How did that get there?' I said.

'Ancient Inca artefacts,' said Tillman. 'Or maybe our buddy Menendez.'

Anton pulled ropes and climbing gear out of his pack. He strapped himself into a harness and clipped on a rope. He fed the end through the steel eye in the cliff.

'Are you sure it'll hold you?' I fretted.

'We'll find out.'

It was dangerous work; Anton made it look easy. Hanging on vines for support, he worked his way up the cliff, chopping and scratching until he'd uncovered a series of steel climbing bolts all the way to the top of the cliff. They held. He clipped into the top ring and dangled there, swiping his machete at the surrounding foliage. Clumps rained down on us.

'Any sign of the carvings?' shouted Drew.

'There's so much crap, the Times Square Coke billboard could be under here and you wouldn't know.'

He kept at it. Tillman and Fabio belayed the rope, while Drew shouted encouragement. I wasn't needed – and I didn't think a dramatic discovery was due any minute. It didn't feel right. I sat on a rock, out of the way, and tried to imagine Diego Alvarado here.

All you have to do is respect history, take it seriously.

Alvarado didn't arrive with a machete and climbing ropes. He'd come here – if he *did* come here – after thirteen days in the jungle. Weak, hungry and alone. He wasn't looking for a lost city: he'd already been there.

Tillman had left his machete leaning against a tree. I picked it up, and started into the woods around the base of the cliff. The others didn't notice me go.

I'd never used a machete before. My technique was crude, but then it's a crude tool. Hack, slash; hack, slash. And I had plenty of energy. After a week sitting on boats at other people's mercy, it felt good to do something on my own.

In the sandy soil, the trees didn't grow so thick here. Dead leaves rustled on the ground, like English woods in autumn. Red flies buzzed around me, drawn to the sweat that had soaked my shirt.

Once you're here, you're part of the ecosystem. Fair game. Was that Anton's line? It sounded like the sort of thing he'd have said.

Something caught my eye on the ground ahead. A snake? I stopped dead, jerked back and almost fell over. I lifted the machete two-handed, samurai-style, hardly daring to breathe. Busy cutting my path, I'd almost forgotten I was in the jungle.

The snake didn't move. A little sunlight filtered through the canopy, but none of it touched the snake. I could hardly make it out in the shadows, but I could tell it was a big one.

'Boo,' said Drew's voice behind me. I almost chopped her head off.

I nodded ahead of me. 'Snake,' I mouthed, trying to keep an eye on it.

'Snakes are deaf,' she said. 'And so is wood.'

She stepped past me, brushing my leg, and stooped to pick up the snake. She waved it in my face.

'It's a liana.'

I lowered the machete. All I could hear was Cate's voice: *You think you can run around the jungle playing Indiana Jones?*

'You shouldn't go off on your own without telling us.' She waved the liana in my face, then tossed it into the undergrowth. 'There's more dangerous things out here than vines.'

'I thought maybe the rock carvings might be this way,' I said lamely.

'OK.' She squeezed aside and waved me ahead. 'Lead on, McDuck.'

I didn't really want to. The snake – even though it wasn't a snake – had reminded me I shouldn't be out here. And the machete wasn't cutting so well – the blade must have gone blunt. I hacked and chopped till I was red in the face, and never seemed to get very far. Drew said nothing.

A little way along, the cliff pushed out in a spur. We worked our way round the base, and came to a little seam in the cliff where a rockslide spilled on to the forest floor. It made a sort of slope, steep and broken. It must have been there a long time. The broken rocks were covered in moss and grass; saplings had started to grow through.

Further up, some of the cliff still looked intact. A series of descending ledges almost made a flight of stairs, ending in a jagged edge where the rock had split.

'Could those be steps?'

Drew took off her sunglasses. 'Just natural, I think.'

'I'm going to have a look.'

Before she could argue, I started scrambling up. Walking on eggshells, never sure if the rocks would give way. Heart in mouth in case a snake or a scorpion popped out from between the cracks. I could almost hear my sweat sizzling as it dripped on the stones. The rocks got looser; solid-looking boulders wobbled when I touched them. Pebbles ran off under my feet. A rock came away and bounced down the hill, just missing my head.

'You should wait for Anton,' said Drew.

You might wonder why I went on. I wonder myself. If you'd told me a month ago I'd be climbing a treacherous cliff in the rainforest, just right for every poisonous creature in the jungle, I'd have laughed in your face. But give me something to aim for, a concrete situation, and my brain locks on. Reality's never worse than your imagination (I thought).

Drew being there watching might also have had something to do with it.

I reached up and stretched my fingertips over the edge of the ledge I'd seen. Sharp edges dug into me; I was at full stretch. I kicked up with my leg and—

The rock gave under me. I tried to hold on, but my fingers didn't have the grip. A tide of stones dragged me down, tumbling and sliding. I put my hands over my head and hunched into a ball. Falling stones bounced off me like pinballs.

I rolled to a stop in a heap of dust and stones. The cliff was still moving: I could hear stones falling all round me. Some hit me. I cowered in my ball and wondered if the whole cliff would come down on top of me. Would they be able to dig me out?

A tug on my shoulder. I peeled my arms off my face and looked up. Drew's face was white.

'Don't you ever give me a fright like that. Are you OK?'

I stretched my arms and legs experimentally. I patted myself down, then tried to stand. Wobbly; bruised all over. My right ankle hurt like a bastard. I could already feel it swelling against my boot. But—

'Nothing broken.'

'You were insanely lucky.'

I looked up, at the fresh scar I'd carved down the slope.

'I'm thinking Alvarado didn't come that way.'

My voice was a croak. Drew offered me water from her bottle. I rinsed dust out of my mouth, then poured the rest over my face to sluice off the dirt. Half a dozen cuts stung in protest. I shook my head like a dog to clear the water.

And that was when I saw it. Out of the corner of my eye, on a low part of the rock face I must have climbed right past. Perhaps my little landslide had torn off some covering vegetation. Perhaps it had been in plain sight, and I hadn't noticed. Certainly, the marks were faint, shallow impressions worn smooth by hundreds of years. How they'd survived at all was a miracle. But there they were.

A spiral, with thirteen strokes radiating out from it.

Four zigzag lines nested together.

A labyrinth.

I ran over. Drew started to say something, then shut up and came after me. Side by side, we traced the marks with our hands, careless fingers brushing each other.

'It's all here. Just like Alvarado said.'

Neither of us moved. We shared the moment, the two of us drunk on a kind of wonder. The strange figures with their heart-shaped faces; the zigzag lines like one of Peggy's drawings of the sea; an angular mask that made me think of Boba Fett. I never wanted it to end.

Our hands were still touching. My body buzzed with possibilities, and some had nothing to do with petroglyphs and lost cities.

'We'd better get the others,' I said.

Every bad thing that had happened was forgotten. Drew ran back for the others, while I nursed my ankle. When Anton saw the marks, compared them one by one with Alvarado's drawing, it was like scoring the winning goal with your dad watching. He slapped me on the back, and passed around a bottle of rum. Even Tillman looked impressed.

Anton kept asking about how I'd cut the path. 'You're sure no one else could have gotten through?' I shrugged, and said I didn't think so.

'Then Menendez missed them completely,' he crowed.

'He wasn't looking for them,' said Zia wearily.

Tillman put his hand in front of his mouth and gave a theatrical cough. 'Bullshit.'

'Doesn't matter,' said Anton. 'We can use his climbing route to get up the cliff. Safer than breaking our necks on this crap.' He kicked the loose stones that had tumbled down the rockfall. 'Then it's a straight line to Paititi.'

'Above the cliffs the terrain will be harder,' Fabio warned. 'Slower to make progress.'

Anton looked around, each of us in turn. In the green gloom under the canopy, when his eyes fixed on yours, you felt like someone had switched on a searchlight.

'I'm not going to lie to you. It'll be tough – probably tougher than anything you've ever done. Without the *Sierra Madre*, it's not ideal. No backup.'

Tillman shaved a stick with his knife, whittling it to a fine point. 'Tell me something I don't know.'

'We've come this far,' said Drew.

'Kel?'

I stood, swaying slightly under the influence of adrenalin, malaria pills and the rum. I felt giddy and happy. Looking at the others, I felt these were the best friends I'd had in my life.

'I don't know about the rest of you,' I said, 'but this is what I signed up for. Fortune and glory.'

Tillman jabbed his stick in the ground. 'Fuck, yeah.'

Fabio nodded. 'Sure, whatever.'

'OK,' said Howie.

The rum bottle was empty. Anton hurled it against the cliff. Shattered glass fell mute on the forest floor.

'Jonestown, here we come,' said Tillman.

Four

Bandit Country

22

A funny thing happened when Peggy was born. If you've got kids, you'll know what I'm talking about, (if you don't, skip ahead). I'd read all the books, thanks to Cate, heard all the advice, and sat through enough courses to qualify as a midwife.

And you know what? I learned a lot. Nothing happened in those first few weeks I hadn't been told about, nothing you could call a surprise. But at the same time, nothing was how I thought it would be. It was as if all those courses and books had handed me a thousand pieces of jigsaw, but I couldn't begin putting them together until Peggy arrived. She gave me the picture to work from.

That's what it was like, that first day in the jungle. Everything *that* I expected, nothing *as* I expected. You can collect all the facts you like about the rainforest, but until you're there, you don't understand. You think it's going to overwhelm you: a green riot of leaves, vines and branches; screeches, teeth and fangs coming at you from every direction. And it's all there – just much more spread out, so it doesn't hit you all at once. It absorbs you slowly until, like a gambler on a losing streak, you realise you're all in.

One thing I'd got right: it was bloody hard work. There were the packs, for a start. I thought we'd been ruthless with our gear when we lost the *Sierra Madre*, but that was five-star Kuoni compared to what we had now. Only what we could carry on our backs – including ropes, rifles and ammunition, hammocks and flysheets, and food. Anton insisted on bringing all three pack rafts, too: 'Never know what rivers we might have to cross.'

The food was what really worried me. I'd watched Zia measure it out, package it up in plastic bags and divide it among us. It didn't look like much.

'How long we going for?' Howie asked doubtfully.

'We find game in the jungle,' Fabio promised.

'And if we find Indians, we can trade with them,' Anton added.

'Alvarado said thirteen days just to get there.'

'No sweat.' Tillman hefted his gun, action-hero style. 'It's gonna be like the butcher counter in Stop'n'Shop.'

The irony is, we were totally underequipped, but also overloaded. After five minutes on the trail, I thought I'd have a heart attack. The pack's straps dug into my shoulders; the muscles in my back were knotted like a rubber band.

'It's OK,' Zia told me, on our first break. 'It'll get lighter as we eat up the food.'

I sat on my pack, staring at a column of leafcutter ants that painted a green stripe across the jungle floor. My clothes were as wet as if I'd been swimming, though we hadn't seen water since we left the river. My feet ached, and my ankle still twinged from my fall on the rockslide. My stomach was telling me it needed something to eat. I wasn't sure we'd even get lunch.

Fabio studied his compass, then peered upwards, at the distant sun somewhere beyond the canopy.

'We're too much north,' he said. 'We need to go more west.'

Anton shook his head. 'GPS says we're right on track.'

'You got Paititi programmed into that thing?' asked Howie.

'Too much north,' Fabio repeated. 'We keep going this way, we arrive maybe fifty kilometres away from where we want.' He reached for the GPS. Anton whipped it out of reach, holding it above his head like the school bully stealing a kid's lunch.

'Have a little faith.'

We camped that evening by a small stream. When Anton called a halt, I almost fell over. I sat on a log, head in my hands, while Zia made a fire and Drew started stringing the hammocks. Fabio and Tillman went off to hunt. My legs hurt, my shoulders hurt, my head hurt, and my feet were blistered to pieces. They were also soaked from the mud and puddles we'd waded through – some waist-deep. I didn't like to think what invisible nasties could have crawled into me.

I was still sitting there when Howie arrived. Whatever I was suffering, he had it worse. His pack must have weighed ten kilos more than mine, and he was out of shape. His face was so white, I worried he'd suffered a heart attack. He stumbled into the clearing, looked around wild-eyed, and fell over backwards. He lay spreadeagled on his pack, like a patient on an operating table. If it wasn't for his heaving chest, and the fresh sweat pumping out, I'd have felt obliged to take his pulse.

'How far did we go today?' I asked Anton.

'Six point eight clicks.'

He didn't even have to check the GPS. He'd been holding it all day, like a prayer book, shouting directions to Tillman and Fabio at the front each time they veered off the course he wanted.

'Is that good?'

'We have to do more tomorrow.' A loud groan from Howie; at least he was still alive. 'I figure it has to be about fifty, fifty-five k's. We want to do it in under a week.'

'You worked that out from the manuscript?'

Anton gave me a sly look. 'Alvarado's ghost told me.'

A sharp bang echoed through the woods. Birds flew screeching out of the trees; Howie jerked up like a hooked fish. 'What was that?'

'Dinner.'

Howie flopped back. 'I'd give everything the good Lord gave me for a Big Mac and Coke right now.'

I went down to the stream to wash myself off and rinse my clothes. It didn't make much difference: when I'd finished, the clothes were still soaked, and I didn't stink much less.

I had to laugh. None of it, even the hardship, was like anything I'd ever imagined. Even if we never found anything, I was glad to have come.

A rustle of bushes spun me round. It was Drew, coming down the slope with a cooking pot. I grabbed my trousers and wriggled into them, the damp fabric fighting me all the way. She grinned, and didn't avert her gaze.

'You've lost weight. You look good.'

I felt ridiculously pleased with the compliment. I tried to play it cool.

'The jungle diet. Better than the five-two.'

I pulled on my fresh shirt. For thirty seconds, I almost felt clean. Drew knelt upstream from where I'd bathed and filled the pan with water. She groaned as she lifted it out.

'Tough day,' I sympathised.

'That pack. My shoulders are killing me.'

'Do you want a back rub?' I held up my hands, all innocence. 'I give really good back rubs.'

She flashed a smile. 'That would be great.'

She sat on the edge of the stream, dangling her bare feet in the water. I sat on a rock behind her. She leaned back into me as I kneaded her shoulders, feeling the knots under the skin.

'Is it what you expected?' she asked.

I looked at the jungle and had to laugh. 'Not really.'

'Me either. It's so much bigger than I thought it would be.'

'I thought you were an expert.'

'First time, just like you. I'm a city girl.' She groaned. 'That's good. And a bit lower.'

'How do you get from a Yale PhD to here?'

'It's a master's, actually. I keep telling Anton, but he still tells everyone it's a PhD.'

'He wants everything to be that bit better than it is.'

'Exactly. Don't tell him I told you.'

'It'll be our secret.'

A dazzling blue butterfly fluttered along the stream bank. So close, I could almost touch it. After the relentless drab green of the forest, the colour was like a bolt of lightning.

'Seriously,' I said. 'How did you get here?'

'I wanted to get out in the world. Make a difference. Right after graduation, I volunteered for USAID. Just for the summer – I had a boyfriend in New York waiting for me, a lease on an apartment, a place at law school. Real life all lined up. My parents are both dentists, so they were thrilled. But . . .' She smiled, bashfully. 'I got the bug. Two months in Guatemala, I found I couldn't go back.' She laughed self-consciously. 'You probably think that sounds really dumb.'

'I think you're incredible,' I told her. 'When I was twenty-two, I did my elective in the Philippines: that street-kid clinic I mentioned. I only went home because I had to do my final year to qualify. I promised myself as soon as I was Doctor MacDonald, I'd be on the first plane back to Manila.'

'What happened?'

'I met Cate. She already had a job to go to, and I didn't

want to leave her. I told myself I'd do my residency, get some experience under my belt. People like Médecins sans Frontières don't want newly qualified doctors. It sort of made sense. I gave myself three years, five years tops.' I sighed. 'It just never seemed the right time. Every year, something came up. We were moving jobs, getting married, buying a house. Then Peggy arrived – and that was that.'

I worked my way down her spine. 'To be honest, I'm amazed Cate let me come here.'

Drew gave a happy sigh and tipped her head back. She closed her eyes. 'I'm glad you're here.'

'Me too.'

Drew's lips were right under mine. I wished I could read her mind. I'd spent far too long thinking about her already that day, mind drifting in dangerous ways to distract myself from the monotony of the jungle and my aches. That moment finding the petroglyphs, hands touching. Dancing on the beach. Every so often, I caught myself; I told myself to think of Cate, to pay attention to the jungle. For a few minutes, that worked. And then my mind spun off again, like a child slipping his parent's hand and running back to the toy shop.

I stood and picked up the pot.

'I'll carry that back for you.'

A horrible smell hit me as we walked into camp. Acrid, like burning plastic. Black smoke curdled off the campfire.

Fabio and Tillman had come back. All smiles; I saw them laughing and joking through the greasy air around the fire. They'd made a small criss-crossed pile of logs next to the fire, with something laid out on top. Dinner, I presumed, though I couldn't see what it was.

I carried the pot towards the fire. Tillman saw me coming and gave a big thumbs-up. He nodded to the kill on the log pile.

I still couldn't see it properly. Smoke stung my eyes, playing tricks on my mind. It couldn't be what it looked like. Tiny arms and legs splayed over the logs; a head tipped back where they'd slit its throat. Naked skin.

The picture didn't change. I could make out fingers, toes, ears. Tillman lifted his machete and drew it in front of his throat with a grin.

He pointed down. At the charred, tiny corpse that was unmistakeably a child.

23

I dropped the pot. Water splashed over my feet. Drew ran past and started screaming at Tillman. '*What have you done? What have you fucking done?*'

Like something from a nightmare, Tillman picked up the corpse by its arms and dangled it in front of Drew like a puppet.

'What's the matter?' he said nonchalantly. 'Never eaten monkey before?'

I looked again. Knowing what it was didn't make it look any better. With the fur burned off, the limbs and body were just the size of a young child.

The last thing I wanted to think of then was Peggy – so of course I did. Three years old, hanging from the monkey bars in the playground and bawling, while I stood next to her and told her she could do it.

'That's disgusting,' said Drew.

'It's meat.' Fabio looked bored. I suppose he couldn't see what the fuss was about. Even so. I'd defy anyone who has kids to look at that thing.

Drew turned to Anton. 'I'm not eating it.'

He looked irritated. 'Whatever.'

'You shouldn't eat it either.'

'Monkeys can carry some nasty diseases,' I said. Anton shot me a dirty look.

'We're in the jungle. We eat game.'

'It's depraved,' said Drew. 'Look at it. It's like a fucking child.'

'Under the skin, we're all meat,' said Tillman.

'Calm down,' Anton said to Drew.

'Don't tell me to calm down.' She was starting to sound hysterical.

'Well, I'm eating,' said Howie. 'You all can die of hunger if you want, or suck on worms and roots. I'm starving.'

Nobody had asked me – which suited me fine. Of course, Tillman noticed.

'Doc?' He leered at me, daring me to say no. 'You in?'

Part of me would have loved to say yes, just to deny him his victory. But then I looked at the carcass, and I thought of Peggy, and I almost vomited right there.

Drew and Anton were both staring at me. Willing me to join them, daring me to take sides; divorcing parents fighting a proxy war through their children. Anton was the boss: I wouldn't be there without him. But . . .

'If I eat monkey, I'll be farting all night.'

Fabio laughed; Anton narrowed his eyes. I picked up the pot I'd dropped.

'I'll get some more water for the rice.'

The second day was like the first, minus the novelty value. Stupid as it was, the monkey incident had drawn a line through us. When supper was ready, we'd eaten separately: Anton, Tillman, Fabio and Howie on one side of the camp; me with the girls on the other, chewing over my bowl of plain rice. Even at breakfast, nobody spoke much. And then we were back under our packs, and no one had strength for anything except carrying on.

We made better progress that day. Around eleven o'clock, we found a dried-up river bed that led in approximately the right direction, and Anton decided to follow it. With no need to open a path, we could stretch our legs. The packs felt lighter. Sandflies buzzed around my legs; iridescent butterflies with electric green markings fluttered around us. I tried to take a photo for Peggy. All I did was waste battery.

Our line became more fluid (except for Howie, anchored at the back). Mid-afternoon, I found myself walking alongside Anton.

'You doing OK?' he asked me.

I nodded, breathing hard. There was no shade in the river bed and the sun was livid.

'Now I know how my shirts feel when I run them through the hot cycle.'

He pointed ahead. In the distance, forested slopes rose out of the jungle and made a rampart across the horizon, until they disappeared in the white mist steaming off them.

'We're so close.'

I couldn't admire the view for long. Stones littered the ground, waiting to twist my ankle. The sand in between was mostly firm, but every so often it would give way without warning and suck you in up to your knee. I tramped on, trying to forget the heat and the weight on my back.

'What's on your mind?' said Anton.

Heat broke down barriers, made me say things I might have kept to myself.

'I'm worried about Tillman.'

It was what I'd been thinking about all day. Now, with Tillman a hundred yards safely ahead, seemed a good moment to bring it up.

'How come?'

'That thing with the monkey.'

Anton looked surprised. 'That was just some dumb shit. Drew shouldn't have taken it so personal.'

'It's not just the monkey.' I remembered the force of Tillman's gaze, wanting me to choose. The savage glee on his face when I sided with Drew, as if it proved everything he ever thought about me. 'Don't you think he's a negative presence?'

Anton swatted a fly off his sleeve. 'You think we'd find Paititi if Howie was cutting the trail?'

'It's a small group. No rotten apples, remember?'

'If we get into trouble up-country, Tillman's the one guy I would absolutely want with me to get me out. One hundred per cent.'

That was hard to imagine. 'How did you meet?'

'We did a job together in Florida. Shipwreck. Turned out one of the guys in our crew had links with the Cuban mob, wanted us to cut them in. Tillman went around to his apartment and beat the shit out of him. Next day, the Cuban came back with some of his buddies. Tillman got some of our buddies together, and beat the shit out of them again.' He laughed to himself. 'Funny thing is, we never did get anything out of that wreck. But that's the kind of guy he is.'

'Good to know.' I wasn't at all reassured.

'I needed someone reliable for this. Everyone else is a first-timer.'

'Is that normal?'

'It's not, like, un-normal. This business, no one's exactly getting retirement benefits. You meet some people, you work together a while, you move on. Most guys try it and quit. Or they don't quit, but it's something they never get back to. They can't raise the funds, they can't get the time off work, they get married and have kids.'

Sounded familiar. 'You're aiming to get to be an old-timer?'

He laughed. 'Me? I *am* an old-timer. I'm gonna be forty in a couple of years. I got to get back, spend some time with my kid before he grows up.'

My kid? My jaw dropped so far I almost burned it on the sand. 'How old?'

'Fifteen. Lives with his mom outside San Diego. She and I, we're not together any more. Obviously.'

He took off his sunglasses and wiped his face. For the first time, I noticed the wrinkles round those blue eyes.

'Maybe I'll try and make it right with her after this.'

'What about Drew?'

It came out far too quickly. Luckily, Anton was too preoccupied with his own thoughts to notice.

'Drew's just a kid figuring things out. I mean, she's great, but she's not going to hang out with an old fart like me for ever.'

'Are you two having problems?' I know I shouldn't have asked it. I couldn't help myself. She hadn't spoken to Anton all day (I'd been watching); had been deliberately lagging behind him. A couple of times, he'd dropped back to walk with her – at which point she stormed ahead.

'It's a tough situation. Magnifies stress.' He chopped at a branch Fabio had left dangling. 'Tillman told me not to bring her.'

I couldn't think of anything to say to that – not without giving myself away.

Anton gave me a look I couldn't decipher. 'You wouldn't understand. You've got the perfect life: great wife, beautiful kid, big-shot job. Me, I've really fucked things up.'

It was envy. The look he was giving me: he actually envied me. This man who was my age (and I'd thought he was ten years younger), who lived his life in the most exotic places on the planet – and he envied a house in Putney, a nanny and a commute.

'Say that again when we find Paititi,' I told him.

But I brooded on what he'd said all afternoon. I suppose I should have been flattered, but it didn't come out like that.

No one wants to believe the life they have is the best they can get. That's why we go looking for golden cities.

By the fourth day, I was actually starting to enjoy myself. Things I'd only ever seen in films had become normal. To cross a gully, Fabio would fell a tree, walk across unaided, then toss us a rope to tie off as a handrail. Edging across those slippy, knotted trunks, pack shifting on my back and the rope not much better than a washing line, I felt like Indiana Jones. *Better* than Indiana Jones. I felt so alive. A couple of times, when Tillman wanted a rest, Anton tossed me the machete and let me take a turn cutting the path. Even when my arm ached (Tillman made it look easy, but it wasn't) and the sweat stung my eyes, I never lost sight of the fact that I might be the first person ever to walk here. Every step was giddy with the chance I might brush past a branch and find the lost city behind it. Every time I sliced through a vine, I waited to feel the blade shiver on stone.

I'd forgotten I didn't believe in lost cities. How could I, when every day I was surrounded by unbelievable sights? Kapok trees you could have built a house in; ficus trees with buttresses like rocket fins; palms jacked up on wigwam roots that held them high above the soil. And every time we came to a clearing, or crossed an open river bed, I'd look up to the horizon and see the mist on the mountains, looming ever closer like something from a dream. When Anton checked the GPS and said we should be there in two days, in my mind I was already past the guardian and halfway across the anaconda bridge.

Not that it was easy. From space, Google's cameras showed it as a flat sea of green; on the ground, that translated as a sadistic assault course of steep ridges and sharp drops. When I wasn't leading, I was usually near the back of the line, so that by the time I reached a climb the path had been churned to a mud chute, and the only plants you could grab tended to harbour wicked thorns or biting ants. Going down wasn't any easier. Our machetes left sharp spikes sticking out from the ground, waiting to impale you if you slipped or tripped. Out there, even a broken leg could become a death sentence.

And those were the things that couldn't move. One afternoon, Fabio found a black snake right on the path, twisted like a carved stick. The first I knew was when he raised the machete and chopped its head off. Tillman had walked straight past it. At night, vampire bats buzzed our hammocks, while mosquitoes, ticks and flies feasted on any inch of skin we left exposed. My feet, constantly wet, had started shooting hot prickles of pain every time I put weight on them.

Then there was Drew. She kept me in a peculiar kind of agony, like a drug I didn't want to quit. I was obsessed. If she stopped to tie her shoelace when I was coming up behind, if she offered me a sip from her water bottle; if she took my hand to get up a slope: I could spend hours analysing it, replaying it from every angle like Sky Sports.

Something was going on between her and Anton. Since the monkey argument, she'd barely said a word to him. She avoided him on the trail, and when we called a halt she'd pitch her hammock on the opposite side of camp from him.

Everybody noticed. 'That time of the month,' said Tillman, to no one in particular. 'This is why you shouldn't bring chicks to the jungle.' Anton glowered at him; I tried not to catch his eye.

It was all worth it. The bleeding and itching, the hunger

(and every night, Zia worried we were using up our supplies too fast), the crushing pack and the sore legs. It was the price of adventure, the sensation that said *this is really happening.*

The price of adventure. I can't believe I actually said that.

24

On the fifth day, we entered a bamboo forest, thick trunks growing at crazy angles that reminded me of a post-apocalyptic cityscape. Hard going: Tillman had been swearing for an hour straight. Suddenly, he shut up.

One by one, we caught up with him. When I got there, Fabio was holding what looked like a stick of bamboo, stripping its outer layer with his machete. Not bamboo, I realised: the inside wasn't hollow, but a pulpy white stick like a peeled apple.

Fabio hacked off a few pieces and handed them round.

'Chew, don't swallow.'

The moment I bit down, a wonderful sweetness squeezed into my mouth. My body shuddered with the sugar rush. I chewed greedily, sucking out every drop.

'You think this could be the plant the Incas gave Alvarado?' said Drew. 'The one he said tasted like honey?'

'It's sugar cane,' said Anton. 'And it doesn't grow wild.'

I sucked it dry and spat out the pulp. The moment it landed, ants mobbed it to get what I had missed.

'You're saying someone planted it?'

'I'm saying we're not alone.'

We walked slowly, scanning the undergrowth in every direction. Five minutes later, Tillman stopped again. He swung his machete in a long arc from left to right.

'Crossroads.'

I wouldn't have spotted it myself. Too narrow, too much foliage pressing into the narrow space. But he was right. A small trail, no bigger than an animal track, cutting across our path on a diagonal. Tillman looked at Anton.

'What do you want to do, boss?'

Fabio squatted and examined the ground. 'No footprints. Maybe an old track.'

'See those banana trees up there?' Tillman pointed up the path. 'They don't space out like that on their own. Someone's farming them.'

Anton took a long look up the track. He rubbed his shark's tooth.

'It's brighter up there,' said Drew. 'Maybe a clearing?'

I remembered the sign by the riverside. I remembered those explorers immortalised on Wikipedia: *killed by wild Indians*. I remembered the chief at Esperanza's throat-slitting gesture.

'We've got guns,' Tillman said. He must have read my thoughts.

'And we're going to massacre them?' Fabio spat out the piece of sugar cane he'd been working over. 'And fight our way back to the boat?'

'Who says they're gonna fight?' said Howie. The last person I'd expect to supply optimism. 'We go in, we act friendly, we offer them some cook-pots or knives. Maybe they know something about some ruins around here.'

'It's not worth the risk,' said Fabio.

'Yeah,' said Anton, non-committal.

'You told me we were going to see Indians.' Howie stood his ground, like a tourist who's had the itinerary changed.

'I told you we were going to find Paititi.'

'I want to talk to them.'

Anton looked tempted. I think he'd have done it, too, if Howie hadn't added unnecessarily, 'Who calls the shots here?'

Anton's face went dark. Without a second glance, he hoiked his pack up on his shoulders, grabbed a machete and started cutting a trail away from the Indian path. The rest of us fell in behind, with Fabio last, just in case.

We pitched our hammocks close together that night, and Anton assigned us shifts for guard duty. None of us could stop thinking about what might be coming down the path. I took the first shift, but even after that, dog-tired from the hiking, I couldn't sleep. That night-before-a-flight feeling, when knowing you have to get up early only keeps you awake. Though I've never had to listen out for a wild Indian attack the night before a flight.

A rainforest at night is the wrong place to listen for danger. A hundred million sounds, and my brain wanted to know about every one of them. It took me half an hour to get up my courage to go for a wee. Standing in the dark forest, shorts down, every muscle was so tense I could hardly get it out.

Something moved behind me. I spun around, splashing piss on my hands, and saw a light moving away between the trees. I didn't think an Indian would make that much noise, and I didn't think he'd wear a head-torch either. I pulled up my shorts and ran after him.

He heard me coming and spun around. The face cupped in the glow of the head-torch was more frightened than mine.

'Howie?' He was fully dressed, boots and everything, with a backpack and even a rifle slung over his shoulder. 'Where are you going?'

'I thought I heard something.' He tapped the rifle. 'It's my shift.'

It *was* his shift – but Howie wasn't the type to go chasing bumps in the night. 'You're not going back to that Indian path?'

'No.' He shifted on his feet. He was a terrible liar. 'Don't tell Anton.'

'By yourself? In the dark? Christ.'

He frowned. He may have had three degrees in linguistics, but he still looked like a mopey child. 'You can come, if you want.'

I don't suppose he thought I would. Maybe he wanted backup, and maybe he wanted privacy for his little mission. But I couldn't let him go alone. And I was curious.

'As long as we make it back before the others wake up.'

I got my boots, and a rifle, and a few other things. Even in the dark, we had no trouble retracing the way we'd come that afternoon. You don't need chainsaws or bulldozers: seven people walking leave quite enough of a trail. An owl hooted; frogs chirruped; my whole nervous system snapped, crackled and popped. I concentrated on the path, and tried not to imagine poison arrows whizzing out of the undergrowth. I let Howie go first.

It was further than I'd remembered. I'd just started wondering about how we'd find the trail, and how we'd get back, and how I was going to walk another ten kilometres tomorrow after our little night hike, when Howie stopped and stooped. A foil chewing gum wrapper shone in the torchlight where it had been stuck on a palm spike.

'You knew you'd be coming back,' I said. I almost admired him.

We turned up the Indian trail Tillman had spotted. This was harder, not nearly so well trodden. Leaves and branches snatched at my sleeves. I took the rifle off my shoulder and held it two-handed in front of me. I'd already decided that if it came to it, I wouldn't mess around with warning shots. A choice between a Stone Age Indian and never seeing Cate or Peggy again: that didn't trouble my conscience one bit.

I tapped Howie on the shoulder. The speed he turned reminded me I wasn't the only one with a panicky trigger finger.

'Shouldn't we turn off our lights? So they don't see us coming?'

'If we look like we're sneaking up, they'll think we're the bad guys.'

'Maybe we are. From their point of view.' The enormity of what we were doing was just starting to sink in. And yes, I do know the correct definition of 'enormity'.

'Nobody told me . . . that the road . . . would be easy.'

A new sound echoed through the forest, so unexpected I almost let off the gun. An off-key baritone, full of fake soul.

Howie was singing.

'What the hell are you doing?' I hissed.

'Letting them know we come in peace.'

I almost shot him for being an idiot. If the path had been any longer, I'd have turned back. But at that moment, it ended abruptly in a clearing. The moon lit it up like a football ground: over Howie's shoulder, I saw the shapes of buildings.

Howie stepped out, arms spread wide, still singing his heart out. I switched off my head-torch and waited just inside the shadow of the treeline.

It was a village. I'd thought Esperanza was primitive, but that was Manhattan compared with this place. Half a dozen lean-to huts stood around a central clearing, thatch laid over simple wooden frames. An empty fire pit sat in the centre, piles of brush and drying palm fronds on the ground.

Saying it now, it sounds incredible. Something no outsider had seen before, an untouched fossil from the Stone Age. At the time, I had other concerns.

Howie lowered his arms and turned around. 'Nobody's home.'

That sounded like tempting fate. I waited for the inevitable riposte, a spear from behind bursting through his chest.

Nothing happened.

Howie ambled over to the nearest hut and looked in. I imagined a sleeping Indian getting the fright of his life. Or not. Howie disappeared inside. I heard his pack rustle as he opened it. Was he taking souvenirs?

Curiosity got the better of me. I stepped out into the clearing, rifle ready. Howie came out of the hut and moved on to the next.

Something snapped under my foot. I jumped back.

A pile of bones lay on the ground, ghost white in the moonlight. So thin, I might have mistaken them for twigs – if I hadn't been to medical school. So many, they couldn't possibly have come from one skeleton. I could see my bootprint in the powder where I'd crushed a couple of ribs. A carved wooden doll smiled at me from next to a skull.

I took four deep breaths and counted to ten. *Monkey bones*, I told myself, trying to ignore the doll. *Monkey bones.* I'd already seen how childlike they looked under the fur. I couldn't believe how many there were.

Using a dead leaf as a glove, I picked one up and put it in the plastic bag I'd wrapped my notebook in. A macabre souvenir. Weird, you might think – but I could get it analysed when I got home. Just to be sure.

I didn't like being alone out there. I thought I heard sounds, voices from the forest where no moon penetrated. My imagination, of course. Yellow light glowed from one of the huts where Howie was exploring, spilling through the cracks in the wattle wall. Suddenly, I was desperate to get out of the open.

I ducked in the door. It didn't look as if it had been lived in for months. Gourds hung from pegs on the walls; a wooden bowl lay on the earth floor as if someone had dropped it. Howie was examining a wooden platform at the far end that made a sort of bed or table, covered in animal skins. At the other end, five stones surrounded the remains of a fire. It hadn't burned recently. Even the ashes had gathered dust.

I took another step, and kicked something with the toe of my boot. It rolled away across the floor. A hollow sound, too light to be wood or stone or even bone.

It bounced off the wall and rolled back towards me. I picked it up. The night and the village got a whole lot stranger.

'Is this yours?' I called to Howie.

He turned. Maybe it was the surroundings, or the dazzle as he turned the light on me, but I saw his face differently. His beard had grown fast; the skin underneath was peeling from sunburn. His eyes and cheeks had sunk in.

He squinted. 'Is that . . .?'

I held it out so he could see. A clear plastic bottle, about a hundred mil. Cap missing. I turned it around and read the label.

Blackwater 102b Active Vaccine.

'Not mine,' said Howie. 'Maybe it belonged to that guy Menendez.'

I slipped it in my pocket with the monkey bone. 'So much for uncontacted Indians. We—'

I stopped.

'Turn off the light.'

Without the head-torch, we were in total darkness. I waited for my eyes to adjust, listening to the darkness. Insects buzzed; the forest murmured. For a moment I thought I'd jumped at nothing.

Then I heard it again. Voices. I peered through a crack in the stick wall and saw figures in the moonlight. Already in the clearing. One of them looked like he was carrying a spear.

They must have seen the light go out in our hut. They

walked straight for us, spread out in a loose line. I counted five.

My hands shook so much I could hardly get the rifle off my shoulder. I crouched next to the door. Howie was on his knees behind me, muttering something over and over.

They must have seen my movement, or the moonlight on the gun barrel. They stopped, about ten metres short of the door. I aimed the rifle at the one with the spear. *One more step . . .*

'You two faggots going to come out already?' said Tillman.

25

'That was the dumbest fucking thing I've ever seen. If I could, I'd send you both back to P-T this instant. You two want to play George of the Jungle by yourselves? See how long you stay alive?'

I'd never seen Anton so angry. 'It was stupid,' I admitted. 'We—'

Anton ignored me. 'You,' he shouted at Howie. 'You knew the deal.'

Howie stood his ground. 'Deal was, I get to see the Indians.'

'This is not a democracy. This is not a town hall fucking meeting. This is survival, and I am in charge. What if there'd been Indians here, and what if they decided they didn't want your company?'

Always a big lad, he looked bigger now: a monster in the dark. He also had a knife on his belt, and a machete on the ground beside him.

'I took a risk,' said Howie.

'You were meant to be keeping guard. Protecting *us*.' Anton put his hands on his hips. Breath ragged, red face black in the moonlight. In a funny way, he reminded me of Peggy, wearing herself out at the end of some spectacular tantrum.

'If this was the army, you'd both be shot.'

He might have gone on longer. But just then, I heard Tillman swearing inside one of the huts. He came out, waving a small box at us.

'What is this? A fucking reading group?'

It wasn't a box; it was a book. Howie snatched it off Tillman and clutched it to his chest, mumbling something. The cover had no writing, just an embossed cross.

'Is this the Bible?' said Drew. She'd opened Howie's back-pack and was holding an identical cross-stamped book. *How many did he have?*

Howie nodded. Tillman laughed in disbelief.

'It's the fucking Gideons.'

Howie stared at Anton. He looked like someone determined not to cry. 'Are you going to tell them?'

'Sure.' Anton ground an ant into the dirt with his heel. For once, he looked as if he didn't relish the attention. In fact, he looked downright embarrassed.

'I'm a missionary,' said Howie. 'My church sent me here to evangelise the natives.'

'Jesus fucking Christ,' snorted Tillman. Howie shot him a foul look.

'I can't believe you did this,' Zia said to Anton. 'You know what these people are like.'

'Living like a hog, back in the Dark Ages, that's any better? We're ennobling their souls.'

'Like those people in Esperanza were ennobled?'

'Can we talk about this later?' I gestured around the little village. 'Noble or not, they might come back.'

Tillman picked up one of the feathers from the hut and stuck it in his hair.

'Maybe they heard God-Boy coming and ran off.'

Howie stuck his chin out. 'I'm not listening to you persecuting me.'

'Persecuting? *Persecuting*?' Tillman picked up a stone and shied it at Howie. It hit him on the arm. 'You do something dumb like that again and I'll fucking persecute you. *Jesus*.'

'The village must have been abandoned weeks ago,' said Drew.

'Where'd they go, then?'

'They're nomads. They'll trek days just to go fishing, or to visit relatives in another tribe. The same way you or I'd go down to the store.'

I took out the plastic bottle I'd picked up. 'I think this belonged to Menendez.' I showed it to Zia; she nodded. 'He must have been here.'

'*Hey*.'

Fabio waved to us from the far side of the clearing, where he'd been exploring. We trooped over, guns ready. He poked his machete into a dark gap between the trees.

'A trail.'

'Isn't there a risk we'll run into the Indians?' I worried.

'Maybe the trail leads to Paititi,' said Tillman. I thought he was joking. Anton nodded.

'Every "lost" city that's ever been found, the locals knew where it was. We're in the right neck of the woods. If Paititi's near here, stands to reason there'd be an Indian trail leading to it.'

'Yesterday you didn't want to follow Indian trails,' I reminded him. I couldn't understand his change of heart.

'And now I do.' Anton gave Howie a thumbs-up. 'Maybe we'll even find some Indians for you to save.'

Zia and Fabio stayed in the village, while the rest of us tramped back to the campsite to retrieve our kit. By the time we got back, my feet were in agony. I'd walked that stretch of jungle four times in twelve hours. This time, Anton made Howie and me carry the extra packs on a stick between us as punishment.

TOM HARPER

I smelled food as we came back to the village. Fabio and Zia had got a fire going, and were frying up some wild bananas with sachets of instant porridge. I ate it so fast it made me sick.

'Go easy,' said Zia. 'This is the food that was supposed to get us home.'

'That came around fast,' said Drew.

Zia ticked it off on her fingers. 'We lost a whole bag of rice when Howie fell in that creek. We haven't caught any game since the monkey. There's a few more bananas we can scavenge from the plantation, maybe some nuts. That's it.'

Clouds of smoke hissed out of the frying pan. Anton looked around the circle.

'I don't know about you guys,' he said, 'but I came here to find a lost city. I don't mind going hungry for a few days.'

'I mind *dying* of hunger,' said Howie.

'If you hadn't brought so many goddamned Bibles, maybe you could have carried more food,' said Tillman. He sliced his knife through the air, as if he was imagining cutting a hunk off Howie.

No one was in a hurry to move off. The broken night had left us all exhausted and bad-tempered. Even the possibility the Indians might come back had receded with daylight. The village didn't look exotic or romantic. It looked dirty and Third World.

Anton and Fabio went to forage for sugar cane in the woods. While they were gone, I got the GPS and the map from Anton's pack.

'Planning your escape?' said Drew. She smiled, but she looked tired.

'I want to plot the village.'

I spread the map on the ground while Drew took the GPS fix. No problems with the signal in the clearing.

'12° 28' 12" South; 71° 37' 44" West,' she read.

172

I pencilled it in on the map, then got out my notebook and copied the position there, too. 12 28 12 71 . . .

I stopped writing.

'You hear something?' asked Drew.

'I just had a massive déjà vu.'

I flipped back through my notebook's waxy pages. Notes, observations, journal entries, half-cocked attempts at sketches. And near the beginning . . .

12 28 47 71 37 09

'The man we rescued from the river.' I was speaking in a whisper, pulse racing. 'Those were the numbers he'd carved on his arm.' I held it next to the GPS, showing our current position. The numbers were nearly identical. 'They were coordinates.'

I found the scale on the edge of the map and ran my finger along the right line of latitude. Drew knelt beside me and traced the longitude.

Our fingers met – almost on top of the pencil mark where I'd plotted the village.

'We can't be more than a mile away.' I oriented the map to the GPS's compass. '*That* way.'

We both stared. I was pointing across the clearing, right towards the trail Fabio had found.

Footsteps crunched the dead leaves behind us. 'You got something?' said Anton.

I stood. My legs trembled; I felt light-headed. I wished I'd had more food.

'Where are you taking us?'

26

Anton stared at the map, the notebook and the GPS. His hand strayed to the shark's-tooth necklace, rubbing it where it had already been rubbed smooth.

'Those coordinates are the numbers from Roberto's arm,' I said. Dangerously calm. 'And this is where we are now. See any similarities? Four numbers out of six still wins you a prize.'

His blue eyes stared at me, as if looking for an answer that would satisfy me. Then he shrugged.

'Sure. You're right. I thought the numbers looked like they might be a grid reference, so I checked them on the map. It seemed about the right neighbourhood for Paititi, and I guessed the guy had come from the Menendez expedition. So I took a shot at it.'

'Without telling us?' said Drew. 'Without any discussion?'

His back straightened. His chest puffed out. 'It's my call; my expedition. I want to find Paititi worse than any of you. If we don't, it's my balls on the block.'

'You stupid *asshole*.' Fabio had come up behind him and overheard. He picked up the map and shook it in Anton's face. 'This is why you would not let me have the GPS. I told you we went wrong. We agreed to go west, due west from the falls. We should be *here* by now.' His finger stabbed into virgin white space. 'Thirty, forty kilometres away. How do we get there now?'

He threw down the map and grabbed the GPS from Drew.

'Give me that,' said Anton.

'Why? So you can lead us more wrong?' He held it up out of Anton's reach. 'Why do you hire me as a guide if you don't want me to guide you?'

'I hired you to take me where I tell you to go.'

'Then why don't you *tell* me?'

'Maybe I don't trust you.'

Anton wasn't made for waiting. He lunged. Fabio whipped his arm out of the way.

Whether he meant to throw, or if it was just sweaty fingers,

I don't know. The GPS flew out of his hand, spun high into the air and landed on a rock. We all heard the crack.

'Mother*fucker*.' Anton ran to it. He picked it up, frantically pressing the buttons. 'You broke it.'

'Try the batteries,' said Drew. 'Maybe they got shaken loose.'

'I've got some spares,' I volunteered.

'It's not the batteries,' said Anton. 'I replaced them yesterday.'

'They could have been duds.'

'It's not the fucking batteries.'

I'd never seen him like this. He held up the GPS so we could see. The screen had cracked, and a broken piece of plastic hung off the casing.

'It's not the batteries.'

With a roar, Anton charged straight into Fabio. They grappled and went down, rolling in the mud like a pair of pigs. Drew screamed at them to stop. Zia tried to pull them apart. Behind me, I heard a rasp as Tillman unsheathed his machete.

Everything was happening too fast: action, reaction, and no one to stop it. Around us, the abandoned huts watched us with empty eyes. They wanted blood; I could feel it. Whatever had happened to the Indians, it hadn't been good.

Zia and Drew had managed to pull Anton back. Fabio crouched on all fours, hair matted with mud, panting hard. He drew his knife.

I stepped into the ring between them.

'Are you insane?' I said. 'Beating each other up won't mend the GPS, or find Paititi. Or get us home.'

Anton's biceps twitched. The sun bowed off Fabio's blade and shot right into my brain. I braced myself for a knife or a punch in the gut. I didn't dare blink.

'We've come this far. We're only a mile off those coordinates.'

I pointed down the path, a narrow gap vanishing into the jungle.

'Don't you want to see what's at the end of the rainbow?'

I'd measured the distance at about a mile on the map. Some days, that might have taken all morning. With the Indian trail, we made good speed. At every bend, I found my hopes rising, only to fall back when we turned the corner and saw more trees. I wished we hadn't broken the GPS.

And suddenly the path ended at a high cliff. A fringe of rust-red moss hung over it; bird droppings ran down the face. Trees crowded along the top like condemned prisoners. A sickly green light seeped through the canopy, while the thick-fallen leaves deadened any sound. A bad place.

And none of us cared.

Staring out at us, front and centre, a cave yawned in the cliff. Anton ran to it. He stopped on the threshold with a cry, reached out his machete and scraped off some moss above the entrance.

I think my pulse stopped for a moment. Perhaps everyone's did. For that moment, not even the jungle dared to breathe.

We weren't alone. Carved in the rock above the opening, watching us, was one of those otherworldly figures with a heart-shaped head and a spiral body.

'They're everywhere.' Drew stepped back, pointing along the cliff face. The whole cliff was decorated like a Gaudí cathedral. Spirals and circles, diamonds and labyrinths; sun symbols and stick-figures and three-eyed heart faces: all flowing into and over each other like a psychedelic dream. So complete, I'd taken them for the texture of the rock.

And in the middle, the cave. A black hole, sucking in the light.

'You crazy fucker.' Tillman punched Anton on the back. 'I don't believe you did this.'

We shrugged off our packs and left them on the ground. We put on our head-torches; Fabio started filming the carvings with the video camera.

'Save the batteries for what's inside,' said Anton. Half an hour ago, they'd been ready to kill each other. Now, Fabio turned off the screen without a murmur. Anton had earned the right.

Tillman hefted the shotgun.

'Let's see who's home.'

27

Rank air enveloped us as we passed into the darkness. Our torch beams chased over the rock walls like so many fireflies, darting and crossing as we craned our heads.

'You can turn the camera on now,' said Anton, slicing through a cobweb with his machete.

The demented shapes from the cliff continued inside, covering every inch of rock up the walls and over the ceiling. Painted here, not carved, in thick brown lines that reminded me of CAT scans I've seen of patients. Like walking through somebody's brain.

'How old do you think these are?' I wondered. A spider scuttled past my feet.

'Impossible to tell,' said Drew. 'Humidity ages it so fast. Plus, it could be the Indians copied over older designs that were there already, keeping them fresh. Or—' She broke off. '*What?*'

Anton had stopped. We crowded round him and looked where he was pointing his torch on the floor.

'We're not the first people here.'

In the red mud that caked the floor, Anton's light picked out a footprint. Scratch that: a *boot*print. Heavy rubber soles, rugged treads that had scored deep marks into the mud.

'Indians wear Timberland?' said Tillman.

Anton moved on. Tillman went next, jerking the shotgun from side to side like a man who'd played too much Xbox. Other chambers opened off on both sides of the main tunnel, yawning holes hiding who knows what. Some of them seemed to have been barricaded off, with sticks and logs jammed across the openings.

Something moved at the back of the cave. Seven torch beams leapt to one place. So did Tillman's shotgun. A deafening bang shook the cave; the flash blinded me. Like being inside a cannon when it went off. Pebbles and sand cascaded down from the roof. I flung up my hands, waiting for the whole tunnel to bury us.

The debris coming down from the roof eased off into a trickle of dust. I opened my eyes.

All the others were crouched in similar protective positions. Howie had sprawled flat on the floor. Smoke and grit choked my lungs. My ears whined like a dog whistle. In front of us, a dead bat lay in pieces on the ground.

'*Fuck*,' said Anton. His voice sounded as if it was under water. 'This is historic. Show some respect.'

He grabbed the shotgun from Tillman and moved forward. Not far. The cave ended after another few metres in a solid wall, etched with more carvings. A large, flat-cut boulder made a table in front. And on it, straight out of Indiana Jones . . .

'Un-*fucking*-believable,' said Tillman.

It was an idol. That's the only word for it. A block of white stone, the size of a dictionary, cut with the swirls and patterns that had become so familiar. Deftly carved, more structured than the chaos on the walls: like seeing a printed page after a child's scribble.

Anton stepped towards it. Tillman turned the torch on the

floor. Zia shrieked; Howie recoiled. He knocked into me; I flailed for balance, and we nearly all went over.

'Please tell me those aren't human,' said Drew. She sounded as if she was struggling to hold down something in her throat.

A row of white skulls sat on the floor in front of the idol, all different shapes and sizes. Dried leaves and flowers scattered the floor around them, or ran braided through the eye sockets.

'They're animals,' said Fabio. 'Offerings.' He picked one up, articulating the jaw so that it snapped at Howie. 'Capybara.'

'That is obscene.' Howie pushed it away.

I put my hands on the idol, tracing the labyrinth in the centre. I felt a surge of illicit power, the thrill of the grave robber. Back home, it would have been behind three inches of plexiglas.

'Can we take this with us?'

Anton and I tried to lift it. Even between us, we could hardly get it off the bench.

'We're not carrying that back through the jungle.'

Anton leaned against the idol and put his head against it. He held out his camera one-handed and flashed a shot.

'Idol selfie.'

'So – what?' said Howie. 'Is this it? Did we find Paititi?'

'I don't think so,' said Drew. 'Alvarado mentioned carved waymarkers on the road he took to the falls. This could be one of those.' She tapped the labyrinth symbol. '*Paititi, five miles*. Maybe the Indians found it and set it up here in their shrine.'

Anton's face shone with excitement. 'We have to be close.'

'They could have brought that stone from anywhere,' Drew cautioned. Anton ignored her.

'Check the rest of the caves.'

We worked our way back. None of the caves went very far: more like side-rooms off a central corridor. Plenty of movement – rats, bats, spiders and other nasties – but nothing worth taking.

Tillman kicked away a pile of branches that blocked the next doorway. He stooped in and shone the light around.

'You guys.'

We all crowded in behind him. Our head-torches lit up the chamber. On the floor, totally incongruous, lay two olive-green duffel bags.

'What the—?'

Tillman knelt and unzipped one. He reached in and pulled out a battered magazine, pages limp with damp. He tossed it back to us.

'We found their secret stash.'

I caught it instinctively. Pamela Anderson pouted from the cover, wearing a striped blazer and a tie and not much else. *Playboy: Entertainment for Men.*

It was about the strangest thing I could have imagined finding there. I held it like a fragment of the Bible, not sure what to do with it.

'Only you, Tillman,' said Anton, laughing.

'Any more?' asked Fabio.

'No more pornos. But . . . check *this* out.'

Tillman reached in the bag again and held up a cellophane packet. Inside was a white brick, like a block of putty. We all leaned closer.

'Is that . . .?'

It was so obvious, it took me a moment to process what I was seeing. Like a cop in a film, Tillman stuck his bush knife through the cellophane. The blade came out coated with white residue. He licked it off.

'Why is it that coke in Peru always tastes way better than anywhere else?'

I remembered two burning eyes on the poster at the airport: *No a la Droga*. The American in the bar in Puerto Tordoya: *What Thailand is for mail-order brides, that place is for cocaine.*

'Are the *narcos* using this place for drug running?'

'If they did, they're not in a hurry to get it back.' Tillman pointed to the date on the magazine. *September, 1991*. 'This stuff's been here since Reagan was president.'

I stared at the packet, the glossy shrink-wrap still crackling after so many years in the darkness. I couldn't imagine how it had got here. Captured by the Indians, abandoned by the traffickers . . . Maybe it just fell from the sky.

Tillman dug through the bag. More cellophane crinkled. 'Gotta be twenty keys in here, easy.' He stuffed two of the bricks in his pockets, and loaded another half dozen into his arms.

'You're not really going to take those?' said Drew. She looked at Anton. 'You know how much *trouble* we could get in?'

'You know how much *money* this is worth?' Tillman retorted. 'You may have come for the glory of mankind, all that world heritage crap. I came to get rich.'

Anton hesitated.

'Remember Aguas Verdes,' said Tillman. 'Never leave money on the table.'

'Right.' Anton nodded. 'Take what you can carry.'

Drew started to protest, but I didn't think she'd change his mind. I'd seen the gleam in Anton's eyes. He was a fortune hunter, after all. And even after twenty-five years, that must be worth a fortune.

I shivered. The wonder had worn off. My head hurt from the shotgun blast, and the foul air was making me sick. The surprise of finding those drugs, all the questions it raised, made me dizzy.

I realised I was still holding the *Playboy*. I passed it to

Fabio and headed for the exit. I needed air – but there was one more chamber we hadn't checked yet.

Curiosity got the better of me. I peered in.

Half a dozen bags lay on the floor. Rucksacks and day bags, all piled up ready for someone's gap year.

'You find something?' said Fabio, behind me.

'I think it's the lost property office.'

But that wasn't right. They weren't lost. As they lay pinned in the torch beam, I knew exactly who they belonged to.

28

We dragged the bags out. In the light, we could all read the block letters drawn on the fabric in felt tip. EXPEDITION PACHACAMAC MENENDEZ CLINIC.

Drew got the stove and started boiling water. 'Maybe they camped here. Found the cave, left their gear for when they got back.'

'Yeah,' said Anton doubtfully. Zia sat with her arms wrapped around her legs, staring into the cave as if she wanted it to swallow her.

'Let's see what they left behind.' Tillman opened the pack and rummaged inside. I glanced at Zia. It felt heartless doing it there, like a public autopsy. But let's be honest: they disappeared months ago. They probably weren't coming back for it.

Menendez's expedition had travelled light. A few clothes and personal effects, an empty can of bug spray. Tillman found a khaki bush hat and put it on. He twisted his head, admiring the shadow he cast on the sand.

'You think I look like Indiana Jones?'

'You're not really going to wear that?' said Drew.

'Until Fabio buys me a new one for the one I lost in the river.'

Fabio muttered something and passed me a vinyl bag with a Red Cross sticker on top. It clinked when he moved it.

'Medical supplies?'

A familiar smell hit me as I unzipped it – the wet, iron smell of blood. The inside of the bag was splashed red, glinting with jagged shards of glass as if someone had gone through a window. I braced myself for some new horror: a severed head or hand, fleshy organs still pulsing blood.

All I saw was a rack of vials, the sort you use for blood samples. Most had smashed, which accounted for the glass and the blood; a few had survived.

'Where's our first aid kit?'

Fabio tossed it to me. I ripped open a pack of latex gloves and pulled them on. Very carefully, I pulled one of the intact vials out of its rack. It was labelled with a barcode and a reference number that must have meant something to someone. Very professional.

My hand was shaking. Not surprising, when you think what I'd seen that day. The vial slipped out of my fingers and smashed on a stone.

'*Shit.*'

I jumped back. The sandflies that had been torturing me abandoned my arms and descended on the pool of blood spreading across the stone.

'Looks like the story about the vaccination programme was true.'

'Of course it was true,' said Zia, tired fury in her voice.

I zipped the bag shut. I could hear flies buzzing, trapped inside, and I took cruel pleasure from that. 'You don't usually take blood samples when you're giving vaccines.'

'I've figured it out,' said Tillman. 'Menendez was a vampire. Lived in a cave, drank blood, kept company with bats . . .'

'Shut up.' The water had boiled. Drew made a cup of coffee and gave it to Zia. 'It was her fiancé, for God's sake.'

Tillman gave her a lazy look. 'Keep your panties on.'

'Check this out.' Fabio lifted a camera out of the pack he was going through. The camera had survived, and it still worked. When Anton pressed the button, the screen lit up with a digital chirp that felt horribly out of place. He hit 'play'. We all crowded round to see.

A picture appeared, a man about my age, with short dark hair plastered to his forehead. He wore a sweaty khaki shirt, a red bandana round his neck and the bush hat Tillman had taken. Tired but smiling, giving the camera a big thumbs-up.

'Dr Menendez, I presume,' said Drew.

Anton tabbed through the pictures on the camera. A flip-book travelogue: Menendez lounging on a boat with a fish he'd caught; Menendez in a harness scaling the cliffs by the waterfall; Menendez in the jungle, bandana round his neck and machete in hand. Menendez with a group of grinning men, with a monkey they'd shot dangling from a tree. Chillingly like watching the last weeks of my own life re-enacted by other people.

The camera bleeped a battery warning. The screen died. Anton popped out the memory card. Zia held out her hand expectantly.

'I'll look after it,' said Anton.

'It belonged to Felix.'

'*I'll look after it*,' he repeated. 'And when we find Menendez, I'll give it back to him myself.'

He slid it into a ziplock bag, and then into the camouflage wallet he kept in his pocket. Zia looked as if she wanted to hit him, if she'd had the strength.

'So where is he now?' said Howie.

The question hung in the space between us. No one looked at Zia.

'They might be alive,' I said. It came out sounding about as hopeful as I felt.

'Sure,' said Fabio.

'Here's what I think,' said Anton, and the way he said it,
I knew it was leading somewhere. 'The Indians caught
Menendez and his buddies and locked them up in the cave.
Then our buddy Roberto escaped. Somehow, he'd gotten a
GPS fix, and he wrote it on his wrist.'

'The camera,' I said. 'I bet that had built-in GPS.'

'Point is, if Roberto wrote down that position before he
escaped he must have been planning on coming back here.
Like with a rescue party. That means Menendez and the
others must have been alive.'

'Back then,' said Tillman.

'After he escaped, the Indians knew the cave wasn't secure.
So they moved the prisoners someplace else.'

'We have to look for them.' Hope was agony for Zia. She
squeezed her mug so hard I thought she'd crack it.

Tillman chewed a piece of sugar cane. 'In a hundred million
miles of jungle?'

'No chance,' said Fabio.

'Fuck you,' said Zia. 'I'll go by myself, if I have to.'

'Then you'll die in the jungle.'

We were so tired, anger was never far off. We'd already
nearly killed each other once that morning.

'Are we really arguing about this? Really?' I looked around
the circle, throwing down the challenge. 'If Menendez's out
there – and I haven't seen anything to make me think he's not
alive – don't we owe it to him to try? It's just common humanity.'

'Fuck humanity,' said Tillman. 'If we go off in the jungle
and get lost and starve, that's not going to help him and it's
not going to help us.'

'I've got this.' I unclipped the emergency beacon from my
belt loop and showed it to the others. 'If I press this button,
we'll have a rescue within twenty-four hours.'

Howie looked so desperate I thought he'd snatch it out of
my hand.

'If it works,' said Anton. 'And if we're in range. And this is a no-fly zone, remember?'

'How about food?' said Howie. 'You already said we're eating what's supposed to get us back.'

Tillman cuffed him. 'Nice attitude, God-Boy.'

'But it's true.' Fabio stuffed clothes back in Menendez's rucksack.

'Three days,' said Anton. 'We'll give it three days. We can stretch supplies that long. If we don't find them, we'll go back, raise the alarm in P-T.'

'Aren't you forgetting something?' said Tillman. 'Fabio fucked the GPS. You want to go walking in these woods without GPS? We'll get more lost than Menendez.'

'The camera might have GPS,' I reminded them. 'Can we get it working again?'

Fabio thumbed open the battery compartment. No joy. 'You need a special battery.'

'Does anyone else's camera have a built-in GPS?' Negative. 'Anyone's phone?'

Mine did, of course, but that had been smashed in the square at Puerto Tordoya. Anton had some relic that still used buttons; Drew had an iPhone, but the battery had died days ago. No one else had brought theirs.

'It's fine,' said Anton. 'People came to this jungle for hundreds of years before there was GPS.'

'Some of them even got out again,' said Fabio.

Anton jumped up. 'We won't get anywhere sitting on our asses. Let's grab and go.' He put his arm round Zia. 'I promise you, if Menendez's out there, we'll get him.'

He turned away. 'Maybe we'll even find Paititi.'

He said it like a joke. But I remembered how he looked when we found the idol: like a gambler who's found his lucky dice. He still believed – more than ever.

He didn't care about Menendez. He was a fortune

hunter. And to get that fortune, he'd drive us over a cliff if he had to.

29

'If the Indians took them someplace else, maybe they left a path,' Anton reasoned.

We spread out and searched the glade around the cliff. I poked around some bushes without really concentrating. All I could think about was whether we'd escape the same fate as Menendez.

I hadn't gone far when Anton gave a shout.

'Over here.'

I found him knee-deep in a patch of ferns, dangling a piece of red fabric between finger and thumb. A bandana, a lot like the one I'd seen Menendez wearing in the photos. A *lot* like it.

Anton gave it to Zia. 'His?'

She clutched it to her face and nodded. Anton cupped his hand under her chin, like talking to a child.

'It's good news. It means he was alive. And heading in this direction.' Anton surveyed the forest. 'Anyone see a trail?'

Tillman pointed to a gap between some trees. To me, it looked like any other gap.

'That?'

'Maybe,' said Fabio. 'But good luck if you try to follow it.'

Anton got out his compass and studied it.

'If you draw a line from the cave to here, it heads kind of west. We'll take a bearing and follow that.'

'Hold on,' said Tillman. 'What makes you think they went straight? You think the Indians never discovered left and right?'

'But they know which way the sun sets. And seeing as they

didn't draw us a map, and we don't have a GPS, following a bearing seems like the only way we're going to get out again. Unless you want to leave a trail of breadcrumbs?'

He snapped the compass shut.

'I know this is a one-in-a-million shot. But we have to try something.'

We could have tried something easier. The map showed nothing, but all the rest of that day we climbed steadily up. Some unmarked, unremarkable spur of the Andes; in England, it would have been the sort of peak people do for charity.

In the heat, the only noise that broke the tedious hum of insects was Howie complaining. Fabio and Tillman cut the path with no obvious enthusiasm; Zia walked alone. Drew was in a bad mood too. She kept her thoughts behind her sunglasses, and herself out of everyone's way. I watched, and wondered.

The second day, the terrain changed. Not for the better. The trees that grew out of that sticky red soil were sharper, spikier and thicker than anything we'd seen yet. They blunted the machetes almost as fast as Tillman and Fabio could sharpen them. Maybe because of that, or because they didn't much care, they did a sloppy job on the path, leaving branches trailing everywhere.

Optimism was in short supply. It's hard to be positive when you're starving. Hunger's a concept that's almost obsolete in the West: we see it on TV, emaciated children with fly-bitten eyes, and reach for another bag of crisps. I don't want to overstate it – we weren't dying or anything. But my stomach had shrunk to a wet knot twisting inside me; I felt nauseous and light-headed. I got clumsy, slipping and tripping too often. Sometimes I almost impaled myself on a spike the machetes had left, or stumbled past a palm bristling with foot-long thorns; then I'd start thinking, *Someone's going to die out here.*

Clouds massed, kettling in the heat; we heard distant rumbles, which might have been thunder or trees falling. The only rest we got was waiting for Howie, who fell further and further behind, sometimes as much as half an hour. He said he was feeling poorly: sore throat, dodgy tummy. I thought it was probably psychosomatic, the prospect of more days in the jungle.

'Trust fucking Anton to bring an interpreter like Howie, when there isn't one goddam Indian on the entire reservation,' said Tillman. Anton had spelled him on trail-blazing duties, so he'd dropped back and was walking in front of me. Even he looked exhausted by the effort.

I didn't want to bad-mouth Howie. If he hadn't been there, I'd have been the weakest link. 'What do you think happened to the Indians?'

'Gone to join the twenty-first century? Maybe they heard they were missing *Jersey Shore.*'

I laughed. Tillman spat on the ground.

'Seriously? I think they're out there right now.'

If Howie had been there, I'd have assumed it was a wind-up. But Tillman didn't make a spooky voice, or look goggle-eyed into the trees.

'These guys have spent the last five hundred years avoiding civilisation. Like they're really going to come out now, shake our hands, because Howie wants to tell them about Jesus?' He sliced at a sapling Fabio hadn't completely cut through. 'These fucking Indians, they're all the same . . .'

I got that sinking feeling you get when a taxi driver starts talking about immigration.

'I mean, basically, they're cowards. Always have been. You know why there's so many blacks in Brazil, the Caribbean? Because the Indians weren't strong enough to work the plantations. They're weak. Instead of confronting you, they run and hide.'

He tapped the side of his head. 'I'm not saying that's dumb. You gotta pick your fights. But they're sneaky fuckers, always watching, waiting for you to make a mistake. Then they get you. Like this one time, at Aguas Verdes . . .'

My ears pricked up. 'Where's Aguas Verdes?'

'Mexico,' said Anton. We'd caught him up; stuck behind Tillman, I hadn't noticed. He sat on a rock, a strange expression on his face. 'Tillman and I did a job there, a while back.'

'What happened?'

Tillman and Anton exchanged a look. 'You'd better tell this story, boss,' Tillman said.

Anton stretched out his legs. He looked up at a vulture, circling in the sky.

'Aguas Verdes was an Aztec gold mine. Way back, before the Spanish; legend says half of Montezuma's treasure hoard came out of it. After the conquest, the Spanish worked it for a while, but the Indians had put a curse on it. Each time a new guy came to work it, he died some horrible death. Eventually, they stopped coming. Later, no one even remembered where it was. A couple of years back, I was playing poker with an old mestizo guy in Mexico. He told me about his Indian buddy who had a map, an old old map from conquest times. We went to see him, took a look and I thought it might be genuine. The Indian said he'd sell it to us, but only if we took his two sons as guides.'

'Chico and Jorge,' said Tillman.

'Well, those guys were terrible. We said left, they went right; we wanted up, they led us down. Kept that up until we were down to our last day's food.'

'This sounds familiar.'

'Then all of a sudden, they couldn't do enough for us. Suddenly, there was a path exactly where we wanted to go. And you know what? That night, just at sunset, we come down this little gully and there's the mine. Big hole in the cliff, spoil heap out the front, like the conquistadors just abandoned it yesterday.'

'Wow.'

'Now, we didn't go there to work the mine. That's hard labour. You need special equipment, trucks to get it out; you've got to pay off the mayor of every one-horse town you pass through, even if you do have a permit. Which we didn't. But there's always a few crumbs around the cookie jar. Tillman and I got down on our knees and dug in the dirt for any nuggets. Not like we were going to buy Porsches and swimming pools, but enough we could kit ourselves out for a proper expedition and come back. Maybe hit the mother lode.

'Then we turned around, and we weren't alone. Chico and Jorge had brought their buddies. God knows how they found us. We'd been in those mountains ten days, never seen a living soul. But suddenly those Indians were there, ten or twelve of them, all with knives and guns.'

'We didn't have guns,' said Tillman.

'Whole thing was a con. Montezuma never went near that place: it was some wildcat mine that got worked out years ago. Chico and Jorge took our cameras, our GPS, our money and the map. Just left us the compass and a couple of granola bars. Then they told us to start walking, and if we ever came back they'd kill us.'

I tried to imagine it. 'It sounds like something from a film.'

Anton waved at the jungle, the white steam snaking through the valley below. 'Like this doesn't?'

Thunder rumbled in the clouds. A hundred yards back, Howie trudged into view. Anton jumped to his feet.

'Let's get going. We're nomads too, remember.'

The rain came five minutes later. I tried my poncho, but the thorny bushes shredded it in no time. I took it off to save what was left. In two minutes, I was soaked through. At least I had a dry-bag lining the inside of my pack. One of Anton's better pieces of advice.

It was a long, miserable afternoon. The ground levelled out on to some kind of plateau: thick, featureless forest. Raindrops dripped through the canopy; green moss hung like cobwebs from the vines. It felt ancient, primitive: if a triceratops had come grazing through the trees, it wouldn't entirely have surprised me.

'There's no way Menendez came here,' said Drew, on one of our breaks. 'I haven't seen anything that looks like a trail since we left the cave.'

I shushed her and looked back, hoping Zia hadn't heard. The forest stretched away in every direction.

'I can't even see our own tracks.'

'Let's hope Anton's compass is working.'

We hurried on. 'Make sure we don't lose Howie,' Anton told me, so I was the one who had to hang back, while the light faded and the path got harder to follow. Sometimes, I couldn't even hear the swipe of the machetes at the front.

We nearly made it. I'd reached the top of an embankment that led down to a stream. The others had crossed and had started making camp on a patch of shingle on the far bank. In the gloom, I could see Zia setting up her cookware, Tillman dragging in a branch for firewood and Anton stringing his hammock.

I started down the slope, grabbing on to the stumps that Tillman and Fabio had left. Five pairs of boots had churned the wet ground into a mudslide.

'Careful,' shouted Drew from below. 'It's tricky.'

I slipped and slithered down the slope. Howie stood at the top, watching unhappily.

'Come on,' I called.

Howie grunted. 'The path of the righteous is beset with thorns,' he said piously. And then: '*Ow!*'

I laughed; I thought he was joking. Then I turned, and saw him curled up on the ground, writhing in pain and clutching his bottom.

'What——?'

Before I could speak, I saw what must have happened. Tillman or Fabio had lopped one of the saplings with their machete, leaving a foot-high spike sticking out of the earth. Howie had slipped and landed right on top of it.

The others, watching, thought it was funny. 'Stuck him up the ass,' Tillman hooted.

I crawled back up to Howie and put my arm around his shoulder to lift him. I could see the hole torn in the seat of his trousers, and blood seeping out around the edges.

'I don't think I'm going to make it,' he whispered.

30

'Can he walk?' said Anton.

We sat round the fire, licking fat from our fingers. Despite the rain, Tillman had managed to get it lit by splitting logs and scooping out the dry wood inside. Better still, Fabio had shot a bird, a jungle turkey. Welcome calories, though it didn't go far between seven people. Howie lay in his hammock, groaning occasionally to let us know he was still alive.

There was no nice way to say it. 'The stick went up his anus.'

Tillman sniggered.

'There's some internal bleeding. God knows what might be ruptured – or if there'll be any infection. If that stump had been six inches longer, he might be dead.'

'But can he walk?' Anton repeated.

'Maybe. Slowly.'

'Slower than before?' said Tillman incredulously. 'He'll be going backwards.'

'The point is, he needs proper medical attention.'

'You can give him a rectal exam, can't you, Doc?'

'I'm worried about infection. I don't have a lot of antibiotics left. If something takes hold . . .'

'There are plants we use for infections,' said Fabio.

I'm not big on homeopathy. But I was tired, and out of options. 'Does it grow near here?'

'Maybe I can find it.'

He took his machete and his head torch and walked into the jungle. I watched the light flit through the trees like a will-o'-the-wisp, dipping here and there as he stooped to examine some leaf or flower.

Anton looked at Zia. 'Go with him, see if he needs a hand.'

'He's fine.'

'*Go.*'

Zia put down the pot she'd been scrubbing and left. Perhaps she guessed what we needed to talk about.

'Howie can't go on, can he?' said Anton, as soon as she was out of sight.

'If he makes it back to the waterfall, I'm seriously going to consider investing in one of his Bibles.'

Anton stared into the fire. I knew what he was thinking about, and it wasn't Menendez. Cities of gold, going up in smoke.

'You could stay here with Howie a few days,' he tried. 'Fabio, Tillman and me can keep looking.'

'We're not splitting up. We don't have a GPS, and there's a village full of Indians somewhere out here unaccounted for. In fact . . .' I pulled Cate's emergency beacon out of its case. Since we'd left the boats, I'd worn it on my belt the whole time, even in my sleep. *Pull only in emergency*, said the red cap.

'I should probably pull this right now.'

One button, and it really would be over.

'Don't do that,' said Anton. No mistaking the warning in his voice, but I didn't care.

'Don't you understand? Howie's life's at stake. This isn't running around playing cowboys and Indians any more.'

'It was never that. But think about it – think how far we've come. If we leave now, we'll never come back.'

I stared at him across the flames. Sparks blew into the air and died in the darkness.

'At least sleep on it. See how Howie does.' A bush rustled; I saw the light of a head-torch approaching. 'Maybe Fabio's jungle medicine can fix him up.'

Fabio emerged from the trees carrying a fistful of leaves in one hand, and a length of vine in the other. He mashed the leaves between two stones, while Zia boiled water from the stream, then mixed them together into a paste.

'You put this on the bleeding.' He smirked at me and made a crude gesture. 'This is why they pay doctors so much money, no?'

We spread one of the ponchos on sticks as a screen. Zia helped me get Howie's trousers down. We cleaned him off, and I applied Fabio's potion. As unpleasant as you would imagine: I won't disgust you with the details.

When I went to wash my hands, Fabio was busy with the vine he'd found. He'd stripped its bark and sliced it into sections, which he threw in the boiling water. He added some leaves and stirred. A head of white foam started to bubble up.

'What is that?' I asked.

'Jungle beer.' Fabio skimmed off the froth with his machete, then strained it through his mosquito net into a water bottle. He offered it to me.

'Drink. It makes you feel good.'

I was susceptible. The word 'beer' had gone off in my head

like a minor earthquake: every advert I'd ever seen funnelled into a Proustian rush of frosty glasses, hot summer's days and ice-cold liquid sliding down my throat. God knows, I needed a drink right then. I'd just had to stick my hand up Howie's bloody arse, remember.

I sniffed the bottle. It smelled horribly bitter. Still steaming, with specks of plant matter floating on the surface. A long way from the pint of my dreams.

'Live a little,' said Drew.

I drank.

At first I felt nothing. I sat by the fire, listening to the others, watching the flames make animal shapes. The stars got brighter; the conversation drifted away.

Then the bottom dropped out of my stomach. I sprawled forward. The fire was inside me, burning me out. I needed water.

I crawled to the stream like an animal going to drink. The fire inside me burned so hot I thought I'd split open. Burning away my soul. The river had stretched out a mile wide. My lips bent to the black water: I knew it would cure me, if I could only drink it.

A great scaly body rose out of the water, swallowing the stars. I fell back.

'What have you been doing?' said Cate.

The snake struck forward. Its smooth belly slid over mine. I wrestled it, writhing against its coils until I forced myself on top.

It wasn't a snake. It was a vine, winding around my throat, forcing itself into my mouth, my ears, my nose. Leaves sprouted. I snapped them off, but each time two more tendrils sprouted.

'No regrets?' whispered Drew. So close, I felt her tongue flick my ear. She writhed on top of me, in the white bikini she wore in Mexico. I undid the clasp. The two halves hung open round her breasts as she rocked against my hips. She lunged forward, but I rolled her over so I was on top. I needed to remember something important, something about Cate, but every time I had it it slipped away.

'I've been wanting to do this since the day we met,' I told her.

31

Running water woke me. Surprisingly loud. I opened my eyes, and saw why. I was lying on my front on the edge of the stream. So close, it ran right under my nose. My stomach felt empty. Not hungry, just void. From the smell on my shirt, I gathered I'd been sick.

I'd be lying if I said it had never happened before. Waking up on the floor the worse for wear, braced to remember how I got there. But not since Peggy was born. And never in the back end of an unexplored rainforest.

Something else was different. My bones hurt from lying on the stones; my muscles felt as if I'd run a marathon. But there was no headache. My mind felt clear, and I don't mean just OK: I mean the sort of sharp, bright clarity that makes you sit up and take notice. The colours around me popped out of the jungle; every sound seemed to resonate inside me like a loudspeaker. As if I'd been looking at life through a dirty window that had suddenly been wiped so clean I could put my hand through it.

I smelled smoke. I sat up. The others were all awake, breaking camp. Howie sat against a tree, while Zia tended the fire where the kettle was boiling. Fabio wound vines between a pair of saplings, weaving a sort of makeshift stretcher.

He grinned at me. 'You OK?'

I rubbed my head. I expected to hear it squeak. 'What was in that beer?'

'You liked it?'

'I'm not sure.'

I started unbuttoning my shirt to rinse it out. I noticed Drew looking at me, and blushed as I remembered my dream. What if I'd said something? Or *done* something?

Instinctively, my hand went to my pockets to check I had everything. Like when I leave the house: *wallet, keys, phone.* Here the trinity was knife, malaria pills and the emergency beacon.

I touched the pouch on my belt. Felt an open zip and rubberised fabric. Did I put the beacon away last night, after I'd had it out?

It wasn't there.

I ran back to the campfire, scanning the ground all around. Heavy marks churned the earth, as if an enormous dog had been pawing it. Had I done that? No sign of the beacon.

'Lost something?' said Anton. All innocence.

I flew at him.

'What have you done with it?' Flashes of conversation came back from the night before. 'Did you think I was going to set it off in the night? Bring the curtain down on your kamikaze *Boy's Own* adventure? Force you to confront *reality*?'

Tillman grabbed me from behind and wrestled me back.

'Calm down, Doc,' he hissed in my ear.

Anton wiped off a streak of mud I'd left on his face.

'Relax,' he said, and the tone of his voice was sufficiently unrelaxed that I stopped struggling. 'I didn't get you drunk, and I didn't take your beacon.'

'Then where is it?'

Everyone else had stopped what they were doing to watch.

'In the mud?' said Zia.

'I looked.'

'Does it float?' asked Fabio.

I tried to remember the instruction manual. I skimmed it the night before we left. 'I think so.'

Fabio nodded to the stream. 'Maybe it fell in.'

I pulled myself away from Tillman and waded out into the stream. I searched for a flash of yellow among the rocks and branches. Nothing.

The buzz from Fabio's drink had gone. That clear brilliant window in my mind had shattered. I picked up a stone and hurled it into the water.

'We have to go back.' I ran to my pack and picked it up. I hadn't zipped it up: everything spilled out. '*Fuck.*' I threw down the pack and scrabbled in the mud, jamming things back in like someone was timing me. '*Shit.* My only change of clothes.'

'Easy, tiger,' said Anton. 'We talked it through last night. We're going on.'

'Are you insane? We just lost our last link to the outside world. We have to go back right now. Howie can't even walk.'

'Howie's doing fine. Fabio's medicine-man shit worked. And we can carry him till his ass gets better.'

I looked at my bulging pack, thought of the weight we were carrying already. 'How far can we do that?'

'Not far. If we don't find anything by noon today, we turn around.'

It was a hot day. After yesterday's rain, the jungle steamed. Stuffing my pack, I'd unbalanced it in some subtle way that put all the weight on my left shoulder. However much I fiddled with the straps, I couldn't shift it. There were no rest breaks. Anton took the lead, slashing the jungle as if he could drive his way to Paititi's front gate by sheer force of will.

We took turns carrying Howie, like a Roman emperor on his litter. I hated him for that. I suspected he could have walked if he wanted: the wound wasn't as deep as I'd suspected, and Fabio's poultice had cleaned it up. When I checked him over, he was running a slight temperature, but that was probably sunstroke from the ridge yesterday.

Mid-morning, I found myself walking with Drew while Tillman and Zia took their turn with Howie. I couldn't look at her without vivid images from the dream popping up in front of my eyes. There was something I had to ask.

'Last night. After I drank Fabio's magic potion. Did I say anything, um, revealing?'

The way Drew looked at me, I think she knew exactly what I meant. 'Don't worry. Your deep dark secrets are safe.'

That didn't exactly reassure me.

We walked for about two hours. It was like waiting for a delayed train: checking my watch every five minutes, counting time, watching it fail to pass. I couldn't see the sun, but I guessed from the heat it must be close to noon. The end of the line.

Anton shouted something from up ahead. I checked my watch, but there were still twenty-five minutes until twelve. We ran up to join him.

He pointed his machete at the ground, and I forgot all about clock-watching.

'Footprints.'

Even I could see them: clear as the Hollywood Walk of Fame. Not barefoot Indians, but heavy jungle boots. Like in the cave.

We stared at each other. 'You think it could be . . .?'

'There can't be another gringo who's been through this forest since Alvarado. Not wearing size-eleven boots.'

'The prints are fresh,' said Fabio. 'Since after the rain.'

'They came through this morning?' The hope on Zia's face was painful to watch.

There must have been a few of them. Even where leaves hid the footprints, snapped sticks and lopped branches told us where to go. Tillman and Zia left Howie on the ground; we all ran down the trail. From the corner of my eye, I noticed a mossy branch at the side of the path, with a sharp point and a round knot that looked exactly like a heron's beak and face.

I stopped. Drew almost cannoned into me.

'You see something?'

'Massive déjà vu. Unless . . .'

I looked around. Up ahead, Fabio and Anton had paused for breath. It wasn't easy running with the packs on our backs. A hundred metres back, Howie sat up on his stretcher shouting not to be left behind.

I found one of the prints and put my foot down next to it. I pressed heavily, until I'd made a firm impression in the mud. I lifted my foot and compared the two prints side by side.

Identical.

'Anton,' I called. 'You need to see this.'

'The GPS is fucked. The compass is fucked. We're *totally* fucked.'

Splinters flew in the air. Each *fucked* came punctuated by the thud of a machete as Tillman took out his frustration on a balsa tree.

'*Fucked.*'

I shivered. I actually felt quite calm, all things considered. Like being in an operation, a crisis seems to turn down my emotions and amp up the calm. It's only afterwards I shake so badly I can hardly pour a drink.

'How did we end up chasing ourselves round in circles?'

'I don't understand.' Anton sounded bewildered. That was scarier than anything. 'I followed the compass.'

'Iron in the trees,' said Fabio. 'It fucks up the compass.'

Drew covered her eyes. 'Seriously?'

'It can happen. Very big trees, here.'

'So how do we get out?' I looked around the group. 'If anyone has my emergency beacon, now would be a good time to come forward. No questions asked.'

No one volunteered it.

'Not like Domino's deliver here anyway,' said Anton.

Drew glared at him. 'You think this is funny? If we've been going around in circles, we can't even trace our path back.'

'So long as we head east, we'll be OK. We'll hit the river, eventually.'

'Head east how? Following the compass, like we did to get here?'

'We'll check it against the sun.'

We all looked up. Through the tangle of vines and branches, we could barely see the canopy. The sky was nothing more than a well-kept secret.

'We've got food for three days,' said Zia.

'Tarantulas can live two years without eating,' said Fabio, apropos of nothing.

'We'll hunt.'

'Hunt what?' said Tillman. 'In case you didn't notice, this ain't exactly the Bronx Zoo. I haven't even seen a monkey in days. These guns are getting rusty.'

'There's always your cocaine,' said Drew viciously. 'That's a stimulant.'

Fabio jumped to his feet. He turned this way and that, sniffing the air.

'You smell that?'

I didn't, and then I did. A musty, musky smell, blowing in on a warm breeze.

'Peccary,' said Fabio. 'Wild pig.'

He took the rifle leaning against his pack and peered into the trees. Maybe he saw something; all I could make out was leaves and branches. But I heard it: branches snapping, leaves rustling, high-pitched squeals and a clack-clack sound like running a stick along a fence.

'We're lost. But we can eat.'

Tillman and Fabio waded into the undergrowth. Anton unstrapped the two shotguns, then looked at me.

'You in?'

A thrill of power ran up my arm when he handed me the gun. The virgin jungle tore and tugged at me as we followed the others, but I didn't care. I had the gun; I had the strength. Up a rise, over a low ridge and down the other side. The smell got worse: something between a locker room and an old fridge.

At the bottom of the slope, Fabio waved us to stop. The noises got louder. The ground rumbled under my feet, like being at the races when the horses come into the final straight. I saw flashes of black and white, legs and snouts and hair and hooves trotting through the undergrowth. There must have been dozens of them.

Tillman, Fabio and Anton wriggled closer. The pigs can't have smelled us – we were downwind – and they surely couldn't hear us over the racket they were making, but they must have sensed something. The rumble quickened.

Tillman knelt and put the rifle to his shoulder. I aimed the shotgun. My chest was so tight I thought I'd crush my lungs.

'Sooooooo-eeeeeeeee.'

The first shot was like the cork coming out of a bottle. After that, all I heard was noise. The shotgun recoil almost broke my shoulder; I nearly dropped it. No one had shown me how to use it. I squeezed my hand around the stock, jerked it forward and pumped out the shell. Just like in the movies – it felt obscenely good. I fired again. The leaves in front of me disintegrated in a green spray. A scream ripped the air, a whoop of savage delight. It took a long time to realise it was me.

We kept firing longer than I thought possible. My shotgun ran out after five shots, but the others seemed to have brought unlimited ammunition. It was like watching *Zulu*, hundreds of poor brutes facing an impossible mismatch. Instead of the pigs, all I smelled now was cordite and gunsmoke. I glimpsed Tillman, and the look on Tillman's face was pure bliss. A small piglet struggled to keep up with its mother. Tillman drew a bead, tracked it and fired. The piglet went down with a wail and a spurt of blood. The mother didn't even look back.

'Young meat tastes sweetest,' Tillman shouted. I don't know how I heard him. He jacked the bolt, ejected the cartridge and loaded again. Squeezed the trigger, jacked the bolt. In some kind of ecstasy.

Something changed. Kel the doctor wouldn't have noticed, but Kel the hunter read it in the foliage, a difference in the pattern like ripples on water. The pulse in the earth quickened.

'They're coming at us,' Anton yelled.

The pigs charged out of the forest: whether from confusion or desperate courage, I don't know. It sounds comical, something from a cartoon. In reality, a hundred animals coming at you full tilt is absolutely bloody terrifying. Like being charged by a hundred prop forwards – except at fifty kilometres an hour, and each one wielding a vicious pair of tusks.

Fabio saw me standing there.

'Get in a tree,' he yelled.

Panic took over. I looked round wildly. Trees everywhere, of course, but none with branches low enough to grab. It was a long time since I'd climbed a tree, and I didn't have time to get it wrong. Ignoring Fabio's advice, I ran.

It's not easy running through a rainforest – but fear's a great performance enhancer. I pushed past branches and tore through brambles I wouldn't have dared touch in normal life. Thorns sliced me; roots tripped and bruised me. On the muddy uphill, my feet kept slipping back, like a bad dream where you run like you're made of rubber.

The pounding got louder. The hill got steeper. I was on all fours, now, scrabbling and grabbing, hauling myself up on roots and branches. A pig's-eye view of the jungle. I wondered if Tillman would recognise me if he saw me, and if he'd care before he pulled the trigger.

There was daylight ahead. The mud under me turned to rock. I hauled myself up the last, steepest section and came out on a ledge under a high cliff.

The energy left me. I sprawled on the mossy rock, too tired even to look back. Everything hurt, everything bled, and I was shaking as if someone had cut the elastic holding me together.

A branch snapped behind me. Something was coming up the slope. I dragged myself to my feet and turned round. My back to the cliff, no way out. I'd dropped the shotgun some-where in the forest. I grabbed a fallen branch and jabbed it in front of me, brandishing it like a club.

'Calm down, Rambo.'

Anton came out of the bushes. Sweat had cut channels through the dirt on his face; his T-shirt had lost an arm. At least he'd kept hold of his rifle.

'You look like I feel,' I said.

He didn't say anything – just stared at me. I wasn't a pretty sight. My trousers were shredded, my arms covered in cuts, and I had a nasty gash on my calf. I wiped a dribble of sweat off my face, and my hand came away covered in blood. How did that get there?

I grinned. 'Next time, I'll climb a tree.'

He didn't even care. He was looking right past me, at something over my shoulder.

I turned round. The cliff ended in a rocky overhang, with a narrow ledge leading round the corner. If you looked at the bottom, all you saw was rock. But when you looked up, you started to think that the outcrop looked a bit funny, almost like a nose. And the crack underneath it, and the bulge under that, were a lot like a mouth and chin. And then you looked higher, and just where you thought the eyes should be, there was an oval hollow staring straight ahead. A diagonal crease sketched the hairline, with cheekbones curving away beneath it.

It was a human face, carved out of the cliff like Mount Rushmore. I squinted, not really believing, but it didn't go away. It stared across the valley, too monumental to care about the humans beneath its gaze.

At that moment, I believed everything Anton had ever told me. I believed I'd lifted the curtain and seen the secret truth of the universe.

'The guardian.'

We didn't wait for the others. The ledge curved around past the guardian, and we followed it, past that implacable gaze. A roosting bird flapped out from the eye socket, shrieking in alarm. I shivered.

The ledge funnelled us into a gully, not much more than a crack in the rocks. The rough sides scraped my arms and reopened my cuts, smearing blood along the walls. My shoulder bumped a clump of moss and dislodged it.

'Oh . . .'

It was hard to see. Not a lot of light came in, and the moss had stained the rock black. But my eye caught it. Lines in the rock, the same smooth designs as at the waterfall. Anton and I peeled off more moss, until we'd torn a three-metre strip off the wall. These petroglyphs were longer, more shapes and more involved. I stuck my finger in and traced the design. Not quite daring to believe.

'Do you think it's a warning?'

If it was, we didn't care. The path took a turn to the right, then immediately left again, and suddenly there was daylight.

'Whoa, there.'

I stopped just in time. We were on the edge of a deep, steep gorge. A silver river ran at the bottom, winding through fallen boulders towards a junction with another river. On the far side, sheer cliffs climbed to the top of a plateau. Trees and vegetation covered it right to the edge, like a mop of hair, with strange lumps thrusting up to form an irregular skyline. They didn't look like hills.

A rope bridge stretched across the chasm to the plateau. The hawsers were made from some fibrous vine, split and frayed, spliced on to two stone outcroppings. I had to kneel down and touch it, working my fingers between the strands, to be sure it was real. Even then, I wondered if Fabio's potion had thrown me into some sort of hallucination.

The sun dipped below the clouds. A shaft of sunlight escaped and hit us face-on. Anton's face lit up gold; I suppose mine was the same. We stared at each other with wild eyes, then threw our arms round each other. I don't think I ever hugged Cate or Peggy harder.

'This is it.'

32

We went to find the others. It wasn't easy: they'd all split up to find us. In the end, it was Zia who brought us together. She'd lit a fire to smoke peccary meat; one by one, the smell brought us in. Five pigs in all, lined up like bodies from a war zone. Flies swarmed over them. It seemed like a poor return for all the ammunition we'd spent.

'Even dried and smoked, we can't take it all with us,' said Zia, up to her elbows in blood from skinning a carcass.

'Doesn't matter,' said Anton. 'We're going to be here a while.'

I was burning to get back to the cliff. Anton insisted we had to find our bags where we'd dropped them: 'We'll need our stuff.' We trussed the larger pigs and strung them up from branches, to keep the ants off. Then Anton and I led the way back to the gorge.

I worried we wouldn't find our way – that the city we'd glimpsed would disappear like Brigadoon. Up the slope and on to the ledge. Howie groaned and swore he couldn't make it, but even he shut up when he saw the guardian. Down the passage, past the petroglyphs and out on to the clearing that overlooked the gorge. I held my breath as I made that last turn, ready to be disappointed. That it had all been a trick of the light, or a funny-shaped hill, or my imagination run riot.

I didn't have to worry. One by one, the others came out on the cliff and stared in awe.

'You'd think it could still be inhabited.' I peered into the jungle, as if I expected to see a lost Inca waving at me from across the ravine. Why not? It wouldn't have been the most surprising thing that day.

Drew knelt at the bridge, just the way I had.

'The anaconda bridge. It's all true.'

'You're not thinking of walking across that thing,' said Howie. 'I mean, there's no way it'll hold us.'

Looking down it, the bridge's shortcomings were obvious. More air than bridge, with some terrifyingly wide holes between the slats. They wouldn't look any smaller when you stood over them.

'Maybe go along the river, see if we can cross further down,' suggested Fabio.

Anton stared along the gorge. A couple of hundred metres downstream, another river joined it from the far side, flowing on into a canyon that looked, if anything, deeper.

'Alvarado said the city was on an island. A hundred bucks says if we crossed the river downstream and came back, we'd find exactly the same situation on the other side. Minus the bridge.'

Anton opened his pack and started pulling out ropes. He tied one off on the rock outcrop and buckled himself into a climbing harness.

'You're not really going over there?' said Drew.

Anton brushed dust off his trousers. 'You're supposed to cross the anaconda bridge to get to Paititi, right?'

He stepped on to the bridge. Tillman paid out the rope, while Fabio filmed from one side. Anton wiped his hands on his shirt. He half turned and gave the camera a thumbs-up.

'See you on the other side.'

I don't think I ever held my breath so long. Every step he took, a ripple went through the bridge. A couple of times, he took leaps over missing slats that made the ropes creak and strain. The bridge sagged lower as he got towards the middle. He crouched, then crawled, testing each plank with his hand before putting his weight on it.

He slipped. Drew gasped; Tillman swore and jerked the safety line. I waited to see the body tumbling like a stunt dummy. Actually, I think I closed my eyes.

Anton was still there when I opened them. He hadn't fallen. He'd grabbed on to one of the hawsers and was pulling himself along it like a monkey, where the gap was too big to jump. The bridge twisted to one side; another plank pulled loose and fell to the river.

'Say what you like about Anton,' I said, 'but life's never dull when he's around.'

Anton reached the next slat and somehow managed to haul or twist himself back on to the bridge. Now the going was easier, the slats better preserved. He could walk again, almost skipping across.

'Don't get cocky,' muttered Tillman.

The sag of the bridge made the last few metres a scramble. Drew turned away, unable to watch. I thought I might puke from the tension. Anton ran up it like a cat, hurdled one last gap and landed on terra firma. He turned to face us, spread his arms and shouted loud enough to reach the Atlantic:

'Welcome to Paititi.'

Five

Jonestown

33

Thank God, none of us had to copy Anton's high-wire act – quite. He tied off the safety rope to a tree on the far side, so we could clip ourselves on without relying on the bridge. Our feet hardly touched it. When it was my turn, I felt like one of those Hong Kong action heroes, skimming over rooftops and walls with balletic, wire-assisted grace. That didn't make it less terrifying. I've never suffered from vertigo, but looking down through a hole in the bridge at the river far below was the most terrifying thing I'd ever done. I let go my grip on the wire, dangling by the harness like a game bird. It took all my strength to pull myself back up.

And then I was there. The other side. I looked around in wonder, waiting for my legs to stop shaking, while the others took their turns crossing. I wished Cate was there, so I could show her it was all true. I'd done it.

A path led off from the bridgehead into the jungle. I stared down it, into the darkness, while I waited for Howie.

He didn't want to come. In the end, Anton had to cross back and more or less manhandle him on to the rope. He and Fabio tied our two ropes together and made a sort of pulley, like a laundry line. He clipped Howie on and we all dragged him across. The backpacks came the same way. Anton unpacked the guns.

211

'Let's see who's home.'

He said it lightly, but I could hear the tension. The path was clear and well trodden. We weren't the first people here.

Anton took the lead, rolling the machete in his wrist to lop off any stray branches. Fabio went next, filming every step, then Tillman with a shotgun. Even Howie came, limping along with the walking stick Fabio cut for him. No one wanted to miss this.

The path led a little way in, then turned right, parallel with the river, into a defile between two of the hills we'd seen from the far side. The jungle rose up; parrots shrieked from the undergrowth.

'Those hills look natural to you?' said Anton.

Without waiting for an answer, he veered off the path, hacking his way to the base of the mound. Where the ground sloped up, he plunged the machete into the earth, like King Arthur or something. It went in about a foot and stopped, quivering.

'Stone.'

Using the machete as a shovel, Anton chopped and scraped the soil until he'd gouged a hole about three feet wide. The blade rasped on rock. We brushed the soil away. A square-edged block emerged, black and proud in the red earth.

'You crazy motherfucker,' said Tillman. 'You really did it.'

'One stone doesn't make a city,' warned Drew. But the incautious light in her eyes said she'd drunk the Kool-Aid like the rest of us.

I started scooping more earth to widen the hole. But Anton was already up and off again, flitting up the path like a butterfly. All we could do was try to keep up.

How to describe that first hour in the city? Like Christmas morning, the last day of school, the birth of your child; like waking up the morning after you lost your virginity, knowing whatever else happens, no one can take that away from you. Just – awe. Walking between the mounds, dwarfed by them and the jungle that crowned them; macaws and parrots that seemed brighter than any we'd seen before; debating among ourselves what the different buildings might have been. Anton gave them fanciful names – 'the armoury', 'the guard room', 'the priests' quarters' – jotting them down on a scrap of paper with a rudimentary map.

'Like I'm going to wait for some archaeologist to tell me what they are? You name it, you own it. Bingham, Schliemann, those guys didn't know jack about what they were digging up – just legends and guesswork. But the names stuck.'

'Don't you think you should at least make sure they're buildings?'

'There's time for that later,' he said. 'Right now, I want it all.'

The path took us between two small mounds – so close together Anton called them 'the gatehouses' – and on to the edge of a clearing. We hung back – even Anton hesitated, reluctant to step into the open. We all felt we'd come to the heart of something, the secret centre of the city. Two squat mounds boxed the sides, while in front of us loomed the biggest of them all. A vine with blood-red flowers spread over it like a network of veins.

'The high temple,' said Anton, and no one contradicted him. 'This must have been the central plaza.'

He walked out, arms spread out and blade bared. If I squinted, I could see him in armour, a battle-hardened conquistador claiming the city he'd taken. He knelt in the centre of the circle and cleared a stretch of ground with his machete. Again, the blade rang on stone.

Anton hardly cared. He looked up at the high temple in front of him.

'Race you.'

I remembered that morning in Mexico, scrambling after Anton up the steps of the Maya pyramid. This was nothing like that – except for the sense of wonder. Here, we went on all fours, swinging our way like monkeys through a magic forest that had been tipped at a forty-five-degree angle. Trees became handholds, vines ropes for hanging on to while we hauled ourselves up the slope.

By the time we reached the top I was grimy, scratched and sore from trying to keep up with Anton. Even my scabs had scabs. Wiping the sweat off my face did nothing, because my sleeve was soaked. Then there was light and air and height around me. The foliage fell away, the slope levelled off. I scrambled out on a carpet of thickly knotted vines, so deep I couldn't touch the earth below. In the centre, a solitary ficus tree spread its shade. I crawled into it hungrily and slurped water out of my canteen. Then I turned round.

It was like being back in the aeroplane. High above the jungle, looking down on a green ocean that had flooded the world. From here, you could see the whole layout. The city was an island, just like Alvarado said, a plateau maybe half a mile long in the middle of the river. Cut off completely, apart from the bridge, which I could see swaying far below. Downstream, the canyon disappeared round a bend.

The mounds we'd seen covered almost the whole island, like an upturned egg carton, too regular and tight packed to have ever been natural. I counted more than twenty. Easy, in the mind's eye, to strip off the vegetation and see houses, temples, courtyards and streets. Blink again, and you could see people, proud Incas who'd come down from the mountains to the very depths of the jungle, rather than submit to the conquest.

And now we'd found them.

I took in the whole three-sixty. Behind me – west, I suppose – the mountains came down much closer than I'd expected. White mist hung on the slopes, until it merged with the clouds that hid the peaks from view.

One by one, the others came over the top and joined us under the tree. Fabio started filming. Drew picked one of the red flowers and tucked it in her hair, like Peggy does sometimes on Putney Heath. Her face shone. Anton put his arm around her waist and kissed her, until Tillman made a puking noise.

I gestured at the view. 'When I signed up for this, I never imagined . . . *this*.'

'Yeah.' The moment was so far beyond words, saying anything was pointless. We drank it in.

Tillman took out his knife. He pressed the flat of the blade against his palm so it made a welt.

'You know what we should do? Blood brothers. Seal the deal.'

'Forget it,' said Drew sharply. 'God knows what's in your blood by now.'

I nodded. 'The last thing we need is more cuts to get infected.'

Tillman flushed; he muttered something and looked at the ground. He was embarrassed, I realised. I almost felt bad.

'He's right, though.' Anton took the knife and made a small cut in his thumb. Didn't flinch. He squeezed it until the blood dribbled out over the ground. He wiped the knife and gave it back to Tillman, who did the same, as did Fabio.

I sighed, and got out my own penknife. Before I made the cut, I rubbed antibacterial gel from the bottle in my pocket over the blade. My blood dripped between the vines underfoot, down through the gaps and on to who knows what. Flies swarmed on to it like Coca-Cola.

While Drew added her blood (Zia refused), Anton took his knife and scarred 'A.M.' into the bark of the lone tree. One by one, we all added our own initials. The first time I'd carved my initials in anything since I was fifteen.

'How about Howie?'

Howie had stayed below. I looked down at the plaza, our small pile of bags in the centre. Couldn't see him: he'd probably gone looking for shade.

'He made it too. Stick him on there.'

From the pocket of his trousers, Anton pulled out a miniature bottle of Captain Morgan's rum. He cracked the seal and poured it out on the ground. It dribbled down through the tangled vines.

'I claim this city in the name of the El Dorado Exploration Expedition,' he declared. 'Paid for with our blood, sweat and spirit.'

'Amen,' said Tillman.

We huddled together the best we could on that twisted ground. Arms round each other's shoulders, sweat to sweat, sharing the moment. Everything else that had happened – Nolberto, Menendez, Roberto, Howie's injury, the food situation – didn't exist. Drew, next to me, squeezed my arm and I squeezed back.

Later – a lot later – when the others had started to go down, I ended up alone at the top with Tillman. He shaded his eyes and looked east, to the far horizon.

'You see something?'

He shook his head. 'Just thinking – it's a long way back from here.'

34

By the time we'd reached the bottom, we all remembered we hadn't eaten since breakfast. We gathered wood and built a fire on the edge of the plaza.

'Ham again,' said Howie. He looked bad. Sweating badly – worse than usual, I mean – and his face sickly grey, apart from a red welt on his cheek. I wondered if his wound had got infected: I didn't fancy having to examine it. He barely nibbled his food.

'Better get used to the taste,' said Zia. 'We'll be eating this all the way back to Puerto Tordoya.'

'First thing I do when I get there, I'm going to order the biggest pizza they have, all the toppings, and an ice-cold beer,' I announced.

There was a moment's silence. The human mind's a fickle thing. Do something, move on. An hour ago, we'd been on top of the world. Now our thoughts had already begun turning home.

'You think they ever did human sacrifices here?' said Tillman.

'Inca didn't do human sacrifice,' said Anton. 'That was Aztecs and Maya.'

'Not true.' Drew scratched a bite on her shoulder and hitched her bra strap. 'Incas sacrificed plenty. Thousands of people, each time one of the emperors died.'

'Thanks, Wikipedia.'

'They've also found hundreds of mummified kids that look like they were killed in some kind of ritual.'

'How about the mummies of the fourteen Inca emperors?' said Fabio. 'They are supposed to be here, when the Incas ran away from the Spanish.'

Tillman snorted. 'I'd rather find the golden sun from Cuzco. And Huascar's golden chain. It's supposed to be a thousand feet long, each link as thick as a man's arm.'

'"Seek and you shall find." Isn't that what the Bible says?' Anton put down his plate and tousled Howie's hair. 'Let's go seek.'

We split up. Without planning: we just drifted away from the square in different directions. I think each of us needed to process the moment in our own way. Plus, after three weeks trapped in each other's company, solitude was almost as precious as a hot shower. We felt safe on the island. Too small to get lost for long, and if any Indians had been there, we'd have found them by now (or they'd have found us).

Even so. Someone had made the path that brought us to the plaza. I kept my eyes open, and a shotgun on my shoulder.

Grey clouds had come over. The jungle steamed; it felt like walking inside a kettle. Even the insects had gone quiet. I cut a little trail between two of the smaller mounds, enjoying the silence and the easy swing of the machete in my hands. I hadn't seen a mirror since we left the boats, but I knew I must look different. More hair, less of everything else. The paunch that had been spreading since Peggy was born had shrunk tight to my hips. My body was battered and weary, but I felt stronger than I had in years – as if all the calcified bullshit of modern life was scaling off, revealing the real me inside, shiny and new.

'*Peso d'ocho* for your thoughts?'

Drew had come round the corner of one of the mounds. There weren't any trees here, just tall grass; she moved like a cat.

I laughed. 'I was thinking about my little brother. He's a glaciologist, spends six months of every year in Svalbard, Greenland, places like that. You see his Facebook, it's like scenes from a James Bond set, while I'm at home trying to arrange a babysitter. This is the first time since he was eighteen I don't feel envious.'

'Wait till you get home before you feel too smug.'

I remembered that vast ocean of green from the top of the temple. 'True.'

She grabbed my hand. 'I've got something to show you.'

She led me through the grass, back the way she'd come. Into a small open space between four squat mounds. She waved her hand in an arc around the perimeter.

'Look at the plant cover.'

Even I could see the difference: the scrub in the middle was totally different, lower and browner, perfectly round like a crop circle.

'This place is incredible,' she said. 'So many secrets below the surface, waiting to be dug up. There must be a fountain under here, or maybe a ceremonial platform. They found one like it in Templo Mayor, in Mexico, a few years ago.'

She squatted by the circle and started pulling up plants by the roots, probing the dirt with her knife. I sat on the hot ground and watched her. The cut on my thumb throbbed.

'You think Zia's OK?' she said.

I shrugged. 'Even if Menendez survived this long, finding him would be a million to one.'

'So was finding Paititi.'

I pondered that, and a few other things, while the sweat ran down my face and Drew dug in the soil with her knife. I looked up at the sky. A black speck hovered in front of the cloud, bug-sized at this distance.

'Condor?' I guessed.

Drew followed my gaze. 'Too far from the mountains. Maybe a hawk.'

I stared. From this distance, it could have been anything. But the way it moved wasn't right. Too perfect, almost – *artificial*.

'I met a man in Puerto Tordoya. He said American drones patrol this area.'

Drew nodded. 'Against the *narcos*. Makes sense.'

I wished it would go away. I hated the thought of being watched, the outside world intruding on our discovery already. Was some twenty-year-old kid in Nevada going to tell the world we'd found Paititi, beat us to the punchline?

Or perhaps I imagined it. When I blinked, the speck had vanished in the clouds.

Suddenly, Drew let out a little 'oof' of discovery.

'Look at this.'

She worked her knife into the ground and levered out a clod of red earth. Working with her fingers, she rubbed the soil away. Shapes emerged: black, stubby legs; a long neck; a pointed ear. So detailed, you could see the cloven hoofs.

Drew gave it a squirt from her water bottle. The last smears of earth washed away, and it lay naked in her hand. She held it out to me, like a child offering a toy.

'You know what this means?'

'It's a llama,' I said. One leg and one ear missing, a crack along its belly. Otherwise, not so different from the souvenirs I'd seen at Lima airport.

Our faces were inches apart. She stared at me, eyes wild and shining.

'There aren't any llamas in the Amazon. It means the Incas were here. It proves *everything*.'

I stared at the figurine: about the size of Peggy's My Little Pony dolls. It seemed an awful lot of weight to put on its tiny, broken back.

The sunlight fell on Drew's face and made her skin glow. 'We have to tell Anton.'

I didn't want to share this with Anton. I didn't want to share her with anyone.

I closed my eyes, leaned in and kissed her.

Her lips were warm and salty. God, it had been so long. The moment I tasted her, I wanted more. I pushed forward, spreading her back on the ground. I rubbed against her. Loneliness and isolation flooded out of me; I was drunk in a golden daze.

Drew pushed my shoulders back. Obediently, I rolled over. She sat up.

I met her eyes, wanting to seal the moment. The look on her face stopped me dead.

'We can't,' she whispered.

'I love you.'

Such a simple phrase: I use it all the time. A sign-off on phone calls and texts, or when I come in from work when Cate's heading out to Pilates and we pass in the hall. Just a convention, a verbal tic. Here it sounded fierce and raw, the way it's meant to sound. The way, when you're sixteen, you think it'll sound for ever.

I tried to kiss her again. Clumsily – she ducked away. She pushed me back, gently but firmly. 'You're an amazing person, Kel. Don't think I haven't thought . . . that I don't want . . . But this isn't the right time.'

I knew I should stop there, before I made myself look a fool. I couldn't.

'Nobody has to know.'

'You know that's not true.' She ran her fingers through her hair, combing out grass and leaves.

'Is it Anton?'

She shook her head. 'Not how you think. But this is his day. I'm not going to break his heart.'

Jealous thoughts crowded my head. That she wanted to be the one photographed on Anton's arm when *National Geographic* broke this. That she'd led me on, teasing me with her youth just for the kick of it. Did she think I was too old? Anton and I were the same age, for Christ's sake.

I know that probably sounds pathetic to you now. Jungle fever spiced with midlife crisis. Maybe you're thinking I should have spared a thought for Cate.

A gunshot broke the silence like the wrath of God. *Caught in the act.* The llama spilled out of my hands; my head snapped up. I expected to see Anton there, brandishing his gun. *What the hell was I thinking?*

There was no one there. The shot had come from further away, back towards the plaza.

'Let me go first.'

I dusted myself off and ran back to the main plaza. The others had already arrived. They didn't look too concerned, though Tillman had his shotgun ready. I straightened up and sauntered across; Drew followed a few moments later from the other side of the mound.

'Was that you shooting off?' Tillman called to me.

'I thought it was you.'

'Where's Anton?'

Bang on cue, Anton came out from the left-hand side of the square. He was running, which was unusual, his front absolutely covered in mud.

'You find something?'

'Grab those shovels,' he ordered us. 'And bring the camera.'

Drew took a triangular archaeologist's trowel from her pack. Tillman grabbed the two short shovels we used for latrines, and Fabio got the camera. We followed Anton back the way he'd come, along a path that skirted round the base of the temple, to a smaller mound behind it. Better defined than the others: I could see stone under the creepers that shrouded it. Halfway along, a mound of stones and red earth stood piled up against the base.

'I just followed the path,' Anton was saying. 'Then I found this. Help me out.'

He and Tillman lifted one of the stones off the pile and laid it on the ground. We knelt around it. The edge had been chiselled square; on the front, another one of the heart-headed figures stared out at us.

'That's proof,' said Drew. 'Not like we needed it, but – *my God*.' She turned to Fabio, who had the camera. 'Can you get it with this light?'

'You're missing the point.' Anton had turned back to the spoil heap and was pulling out rocks, tossing them back into the jungle. 'No way that earth fell here.'

I understood. 'Somebody dug that out and piled it up here.'

'Who?'

'Question is: why?'

Anton grabbed one of the spades and attacked the pile. Tillman joined him. They unearthed more heavy blocks, salted in the mix like plums in a pudding. They pried them out, and Fabio and I dragged them away.

No one spoke. No one had to. As the mound shrank, we could all begin to see what was behind it.

Nothing. Black space, framed between stone posts that emerged as the heap went down. A doorway.

'Run back and get the flashlights,' Anton told Zia.

I don't think any of us underestimated what we'd found since we crossed the bridge. But this was a whole new level.

Zia returned with the head-torches – and Howie, limping on his stick. By now, the pile had come down to knee level. Anton threw down his spade and grabbed a head-torch. He shone it inside.

We all stared in.

'Paydirt,' whispered Anton.

'Shit just got real,' said Tillman.

'Don't move those flashlights,' Anton ordered. 'I don't want this to disappear.'

'It's not going anywhere,' I promised.

From the gloom within, a group of human skeletons stared back at us.

35

The torch shone into a stone chamber, not much bigger than my living room. It looked intact. Unlike the skeletons, which had collapsed into a ragbag pile so you couldn't be sure which bone went with which.

'Are there fourteen?' The torch beam wobbled. Even Anton couldn't help trembling.

'Fuck you,' said Tillman incredulously.

'Count them.'

'The legend says we're looking for the mummies of the Inca emperors,' Drew cautioned. 'Those are just skeletons.'

'Let's take a closer look.' Tillman stepped forward. Drew put out her arm, blocking his way.

'We're not going in.'

'Come back when it's light,' reasoned Fabio. The dark sky had got darker. Somewhere beyond the mountains, the sun was setting.

'I'm not afraid of King Tut's ghost,' said Tillman.

'No one goes in until we've done a proper survey.'

She looked at Anton, in a way that made my heart twist in my chest. 'This is the find of the century. Don't you want to do it right?'

Anton nodded slowly, like a man coming out of a dream. 'Yeah.'

'Are you fucking kidding?' said Tillman. 'I thought we came for the treasure. To get rich. Huascar's golden chain could be six inches under that dirt.'

'We're going to do this right,' Anton repeated. 'This isn't digging up bullets on Omaha beach for tourists. If we go back and tell the world we fucked up the site, our names'll be mud in every textbook till the end of time. Don't you want to be a hero, for once?'

'I'd rather be rich.'

'Come on,' said Fabio. 'Too dark now, anyway. We need to make camp.' He took Tillman's arms and tried to steer him away, like a bouncer escorting a drunk to the door. Tillman shook him off.

'Get the fuck off of me.'

'Children!' said Drew.

I stepped into the space Tillman had left to get a closer
look. A foul smell breezed out and made me gag. Something
had died in there more recently than five hundred years ago.
I covered my nose with my shirt collar and shone my torch
around the chamber.

More stones and small piles of earth lay on the floor, radiating
out from the doorway. I didn't think we'd done that. Some animal
must have been trapped inside, frantically trying to burrow out.
I wondered if it had found a way – or if that explained the smell.

I aimed the torch further back towards the skeletons. I
counted the skulls. Hard to see from the doorway, and in
that condition. But:

'Didn't you say fourteen Inca mummies?'

Anton spun round. 'What do you mean?'

'I only count eight.'

'I assume some could have fallen over, gotten buried in
the dirt.'

'Never assume,' said Tillman. 'It makes an asshole out of
you and me.'

Anton hefted both spades and jammed them into the earth
in the doorway. He angled them so their handles crossed.

'We'll come back in the morning.'

'What's the greatest thing you've ever done?'

The fire crackled; sparks and smoke spun into the air. I
could feel the city all around me, pressing in from the darkness. I knew what Anton wanted me to say.

'This.'

'Yeah?'

I didn't dare look at Drew. Everything had happened so
fast, I was in danger of losing my grip. I felt guilty and
embarrassed, and at the same time I wanted her more than
ever. The memory of that kiss played over in my head like
some kind of torture.

'Truly. This is the greatest moment of my life.'

'Not the birth of your daughter?'

'I might have another child. But this . . .' I waved my hand at the darkness. 'This is one of a kind.'

I licked my fingers. Fabio had shot an agouti, a jungle rodent like an overgrown rat. Not something I'd have touched back home; here I gnawed every ounce of meat off its tiny ribs.

Anton smiled. 'True that.'

'Remember that time me and you went to that riverboat casino?' said Tillman.

'Natchez.' Anton savoured the word like a connoisseur swilling his favourite wine.

'We ran the table. Everything we touched turned to gold – sevens every throw. I kept saying to quit while we were ahead, and you always said—'

'"One more throw."'

'We went home next morning ten thousand dollars richer.'

'Yeah.' Anton leaned back and stared up at the stars. 'And the next week we blew it all on that gold-mine tip in Arizona.'

'This is like that. But better.'

The memory had brought a funny expression to Tillman's face. I think it might have been happiness.

Anton laughed. 'Listen to us. We sound like a pair of fags.'

I threw another log on the fire. 'So what next?'

'We'll stay a while, take a look around.'

'How about food?' said Howie.

'We've got the pigs. All you can eat.'

We looked at Zia. She'd said nothing until then – no doubt thinking about Menendez.

'We left the pigs on the other side of the ravine,' she said.

Anton's gaze dropped off the stars. 'I told you to bring them.'

'You didn't.'

No missing the edge in her voice, the way I speak to Peggy when she claims she can't find her loom bands. Anton didn't like it either.

'You're the fucking cook. You look after the food.'

'We go back and get them tomorrow,' said Fabio calmly. Letting the pressure out of the situation, as usual. 'Plenty of food, plenty of time.'

'Plenty of time?' repeated Howie. He lay flat on his back, close to the fire, eyes closed and groaning every few minutes. Something had taken hold of him: his temperature was up, and he had a red rash spreading over his arms and face. Antihistamine cream hadn't helped. He hadn't moved all evening. 'How long we staying here?'

'When Columbus landed in Cuba, did he head home next morning?' said Anton. 'We need to make a full survey. See if we can open up any of the other buildings. And clear one off – one of the small ones. It'll look a million dollars in the pictures.'

'What about the mummies?' I said.

Anton fiddled with the shark's-tooth necklace. I'd never seen him so reticent – almost as if he was frightened of something in the treasure house.

'I guess you know about doctoring, but you've got a lot to learn about this business. You don't sell people on what you found. You sell them on the hope. If we show people what we found so far, I can talk them into funding us to keep coming back another ten years.'

'Paititi is real,' said Drew. 'No one can take that away from you. The mummies are just the icing on the cake.'

'They'll put up a statue of you in Puerto Tordoya,' I said.

'If you're worried about keeping the site intact, I can do a quick survey, very low-impact,' said Drew. 'We've got tools, we've got the cameras, we'll document everything. Take one level off the ground, just to see what's there.'

'She's right, boss,' said Tillman. 'If those are the mummies, then that's got to be the treasure house. You know what else might be there? Because I've got some ideas. You're gonna tell the world you found the Lost City of Gold, it'll look good to have some actual gold to show.'

'Plus, we can take a bone sample from one of the skeletons to run a DNA check when we get home,' I pointed out. 'Analyse it for traces of Inca ancestry.'

Anton put a finger in his mouth and mimed throwing up. 'You know, I stopped watching cop shows when they invented DNA. All that CSI crap. I like the old-timers, guys who use their intuition.'

Drew gave him a level stare. 'You're going back to the world to announce that your *intuition* says you've found the fourteen Inca emperors? You don't know how big this is going to be.'

'Trust me, I know.' He looked around the fire, fixing his eyes on a patch of darkness between me and Fabio. Knowing he was beaten. Not really wanting to win.

At last I understood. Anton was a dreamer. He'd wade through swamps and jungles, clamber across that rope bridge, all without a second thought, because he believed in the dream. And now he'd got here, he didn't know what to do with it.

He turned to me. 'What do you think?'

I laughed. 'I came here to find some treasure.'

A noise woke me in the night. I'd been dreaming, and as soon as I woke I couldn't tell if the noise had spilled out of the dream, or intruded from reality. I lay under my net, tense and listening. In the jungle, that's a recipe for madness.

A white light glowed through the bushes, near where the path from the bridge came out. Too bright for the moon. I fumbled for the knife on my belt and got up.

I crept towards the bushes. Across the plaza, the moon

shone behind the top of the temple pyramid. I stepped on a branch that snapped underfoot. The light stopped. Turned.

'It's Kel,' I called.

Fabio stepped out of the bushes. I breathed again.

'Can't sleep?'

He jerked his thumb down the path. 'Checking the bridge. I keep dreaming how easy it would be for someone to cut the rope.'

I looked around the campsite. Five sagging hammocks, all present and correct. All around, the ruined buildings loomed vast in the night sky.

'Do you think one day New York and London will look like this?'

Fabio laughed softly. 'You feel it too? The fear?'

'I'm a long way out of my comfort zone.'

He picked at his teeth. 'You know how the Indians go fishing? The fish, they like still water, so the Indians build a dam, make a pool where the fish can come, swim around. Then, very quiet, the Indians come down to the edge and pour in poison. Not so much to kill; the fish don't even know it. They drink it through their gills, and then suddenly they float to the surface and the Indians can pick them up with their bare hands.'

'Clever.' I wondered why he was telling me that.

'This place is poison. We don't taste it, but the longer time we stay here, the more it gets inside us. And one day we'll wake up and find we can't get out.'

36

Whatever nightmares haunted that city, we woke next morning to clear skies. The only clouds were far on the horizon, the white mist climbing up the face of the mountains.

'Doesn't that ever shift?' I wondered.

'Transpiration,' said Fabio. 'That's a billion trees all breathing out.'

Some things were fine that morning, and some things were worse. Howie's temperature hadn't come down; his rash had started to blister, and his eyes were bloodshot. I changed the dressing and pretended everything was normal, best bedside manner. In fact, my medical kit was so low I didn't know how long I could even offer him clean bandages. I hadn't expected to need so much.

It was a bright hot day – but the light didn't reach inside the treasure house (as Tillman had optimistically christened it). We stood on the mound of trampled red earth by the entrance, watching the skeletons watching us. *Et in arcadia ego*. Doctors don't suffer many illusions: we know humans are meat, gifted a short span before the bolt between the eyes. I confront that every day. Even so, I avoided looking too closely.

I'd brought a couple of paper surgical masks in the first-aid kit, which Drew and I put on. I told the others it was to prevent contamination of the site, which sounded scientific. Truth is, the smell was so bad nobody could have worked in there without protection.

Drew took the lead. I followed as her designated assistant. Fabio waited just inside the door with the video camera, recording everything. Flies swarmed in the cones of light that our torches cut through the gloom. I felt like a deep-sea diver entering a wreck.

The other three (not Howie: he was still unwell) crowded around the door. Anton flapped them back with his free hand. 'You're blocking the light.'

Drew unravelled a tape measure. We stretched it between us from the door to the far wall of the cave, every step like treading through a minefield. Called the measurement back to Anton, then measured again, a metre away, then another, until we'd marked a grid covering the whole room. I tried to stop myself looking at Drew; when we swapped tools, I cringed in case I touched her. Having Anton watching was worse than the skeletons.

The whole process took nearly three-quarters of an hour.

'Archaeology goes a whole lot faster in the movies,' Tillman said from the door. Zia had already drifted off. Even Anton looked bored.

'We said we wanted to do this right,' Drew reminded them, sketching the grid in her notebook. She labelled each box like the squares on a chessboard, A1, A2 and so on. The skeletons were mostly in the back left corner, with a few in the back right. Eight in all. Some had shreds of cloth hanging off the bones, but not even Anton could have dressed that up as a mummy.

Rats scuttled around the edge of the room, always one step ahead of the light. Flies buzzed and drove me mad. Sweat soaked my mask so it nearly smothered me, but if I took it off I knew I'd gag on the smell.

'It's all a bit *Scooby Doo*,' I said, trying to lift the atmosphere, but nobody laughed. I glanced at Drew's notebook and saw she'd written the date. Friday, 13 June (I'd completely lost track). Six hours ahead of us, Cate would be bringing Peggy home from school and making tea. Perhaps they'd curl up together on the sofa with popcorn and watch a video, a girls' night in.

I closed my eyes and shook my head to dislodge the thought. I didn't want to bring Peggy into that place.

'There's your smell.'

Drew's torch shone on a dead bat lying on the ground. Between its loose wings, I could see tiny ribs where its stomach had been eviscerated. I took a photo, for thoroughness, then scooped it up with a spade and disposed of it under a bush outside. Anton paced about like an anxious father who can't stand the delivery room.

'Nothing yet,' I told him.

We worked all morning, beginning at square A1 and working our way along the grid. Drew insisted. I wondered if that was best practice, or if she was just delaying the moment of truth with the skeletons. She squatted on the ground, scraping back minuscule layers of earth with her trowel. I held the bucket, and watched for anything coming out of the ground.

Fabio put the camera on a rock and left it running. 'I come back in an hour to change the memory card.'

We were alone. Outside, even Anton had given up. The only sound was the buzz of the flies, and the squelch of Drew's trowel stabbing moist earth. I looked at the skulls, and thought of the cave in Mexico. The reason I was here.

'We really must stop meeting like this,' I said. So awkward. I tried to pull myself together. *Not like you slept with her*, I rationalised. Sweat poured off me by the gallon. Drew didn't seem to notice.

The trowel scraped something. A different sound from the stones she'd hit before. I picked up the camera and aimed it at the floor, while Drew dug out the find with small, delicate flicks of her trowel. Soon, she'd exposed a clay figurine about ten centimetres high, simply made, with a long face painted with black accents. Lying spreadeagled on the floor, it reminded me of the poor bat.

'Is that Inca?'

'Too crude. Could be pre-Inca, which would be interesting. Possibly Tiwanaku, which would be very interesting, historic- ally speaking.'

She tipped it into a ziplock bag and put it in my hand. It looked like a child's toy.

'Or it could be from any time in the last ten thousand

years – up to and including last week. Without carbon dating, no way to tell.'

We worked all morning. The whole time, I could feel the skeletons waiting for us like a final exam. When we eventually reached that grid square, it almost came as a relief. Drew started removing the soil around them, while I filmed the bones in close-up.

'They seem quite pale,' I noted for the camera. 'I'd expect bones that old to be browner.'

'Maybe something to do with the mummification process.'

'Maybe. Didn't do anything for their dentistry.'

All the skeletons were missing teeth. They must have fallen out post-mortem: I could see a few glinting on the ground, like spilled food. I videoed them all.

'How about those marks on the bones?' All the arms and legs were badly scarred, strange red marks etched into the bone like acid. 'Is that normal?'

'You tell me, Doctor.'

I got a plastic bag. Using the tip of my knife, I dug out three small pieces of finger bone and tipped them in. Sealed it up. We could take it to the lab when we got back, and maybe find out something about when these people had lived – and how they'd died.

Drew had something. She poked the tip of her trowel into the ground, probing the contours. Leaned forward and brushed the soil aside with gloved fingers.

'Oh my God.'

A bright spot had appeared in the earth. Smooth metal, reflecting our torches back at us with the serene perfection of something rich and valuable. The colour of dreams. The reason we'd come.

Gold.

I swung the camera around and aimed it at the spot,

zooming right in. The gold flickered in the viewfinder, grainy in the dim light.

'We should get Anton,' I said. But I didn't move. Drew's trowel flicked and smoothed the earth like an artist's paintbrush. More gold appeared, rectangular panels joined by wire into a loop.

'Some kind of bracelet?' I guessed.

A noise at the door almost made my heart stop. Fabio ducked his head in, holding a bandana over his nose.

'Zia says lunch is ready.'

I didn't answer. Now Drew's trowel had cleared the earth around the find, I could see it for what it was. I didn't need a handbook of Inca archaeology to explain it.

'Switch off the camera,' said Drew.

Fabio took a couple of steps closer. 'Is that—?'

'Switch off the camera,' she said again.

It was a watch. A gold slip-on band, gold hands scissored on a white dial. So out of place, I don't know how long I stared at it before I realised the hands were moving. I checked my own watch instinctively, and realised it said the same. Buried in the mud, the gold watch had been keeping perfect time, ticking by the hours long after its owner had stopped.

How long?

I grabbed the watch and stumbled out of the cave. I needed Anton – and I didn't have to look far. Everyone had gathered outside the treasure house, even Howie, watching the door from a safe distance. As if they'd known.

I ripped off my face mask and swallowed fresh air. I held up the watch, like a priest showing the entrails. Some of them only saw gold – they whooped and clapped. Others saw it for what it was.

The scream was loud enough to wake the whole city from the dead. Everybody forgot the watch and stared at Zia.

Her screams tailed off into sobs, each one as if her soul

was being ripped out of her. I was aware of voices crowding the clearing, everyone wanting to know everything at once. Zia could hardly breathe, let alone speak.

She didn't have to. The truth was obvious in every choking sob.

We'd found Menendez.

37

'But how did they get . . . like *that*?' Drew lowered her voice, her eyes darting towards Zia, who sat by the campfire wrapped in a sleeping bag. Her eyes looked as if they'd been drilled out and filled with wax.

'The biggest factor that speeds decomposition is heat,' I said. 'It must have been close to forty degrees in there, and so humid. Plus . . .' I trailed off, in deference to Zia. In my mind's eye, all I could see were swarming flies, and rats scurrying from the light.

Howie sat bolt upright. 'You think that agouti we ate last night could've—'

'Shut up,' said Drew.

'I mean, that would be like cannibalism.' Howie looked properly horrified. I wanted to punch him. Though I'd be lying if I said the thought hadn't crossed my mind. All the meat on those tiny ribs.

Zia didn't flinch. I'd given her a couple of pills to calm her down. Erred on the generous side.

'We should give them a proper burial,' said Drew.

'We should get the heck out of Dodge,' said Howie. 'Were you guys not paying attention? Someone already buried them. Probably the same folks who killed them.'

'I don't think so,' said Fabio.

Howie's bloodshot eyes nearly popped out of his head.

'You don't think the Indians killed them? They looked pretty dead to me.'

'All the rocks they piled up. Why so many, if Menendez was dead already? And the earth we found inside. It was not rats trying to dig themselves out.'

He lowered his voice, as if that would make anything better. 'It was Menendez.'

'Buried alive,' said Howie, borderline hysterical. 'This gets better and better.'

'What I don't understand,' said Tillman, 'is if they were alive when they went in, why they didn't fight their way out? I mean, eight of them, and the only thing blocking the door was dirt and stones. If your life depended on it, you'd pull that down with your bare hands. It's like they just gave up.'

'Maybe the Indians were guarding it.'

'There were blood-marks on the bones,' I said. 'Consistent with some sort of illness. They'd been in the jungle God knows how long, maybe held captive for weeks. They were probably in a pretty bad way.'

'We need to get out of here right now,' said Drew. 'If those Indians come back, there'll be seven more skeletons for the next explorers to find.'

Tillman patted his shotgun. 'Let them try.'

'Menendez and his men had guns.' I glanced at Zia for confirmation. A sluggish nod. 'Didn't help them.'

'What if we put a guard on the cliff with a rifle. Our side. Anyone comes within ten feet of the bridge, we pop a cap in his ass.'

I couldn't believe Tillman was serious. 'And who's the sniper? You?'

'Better believe it.'

'I bet you're a real ace at *Call of Duty*.' I turned to Anton. 'This is a survival situation—'

236

'It's been a survival situation since Pedro and Pablo checked out,' said Tillman.

'Am I the only one who doesn't want to get trapped on an island waiting for a bunch of homicidal Indians to show up?'

'Shut the fuck up,' shouted Anton. 'I can't hear myself think.'

He twisted his shark's tooth on its cord.

'Way I figure it is this. The Indians captured Menendez and his men. Locked them in that cave near the village for a while, but it wasn't strong enough. Roberto escaped. So they brought them here. They probably used the city already as some kind of religious centre.'

'If Menendez was sick, perhaps they thought the gods would cure them or something,' said Drew.

'Maybe. Didn't work.'

'We haven't seen any Indians,' Tillman pointed out.

'But maybe they see us,' said Fabio. 'And now they got us right where they want us.' I remembered his story about the fish traps. *Fish don't even feel the poison.*

'Please,' I begged Anton. 'Think of my child. Think of yours.'

Anton looked around at the city. Those clear blue eyes might have wanted to cry. He'd found everything he ever wanted, and now it was being ripped away.

'Kel's right.'

We packed up the camp as fast as we could. We should have had it down to an art, by then, but we'd been sloppy, relieved to think we'd be there a few days. It's amazing how much stuff you cling to, even when you're carrying it yourself through the jungle.

'These?' Fabio indicated the artefacts we'd found. As well as the clay figurine from the treasure house, we had a stone axe, two sharp pieces of palm wood that Drew said were arrowheads, and the llama she and I had found. Not forgetting Menendez's watch.

'Take them,' said Tillman. 'They'll be worth something in Puerto Tordoya.'

'I said no looting,' said Anton.

'The way this is going, we'll need whatever we can get when we're back there.'

Tillman stuffed them in his pack. Fabio doused the fire. I looked at the smoke trailing into the blue sky, and wondered who else could see it. No sign of the drone from yesterday. Today, I'd have been glad of the company, the promise that somewhere civilisation was watching over us.

The sun had dropped well past noon, but nobody thought about lunch. I took a last look around the plaza, trying to remember every detail. In an hour, I knew, it would seem impossible I'd ever been here.

'Wait,' said Anton. 'We forgot one thing.'

He made us go back into the middle of the plaza. Even Howie. We lined up in front of the temple, arms awkwardly around each other's shoulders, while Anton balanced the camera on top of his pack. A red light counted down the timer as he ran back and squeezed in between us.

'Say "Paititi".'

'Paititi,' we chorused. Fabio made a peace sign. Tillman flipped the bird.

'Now let's get out of here.'

We hiked back between the silent mounds, lost in our thoughts. Zia looked as if she'd sit down and cry if we let her; Drew had to take her hand and lead her like a toddler. Howie needed two of us just to keep him upright. For the first and only time on that entire expedition, Anton brought up the rear. I think that slowed us more than anything. Like monkeys in a tribe, we relied on him to give us our lead.

At last the path turned, and I saw light and space. I hurried ahead: I felt a sort of dread, as if the island's evil gravity would pull me back if I didn't run fast enough.

I came out on the bluffs and stopped. Everything was as I remembered it: the red cliffs and the silver river below; the rocks on the opposite side, and the cleft we'd squeezed through that day we shot the pigs. The stump where we'd tied the safety rope, and the rock eyelets that had held the bridge. All present and correct.

Except for one thing.

We weren't going anywhere.

38

We lined up on the clifftop and stared down, like mourners at the graveside. No hope of resurrection. Even Howie crawled over, peering over the cliff on his belly.

The bridge hung down the opposite cliff and spread across the bottom of the ravine. It straddled the river like a weir, ruffling the water behind it. As I watched, the current wrestled one of the planks free from the vines and carried it away. One less ripple to disturb the river.

Howie said what we were all thinking. 'How did this happen?'

Fabio kicked the stone rings. The bridge hawsers were still tied through them, trailing off after a couple of feet where they'd broken.

'Frayed on the cliff edge?'

'Both the hawsers at once? And how do you explain the safety rope?'

Anton pointed straight down. So tight, I had to lean way out to spot it, painfully aware that one nudge or jostle would tip me off. Did I trust the people behind me? All of them?

The rope we'd strung across the gorge lay in a heap at the foot of the cliff.

'Maybe it got tangled when the bridge fell?'

'That rope's rated a thousand kilos. No way the bridge could have dragged it down. I tied it off myself.'

'Indians,' said Fabio. 'They got us on the island, then they cut the bridge. We walked right into their trap.'

Silence. I took a step back from the cliff. Around me, the others shuffled back too. Only Howie stayed where he was, staring like a man who's just dropped his keys down the drain.

'How are we gonna get off?'

Anton picked up the dead rope still tied to the stone ring. A few stray fibres tickled out from the end, but otherwise it was a clean break.

'That's not our biggest problem.'

He was one step ahead – as usual. You could see the pennies dropping as each of us spun round and stared into the bushes behind us. Tillman chambered a round; Fabio brandished his machete.

'Whoever did this, they must still be on the island.'

Tillman wanted to search the city and, as he put it, 'String that motherfucker up by his balls.' Anton nixed it.

'No way we'd keep sight of each other. We'd get separated, they could pick us off one by one.'

Drew raised an eyebrow. 'They?'

'Who says there's only one?'

'Bad,' moaned Howie. 'Really, really bad.'

He was in shock. We all were. Zia hadn't said a word,

Tillman hadn't stopped swearing, and Fabio's thumb was bleeding from pressing it against his machete. Never mind the Indians. Never mind the bridge, or the hundreds of miles of jungle all around us. I doubted our group could hold together twenty-four hours. And if we didn't . . .

Anton looked at me as if he'd read my mind. 'You seem pretty cool.'

'Detachment comes with the job.'

'Good. We'll need that.'

Drew looked down, then across the ravine at the rocks on the far side. She shivered. 'Let's get away from here. We're too exposed.'

We retreated a little way, behind the first of the buildings. On Anton's sketch map, he'd labelled it the watchtower.

'We'll make camp here,' said Anton. 'Clear the jungle to make a perimeter. Cut a path up to the top of the watchtower, too, so we can use it as a lookout point.'

'What about water?' said Drew.

'I'm going down to the river to check out the bridge. I'll fetch some.'

'*Going down to the river?*' I repeated. 'Just like that?'

'Just like that.' He grinned at me – as if he was enjoying this, thriving on the drama. The possibility we might not make it out alive didn't seem to have crossed his mind. 'And you're coming too.'

Tillman and Fabio started laying into the brush with their machetes. Tillman, in particular, looked as if he'd do someone an injury, hacking and slashing like a pissed-off Viking. I wouldn't want to get in his way.

'Zia, stay here with Howie. Drew, grab a gun.'

'I've never fired a gun in my life.'

'But the Indians don't know that.' He tossed her his rifle. She only just caught it, bending double with the weight. 'Point the round end at them.'

Anton pulled an armful of climbing gear out of his pack and headed back to the cliff. I grabbed our water bottles and followed.

We rappelled down into the ravine. Loose rock came away every time my feet touched the crumbling cliffs; with my back to the river, I felt horribly exposed. And it was our last rope. If it broke – or was cut – there was no way back.

I landed on the riverbank and unclipped myself. The river flowed close to the cliffs on that side, leaving only a narrow rim of boulders to balance on.

Anton had come down first. He'd found the safety rope where it had fallen in a hollow between the boulders. He swore.

'Won't be using this again.'

He picked up two lengths, each not much more than a couple of metres. More lay tangled at his feet. It hadn't just been severed: it had been cut into pieces, so many that if you tied them all together you'd have more knots than rope.

'They knew what they were doing.'

Anton dropped the useless rope. We waded out a little way into the river and examined the bridge. There wasn't much to see. The fall had smashed it, and the river had done the rest. Not more than a dozen planks survived.

'Still keeping cool?'

I gave a weak smile. 'As much as I can, marooned on an island in the jungle with no way out, and some homicidal Indians for company.' I didn't mention I'd also popped a Valium. Professional detachment only takes you so far. 'I'm amazed how calm you're keeping.'

Anton shrugged. 'Truth is, I was afraid something like this might happen.'

Even the Valium didn't get me ready for that. 'You *what?*'

'I've read about this kind of thing. Big find, pressure situation. Some people don't want to share the glory.'

'You think it could have been . . .?' I lowered my voice and nodded up to the clifftop. 'One of *them*?'

'Wouldn't surprise me.' And he thought *I* was detached. 'We haven't seen one trace of the Indians since we came up the Pachacamac.'

'But why would one of them . . . one of *us* . . . I mean, we're all stuck on the island together.'

'So you don't suspect him, right? But I guarantee you he has an escape plan.'

'*He?*' I tried to keep my voice level. 'Is there someone . . . in particular . . .?'

'The bridge was A-OK this morning. I checked it after breakfast. That means it must have been cut while you and Drew were in the treasure house. Howie can't hardly move. That gives you Tillman, Fabio and Zia.'

'You know Tillman. You've worked with him before.'

'Yeah,' said Anton slowly. 'But never where we found something like this. Guys change when they see an opportunity. You can see it happening already.'

I thought of how Tillman had shortchanged Anton when we bought the guns from Lorenzo. The stupid risk he'd taken for five hundred dollars. What would he do for a thousand times that much?

'Fabio?'

'There were a few things I heard.'

'What sort of things?'

'Nothing concrete. Some guys in Puerto told me I shouldn't take him, couple of stories about jobs that ended badly. One time, they said, he walked out and left some people stranded. Another time, an Indian tribe ran him out of town because they said he stole something from them. But . . .' He shrugged. 'I thought any guy tough enough to make it out here, he's going to piss some people off along the line. Maybe I should have paid more attention.'

'That leaves Zia.'

'Yeah.' One word, heavy with meaning.

'Did you see any of them? Where they were, while Drew and I were excavating?'

'We were all kind of wandering about.'

'Should we confront them?'

Anton shook his head. 'We'll let this play out a while. Keep your friends close, and your enemies closer.'

I scooped up a handful of river water and tipped it over my face. 'Doesn't that scare you?'

'What scares me is thinking that all this . . .' – he swept his arm in an expansive three-sixty – '. . . that we might not get to show it to the world.'

'What scares me,' I said truthfully, 'is thinking I might never see my daughter again.'

Anton reached behind his head and fumbled with the leather cord that held his shark's tooth. He undid the knot and handed it to me.

'Take it. It's my lucky charm.'

The leather was slick with his sweat, but I tied it around my neck and felt absurdly grateful. 'What about you?'

'I make my own luck.' He grinned, and looked up at the cliff. 'Let's give it a go.'

He might make his own luck, but on the far side of the river even Anton couldn't make climbing screws stick in that cliff. It crumbled like plaster at the least touch; the cams pulled out as fast as he could jam them in.

'You made it up at the waterfall,' I said hopefully, after he'd slid down for about the tenth time.

'It's a different kind of rock.' Anton took a long swig from his water bottle. Sweat and dust made a warpaint stripe across his forehead. 'Flaky as hell.'

He put his weight on one of the bridge hawsers, dangling

down the cliff. A few of the planks had survived the collapse: perpendicular, they made a sort of Jacob's ladder up the cliff face.

'Could you use that?'

I'd seen it done – by Indiana Jones. The moment Anton touched the lowest plank, it pulled loose and almost fell on our heads. He tried hauling himself up the vine rope, hand over hand, but the dry fibres came away in clumps until the rope was barely as thick as a pencil. He slid down before it snapped.

Eventually, even Anton had to admit reality. 'We're not getting out this way.'

We abandoned the attempt, and made the long climb back up the other side to the city.

At the watchtower, Tillman and Fabio had cleared a swathe of jungle around the pyramid. They'd stacked the brush around the perimeter, making a rough stockade. Tillman's stars-and-stripes bandana fluttered from a sapling he'd erected on the top of the pyramid. Zia had got the fire going.

I poured the water bottle I'd filled into a pot, and waited for it to boil. Fabio had found some wild potatoes, which we cooked on the coals. Zia doled out slivers of dried pork, not much thicker than bacon.

'Is that all we get?' complained Tillman. 'Clearing jungle's hungry work.'

Zia didn't bother to reply. We all knew the answer.

'We can always eat bugs,' said Fabio, slapping his face. The mosquito left a bloody smear across his cheek.

'I don't know about you guys, but I don't plan on being here too long,' said Anton.

'And how's that work? We're gonna stitch our ponchos together, make a hot-air balloon and just float off into the sunset?'

'Swing across the river on vines, like Tarzan?' suggested Fabio.

Anton toyed with his knife, spinning its point in the earth.

'There is another possibility.'

'No way,' said Tillman.

'We knew it might be an option. That's why we carried the pack rafts all this way.'

I was a few steps behind. 'The river?'

'Alvarado said it was impassable,' said Drew. 'That's why he hiked cross-country to the Pachacamac.'

Fabio drew a pattern in the ground. 'Why not? You think we can survive the jungle? Ten days, no GPS? Howie can't even walk. In the boats, four or five days, a week for sure, we find a village.'

'And we're just going to float down like a church school picnic?' Tillman snorted. 'You ever think there might be a reason why no one ever explored up the top of this river?'

'"The Indians do not navigate it, for they say it will crush any vessel like a serpent,"' said Drew. 'That's what Alvarado said.'

Tillman looked at Howie. 'You think you're good to hike back all the way we came?'

Howie groaned and stared at the fire. 'Just get me out of here.'

Anton jumped up. 'It's too late to decide anything now. We'll sleep on it, and see how we feel in the morning.'

'You're going to sleep?' said Drew.

'We'll keep watch. Two by two, so nobody falls asleep. Or runs off.'

'I'm not going anywhere,' Howie promised.

'You get the night off. Me and Zia first. Then Kel and Fabio. Drew and Tillman last. Two hours apiece.'

He'd kept Tillman, Fabio and Zia apart, I noticed. No escaping the line he'd drawn through our group: I wondered if the others spotted it. I wondered who was supposed to be watching whom.

I wondered how long before we fell apart completely.

*

You're going to sleep? Drew had said. Of course not. I was in survival mode, every sense running at the redline. I lay in my hammock, rifle in reach, and listened to the night. Each time I closed my eyes, it was like twisting up the volume knob the way Peggy does if she gets her hands on the stereo. And in case my imagination ever flagged, I always had the image of those skeletons in the cave to remind me how I might end up.

Worst of all, I wasn't listening to the distant jungle the way I had all those other nights. I didn't have to wonder what might be sniffing around in the undergrowth. The danger was a whole lot closer.

I dozed, and I dreamed, and I wondered, and afterwards I couldn't be sure which was which. I fell asleep with my knife in my hand, and nearly stabbed Anton when he came to wake me up.

'Keep cool,' he told me.

'Anything happening?'

'Nada.' Moonlight turned his hair grey and cast deep shadows around his eyes. He looked tired.

'Zia OK?'

He knew what I meant. 'No problem.'

I picked up the rifle and climbed to the top of the watchtower. Fabio was already there. A cigarette glowed in his mouth.

'I thought you smoked your last one days ago.'

'I found it in the bottom of my bag.' He offered me a puff and I didn't hesitate. Not much danger of getting addicted. With nothing in my stomach, the nicotine hit me like heroin.

'Do I get a blindfold as well?'

Fabio grimaced. 'At least the firing squad would be a quick death.'

I liked Fabio. I liked his no-drama persona, the quiet confidence he brought to the group. Our ballast. I didn't like to think he might have cut the bridge.

I swept my arm over the moonlit city. A lost city, bathed

in moonlight, and the jungle pressing all around it: the most insanely romantic thing I've seen in my life. And all I wanted was for it to go away.

'You think we're going to be rich? If we get out of here, I mean?'

He shrugged. 'No gold.'

'But we found the city. People have got rich for doing less.'

'Famous, maybe.'

'These days, if you're famous you can be rich. Even if you're just famous for being an ugly cat.'

Fabio didn't get that, and I didn't try to explain.

Something rustled in the trees. I scanned them with my torch. A pair of orange eyes jumped out of the darkness, glowing angrily. I yelped and grabbed the rifle.

Fabio's hand pushed the barrel down. I heard a flutter, and the beat of heavy wings as a dark shape flew over us.

'Spectacle owl,' said Fabio.

I let my pulse come back to resting. I saw Fabio squinting at his gun, concentrating on something.

'You know Tenzig?'

I shook my head.

'The first man who climbed Mount Everest. The man who carries his bags is called Tenzig.'

'Oh, right. Sherpa Tenzing.'

'Sí. But in the books, all they say is that the white man climbed Everest. When we go home, do you think the newspapers will write that Anton and Kel and Fabio and four others discovered Paititi? Or will they say it was only Anton?'

'Does that bug you?'

He finished the cigarette and flicked it down into the jungle. 'Without him, none of us are here.'

We lapsed into silence, and the darkness of our thoughts.

'Where's Anton?'

I opened my eyes and saw Drew's face, cloudy through the

plastic sheet spread over my hammock. Wild ideas sprang into my mind; I wondered if I was dreaming. Then I saw Tillman, a few paces back, sniffing the air and cradling a shotgun. There was rain in the air: the world was grey and still. The stars-and-stripes bandana hung limp from its flagpole.

'Where's Anton?' Drew said again.

'He got me for my shift.' I rubbed my eyes. 'Isn't he here?'

'His hammock's empty.'

'Maybe he went for a piss.'

'We've waited ten minutes already. He wouldn't have been gone that long. Not with the Indians out there.'

I rolled out of my hammock and grabbed the rifle. Strange how quickly it had become a compulsion.

'You know what Anton's like. He probably wanted to explore the temple one more time.'

But I was already moving in the opposite direction. I knew where Anton must have gone. Call it a hunch, or instinct, or just having lived in his pocket for three weeks. If there was an obstacle to be overcome, he didn't sit back and stroke his chin, or try coming at it from a different angle. He battered it until it gave.

A small pile of webbing and carabiners lay in the clearing by the ravine. Anton's rifle leaned against a tree, his hat hooked over the muzzle. Our good climbing rope ran from the stone ring and over the cliff.

'Anton,' Drew called. Hysterical echoes repeated it back from the red cliffs.

'Boss?'

We were all hanging back from the cliff. Like animals, feeling the storm before the first rumble of thunder. I got down on my hands and knees, crawled to the edge and peered down. An ant wandered over my finger. I shook it off, getting a stab of pleasure watching it fall into the abyss.

Then I saw Anton. A long way down – but even from that

distance, I knew it could only be him. A broken heap on the rocks, arms flung out and neck bent at an unnatural angle.

Drew and Tillman joined me on the edge. Drew sobbed; Tillman grabbed a fistful of earth and threw it angrily down the cliff.

'You stupid asshole,' he hissed. 'Now we're really fucked.'

39

We held it together long enough to bury Anton. Tillman and I went down into the ravine and hauled him up, wrapped him in his hammock like an old-time sailor, and carried him to the top of the temple mound. We hacked a hole in the roots and vines, and laid him with his head towards the sunrise. I wanted to put his driver's licence in the grave, in case anyone ever found him, but when I checked in his pocket his wallet was gone.

Afterwards, we stood in a circle around the grave, holding hands. The rain got heavier, soaking our clothes and running down our necks.

'Anyone want to say something?' said Drew.

No one rushed to fill the silence.

Drew clasped her hands in front of her. 'Anton used to say, you make your own adventures in life. And he did it better than anyone I knew. The world's more boring without him.'

'He died doing what he wanted,' said Fabio. He gestured to the city around us, the squat mounds poking through the trees and clouds. 'For him, this was heaven.'

Silence. Rain pattered on the ground and dripped through the branches. It soaked the corpse in its makeshift shroud, so that the outlines of Anton's body started pressing through the fabric. As if he was trying to escape.

Tillman coughed and hawked a gob of phlegm.

'I'm not . . . I don't . . .' He balled his fists and started again. 'Anton was like a brother to me. All the bad times in my life, the dumb shit I did, Anton was there to pull me out. And now we're on our own.' He trailed off. He looked as if he wanted to cry, or hit someone.

Suddenly, he leaned forward and shouted into the grave. 'I can't believe you're gone, you crazy motherfucker.'

Drew tried to put her arm around him, but he shook her off. Rain had dribbled into his eyes, and he rubbed it away angrily, in case we thought he was crying. The rest of us stared at the ground. Zia crossed herself and mumbled something I couldn't catch.

'Anyone else?'

I touched the shark's tooth around my neck, but I didn't say anything. There were times, in Anton's company, when he'd felt like the best friend I'd ever had. Now he was in his grave, I didn't feel like I'd known him at all.

Howie started to say a prayer, but Tillman stopped him with a murderous look.

'Not a fucking word, God-Boy.'

We covered Anton with brush, stones and earth. Hard work. Thorns on the branches tore our skin; the earth turned to mud and caked our hands. The wet vines were slick underfoot: Drew slipped, and would have fallen into the grave if I hadn't grabbed her arm in time. I pulled her towards me and she fell, awkwardly, against my chest. She didn't move straight away. It appalled me how much I enjoyed the feeling.

We threw in enough to cover the body and then, by some unspoken agreement, called it a day. In the jungle, there's never enough soil to bury a body deep enough.

As we clambered down, I realised that in all the burying, nobody had asked the most obvious question of all.

Did he fall, or was he pushed?

After the funeral, the arguments began. Too wet to light a fire, we huddled under the trees in our ponchos and tried to work out how to stay alive.

'Inflate the rafts,' said Fabio. 'It's the only choice.'

'If you want to choose suicide,' said Tillman.

'It's what Anton wanted.'

Nobody disputed that. Nobody was crass enough to point out that what Anton thought didn't matter a damn now he was dead.

'Is there any other option?' I said.

'Back the way we came. Through the jungle.'

'I hate to tell you this,' said Howie, 'but the bridge is out.'

'There has to be some place downriver where the cliffs end. Scramble out, and follow the compass cross-country.'

'You make it sound so easy.'

'What about him?' Fabio pointed to Howie. 'No way we get him out through the jungle.'

'Can we not talk about me like I'm not here?' pleaded Howie.

Drew glared at Tillman. 'Maybe if you didn't have five kilos of cocaine in your pack, you could help carry Howie.'

Tillman squatted on his haunches, leaning on his machete. He stared at his reflection in a puddle, then looked around.

'Let me tell you a few things. I'm the only guy thinking ahead here. However we go, even if we get out OK, it won't be worth a damn if we don't have something to show for it. We come out of the jungle empty-handed, we might as well not have tried.'

Drew shook her head in disgust. 'You're still worried about getting *rich*?'

'*Rich?*' Tillman rolled his eyes. 'You don't have a clue. This is about survival.'

'Of course. Cocaine comes in every survival kit.'

'*Shut up!*' I held up my hands. 'Shut up for a second. Is there something we need to know?'

Tillman had gone red in the face.

'Here's the deal,' he said. 'Remember Anton told you about Aguas Verdes?'

'The old mine you found.'

'Right. Well, that was bullshit. Aguas Verdes isn't an Indian gold mine. It's a casino, outside of Cuzco. We went there, Anton and me, a couple of months back with five thousand dollars he borrowed from Lorenzo. He thought he could play it up into enough cash to fund the expedition. Instead, he lost it. This kid hanging around the tables, he comes up and says he knows a guy who can help him out. I said no, but the kid kept bugging us and Anton was desperate. Could see the whole Paititi expedition falling apart. So the kid takes us outside to an old Indian guy, who advances Anton another five. Just to win back what he's lost, right?'

I could see where this was going.

'Ten hours later, Anton's into him for eighty thousand. Plus the five he still owes Lorenzo. Then the Indian's buddies show up with machetes and knives, shouting at us, explaining what happens if we don't pay.'

He rocked back, staring at the ground.

'We had to go back to Lorenzo on our knees and beg for an advance to pay back the Indians, before they started feeding our dicks into our mouths. What we've done these last three weeks, Paititi, everything – it's all bought on credit. And when we get back, they're gonna make us pay.'

The jungle had gone quiet, apart from the drip-drip of rain from the leaves.

'But Anton's dead,' I said at last.

'Don't you get it? They don't let you off for that. They go for the next in line. That's all of us – me, Drew, Howie and you.' He jabbed a finger at me. 'You especially. Lorenzo's met you, he knows who you are. Rich gringo, family to think of. He can make you pay.'

'Are you threatening me?'

'I'm telling you how it's going to be. And why we need every last cent we can get out of this place.'

'We have to get ourselves out first,' said Drew. 'We can deal with Lorenzo when we're back in Puerto.'

The conversation had come full circle. 'So how do we get there?'

Tillman wiped a trail of water off his blade. 'We don't.'

'We don't?' I repeated.

'Let's get real. No way all of us can make it through the jungle. Not with the food we have, and him.' He pointed his machete at Howie. 'Our only shot is if one of us goes alone. Travel light, double-time it to the Pachacamac and back to civilisation. The rest sit tight here and wait for the cavalry.'

'And who's going to go?' said Fabio. 'You?'

'That's right.'

'Maybe you don't come back.'

'Are you accusing me of something?'

Fabio smirked at him.

'I just levelled with you. You're saying you can't trust me?'

'No.'

'Then fuck you too.' Tillman jumped up and walked away, kicking spurts of water off the puddles.

'Stay,' I said, and what I lacked in authority, I made up with desperation. 'We need you. You too,' I said to Fabio. 'If we're going to get out of here alive, the only way we'll do it is sticking together.'

Tillman stopped. Rain danced off the brim of his hat.

'Going alone is too risky,' I said. 'There's a hundred ways you could die in the forest, and the rest of us would never know. How long would we wait? Three weeks? A month?

Two months? By the time we gave up, we'd be two months weaker and hungrier.'

'And the Indians,' said Howie. 'They'd have gotten us for sure by then, same way they got Anton.'

'Either we all go, or no one goes.'

'Kel's right.' Drew backed me up. 'We stick together, or we die alone.'

Tillman glared at her. 'Who died and made you God?'

'We take a vote.'

'You don't take votes in a survival situation. You follow the leader.'

'The leader's dead,' I said. Deliberately brutal. We were still acting as if Anton would come along and settle the debate. We needed to grow up.

'I'm the guide,' sulked Fabio.

'That's right, asshole. You take us where we want to go.'

Before Fabio could retort, I said quickly, 'Where *we* want to go. All of us, collectively.'

I stared around the group. 'River or jungle? What's the choice?'

'You know what I think,' said Tillman. 'The devil you know, all that shit.'

'River,' said Fabio.

'River,' said Drew.

I turned to Zia. She wouldn't meet my eye. I grabbed her arm and squeezed until she gasped with pain. 'Look at me. Look at me. You need to be part of this. No passengers.'

'We don't know where the river goes, and we don't have enough food for the forest. I say let Tillman go fetch help.'

'That's not an option.'

'We can fish in the river,' said Fabio.

'We can hunt in the forest,' retorted Tillman.

Zia stared at her knees. 'Forest.'

'There's Indians in the forest,' said Howie. 'I say let's get on that river. The sooner the better.'

Tillman didn't move. 'Three–two, Doc. What's it gonna be?'

I hesitated.

'You frightened to commit yourself? No passengers, remember?'

I stared him down, determined not to let him intimidate me.

'The river,' I said. I saw the look Tillman gave me and returned it with a chill smile. 'It's what Anton would have wanted.'

We inflated the rafts at the top of the cliff. All through the jungle we'd cursed the extra weight; now, they were a godsend.

'Are they really going to fit all of us?' said Howie, sitting doubled over on his pack under a tree.

'They have to,' I said. In fact, I'd forgotten how small they looked. The tag said they were rated for two people, or one person with baggage.

'Everyone empty out their bags,' I said. 'We're taking the absolute minimum.'

'Food, guns, flashlights and ponchos,' said Fabio. 'Sleeping bags. Mosquito nets. No more.'

'And the medical kit,' I said.

The others didn't even have the strength to complain. I watched carefully as our stuff spilled out, looking for the telltale yellow of my emergency beacon. I remembered Anton's hypothesis. *Whoever cut the bridge, I guarantee he has an escape plan.*

Whoever it was, he (or she) was smart enough to keep it hidden. Soon, we'd made a pile of khaki clothing, hammocks, sodden paper and ripstop nylon. We left the backpacks, and repacked what we were taking in the dry-bags we'd used as liners.

'Did we really carry all that?' I wondered, looking at what we were leaving behind.

'I read a book, once, about the John Franklin expedition

that went missing in the Arctic,' said Drew. 'Their ships got trapped in the ice, so they set off on foot for rescue. Never seen again. All anyone found was the crap they left when they died. Silk handkerchiefs, writing desks, silver spoons. And they were man-hauling that every day across pack ice.'

'Is that the one where they ended up eating their boots?'

Drew lowered her voice so the others couldn't hear. 'They ended up eating each other.'

'Boats are ready,' called Tillman. He pulled up the climbing rope and tied a raft on the end so we could lower it to the river.

'Make sure you tie them up good,' said Howie.

'Yeah,' said Fabio heavily. 'We have shitty luck with ropes.'

Something in the way he said it made me look at him. He caught me and stared back.

I looked around at the others. Realised everyone was doing the same, checking each other out, like the pirates and the redskins and the animals and the Lost Boys stalking each other around Neverland.

Nobody was buying the Indian story. We knew it was one of us.

We lowered the boats, Howie, the gear and finally ourselves. With all of us in, the boats sank so low they grazed the river bed. Rather than risk a puncture, we got out and walked them downstream to where the second branch joined. The rubber floor sagged; even on the flat stretch, water slopped over the hull. I doubted we'd last five minutes in the first rapids.

Fabio took the lead boat, paddling solo with Howie. Tillman and Zia followed, then me and Drew at the rear. I crabbed a few strokes with the paddle, trying not to whack Drew in front of me. The current tugged us on.

'We're on our way home,' I said. No one cheered.

I looked back, but by then the city had disappeared into the mist.

Six

The Back Door

40

There's a reason they call it a rainforest. After two weeks of living in damp clothes, damp pack and damp boots, I thought I'd got used to it. But this was different. The soft rain beat on my skin and blew in my face; the river slopped over the low sides of the boat and threatened to sink us. My hands, gripping the paddle, shrivelled up. Sores spread and opened, blistered by the rain and the relentless effort of steering our little raft. I could hardly see, except to follow the boats ahead. The others sat hunched in their rafts, so low they seemed to be drowning. Their ponchos made pointed steeples over their heads, like strange animals who'd missed the ark.

I couldn't stop thinking about Anton. I desperately wanted to mourn him, but the emotions wouldn't come. Perhaps it was too sudden, or the pressure of the situation limiting me to basic survival. Perhaps it was the guilt. I tormented myself playing silly games of *What If?* Drew's presence right in front of me was a constant rebuke: I couldn't shake the ludicrous idea that if I hadn't kissed her, Anton would still be alive. I'd betrayed him; perhaps, subconsciously, I'd *willed* him to die, and the bloodthirsty gods of Paititi had obliged.

Crazy thoughts. But easier than confronting the alternative: that one of those pointy-hatted figures in front of me had pushed Anton off the cliff.

Someone's going to die out here. I'd thought it so many times those last two weeks, it had lost the power to shock – until it actually happened. Even then, I'd never have believed it would be Anton. He was more alive than any of us: standing on the pyramid, howling at the sunrise, while the rest of us scuttled about in mist and shadows.

Not that it did him any good in the end.

We travelled slowly, too tired to paddle much faster than the current would take us. Even with the rain feeding it, the river ran shallow. Often, we grounded on shingle, and had to splash out to walk the boats along, followed by a mad scramble to get aboard when the current picked up again.

The cliffs never got lower. After a few hours, too miserable to count, we pulled up on a small beach tucked in the elbow of a bend. My legs almost buckled when I touched ground; I felt like a sailor stumbling ashore after a six-month voyage.

'Are we going to camp here?' I asked. Half of me desperately needed to stop. Half couldn't bear any delay.

Fabio shook his head. He was examining a piece of driftwood that had run aground.

'This place is too small. The river is rising.' He beckoned me over. 'Help me with this?'

The log was longer than me. I put my hands round it doubtfully – and almost overbalanced when I tried to lift.

'It's so light.'

'Balsa,' said Fabio. 'We can use to help float the rafts.'

'Our lucky day.'

Fabio and I carried the log to the rafts. Fabio attached it as a makeshift outrigger to the side of his boat, with a cat's cradle of rope and branches. Tillman didn't offer to help. He stood at the back of the beach, staring up at the cliffs as if he wished he could fly.

'You gonna help me?' said Fabio.

Tillman didn't move. 'River was your idea.'

'For Christ's sake.' Drew had taken off her poncho.
Underneath, she'd stripped down to her bra and shorts. She
twisted her hair into a ponytail and wrung out a stream of
water. 'Is this really the time?'

While Fabio worked on the outrigger, Zia and I lifted
Howie out of the boat. We made a lean-to with ponchos and
the paddles, and examined him. Lying in the bottom of a
waterlogged boat, no protection from the rain or the waves,
hadn't done him any good. His exposed skin was cold and
rubbery, but when I put my hand on his forehead I felt a
blazing heat. I rolled up his sleeve, and saw the red rash had
started to blister.

'How do you feel?'

He made a sort of retching noise, flopping out his tongue.
He barely opened his eyes.

'You'll be fine,' I told him, as the next shot of morphine
went in.

Getting back in the boat felt like drowning myself. Easing
myself down into the pool that had collected in the bottom;
the claustrophobia of being squeezed between those thin
rubber walls. A week ago – not even – I'd been dreaming of
the chance to get Drew to myself all day. Now my conscience
couldn't stand it.

As soon as we were back out in the current, she half turned.
I let the hood of my poncho slide forward. I hadn't looked
her in the eye all day.

'Are you going to sit there like a PMS-y eighth-grader all
day? Or are we going to talk about this?'

She said it deliberately, like something she'd been working
up to for a while.

'About what?'

'Anton. And what it means for us.'

Of course, I could hardly think about anything else. I hated myself for it, which is maybe why my reply came out more heated than I meant. 'Is there an *us*?'

The look she gave me made me shrivel. 'I'm not talking about *that*. Jesus.' Her voice softened. 'I'm talking about how we survive.'

She nodded forward, at the other boats in the mist. 'You trust them?'

'Do I have a choice?'

'What do you think happened to Anton?'

'He fell,' I said. Putting it out there, not committing myself.

'Really?'

I thought of Anton balancing on that tree in the river, when we rescued Roberto. All the gullies and streams we'd crossed on fallen trees; dancing across the anaconda bridge without a safety rope.

'Not really.'

'And there were no Indians on that island.'

'Agreed.'

That left one possible conclusion.

'First they cut the bridge; then they went for Anton.' I thought I saw a tear escape Drew's eye – one more drop in the world's biggest river.

'Anton thought it could have been Zia who cut the bridge.' I repeated the conversation I'd had with him in the ravine. *Keep your friends close and your enemies closer.* So much for that plan.

'Or maybe Tillman,' suggested Drew.

'Or Zia *and* Tillman.' Things came together in my mind, the kind of clarity you only get when your life depends on it. 'Tillman had Zia all lined up as soon as Nolberto was out of the way. And she's got the Menendez connection.'

'What's Menendez got to do with anything?'

Everything, I wanted to say. He'd haunted our journey the whole way, from the moment Cate read his name on the news story. Zia; Roberto; the abandoned village and the cave; and at the end of it all those toothless skulls waiting for us in Paititi.

'The bridge was cut while we were in the treasure house. As soon as we found Menendez, that was when they decided to act. And there's Anton's wallet.'

'What about it?'

'It was missing when we buried him.'

'It must have fallen out of his pocket when he fell.'

'I went down to get him, remember? The wallet wasn't there. And his pocket was Velcroed shut.'

'You think someone did this to *rob* him?'

Out of the corner of my eye, I saw something move on the left bank. Too wired, I spun to get a look and nearly capsized the boat. It was a blue heron, flying from rock to rock keeping pace with us.

'Careful,' Drew warned.

I steadied the boat with the flat of my paddle, then dug in to correct our course. My mind raced.

'There must have been something we weren't supposed to find.'

'Like what?'

I paddled harder. 'There's something not right about the Menendez mission. He was supposed to be vaccinating Indians, but we haven't seen a single Indian since we came up the Pachacamac.'

'So?'

'What if it went wrong, somehow? Zia could have come to clean up after him, make sure the scandal never got out. Anton had the memory card from Menendez's camera in his wallet. Maybe that's what she wanted.'

The heron glided low over the water and landed on an outcrop of rock. Flaunting its freedom: I hated it.

'Tillman could have been her contact on the inside.'

'Tillman was Anton's best friend,' said Drew.

'Anton didn't trust him.' *Guys change when they see an opportunity.* 'Think about it. They cut the bridge and get rid of Anton. While they're at it, they take the memory card, in case there's any incriminating evidence in the pictures. Tillman offers to go into the jungle to get help. Zia stays behind and poisons our food. Then Tillman comes back, and they go home together.'

'That's a lot of leaps,' said Drew doubtfully.

The heron was still following us, and I couldn't take it any more. I grabbed the rifle from the pile of gear, aimed and fired. I missed, of course. A patch of rock exploded where the bullet hit; the bang bounced across the canyon, back and forth until I thought it would split my skull. The recoil nearly capsized us.

'What are you doing?' shouted Drew.

'The heron,' I mumbled. I pointed, just in time to see the frightened bird soar over the cliffs and vanish. 'I thought . . . for supper . . .'

I was shaking almost too much to talk. I was frightened by how badly I'd lost control, how the rage had overwhelmed me.

Ahead of us, Tillman had back-paddled so we came alongside.

'What the fuck was that?'

'Kel wants dinner,' said Drew.

'Then learn to fucking shoot.' Tillman glared at me. I imagined the same look on his face as he pushed Anton over the cliff. It was all I could do not to shoot him right there. 'If you're gonna make so much noise every Indian in the Amazon can hear us, at least fucking hit something.'

I didn't have anything to say to that.

Tillman pointed a fist at the darkening sky. Evening would start early in the bottom of the canyon. 'We going all night?'

It was a rhetorical question. Risking the river in the dark, with its sudden shallows and twists, would have been suicide. We'd had an easy day, but nobody was fooled. The longer it lasted, the more we worried.

I'd been scanning the riverbanks for the last hour and seen nothing that looked like a beach. If anything, the cliffs looked steeper and higher than they had that morning. But around the next bend, we found a long strip of shingle where we could pull up the boats. Tillman didn't like it – 'if the river rises, we'll get wet' – but we didn't have a choice. The river had started to run faster, tugging our boats on; I could hear a roar like a distant motorway. It got louder as night fell, and we made our pathetic little camp on the beach.

Fabio worried about the river taking the boats; Tillman suggested tying them up, but no one wanted to trust to ropes. I could see suspicion everywhere, little glances flying about like knives. In the end, we carried the boats to the back of the beach and leaned them against the cliff. If the river rose, it would have to get through us. I made a makeshift lean-to by propping up the raft on the paddles, and spread my sleeping bag under it. Without a word, Drew laid hers next to mine.

The driftwood on the beach was too wet to light a fire. Fabio split some with his machete, but even the inside was waterlogged. Zia boiled water on the gas stove and cooked a cup of rice – not much more than a spoonful each – and the last of the pork. Paranoid theories played in my mind – *Zia stays behind and poisons the food* – but hunger trumped it. I wolfed the meal down in three mouthfuls and wished there was more.

The moment we'd eaten we drifted apart. Everyone felt safer with a bit of space. Tillman sharpened his machete with long, even strokes; Fabio patched our raft where a rock had torn a hole. Drew disappeared behind some rocks to squat.

I checked on Howie. The blister on his cheek had started to bleed.

All I wanted was sleep. I couldn't. With no hammock or mat, I had nothing to lie on: the stones dug into my back, however much I tried to ignore them. My ears strained to hear any noise beyond the rain drumming on the boat; my eyes wouldn't stay shut. A survival instinct had kicked in: a primitive terror of going to sleep and never waking up.

And something was bugging me. I got up and found Fabio. 'Is the camera in your dry-bag?'

'*Sí.*' He looked around the lonely beach and cracked a weary smile. 'You really want to film *this*?'

'Just checking something.'

I picked up his dry-bag. Before I could touch the clip, Fabio tore it out of my hands, so hard he nearly pushed me over.

'Private,' he growled.

I almost attacked him. I was so raw, operating on animal logic: poke me and I hit you. I fought back the impulse and got a hold of my emotions. 'Sorry. Just wanted the camera.'

Turning away so I couldn't see, he unfolded the neck of the dry-bag and got out the camera, wrapped in a clear ziplock bag. I took it back to the semi-shelter of the upturned raft, leaving it in the bag so it wouldn't get wet. I fumbled the controls through the plastic until the screen came alive.

'How can you watch TV at a time like this?'

Drew ducked under the boat and slid in beside me. I angled the camera so she could see the screen.

'There's a show at home Peggy's obsessed with. A game show for kids; it's called *Jungle Run*. You have to do this jungle assault course. They should bring them here.' I shook my head, trying not to cry. 'I don't know why I thought of that.'

She put her arm around me – the first warm thing I'd felt that day. 'You'll see them again.'

TOM HARPER

'Yeah.'

I rewound the video. Not far: it was the last thing we'd filmed. A trio of toothless skulls appeared, lit by the sickly yellow light of our head-torches. I fiddled with the controls, jogging the video back and forth.

'Haven't you seen enough of this?' said Drew.

'I was wondering how Menendez and his team died.'

'They starved.'

I found the place where the camera zoomed in on the skeletons. I hit 'pause'.

'See?' I pointed to one of the dead men's femurs in the foreground. Menendez? Viewed through plastic, reduced to a few hundred pixels, there wasn't much to work with. But I'd remembered it right.

'You see those marks?' I pointed at a brown smudge running down the length of the bone. 'That's bloodstaining.'

'You're sure? Not mud?'

'I've seen it before.'

'So they bled to death?'

'It's consistent with massive bleeding. But there's no other sign of violence. If the Indians had attacked, it would leave marks. Cuts in the bone, probably some fractures. These bones are all intact.'

I pressed 'play'. The picture panned over all eight skeletons, recording every detail. Good camerawork by Fabio.

'The thing is, they all have the bloodstaining.' I paused, to see if she'd got my point. 'They all died of the same thing.'

'Could it have been malaria?'

'You wouldn't get staining like that.' I closed the screen; suddenly, I couldn't look at it any more. Didn't want to think about it either, but a horrible idea was rising inside me and I had to get it out.

'What if they died from the same thing that killed the Indians?'

266

Drew shook her head. 'You're overthinking this. If they were locked in there alive . . . No water, no sanitation. You remember how it stank. They could have caught anything. Typhoid, yellow fever . . . all that Third World stuff you see on the news.'

'They'd have been vaccinated against those before they came.'

'Something else, then. Something this sick fucking jungle threw up all by itself.'

She rolled away, turning her back to me. Perhaps she didn't believe me; perhaps she'd seen too many horrors to be able to comprehend one more. Perhaps, in that situation, she blanked out everything except survival.

Zia might know, but I couldn't exactly ask her straight out. I looked at her, sitting with Tillman in the lee of the cliff. What were they talking about?

A little way off, under the tented poncho we'd put over him, I heard Howie coughing his guts out. I couldn't imagine how lonely he must feel. I knew I ought to go and check on him, squeeze his hand and give him some empty reassurance. I couldn't move. The night was dark and wet; my legs had locked up from kneeling in the raft, and my shoulders ached from paddling. There were things I desperately needed to think about, life-and-death decisions, but they all reduced to one simple sentiment hammering in my brain.

I don't want to die.

41

There was no dawn: the rain drowned it. I hadn't slept more than a few, restless hours when cold water woke me, the rising river snapping at my ankles. Then it was a race in the dark to float the boats, load them and get in before the beach vanished completely. In the chaos, we lost one of the rafts. It was my fault. One minute, I was holding the rope; the next, the current snatched it out of my numb, wet hands. I lunged for it, and almost drowned as it rushed into the darkness. When I managed to get back to shore, I thought Fabio would slit my throat.

'That had the ammunition and fish-hooks,' he shouted, waving his machete. Bloodshot eyes, grey skin: he looked like a zombie. 'You think we get six of us in two boats?'

Automatically, everyone looked at Howie. No one said what we were thinking.

'If we starve, they won't be so overloaded,' said Tillman. He actually seemed to be enjoying it, feeding off our misery. I suppose he felt vindicated.

Howie couldn't stand upright. We loaded him into Fabio's boat, which had the balsa outrigger. I was about to join him, but Fabio told Drew to get in with them. 'No room for pussies on my boat,' he told me. That left me with Tillman and Zia.

From behind Tillman's back, Drew mouthed *You OK?* I nodded. Whatever Tillman and Zia might be up to, they were the least of my worries that morning.

I couldn't believe how fast the river had come up – and still rising. By the time we'd loaded the boats, the last sliver of our beach had vanished. Angry white waves broke where yesterday there had been calm water. The motorway rush sounded louder than ever.

'Maybe the Transocean highway,' joked Fabio. 'We find a bus, back in Puerto Tordoya in ten hours.'

Tillman rolled his eyes. 'Or maybe we get smashed to pieces.'

'Should we wait until it goes down?' I wondered.

'More rain is coming.' Fabio took a long, anxious look at the river. 'Better to go now. We will stop the boats before the rapids and make a look. If it is too dangerous, we portage the boats on foot.'

'That easy, huh?' said Tillman.

We cast off into the main current. Tillman steered; Zia and I bailed. It took all our strength to keep up with the water slopping in over the sides of the overloaded raft. The roar got louder.

The blisters on my hands reopened. My shoulders felt as if they'd drop off.

'Tell me more about Menendez's vaccination programme,' I said to Zia. Anything to take my mind off the situation.

Zia tipped out a panful of water. 'What do you care?'

'I want to understand why he died.'

'Fuck you.'

'Seriously.' It was hard having this conversation with her back, constantly watching for danger. The roar sounded louder, funnelling down the canyon and blowing spray in our faces.

'How much did he tell you about the programme?'

'I worked in the clinic. I saw all the documents.'

I glanced over my shoulder to see if Tillman was listening in. He looked like he was more interested in keeping the boat on course.

'The drug he used: was it a standard vaccination?'

'A new treatment.'

'That he developed?'

'An American company. They invented a new vaccine, they paid Felix to pilot it.'

She paused. Ahead, Fabio had been having real trouble with his outrigger, constantly spinning broadside to the current. It slowed him down so much we'd now come alongside. He waved us by, struggling furiously. I gave Drew a thumbs-up and wished I was with her.

'Did Menendez tell you how the vaccine worked?' I asked Zia.

'Can you shut the fuck up and paddle?' interrupted Tillman. He jabbed his paddle ahead. We'd come around a bend, into a narrow channel. Ahead, the river seemed to end in a wall of white water and a sudden drop to nothing. I kept waiting to see over the edge. We rushed closer and closer, faster and faster. Zia and I grabbed our paddles and dug in where Tillman told us. We still couldn't see anything beyond.

'*There.*' Tillman had spotted a break in the cliffs, a small cove where the water eddied back. The river had us so fast we'd be past it in a few seconds. Tillman and I forced in our paddles, wrenching the boat across the stream. Sweat streamed down my face; I thought my arms would snap. The current rushed us on, ten metres forward for every one we moved sideways. The roar of the rapids beat all around us.

'We're not going to make it,' I shouted. We were so close to the edge, now, I could look through the curl of water and see the rocks underneath, drooling teeth waiting to chew us up.

The river slackened. In the raging cross-currents around the drop, we'd found a back eddy. We paddled for all we were worth, powering the heavy raft towards the cove. Even then, I thought we'd missed it. But Tillman had other ideas. Almost by force of will, he dug in, scooping great holes in the water.

We hit the cliff so hard I almost fell out. Water flooded over the side of the raft. I grabbed one of the vines that trailed down the rock face and held on, wrapping it around my wrist until it cut the blood off. The boat steadied and stopped. Shielded by the cliff, the wind calmed; the noise of the falls dropped off.

'We *made* it.' Still holding the vine, I grabbed Zia's pot and started scooping out water one-handed.

'Where are the others?'

I looked back. Fabio's boat was still out in midstream, nearly past us already. Fabio and Drew were paddling hard, but the outrigger kept dragging them off course. Even Howie had sat up, and was pawing the water with his hands.

'Throw them a rope,' shouted Tillman.

'I don't have a rope.'

I scrabbled in the base of the boat, trying to unpick one of the knots that held the baggage. Numb fingers on wet rope, and no room to move, like something in a nightmare.

'Out of the way.'

Tillman pushed me back, almost out of the boat. He cut the knot with his sheath knife, stood up and hurled the rope. It fell short – well short. He grabbed one of the paddles, knotted the rope round and threw it like a javelin. Drew and Fabio saw what we were doing and tried to steer towards us. The paddle bobbed on the water.

The rope was too short. The only other one we had was lashed to the outrigger in Fabio's boat. Across the water, Fabio had put down his paddle and was trying to cut the log free. The bags on the outrigger fell in the water and were carried over the falls. I think one of them was the food bag.

Tillman was still standing, screaming at Fabio to paddle harder. I pulled him down before he tipped us all in the water. 'It's too late,' I shouted.

Fabio must have felt it: something irrevocable in the current that held the raft. He abandoned the outrigger and threw himself back into the boat. I saw hands clutching the rubber handles, a pile of bodies jammed in the boat like mannequins. Like their own stunt doubles.

The boat reached the lip of the falls. It hung there, balanced like a seesaw, as if time had paused. Perhaps that's my imagination. The river ran so fast, it can't possibly have been there more than a split second.

The boat tipped over the edge and vanished.

For the first time since I'd met him, Tillman looked as if he didn't know what to do. He stared at the rapids in disbelief, as if it was all a movie and he could hit 'reverse' and bring the boat flying back up.

'We have to go after them,' said Zia.

'That's insane.' I still had the vine around my wrist, tying me to the cliff. I clung on.

'They'll die.'

'*We'll* die.'

We were all screaming. And in that moment, I remembered who I was with. Tillman and Zia. They'd cut the bridge, pushed Anton off the cliff. Got rid of the others. Now it was just me.

'We'd better go rescue them,' said Tillman.

A few metres away, a wall of white water boiled over the cliff. I couldn't stop looking at it.

'Isn't there another way?'

'Not any more.'

Tillman filled his dry-bag with as much air as possible, then resealed it as a makeshift flotation device. I copied him, and tied the strap round my wrist. We took off our ponchos to keep our arms and legs free.

'If you go in,' said Tillman, 'try and point your legs downstream. And keep them together,' he added, 'if you ever want kids again.'

He pulled a stroke with his paddle. The boat didn't move.

'You got to let go, Doc.'

'Sorry.' I loosened my grip and let the vine slip off my wrist. The rubber boat bobbed out of the cove. The main current was so strong it actually pushed us back, out of its way; I nearly lost my nerve. But Tillman put in a shove, and the boat broke through, and suddenly we were accelerating at a frightening pace. I gripped my paddle for dear life.

We approached the lip. Tillman paddled furiously, aiming for some gap only he could see. He screamed instructions; all I could hear was the river.

And you know what I was thinking of? The time we took Peggy to Legoland. Sitting in a plastic log, Peggy squeezed between my knees in the red plastic cagoule we'd bought at the turnstile. Her scream of happy terror as we dropped down the chute, and the slap of the landing. Insisting she hated it, demanding to do it again.

This wasn't like that. No rattle of the mechanism that pulled you up, no stage-managed delay as you approached the drop. Just a rush and a roar, sickening helplessness. A moment of savage clarity as the boat bent over the lip.

Time did stand still. I looked down the falls, and I had time to think, *That's too high.* Water frothed in the pool below – except in its centre, the eye of the storm where a still patch of water was so clear I could see right through to the pebbles and sand at the bottom. Ropes trailed off a black log jammed between two rocks – Fabio's outrigger.

Then we went over.

42

The first drop nearly finished us. The raft tipped almost vertical: if Zia hadn't thrown herself back on top of me, I'd have spilled out and been beaten to death on the rocks. The nose of the boat splashed into the water, then porpoised out so violently it almost shook us all off. It bellyflopped down – right side up.

Something hard smacked my face. Tillman's paddle. He

pointed to the water and began paddling furiously. The waterfall was sucking us back. I dug in my paddle, which I'd somehow kept hold of. Not a fair fight: a small plastic blade against tons of water pouring behind us, but we fought and howled and drove and dug and forced the boat forward.

The boat jerked, like a car kicking into gear as the main current snatched us back. No relief: now it was dragging us straight towards a massive rock outcrop that divided the river in two. White water surged around the base and poured over gigantic drops on either side.

'Go right,' hollered Tillman, who must have seen something I hadn't. I did what he said; Zia leaned her weight against the side to turn us.

The boat scraped the outcrop. I imagined the jagged rock opening our rubber hull like a scalpel; I waited for it to pop like a balloon.

The second drop was lower than the first. The boat hit the water hard and slewed us around backwards. Spray slapped me, though I was so wet I hardly noticed. Something harder jabbed me in the chest. Tillman's paddle, again.

'Turn around,' he bellowed.

The boat had spun too far – and the next run of rapids was close. Instead of trying to turn the boat, we turned ourselves round. Now I was in the front, staring at the rocks and surging water, trying to find a way through. Like flying through a meteor field: all I could do was react, paddling frantically to avoid whatever came at me, while Tillman shouted incomprehensible orders from the back.

The river descended in a series of giant steps, twisting through the canyon. Bouncing, splashing, spinning: I lost count of the times we nearly wrecked ourselves. I wanted to stop, find some little nook out of the current to catch my breath. But we couldn't hold back. Going slow cost steerage way, gave the river more time to drag us off course. We had to commit, full pelt, and pray we didn't break our necks.

In the few moments where the river relented, I looked for Fabio and Drew. I saw a black stick floating in a pool of foam, which could have been a paddle or could have been a branch. Otherwise, no trace.

The river spread wider and eased off. I looked ahead, daring to hope we'd passed the worst. No such luck. In front of us, the walls of the canyon curved together like the neck of a wine bottle, squeezing the river into a chasm narrower than anything we'd been through yet.

I glanced back. Tillman was scanning the banks for some-where we could pull in to regroup. Nothing doing. The river rushed on, picking up pace as it funnelled us towards the gorge. A curtain of spray blew up across the mouth and hid the interior from us. All I could guess at beyond was noise and darkness.

The river sucked us through the spray. Now we were in a chute, a non-stop storm. Blinded by the sudden darkness, I didn't see the rock right in front of us. We bounced off it, spun round and on down, bouncing like a tennis ball on a flight of stairs. We'd lost all hope of control, any attempt at steering. I reversed my paddle and used the butt like a bat, fending off rocks and poling us away from the cliff edge. Stuck pieces of trees choked the narrow chasm; once, I had to duck under a whole trunk wedged mid-air between the cliffs before it took my head off. I didn't think Drew and Fabio could have survived this. I didn't think I could.

Something thumped hard against the bottom of the boat, bruising my knee. I looked down. Bubbles fountained up between my feet. I felt around the bottom, until my finger went through a small tear in the fabric.

I looked up, wondering how much longer we could last. Almost had my eye poked out by an overhanging branch

TOM HARPER

that scraped a bloody welt in my cheek. Brightness loomed
ahead. The canyon was opening up. If we could—

I didn't see the rock that got us. The raft hit it a glancing
blow and rode up on its side. The water in the bilge rushed
down. I threw my weight against the roll, but I still had the
dry-bag looped to my wrist. The water caught it and pulled
me off balance, just as a wave from behind caught the
underside of the boat and flipped it.

The boat toppled over on to me, like a coffin lid slamming
shut. Underwater objects kicked and punched me: rocks, or
driftwood, or Tillman and Zia flailing for their lives. I kicked
back, desperate to connect with something solid in the
madness. The boat smothered me. I pushed and fought,
couldn't dislodge it. It would drown me.

A jarring impact shook my spine. Just because I was dying
didn't stop me moving. The river dragged me on, but the boat
held me back. Caught on something? My feet kicked for a
foothold, anywhere to brace myself so I could get it off me.

The boat lifted. I got my hand underneath and heaved. If
I could get it over, perhaps I could scrabble back on. But
something had grabbed my arm, tugging me away. Tillman?
I shouted to him to let go, that I almost had it. Words came
as gurgled gasps; he didn't listen. Pulled harder. I tried to
cling on to the boat; my fingers scrabbled on slick rubber.
Couldn't get a grip. Squeezed – and lost it.

The current dragged me under, drowning my cry of
despair. When I resurfaced, the boat was gone; Tillman's grip
was so strong I thought he'd cut off the blood. 'Stop,' I
shouted, but he didn't let up.

I shook the water from my eyes. It wasn't Tillman. It was
the dry-bag, still looped to my wrist. In all the chaos, it
was the one thing that had worked perfectly. It bobbed
along, dragging me like a fisherman's float. I fumbled with
the rope, but there was no slack. A rock grazed my arm.

Point your legs downstream. A dark shape rushed towards me; I twisted my body, jerking my head away. Just in time. The rock smashed my shoulder. I screamed and took a mouthful of river water. Spun a hundred and eighty degrees, just about got my legs in the right direction before I went over the next fall.

Water splashed and stung my eyes. I forced them open, to see what was next. Red rocks and white water, scribbled black where branches had got caught.

One of the branches moved. *Zia.* She must have hurt herself badly. The water churned around her, spinning her like a feather, and she did nothing to fight it.

I kicked on. The current fought me, tugging me off in all directions. I wrapped one arm round the dry-bag, like a rugby ball, lunging forward with the other. Grabbed for Zia's ankle, but the river spun her wide. Tried again and stubbed my fist on a rock.

Ahead, two rocks stuck out of the river like vampire teeth, a narrow gap between them. Zia slammed into them and went under. Her legs stuck out at an unnatural angle, wedged in the gap. A wave curved back off the rocks and held her down.

I could have left her there. Even in the chaos of that moment, I understood that. *Solve all our problems*, as Anton might have said. As far as I knew, she'd have done it to me. The current split around the rocks, pulling me away from her; in a moment, I'd be past her, and no one could say there was anything I could have done different.

I'd like to say I chose to do the honourable thing. The truth is, if I'd thought about it I'd never have done it. It was sheer instinct. I flailed and kicked, touched bottom; let go of the bag and lunged with both arms, a fullback making a last-ditch tackle.

My hands closed on her leg. The current did the rest,

pulling me forward and wrenching her free. Her head broke the surface. Limp, facedown in the water: perhaps I'd broken her neck. No time to check. One arm on the float, one around her chest, I clung on and tried to get us pointing the right way. Huge boulders littered the river here, any one of them enough to dash my brains out. I cupped her head against my chest.

The current quickened again. I knew what that meant. I let go of the float and pawed at the passing rocks to slow us down, put the brakes on so I could swing our legs downstream. My hand slipped on the slimy rocks; the current roared faster.

A rock jarred my knee and then the river seemed to rise, lifting us over the edge of something. I felt weightless. The world spun. We spun, thrown so far we were actually out of the water in mid-air.

We splashed down, hitting the river so hard I thought my spine would break. The dry-bag, still tied to my wrist, yanked us up again before I touched bottom. I broke the surface, tensing myself for another impact. My nostrils burned from having water shot up them; my ears were ringing.

For the first time since we'd entered the canyon, I felt the current slacken off. I rolled over, treading water. I pulled in the dry-bag and forced it under Zia's chest, so it held her head out of the water. Her arms fastened on to it reflexively, like a newborn baby grasping the breast.

My foot touched solid ground. I could stand. The river had spread out, wide and shallow. The red cliffs had vanished. I saw trees on the banks.

I tasted blood in my mouth, and my left leg howled when I put weight on it. Zia still wasn't moving, but I could feel a pulse. I thumped her back until she'd coughed out a couple of litres of water. That brought her to.

'Are we OK?' She slurred her words so much I worried

about brain damage. How long had she been held under between those rocks?

'We will be.'

I saw a shingle beach where the river made a bend. Half hopping, half swimming, I chested my way through the water. As soon as it was shallow enough, I dropped down on all fours and crawled ashore, dragging Zia until it was safe to collapse. We lay there, half in the water and half in the rain.

Footsteps crunched on the stones. I looked up. Drew stood over me, drenched, in combat trousers and her black bikini top. I stared, then started laughing. So hard, I nearly choked on the water lapping ashore. Even when Fabio appeared beside her, I couldn't stop myself.

'Something funny?' said Fabio.

I pointed to Drew. 'Doesn't she look exactly like Lara Croft?'

43

Drew and Fabio helped me and Zia out of the water and up to the edge of the jungle. We sat there like a row of monkeys, hunched under the trees. They kept the rain off, though we were so wet it made no difference. Fabio scanned the river.

'What happened to Tillman?'

'He went overboard. We all did.' I checked the river. 'He hasn't come down yet?'

'No.'

I touched my shoulder and winced. That had nearly been my head.

'What about Howie?'

I already knew the answer. I'd felt the dead weight when we loaded him in the boat that morning. The rapids would have beaten him to a pulp.

Fabio pointed along the beach. About ten metres down-stream, a blue raft sat half deflated on the shingle. The wind snatched at it, but didn't move it. Something was weighing it down.

'Come and see.'

I hobbled after him and peered into the boat. Howie lay in the bottom, eyes closed, a rope wrapped round his chest. I can't say I was surprised he didn't make it – only that he wasn't the first. Mostly, at that moment, all I felt was selfish joy that it was him and not me.

'Rest in peace,' I murmured.

Howie's eyes snapped open. I almost fell over with surprise. 'Howie?'

He opened his mouth, mumbling something. Blood-streaked spit drooled out of his mouth. He reached out to me, clawing the air. Bloody sores pocked his hands; he seemed to have lost three teeth.

Fabio laughed. 'When we came to the rapids, we tied him down. We fell out, but Howie stayed in. Even when he went over the last fall.' He smiled. 'It makes you believe in God, no?'

'Someone was watching out for him.'

'Fabio was amazing,' said Drew warmly. 'He almost got us through. Just at the end, I lost my balance. He dived in to save me.'

Howie's eyes shut again. I wanted to cover him with a blanket, but of course we had none.

'Have we got sleeping bags? Ponchos?' I took in the expression on their faces. 'What *do* we have?'

We lifted Howie out of the boat and carried him to the shelter of the trees. Fabio spread out what he'd managed to save or salvage. One cooking pot, but no matches to light a fire. One head-torch that had cracked open, but miraculously still worked when we dried off the batteries. A water bottle. A length of rope, one paddle and a machete. Fabio's dry-bag, still sealed, which he kept to one side. The ballpoint pen and notebook zipped in my trouser pocket. And a rifle, which had been tied into the bottom of the boat with Howie.

'But no ammunition,' said Fabio. 'Only what is inside. Two bullets.' He slung the rifle on his shoulder.

'No food?'

'Not even Tillman's cocaine.'

I checked the river again. No sign of Tillman.

'Should we go and look for him?'

I said it because I felt someone ought to. I knew what Fabio would say.

'You want to climb up that cliff? Back up the river and the waterfalls?'

I looked back. From here, the last fall didn't look so high. I wasn't fooled. Behind it, the river disappeared into the red rock canyon, into the heart of an immense dark cloud lowering over it.

'More to the point,' said Drew, and something hard in her voice said we were moving on irrevocably, 'how do we get out of here? One boat for four of us.'

I made a quick count. 'Don't you mean five?'

'You think Howie can make it?' We were standing right over him, but Fabio didn't bother to lower his voice.

'Can't we make a raft or something?'

'If we find some balsa, is possible. But it takes time. The balsa will be wet, float badly.'

'We need rest.'

'No,' said Fabio. 'Rest kills us. With no food, no shelter, every hour is closer to dying. Only the river can save us.'

'We don't even know where it goes.'

'It must join the Santa Maria. After that, we find someone for sure.'

Whether it was adrenalin, or euphoria from surviving the river, he was almost bursting with manic energy. I needed to stop him. I had a theory that had been growing in my mind since yesterday, and it was time to share it.

Before I could work up the courage to say what needed to be said, Zia cut in. 'Four, five, does it make a difference?'

It was the first thing she'd said since we landed. Her voice shook, as if she wasn't sure how to use it any more.

She pointed to the boat. 'If you put more than one person in that, it'll sink.'

'We fix it,' said Fabio.

All three of us stared at him. 'Did you find a repair kit?' said Drew. 'Or were you going to sew it up with jaguar gut?'

Fabio tapped his head with the flat of the machete and grinned. *Perhaps*, thought some cynical part of me that the river hadn't touched, *he's happy we lost Tillman*. Dig down, to the places we don't like to go, perhaps I was happy too. Without Tillman, I thought I could handle Zia.

He pointed the machete at me. The tip hovered drunkenly a few inches from my chest. I wasn't sure he wouldn't run me through.

'Come with me.' He hooked the handle of the cooking pan with the machete and flipped it up in the air. 'Bring this.'

I followed him into the jungle. His energy never flagged: he hacked and slashed like a drunken pirate. His head darted about like a snake, looking for something. I tried to keep a safe distance behind, but each time he saw me he'd scold me, 'Keep up, Kel, or the jaguar will eat you.'

Suddenly, he stopped in front of a tree. 'This one,' he announced, though it looked like any other tree to me. Straight trunk, greyish-green bark and branches sprouting above my head. He made two diagonal cuts in the bark with the machete.

He peeled back the strip between, revealing the bare wood below.

'Pan,' he ordered. I gave it to him. He took the clasp-knife from the pouch on his belt, jammed it into the tree like a peg and hung the cooking pot from it.

Drops of white sap oozed out of the cut he'd made. They ran down the diagonal cut and dribbled into the pan.

'Latex,' said Fabio. 'Maybe later, you get lucky with Drew, we make a condom.'

He giggled and slapped me on the back. I gave a glassy grin. On the forest floor, an army of leafcutter ants went about their business.

I held the pan tight to the tree so the rubber would flow in. Fabio couldn't stand still. He paced around, swiping the undergrowth; he wandered off a little distance. 'Maybe I find a balsa.'

Five minutes later he was back.

'Kel,' he said. 'I can count on you, OK? We do what we have to do.'

The wildness in his eyes made me wonder if he might not have salvaged some of Tillman's cocaine after all.

'Of course,' I said.

'*Esto es guerra*. Survival. We win or we die.'

'Right.'

He obviously wanted something from me. I waited for him to elaborate. He peered into the pot.

'Is enough.'

Without another word, he unhooked the pot, pulled his knife from the tree and set off back towards the river. Just before we reached the beach, he stopped abruptly and turned.

'You still have your medicines?'

'A few.' A strip of paracetamol in my trouser pocket, and one vial of morphine (but no needle to inject it).

'Good. Good.' He leaned close to my ear, though no one

283

could hear us. 'When it happens, you go for the one on the right, OK? I make sure.'

'The right of what?' I asked.

He bounded out on to the beach. The rain had stopped, though not for long. Black clouds massed on the horizon; the wind blew in erratic gusts. Fabio took the pot to the boat and used a twig to smear the gum round the tear in the hull.

'You have your dry-bag?'

I gave it to him. Before I could protest, he slipped his machete inside the bag and sliced it open along the seam.

'That saved my life.'

'Now it will save you again.' He spread the fabric flat over the boat, pressing it against the latex glue. I held it there, while he got down on his knees and blew into the valve until the hull filled enough to stretch the patch tight.

Drew had come to watch. 'It still won't hold more than three people. At best.'

'I have a plan.' Fabio lopped the twigs off a fallen branch and started stripping the bark to make a pole for the boat. He still had the rifle on his shoulder – hadn't taken it off since we landed.

I needed to slow things down. 'You're not going to go now? We're exhausted.' Fabio ignored me. 'At least let's give Tillman a chance. See if he comes down the river.'

'If he doesn't come down already, he is dead.'

'You don't know that.'

'I don't care.'

'How are we going to fit in the boat?' Drew repeated.

Fabio picked up two of the sticks he'd cut off and snapped them roughly in half. He clenched the pieces in his fist, so all you could see were the ends sticking out the top.

'We pick sticks.'

We all stared at him. Even Howie seemed to register it was serious. He opened his eyes, pushing himself up on one arm.

'That's crazy,' I said. I wished I had the gun. 'We all stick together, remember?'

I glanced at Drew. Had they cooked this up between them, while Zia and I were still coming down the rapids? Her face told me nothing.

Fabio thrust out his fist at me. His thumb twitched, tapping the stick nearest it.

'Kel. You choose first.'

When it happens, you go for the one on the right. He'd rigged it. He wanted me with him. I looked at his face, and saw him nodding not so subtly.

And why not? *If you're going in the jungle, the first law is you have to know who you can trust.* But beneath that there's a more brutal law. Anton should have known it: perhaps it would have saved his life.

Survival of the fittest.

Fabio, Zia, Howie: what were they to me? Even Drew. In the final analysis, the only debt I owed was to myself; to stay alive. If Fabio could get me out in the boat, then forget the others and good luck to them.

But that couldn't happen.

'We can't go,' I said. Even in a world of water, my mouth had gone dry. 'There's something else we need to talk about.'

'Not now.'

'Menendez and his men didn't die of hunger.'

'We don't die of hunger either.'

I pushed Fabio's fist away. His smile soured.

'You don't want it? OK. You stay with Howie. Drew and Zia come with me.'

I stood my ground. 'They died of disease,' I said loudly. 'A nasty, infectious disease that killed them horribly. Their teeth fell out; they bled so much it stained their bones.'

I saw anguish on Zia's face. I wondered how much of this she knew already. I had to make the others understand.

'I think Howie has the same thing.'

Everyone looked at Howie. No one spoke.

'That's impossible,' said Drew at last. 'Howie's the only one of us who never went in the temple chamber.'

'So . . .' I let her work it out for herself. I knew she'd got it by the look of horror that crossed her face.

'You think he caught it . . . outside?'

'It's the only possibility. And if he could catch it, so could any of us.'

I avoided Drew's eye. We'd worked longest in the tomb; we'd handled the skeletons. We'd worn gloves and masks, but who was to say that counted for anything.

'We have to find a hospital,' said Zia.

'Where, exactly?'

'Follow the river. Maybe there's a village with a clinic.'

I thought of the clinic in the Indian village. I thought of the desperate faces crowded into Puerto Tordoya's hospital. I spoke very deliberately, and wished I'd managed to get hold of the gun.

'Whatever this is, I've never seen anything like it. It's entirely possible it's unknown to medicine. We don't know how Howie caught it, but the fact he did suggests it's extremely virulent. Possibly airborne.'

I let that sink in.

'We wondered why we didn't see any Indians. Now we know. And if this virus could wipe out an entire village, think what it would do in a place like Puerto Tordoya.'

I'd hoped that giving voice to my fears would make them seem more manageable. A problem shared is a problem halved, all that crap. In fact, I felt as if I'd jumped into the abyss.

Space had opened between us. The terror of the unknown, working on our imaginations. Fabio unslung the rifle and pointed it at Howie's forehead.

'We end this now.'

'Put that down,' I shouted. Thunder growled near by. 'Killing him won't end anything.'

Howie stared up at us, eyes wide and helpless. I remembered the pigs we'd slaughtered, that day we found the city.

'Please don't,' he mouthed.

He fumbled in his pocket and pulled out a penknife. The lesions on his skin broke open as he scrabbled to get the blade out. Fresh blood flowed down his fingers. He was hardly strong enough to prise it open. He sat up, jabbing the blade at Fabio. It was pathetic.

'It's too late,' I said to Fabio. 'We probably all have it by now.'

'Then he's already dead.'

Fabio looked at me. He looked at Zia and Drew. He chambered a bullet.

'We need to study this disease. See how it runs its course.' I tried to keep my voice calm, bleed out the tension. 'If it ever gets out into the world, we need to be ready.'

'Fuck studying it. Cure me, for God's sake.'

Hearing Howie swear might have been the strangest moment of the whole trip. But Fabio was ready to shoot. I threw myself at him. He pulled the trigger. The shot went off so close to my face I thought my teeth would shatter. I went deaf, but I clung on to the rifle barrel, twisting it away from Fabio's grip. He stamped on my foot and kicked my shin. It was like being back in the rapids.

His grip weakened. I yanked the gun and it came free, so fast I sat down on the stones with a bump. I scrambled away.

Drew had saved me. She hung on to Fabio's shoulders, pulling him backwards, the way Peggy does when she wants a piggyback. I shot the bolt on the rifle to chamber another round.

'Now what do you do?' said Fabio. 'Sit there until we all die?'

He shrugged off Drew and stepped away. Back up, shoulders tensed. Heavy animal breaths. We stared each other down, and I was very glad of the gun.

In the pause, Howie got up.

It must have taken everything he had. Before any of us could react, he pushed himself on to his feet, staggered down the beach and flopped against the boat.

'Get him back,' shouted Fabio. 'Don't let him take it.'

But Howie wasn't going anywhere. As we watched, he lifted his penknife and stabbed it into the boat's hull, again and again in a frenzy of destruction.

Fabio moved first. He threw himself at Howie and dragged him off. Howie had no strength left; he came away like a piece of paper. But he'd done his work. The boat shrivelled up. Air wheezed out of the cuts with a sound like dying bagpipes.

'What have you done?' Fabio screamed.

The storm broke.

44

The rain fell so hard, so suddenly, no one could stand it. Arms over our heads, we ran blindly for the trees. Raindrops pricked my skin, like being strafed with needles.

I reached the shelter of the forest. Rain forced its way between the leaves, but at least I could see. Drew and Zia had joined me; Fabio skulked under the trees on the far side of the beach. That left—

'*Howie.*' I could see him, dragging himself across the stony beach like some primordial whale making a bid for evolution. I hesitated. 'We should get him.'

I gave Drew the gun. 'If Fabio looks like he's going to try anything, shoot him.' I glanced at Zia. 'Or anyone else.'

The rain beat so loudly I had to shout in her ear. She nodded. Zia and I ran out into the rain, flinching under the onslaught. Between us, we just about managed to half carry, half drag Howie back to the trees. For someone who'd hardly eaten in a week, he weighed a ton.

'You look after Howie here,' I told Zia. 'We're going over there.'

I pointed to a patch of shelter a little further along the bank. I didn't give a reason, and Zia didn't ask. The river had knocked the fight out of her; she looked half dead.

I settled down a little way off, where I could keep her and Fabio in sight. He'd stayed on the far side of the beach, sitting cross-legged at the forest's edge under a spreading palm, like the Buddha. Whatever he'd been on earlier, that manic energy, he'd got it out of his system. He saw me watching, and raised a hand in an ironic salute.

Drew joined me with the gun.

'What now?'

'I don't know,' I admitted. 'We can't go anywhere.' Even as I said it, I heard a crash like a gunshot from the forest behind me. Sharper and nearer than thunder – a falling tree. 'If we go into the forest, there's a good chance we'll be crushed. If we go on to the river, we'll drown.'

She forced a weary smile. 'When you put it like that . . .'

'Howie's going to die.' It was obvious, but I still felt bad saying it. As if I was betraying hope.

The smile vanished. 'You really think he has the same thing that killed Menendez?'

'It's even worse than that.'

Keeping my voice down, I told her about my conversation with Zia, before the falls. Plus a few more thoughts I'd had since then.

TOM HARPER

'Menendez was trialling some new vaccine.' I looked to
see if she understood. 'A vaccine is just a less powerful version
of the disease it's preventing.'

Drew stared. 'You're saying . . .?'

'If the vaccine somehow was too strong, or mutated . . .'

'*Jesus.*' She balled her fists. 'I've heard about this kind of
thing, Big Pharma testing their drugs in places they don't
need regulatory approval, no FDA breathing down their necks
when things go wrong. I never imagined they'd come here.'

'The Indians must have realised something was wrong.
They caught his expedition and walled them up inside the
temple. Maybe they thought it was a holy site, that the gods
would cleanse or protect them. Maybe they even meant it as
some sort of sacrifice. But by then it was too late. They all
had it.'

'Wouldn't Menendez have known to avoid it?'

'That's what worries me.' *Terrifies,* more like. 'It must have
become infectious, somehow. Menendez caught it; so did
Howie.'

I didn't need to spell out the obvious conclusion.

Drew rubbed her throat, as if it had suddenly started to
ache. 'You think we could have it too?'

I touched my jaw. Did my tooth hurt? Was my forehead
warmer than usual? We're all hypochondriacs at heart, doctors
worst of all. Give us a list of symptoms, and we can convince
ourselves of anything.

'I've felt terrible so long, I've forgotten what health feels
like.'

A tree floated past, waving its roots at me. Surprisingly
close. I rubbed water from my eyes.

Half the beach had disappeared. I don't know when. Now
that I looked, I could see the river had risen fast. Was still
rising. Water trickled between the stones, flowing towards me
like an incoming tide.

'I've seen too much of this,' said Drew suddenly. 'Western companies coming in, grabbing what they want, trampling anyone who gets in the way and then leaving the mess for someone else. Just like what the oil company did to those Indians – but this is a whole other level. We need to tell people.'

'How?'

'I've got contacts with the NGO I worked for. If we can give them evidence, they can make sure it gets seen. Can you prove anything?'

I squinted at Howie. 'A blood sample. If we get home, we could sequence the virus and compare it against Menendez's vaccine. There's also the bone we took for DNA analysis – when we still thought they were Incas. And I assume Zia has Menendez's memory card somewhere. Unless Tillman had it.'

'We can't exactly ask her to hand it over. You said it yourself. If her job is cleaning up Menendez's mess, she's not going to give us the evidence.'

I glanced over. Zia sat beside Howie, leaning against a fallen log, head slumped in sleep or despair. The rain drummed on the leaves and hissed on the water. She couldn't have heard a word we'd said.

'She doesn't look too dangerous.'

'Neither do snakes. Until they bite.'

I stood. 'I'm going to take the blood sample. You cover me.'

Drew raised the rifle. It looked so big in her slim arms. 'Don't do anything stupid.'

Shielding my eyes against the rain, I ran across to Howie. Zia didn't move; with her head bowed, I couldn't see if her eyes were open or shut. Drew's warning echoed in my mind.

I took the pen from my trouser pocket and pulled out the ballpoint insert. My hands trembled. I had to force myself not to keep looking at Zia. I pressed the empty plastic case against one of Howie's sores and let the blood flow in.

'What are you doing?'

Blood spilled over my hands. I almost dropped the pen in the river. Zia's eyes were open, her head up staring at me. *Did she have a knife?* I couldn't see her hands.

'Taking a blood sample.'

I bent down and washed the blood off my hands in the river, which was almost at my feet. Behind her, I saw Drew had the gun ready to fire.

'You're not worried you might catch it?' said Zia.

'I'm terrified,' I admitted. 'But it's too late now.' My throat felt dry; my bones ached. And my heart felt like it was about to explode. *What did she know?*

'Why didn't you let Fabio put the bullet in him? End his pain?'

'The more I can find out about this disease, the more chance someone else won't suffer.'

I looked at her, trying to fathom her dead eyes. Was she really who I thought she was? Could she be responsible for everything that had happened to us? Anton, the bridge . . . She just looked defeated.

'Do you still have the notebook we found in the cave? Menendez's lab book?'

'I lost it in the river.'

Convenient. Over her shoulder, Drew made a gesture with the gun. I shook my head. I tried to do it subtly.

'It was the monkeys,' Zia said suddenly.

'I'm sorry?'

'The vaccination programme. On the raft, before we hit the rapids: you wanted to know how it worked. Felix's big idea. It was the monkeys.'

I waited for her to go on.

'It was the old problem. How do you vaccinate wild Indians

without giving them the diseases you're trying to protect them from? Felix thought if you made a vaccine that could be passed on in food, you solve the problem. Vaccinate the animals, the Indians eat them, they develop immunity. He chose monkeys because their physiology is most similar to humans', to preserve the vaccine intact.'

I thought of the photos we'd seen, Menendez and his men holding up the dead monkey. I wondered why she was telling me this.

'There are some pretty far-reaching ethical problems with doing that.'

She shrugged. 'It's the jungle. Is it better to wait until some illegal logger or *narcotraficante* finds the Indians? Maybe gives them the blankets infected with measles? Maybe rapes the women? Felix knew he had to get there fast or there would be no Indians to protect.'

Big Pharma testing their drugs in places they don't need regulatory approval, no FDA breathing down their necks when things go wrong.

But she didn't sound like a stooge for Big Pharma. Emotion rang through her tired voice, so sincere. I was tired, too; I wanted to trust her.

'This disease Howie has,' she said. 'You really think it killed Felix?'

Why was she doing this? Finding out what I knew? Judging whether I needed to be eliminated? Cleaning up the mess. I was twitching so badly, I almost signalled Drew to shoot.

'I can't tell without proper tests,' I hedged.

'But you think so.'

'Yes.'

'And the Indians?'

'Them too.'

I listened to the water dripping from the trees.

'You think Felix brought it with him, don't you,' she said.

TOM HARPER

Shit shit shit. 'Why do you say that?'

She lowered her voice – though no one except Howie could hear us. 'The questions you were asking in the raft, I can tell what you were thinking. It was a new vaccine. Something could have gone wrong. Maybe injecting it in the monkeys changed it into something dangerous. Something humans could catch.'

Why was she telling me all this? Speaking so softly, she'd made me lean in close to hear her over the rain. I jerked back before she could grab me.

'You said it might be airborne.'

'It's possible,' I said. My teeth wouldn't stop chattering. 'Howie didn't go into the temple.'

'But he was sick before we reached the city.'

'He's been sick since we left Puerto Tordoya. This is different.'

'But that first day in the jungle, after the waterfall. Howie and the others ate that monkey Tillman shot.'

I'd almost forgotten that; it seemed a lifetime ago. I'd lost count of the days, but it couldn't have been much more than two weeks.

'Felix was injecting the vaccine into monkeys,' she went on. 'If the vaccine is the problem, and the monkey was infected . . .'

'Who else ate it?' I thought back. 'Anton, Tillman, Howie . . .' All dead, or well on the way.

'And Fabio.'

I peered across the dark bay that had once been a beach. Night was falling; the jungle's shadow hid Fabio – if he was there. Did he still have the machete? I couldn't remember.

'I'd better get the gun. And thank you,' I added.

'For what?'

'For trusting me.' I tried to find some warmth to put in my voice. 'I didn't think you did.'

294

'I didn't.' No hint of apology. 'I thought you worked for the drug company. Western doctor, last-minute addition. I thought they sent you to find Felix. When everything started going wrong – the boat, the bridge, Anton – I thought perhaps you wanted to hide all trace of him.'

'I thought the same about you,' I admitted. 'You were close to Menendez. The way you came aboard so late, after what happened to Nolberto . . .'

'That's why you gave me so many killer looks.'

'I thought I was more subtle.'

'Not really. But now I think if you wanted me dead, you could have left me to drown in the rapids. So thank you.'

It was a nice moment, but I still wished I could see her face more clearly. Fact was, someone had cut the bridge, and pushed Anton over the cliff. The stuff about Menendez and the monkeys; her thinking I was a drug company agent. Was it even true? Or just some elaborate double bluff?

The world was quieter; the storm seemed to have moved on. The rain hissed on the river, like an old cassette playing out its final seconds.

'You guys OK over there?' called Drew.

'Fine,' I said. 'We need to get Fabio back.'

A wet cough sounded near my feet. Howie, spitting up another bucketload of whatever he had inside him. A black goo with the consistency of coffee grounds. I turned his head so he wouldn't choke. He resisted, pushing back on my hand to force himself upright.

'It's OK,' I told him. 'Just rest.'

'Am I dying?'

'You're doing fine,' I told him.

'Am I dying?' he repeated. The words gurgled out with a gob of bloody phlegm, and another tooth.

'Most likely.'

Leaves rustled as he sagged back down. 'How much longer?'

'Not long.' I said it gently, as if it was a secret between us. 'I've got one vial of morphine left. That would make it quicker.'

Another bout of gagging. 'Suicide . . . It's sin.'

'You'll be with your God soon.' In some ways, I wished I had his faith.

He shook violently. 'I . . . gotta . . . confess.'

'Confess what?'

He pushed himself up so I wouldn't miss what he said. 'Anton.'

45

'*You?*'

I turned on the head-torch and shone it in Howie's face. He shrank away, covering his eyes with his hand. Blood from the open sores on his gums smeared his face.

'You killed Anton?'

'What's going on?'

Drew had come over. The three of us crowded around Howie, staring down at him.

'Turn it off,' he begged, jabbing a finger towards the torch. 'It hurts.'

I kept the light full on his face. 'Tell me exactly what you did.'

'While . . . you were in the tomb. I cut the bridge.'

'You didn't have the strength.'

'God gave me strength.'

'*Why?*'

'My mission.'

'What mission?'

'Make sure . . .' He broke off in a surge of coughing. Spat out more blood. 'No one finds it.'

'Finds what?'

'The city. Cajamarca.'

'Cajamarca's in northern Peru,' said Drew. 'What's that got to do with anything?'

'Cajamarca is the oil company in Puerto Tordoya,' said Zia. 'They have the concession to explore this whole area.'

Howie nodded. 'They . . . paid.'

'Paid who?' I asked. Howie touched his chest. 'You? They paid for you to come?' Another nod. 'I thought you were funded by your church. Converting the natives, all that Victorian nonsense.'

'Cajamarca . . .' The word came out as a jumble of air and spit. 'Pan the church.'

'Why?'

Howie rolled away, moaning in pain. I turned off the torch to save battery. Absolute darkness. Something splashed in the water – probably a fish – and I wondered again about Fabio. Was he out there, waiting for us to drop our guard?

'They wanted Howie to sabotage the expedition,' said Zia, dragging me back to the moment. 'That's why they paid him.'

'Why would they do that?'

'Because they think they'll find four hundred million barrels of oil in the jungle, and an archaeological miracle right on top of it would really screw up their plans.'

I looked at the patch of darkness that I knew was Howie. He didn't deny it.

'You sold us out for oil money?'

'No.' It came out as a howl of pain. Took so much energy, he couldn't continue. I heard his lips smacking and flapping like a dying fish as he fought for breath. 'Save . . . souls.'

'Whose souls?'

'The Indians,' guessed Zia. 'Just like the ones we met. Oil companies and churches have some common interests. The oil companies build roads – roads missionaries can use. They round up the Indians and corral them into settlements, where the missionaries can get at them. And the missionaries teach them how to be good little Westerners. They force the Indians to wear clothes; they tell them to get jobs, so they can put their money in the collection plate. Jobs the oil companies control. It's what they call in biology a symbiotic relationship. Like the crocodile, and the bird that feeds off the rotten meat on its teeth.'

I turned the head-torch back on, aiming it at the ground next to Howie. Flies swarmed in the light, returning after the storm. I wanted to look in his eyes, but they were tight shut.

'Is she right?'

He rocked up and down. I took it as a yes.

'You came here to cover up anything the oil company would find inconvenient?'

'They said . . . no escape. Die in the wilderness.'

'What about you?'

He cracked a ghastly smile. The blood on his face made it seem twice the size.

'Looks like . . . I die too.'

Speaking in a medical capacity, I couldn't disagree.

'And you killed Anton,' said Drew.

'I cut the bridge.'

'And pushed him off next morning?'

'He fell.'

'Don't give me that.' I hadn't bought that at the time, and I wasn't about to buy it now. 'You're supposed to be confessing, remember?'

'I cut the bridge,' he repeated. 'Anton fell.'

'With your help.'

'No. *No.*' He opened his eyes, desperate for me to believe him. 'I wasn't there.'

'Then how did you kill him?'

'The bridge.'

Drew leaned closer to him. 'You mean if you hadn't cut the bridge, he wouldn't have fallen off trying to fix it.'

'Right.'

'How about Menendez?' I said. 'What do you know about him?'

He shook his head.

'Did your pals at the oil company ever mention him?'

'No.'

'Did you cut the boat loose?' Zia asked. 'Back on the Pachacamac?'

'Yeah. If we never got there . . . never find anything.'

'How did you know Pedro and Pablo wouldn't come back?'

'I paid them.'

'And my emergency beacon? That night I drank Fabio's jungle juice – did you take it?'

He nodded. 'No escape.'

'Where is it now?'

'Paititi . . . Threw it off the cliff.'

I looked into his eyes. The whites were yellow, the pupils dark pits into his unravelling soul. Blood seeped out around the eyeball and crusted his eyelids, which were purple with bruises.

'I don't believe you,' I said softly. I leaned in as close as I dared. The smell hit me: he'd already started to rot. 'You didn't want to die a martyr. Once we were out of the way, you wanted to get back to Texas, to your fat fiancée and your pickup truck and your drive-in megachurch. So I'm asking you again. Where is the *fucking* transponder?'

'I'm dying,' he mumbled.

'Not that fast. But if you don't tell me where that trans-ponder is, I'll kill you myself.' I grabbed his shirt and pulled him upright. 'We can still get out of here. Still get you medical treatment. If you refuse, that's pretty much suicide, OK? What's God going to say to that?'

'My mission.'

'Forget it. Anton's dead. Tillman's dead. Do you think I'm going back to civilisation to tell everyone about a lost city that's harbouring an unknown virus? I want it kept hidden more than you do.'

Howie's head lolled back, as if he'd had his throat cut. I gripped his shoulders and leant very close to his face. He smelled so bad, if I'd had anything in my stomach I'd have puked on him.

'The dry-bag.'

'Where is it?'

He flapped his arm.

'Fabio.'

I'd left the head-torch on too long: the batteries were going. The darkness swallowed the little light it put out. Drew and I waded waist-deep across the flooded beach, towards the last place I'd seen Fabio. Zia stayed with Howie. The surface barely rippled, but around my ankles strong currents tried to tug me off balance. Each step was like moving through a minefield, testing the pebble bottom for strength. I clutched the rifle high out of the water. I thought it would probably still shoot if it got wet – but I didn't want to count on it.

Stumbling through the dark water, nothing ahead and nothing behind, I lost my sense of direction. The water had dropped to knee height. At the limits of the torch beam, I heard leaves rustling. I must be near the edge of the beach.

'Fabio?' I called.

For a long time there was no answer. Under the water, something brushed my leg. I panicked. I splashed forward, desperate to be out. Caught my leg on something, tripped – and fell face first into the water. I pushed myself up, stepped forward and promptly sank above my knee in mud.

Cold earth squirmed around me. I fought to get out, but the mud sucked me back and wouldn't let go. Every movement dragged me deeper.

I forced myself to stand still. Mud bubbled and oozed. *Please God don't let me die like this.*

'Kel?'

A branch came out of the darkness and swiped my face. Almost took my eye out, but I grabbed on to it and hauled. Pulled so hard I nearly brought Drew in on top of me. Somehow, she'd managed to get past the mud and up on to solid ground.

'Easy,' she said. 'Use both hands.'

I threw her the gun. That worked better. Hand over hand, I dragged myself forward until the mud released me. I squelched out and crawled up a low embankment.

'Thanks. Bugger.'

'What?'

I rubbed my foot. 'I lost a boot.'

'If Fabio has the transponder, we're nearly out of here anyway.'

I called Fabio again. In reply, a low whistle sounded off to my left.

We walked along the embankment. All things considered, we'd come pretty close. Fabio sat under his tree, legs crossed, exactly the same position I'd last seen him in. He was smiling, as if he was in on a private joke.

'Give me your bag,' I said. The fading torchlight picked it out on the ground beside him.

He turned slowly. A red mark burned livid on his cheek; his forehead glistened with sweat. His eyes seemed to be looking at something far away.

'You want to rob me now? You do it.'

He held out the bag. I snatched it off him and retreated, while Drew covered him with the rifle.

'Did Howie give you something to look after?'

He looked surprised. 'You want to pray or something?'

I delved in the bag. There was more than I expected: half a dozen objects wrapped up in old socks, solid and heavy when I moved them. And, near the bottom, the unlikely outline of a hardback book.

'Is this for Howie's funeral?' said Fabio.

I pulled out the last of Howie's Bibles. The embossed cross on the cover seemed to shimmer in the darkness. It looked intact, but when I opened it I saw that the pages had been gouged out with a knife to make a hollow. Inside, like an egg in a nest, lay the transponder.

My hand trembled so hard I almost dropped it when I pulled it out.

Fabio swore in Spanish. 'Howie had it all the time?'

'He stole it from me.'

Fabio laughed out loud. 'So why he doesn't use it?'

'He wants us all to die out here.'

I threw the Bible away. The transponder sat in the palm of my hand, bright and cheerful yellow. *Fast Find*, said the logo at the top, and I don't think I've ever seen two more magical words. Beneath the logo were two buttons, 'Test' and 'On'.

I pressed 'Test'. The light at the top flashed three times, bright as lightning in the darkness. No problem with the battery.

My thumb hovered over the 'On' button.

'Why are you waiting? You want us to be rescued?'

I slipped the transponder into my pocket. 'You know why I can't do that. Howie's dying of the same disease that killed Menendez.'

'So leave him behind. He dies anyway, for sure.'

'I think he caught it from a monkey.' Out of the corner of my eye, I glimpsed Howie's disembowelled Bible lying on the ground. 'The monkey Tillman shot and cooked near the falls.' I looked him in the eye. The head-torch followed my gaze, bang on his face, and even with the batteries going I could see the light hurt him. He looked a mess, covered in mud and bites and scratches, but even among all that the raw sore on his right cheek was obvious. I thought I saw another forming on his neck.

'How are you feeling, Fabio?'

He looked incredulous. 'You think I have this thing?'

'You know you do.'

'So – what? The rich gringo and his girlfriend fly out, and you leave me here to die with Howie?'

'I told you before. No one's going anywhere until we know who has the disease, and how infectious it is.'

Fabio almost snarled with anger. I was glad I had Drew covering me with the rifle.

He squatted down on his haunches, arms wrapped round his knees.

'OK. You win.'

I touched the dry-bag with my toe. 'What else have you got in there?'

'Some cans of food I saved for an emergency.' He gave me a bleak smile. 'Maybe now is an emergency?'

Unless you've been on a seven-hundred-calorie diet for two weeks, and barely eaten in three days, you have no idea how good the word 'food' can sound. I literally drooled; my stomach flipped. I knelt beside the bag and greedily unwrapped the socks round one of the bundles. In passing, I wondered why he'd needed to wrap up a can. In fact, it felt more like glass than metal.

I pulled off the sock. It was glass – a screw-top jar, with something like a lump of ginger inside it.

'What's this?'

'A root I found. You can eat it.'

I twisted the lid. Either I was too weak, or Fabio had shut it tight. I couldn't budge it.

'You want me?' Fabio offered his hand. I passed him the jar.

I admit, hunger made me stupid. You'd probably have been the same. I even leaned closer as he took the jar, giving him the easiest target you can imagine.

He drove the jar into my face like a glass fist. My head exploded with pain; I reeled backwards, knocking the gun Drew was holding, and fell flat on my back. I lay there stunned – probably only for a few seconds, but that was long enough. I opened my eyes and spat out blood. Felt my teeth with my tongue to see if they were all there. Tried to focus.

The gun lay on the ground. I couldn't have reached it, even if I'd wanted to try. Which I didn't. Fabio stood behind Drew, one hand twisting her arm behind her back, the other holding the machete at her throat. It occurred to me after-wards he must have hidden it in the leaves where he sat.

'Stay there, OK?'

One of my eyes didn't want to open. The other couldn't tear itself off the terror on Drew's face, and the big blade next to her throat. I thought of all the vines and saplings I'd seen Fabio lop, one casual swing of the wrist. Against those, Drew's neck was a twig.

'Get the jar.'

The jar lay on the ground beside me. It hadn't broken. If it had, I'd probably be blind. I picked it up and put it back in the dry-bag.

'And the transponder.'

I hesitated. Drew gasped as Fabio tightened his grip.

I wish I'd had the courage to resist, to strike a moral pose for all mankind. But I was so tired and I hurt too much. And it would make no difference. If I refused, he could kill Drew, kill me, and take whatever he wanted.

I took out the transponder and offered it to Fabio. He shook his head.

'Turn it on.'

I flipped open the safety cap. A thin metal aerial popped up from the top. Trembling, I put my thumb on the 'On' button.

I pressed it. Surprisingly difficult. Whoever designs those things, they don't want them going off by accident.

The light blinked on, strobing white lightning across the beach. A million miles up in space, a satellite registered a new transmission. Somewhere in Europe or America, a new alert flashed up on a computer screen. That was that.

'*Muchas gracias.*'

Fabio pushed Drew away. She stumbled and fell. Before she could get up, he'd scooped up the bag and the rifle and slung them over his shoulder, never letting go of the machete. He pulled the head-torch off my head, and clipped the transponder on to his belt.

'Was this what you wanted all along?' I said. 'To get rid of us? Did you push Anton over the cliff?'

Fabio bared his teeth. 'You're crazy. Without me, you would be dead in the jungle before you ever saw Paititi.'

'Then why are you doing this?'

'Because I want to live.'

Drew had stood up. Fabio put the point of the machete against her back and pushed her away into the forest.

'*Hasta luego,*' he said. He chopped the air with the machete, an inch from Drew's back. 'You don't follow us, OK?'

Prodding Drew, he vanished into the forest. The flash on the transponder blinked among the trees, then faded out of sight like a fairy flying home.

46

With one boot, no weapon and no strength, I didn't try to follow. I couldn't even get up. I lay on the ground, letting the damp seep through me, until I felt my bones had turned to mud. I had so many scrapes and itches, I hardly felt the flies and ants crawling over me. I was out of hope.

The wind had dropped to a gentle breeze. I rolled over. The clouds had parted into thin wisps, with the moon shining through behind. Would it still be dark in England? I imagined Peggy and Cate seeing that same moon. I imagined the satellite flying past in space, blinking back my distress signal to Earth. Would they call Cate and alert her that I was in trouble? Would she sit by the phone, waiting for news, chain-drinking cups of coffee? Never guessing that the only person coming back was Fabio. I hoped he'd tell her a good story about how I died. If he lived that long.

Something splashed in the water behind me. I twisted round, imagining a crocodile, or an anaconda slithering out to devour me. I might have lost the capacity for hope, but fear was very much alive.

There wasn't much moonlight – but a little goes a long way when there's nothing else to see by. A figure rose out of the river a few metres away, climbed the embankment, and I heard Zia's voice calling, 'Is everything OK?'

I moaned loud enough for her to hear. She came and squatted beside me.

'I saw a flashing light.'

'Fabio switched on the transponder.' I explained what had happened. 'He can't have gone far. We have to find him.'

I stared into the forest. No moonlight penetrated there.

'We'd just get lost,' said Zia. 'The river's our only hope now.'

I knew she was right. Still, I couldn't forget the look on Drew's face, the utter terror. I didn't think she figured in Fabio's escape plan.

'How's Howie?'

'He died half an hour ago.'

I didn't grieve. Didn't even flinch. If our positions had been reversed, Howie wouldn't have cried for me – though he might have prayed.

'Just you and me, then.'

I touched my cheek. The left side of my face had swollen up like a basketball where Fabio had clocked it. My shoulder throbbed from being battered by the river, and when I tripped on the root I'd cracked my leg so hard the bruise broke the skin. We had no gun, no machete, no boat and no food. I still didn't know if I trusted her, but that was beside the point. There was no one else.

The sky was getting lighter. I could see the treetops silhouetted against the clouds, black on grey. The long night was ending at last.

'We have to find Drew,' I said. 'We can't leave her out here. If there's any possibility she's alive . . .'

'There's no possibility.'

'She'd do it for us.'

'Would she?' It was light enough now that I could see the scepticism on Zia's face. 'Maybe for you.'

'And we have to stop Fabio. If the helicopter comes, takes him back to civilisation, he could start a pandemic.'

Zia's look didn't change. 'He got it from eating poisoned monkey, remember. No monkeys, no disease.'

'We don't know that,' I cautioned. 'And there's another thing that worries me. How did Menendez catch it?'

Zia stared at me as if I was stupid. 'The monkeys.'

'If he was vaccinating monkeys for the Indians, he wouldn't have eaten one.'

'A jaguar could have bitten the monkey, and then bitten one of Felix's men.'

'All eight of them?'

'Or when they were captured, the Indians fed them something and they didn't know what it was.'

'Maybe. But we still haven't ruled out the possibility that it mutated and became airborne. And if that's the case, we need to keep Fabio away from anyone he could breathe on.'

I pulled myself to my feet. Pain shot up through my leg. While we'd been speaking, the dawn had come up: a flat grey light that cast no shadows on a landscape that was unrecognisable.

I stared. My leg buckled and I sat back down with a bump.

'How are we going to track him in this?' said Zia, bleakly.

The world had turned to water. The river had burst its banks and flooded the forest. A few islands poked through the water, hillocks and embankments like the one where we stood. Apart from those, it was a drowned world.

I forced myself up again, ignoring the pain. 'It can't be more than a few feet deep.'

'And where will you go? No footprints in water.'

I stared into the forest. The glassy water twitched and rippled to the touch of a million insects dancing on the surface. I wondered what happened to the ants. Did they all drown?

'Fabio can't have gone far in this. Plus he needs open space to send a clear GPS position – and so the helicopter can see him.'

'He could find a clearing.'

'Unless he's got Google Earth tucked away somewhere, that's a long shot. I think he'll keep close to the river.'

'Everything's river.'

'Then we can't go wrong.'

I was still missing a boot. I cut the sleeves off my shirt and bound them round my bare foot. Even so, every step through that filthy water was an ordeal. Mud oozed round my feet. Slimy things brushed and clutched my legs; sharp things on the ground went straight through the bindings and hurt so much they must have drawn blood. I wondered if there were piranhas in this stretch of river, or if they'd all been washed away.

Sometimes the ground dropped away and we swam a few strokes. Those were moments of pure relief. I looked longingly at the deep water in the middle, thinking about swimming, but the river flowed fast out there. Great troughs pitted the surface. I couldn't risk being swept away. So we waded, and splashed, and hurt.

We reached an islet that must once have been a bluff and was now a muddy beach. We crawled on to it, dripping, and caught our breath. A mat of tangled branches sat grounded at the water's edge. One stick caught my eye, a small sapling that had been torn up by the roots. I worked it free, got out my penknife and started shaving strips off the end, sharpening it to a point.

'Fabio has the gun,' Zia reminded me.

'Better than nothing. I—'

I stopped. A new sound had entered the jungle, throbbing below the birds and insects and rushing water. Far off, like rolling thunder that never died away.

'Come on.' I grabbed my makeshift spear and pulled her to her feet. We splashed back into the water, pushing on as fast as we could. Now I barely noticed what was underfoot.

The river rounded a bend. A cluster of spiky plants, half under water, forced us out wide; the current threatened to snatch us away. The rumble in the distance got closer.

And then I saw him.

I'd guessed right: he'd stayed with the river. Hadn't even bothered to go far. He stood on a grounded log, about a hundred metres off, staring at the horizon like a shipwrecked mariner. I didn't see Drew.

Fabio was facing downstream. Concentrating on the

helicopter, willing it to come faster. He hadn't noticed us. He still had the machete in his hand, and the rifle on his shoulder. His dry-bag lay at his feet. I gripped my hand-made spear tighter.

I splashed back towards the treeline. Downwind, he didn't hear the noise we made. I kept waiting for him to look round, to check his surroundings; for that sixth sense he'd shown so often in the jungle to kick in. He never took his eyes off the horizon. I don't suppose I blame him. That was the sound of salvation.

I still couldn't see the helicopter. I tried to remember what I'd read about accuracy in the transponder manual. The radio beacon only got you to the nearest couple of kilometres; the GPS to within a few metres. Was it broadcasting both?

The water got shallower. I felt hard rock underfoot. We must have come on to a stretch of shingle, though I couldn't see the bottom. I walked faster, bashing my bare toes on the stones. Ferns sprouted out of the water like fans, and I tried to keep between them as much as I could for cover.

I paused to let Zia catch up with me.

'You stick to the shore,' I said. 'I'll go out in the water where he can see me.'

She looked at me as if I was crazy. 'You think you're going to spear him? Fabio has the gun.'

I told her what I wanted her to do. 'He's only got one bullet. If he shoots me, you do whatever you have to do to make sure he doesn't get on the helicopter.' I grabbed her shoulders. 'You saw what happened to Howie. If Fabio gets home, that could be half of Lima before we know it. And from there . . .'

'I get it.'

She slipped away between the ferns, keeping close to the treeline. I waited as long as I dared, then splashed out into open water towards Fabio's tree.

The noise was getting louder, like a jackhammer next door. I could feel the vibrations in the water. Fabio raised his left hand. Waving to someone? I looked up, still couldn't see anything above the trees.

A thin piece of metal caught the light. The transponder antenna. He held it up, pointing it towards the noise.

Some possessive, childish instinct kicked in. *Mine.* I lumbered out into the river where he could see me, shouting his name and splashing the water. I don't think he heard me over the throb of the helicopter. Gripping my spear like a baseball bat, I took a big swing at the river surface and hit up a sheet of spray.

He turned and saw me. He looked angry – but only for a second. Then he took in the situation and laughed. Him, standing on the tree trunk with the rifle and machete; me, waist-deep in the river with a home-made spear. My head barely came up to his knees.

He stuck the machete in his belt and hefted the rifle. His eyes kept darting to the sky. He hadn't seen Zia. She'd reached the tree trunk now. She edged along it, stepping carefully. If he saw her . . .

I forced myself not to look at her.

I waved the spear, trying to distract Fabio. He bared his teeth and aimed the rifle.

'You've only got one bullet,' I shouted. 'Unless you already used it on Drew.'

He shouted something back. His lips moved, but the helicopter obliterated the sound.

'Going back won't make you safe.' No way he could hear me, but I kept screaming to keep his attention. 'Are you feeling hot? Nauseous? Look at yourself in the mirror. If you take this back to civilisation, it'll be World War Z.'

I checked the sky. The rotor noise had got quieter for a moment, but now it was coming back louder than ever. I didn't dare look at Zia.

She grabbed his ankle. Fabio toppled, lost his balance and fell into the water. I jumped forward, spear raised two-handed. Bloodlust came over me; all I wanted was to stab and stab and stab again, until the river ran red.

An orange helicopter swept in fast and low over the trees. The noise suddenly doubled. For a moment I thought it hadn't seen us. Then it banked and swooped round. A high wind beat down on me.

Fabio's bag bobbed about in the water. While Fabio wrestled Zia, I grabbed it.

'You want this?'

He looked up and gave a howl of rage. He dived towards me. I waited until he was nearly there, then lobbed it over his head to Zia, like a frenzied game of piggy-in-the-middle.

'*Give it to me.*'

We were both shouting at the top of our lungs. We had to. The helicopter hovered over us, buffeting us with its wind. White-capped waves chopped the water. The rotor wash whipped up spray and blew it in my face.

In an abstract corner of my mind, I wondered what the pilots saw, looking down from their air-conditioned bubble. I couldn't imagine. Probably thought Fabio was being held at spearpoint by an Indian. With my torn clothes and filthy skin, I looked wild enough. I wondered if they had a gun on board.

'*Run,*' I shouted to Zia.

Zia splashed through the water towards the trees. Fabio turned, lifting the rifle. I lunged with the spear.

The water weighed me down, slowed me up. I'd forgotten how weak I was. Fabio caught the movement. Turning back, he grabbed the spear one-handed, pushed it out of the way and then wrenched it round. I lost my footing and fell in the water, clinging on to the spear for dear life.

Fabio put the rifle to his shoulder, aimed and fired. Pure

hunter's instinct. I barely heard the shot over the helicopter's roar, but I felt the echo in my chest. Blood puffed from between Zia's shoulder blades. She fell forward into the water.

I stumbled after Fabio. It was like being in a nightmare – the water slowed everything. I stuck out the spear and caught him between his legs. He tripped and sprawled into the water, jerking the spear out of my hands Before he could get up, I ran past. He grabbed for my legs; missed and splashed down again.

I reached Zia. Blood clouded the shallow water where she lay. Dark shapes flitted through it, predators gathering. I rolled her over. More blood gushed from her chest where the bullet had come through. Her eyes were shut. They must have closed in the split second before she hit the water, one last reflex from a body that didn't know it was finished.

I pulled the bag from her dead grip. The helicopter engine pounded in my head like a migraine. I looked back.

Fabio stood about five paces back. Arms out, shoulders tensed. Water dripped off him like some monster from the deep.

'Give me the bag,' he yelled. 'We can both go home.'

He still had the machete. I didn't even have my spear.

I turned and ran.

47

I splashed through the water, weaving between the trees. Didn't look back; didn't hear anything except the thunder of the rotor blades. A hunted animal in a drowned world. I floundered and tripped; my legs felt as if they'd snap. Any moment, I expected to feel the machete sliding into my spine. I almost wanted it.

Suddenly, I was up to my neck in water. The ground had disappeared. Only Fabio's bag kept me from going under.

I thrashed to stay afloat, kicking my legs for something to stand on.

The trees around me had thinned out, like a glade. Except this glade was a lake. Perhaps it had always been a lake, even before the flood made that moot. Hummocks studded the water – dozens of them. Some were smaller than a coffee table, others as big as a room. I didn't understand how they hadn't been covered, until I reached for one. It moved away from my hand, rocking back to expose a black nest of matted branches underneath.

They were floating islands. Some sprouted their own grass; one or two had become so established that saplings grew out of them. A few had got wedged in place between trees, but most floated free.

Off to my right, something broke the water. Something immense and ancient. Black and yellow scales broke the surface and disappeared without a ripple. Only a stone's throw away. So quick, I might have imagined it; but I'd seen that pattern before, coiled on a beach while I sat safe on the deck of the *Sierra Madre*.

Anacondas go for movement in the water. That doesn't help when you're *in* the water. I lunged for the floating island, so hard that the wave I created washed it out of reach. My hands closed on water. I kicked out, waiting to feel those jaws sink into my thigh, the coils crushing my ribcage. Reached for the island again, and this time got a grip. I hauled myself out, praying I wouldn't capsize it. The island rocked and wobbled; when I stood, my foot went straight through. I pulled it free and crouched on hands and knees, clutching the bag.

I glanced back. Fabio stood balanced on a branch, on the edge of the sunken lagoon.

'Why you are doing this?' he shouted. I could hardly hear him. The canopy hid the helicopter, but the noise drummed through the jungle. How much longer could it wait? It had to run out of fuel eventually.

All that mattered was for him to follow me. I stood up, dangling the bag like bait.

'You want it? Come and get it.'

Another island floated a couple of metres away. I jumped. A clumsy, half-arsed jump with no run-up; I landed short, and had to scramble out again. This island was bigger, bound tight with matted grass. I slopped through the soggy turf, feeling the sticks below. On the far side, a fallen tree made a bridge to the next island, which had snagged on its roots. I ran along it.

I heard a splash behind, Fabio coming after me. He wasn't doing much better than I was: he'd got stuck waist-deep in one of the islands. But he pulled himself out, dripping mud, and bounded on to the next.

Now we were in a race, jumping from platform to platform like characters in a video game. The archipelago was a labyrinth, where each wrong choice left you no way out except to swim. Sometimes I walked on what looked like low-spreading bushes, but were actually the tops of submerged trees; sometimes the islands sank under my weight, so I seemed to be walking on water. I kept checking for signs of that anaconda. I *wanted* to see it, just to know where it was. Either it had swum off to find easier prey – or it was biding its time.

Ahead, brightness streamed through a gap in the trees. Without thinking, I found myself heading there, drawn by that primitive logic where light equals hope.

Branches cracked and water splashed behind me. Fabio didn't have choices to slow him down: he only had to follow me. A wave of futility hit me. What was I doing? How did I think this could end? I couldn't outrun him for ever. Still, I had to go on. I sized up my options, and took a flying leap towards a small green island.

I'd misjudged it. I cannonballed into the water, went through and came up *underneath* it, held under by the branches. I forced my eyes open. The tangled branches made a lattice, with air trapped in the gaps. I breathed it in: foul breaths that tasted of mud and rot.

The sticks pressed harder against my shoulders. Something broke the water right in front of me. A hole: a shaft of light – and steel. Fabio must have landed on top of me, plunging the machete through the island to skewer me. Another hole opened as he pulled it out and stabbed again. Another, so close it grazed my arm.

I couldn't stay there waiting for him to sever my neck. Fabio's weight was sinking the island on top of me, pressing out the air. I gulped down what I could, taking half a lung's worth of water, and pushed myself down.

Every instinct and law of survival told me to go up. My aching chest told me to find air. Fabio's bag, buoyant, tugged me to the surface. Fighting them all, I forced myself as deep as I could.

I've never been more certain I would die. The water, or the anaconda, or Fabio – or something lurking I hadn't even imagined. The whole wet world wanted to kill me.

But it hadn't succeeded yet. A furious strength seized me, God knows where from – as if I'd found a lever in the depths of my soul marked 'Emergency Use Only'. I knew I'd die – but until that final moment, I was hell-bent on living. I swam through the water, milling my arms hard enough to make any predator think twice; once I swear I batted a fish from right in front of my face. I swam until my lungs hurt and my head popped, and if the anaconda had wrapped itself around my ribs, I wouldn't have noticed the difference. I swam until I couldn't stand it, and then I swam some more, right to the brink of consciousness.

Something hard grazed my stomach. I recoiled, lost control.

Tried to stay down, but my body refused. I floated up to the light.

I hadn't come as far as I hoped. Fabio stood on the small islet, peering into the water. By the time I'd dragged in a couple of long, desperate breaths, he'd seen me. He raised the machete and bared his teeth.

I'd come up on the other side of the submarine lake, beyond the islands. Here, the water wasn't more than waist deep; I could stand. What I'd grazed my stomach on was the spreading root of a tree. Ahead of me, the forest opened into a wide clearing with a fallen tree in the centre.

A fallen tree. That doesn't do it justice. You probably have an idea what a fallen tree looks like from walking in the woods at home. You're wrong. Instead, think of a downed airliner, or a toppled cathedral. I'd seen these giant kapoks standing in the forest, and marvelled at them; brought down to my level, this one was even more immense. When it fell, it had taken out half an acre of jungle: sycophant trees tangled in its branches, lashed to it by vines, or innocent victims that just couldn't get out the way. Those trees gathered around its trunk and snagged others, fallen logs swept in by the flood, until they piled up like so much matchwood; like the biggest bonfire you've ever seen.

I could see the sky. The kapok had ripped a hole in the canopy so you could see through to the clouds above. Big enough to fly a helicopter through – or at least lower a rope.

I splashed through the water to the logjam around the kapok. I got my knees up on to a log, and was almost rolled back into the water. I lunged for a branch above. It bent, dislodging another branch higher up, which fell hard on my head. It was like being inside a giant game of pick-a-sticks. Every movement moved something else; the whole pile rumbled and shuddered, constantly shifting. I kept waiting for it to collapse on top of me.

I reached the top – still only chest-high to the kapok trunk. The logs under me shuddered; no time to think. I stretched my arms over the trunk to haul myself over.

Pain shot through my hand, so unexpected I screamed. Fabio's face appeared over me – a long way up. I tried to pull back, but his boot crushed my hand in place. He lifted the machete like an executioner. I don't know how he got up there so fast.

'Please,' I begged.

I still had one arm free – and the dry-bag hooked over my shoulder. I shrugged it loose, so that it dropped down my arm. One-handed, I undid the clip and let the neck unroll.

'If this falls, you'll never see it again.' There were plenty of gaps in the brushwood pile for it to fall down – and you'd need a bulldozer to move it all. Black water gleamed at the bottom.

Fabio checked himself. I didn't give him time to think twice. I swiped up with my free arm, got a grip on his ankle and pulled as hard as I could. The wet kapok bark gave no traction. His foot slipped, he lost his balance and fell backwards.

My trapped hand came free. I grabbed a knot in the wood, the size of a medicine ball, and pushed myself up. I wanted to kick him while he was down, at least get the machete away – but Fabio was already up. He swung the blade at me and nearly took off my ear.

I ran down the tree trunk, wide as a hospital corridor. Further down, it spread even wider. Huge buttress roots rose like fins, creating valleys between them. The trunk became knotted and scarred, wounds from its earliest days when it was still small enough to have to fight.

The tree ended in a root ball so big it made a cliff. No way through – and Fabio was right behind me. Instinctively, I went the only way I could: out on to one of the root buttresses that stuck out like an aeroplane wing. Not a good move. Below me, a hollow opened in the woodpile like a well.

I turned. Fabio stood on the trunk, breathing hard.

'It's over.'

I held up the bag.

'One step closer and this goes in the water. Good luck dredging the swamp to find it.'

Fabio stayed put. 'So what – you stand there all day? Until when? Your arm gets so tired it wants to fall off. Maybe you need sleep?' He tapped his temple. Even through the dirt, I could see a horrible ulcerated blister spreading from the side of his nose down his cheek. 'I promise you, you go to sleep before I do.'

The helicopter didn't sound so loud any more. Had it given up? I imagined the pilots in their cockpit, arguing whether they had fuel for one more sweep, if they'd get overtime pay. It couldn't be long now.

Never taking my eyes off him, I reached inside the bag. Felt cool, hard glass. I pulled it out, the jar that Fabio had punched into my face last night.

All that was inside was the white lump I'd seen before, like a peeled potato slightly shrivelled.

'What's so valuable?'

Fabio stiffened. 'Be careful. That is solid gold.'

'I don't know what you're talking about.'

'When the Indians found Alvarado, they gave him the plant that makes him better. Purple flowers, tastes sweet like honey.'

I squinted at it. 'This is that?'

'The root. In the bag I have plants, flowers, cuttings.'

I thought of all the times Fabio had wandered off from the campsites. Crouching down, examining the plants by torchlight.

'So . . . you're a botanist?'

'A businessman. You drink Diet Coke?'

I wasn't sure I'd heard him right. 'Are you offering me a drink?'

'The magic ingredient in Diet Coke. You know what it is?'

'Caffeine?'

'Aspartame.' He said it carefully, pronouncing each unfamiliar syllable. 'You know this?'

'It's an artificial sweetener.'

'Artificial – exactly. And the others, too. The one you put in your coffee is made from methanol. The pink one is made from coal. No good. And the taste is not right, also.'

I glanced at the jar in my hand. 'You think you can make this into an artificial sweetener?'

'A *natural* sweetener. There is a company in United States, they pay millions of dollars for this. In Peru, other countries, people die because they have no food. In United States, they die because they eat too much. Is it true?'

'Pretty much.'

'If they can make food sweet with no calories, no chemicals, no funny taste – is more valuable than gold.'

'Isn't there a word for that?' I dredged it up from the back rooms of memory, one of the websites Cate bombarded me with before I came. 'Biopiracy?'

Fabio shrugged. 'I just want to go home. But maybe live nice life, OK?' He cracked a horrible smile. Two of his teeth had gone black; one was missing. 'Nobody can steal from the jungle. You only take what is there.'

He stretched out his hand. 'Give me. We share the money. All ok.'

The helicopter was coming closer again. The noise shivered through the tree and into my legs. Fabio beckoned me, still grinning. The other hand tightened his grip on the machete.

I was out of options. I held out the bag, dangling it open so he could see inside.

'You want this? Fifty-fifty?'

'Fifty-fifty, sure.' Fabio edged closer.

'Then get it yourself.'

With a twitch of my wrist, I threw the bag as high as I could. It spun in the air, spilling Fabio's jars over the swamp in all directions.

Fabio sprang at me. I'd expected it; invited it: I was ready. I caught his right wrist and bent it, forcing the machete out of his hand. Twisting, I tried to force him over the edge.

It was a good plan. But I was at the end of my strength – and Fabio was a street fighter. He twisted my arm back, grabbed me and pulled me towards him, scratching and kicking. I pulled away but he wouldn't let me go.

A heavy wind beat against my face. A shadow covered the sun. I flung myself towards Fabio, wrapping my arms round him to try to smother the blows. He sank his teeth into my arm. I jerked back, lost my balance . . .

Like a pair of demented lovers, we went over the edge.

48

Fabio landed on top of me. Ironically, that probably saved my life.

We'd fallen into a hollow like a giant bird's nest, a deep bowl in the tangled woodpile. Yellow and white slime streaked the walls; black water lapped at the bottom. Even through my pain, I noticed the stench.

The ground shifted. Like rolling around on a waterbed – except I wasn't moving. Powerful muscles twitched and rippled underneath me. So big, that even though I'd seen it I needed a few seconds to realise what it was.

I'd landed on a snake.

Still pinned under Fabio, I tipped my head back, trying to see where the snake ended. The coils seemed to go on for ever, metre after metre of tight-woven scales patterned black and yellow.

Fabio pushed off me and stood, crouching. The snake was moving away, I realised – I saw its head slithering towards a hole in the wood stack that led to open water. It didn't want to kill us, just to get away. I could identify with that.

Who knows how snakes think? If it changed its mind; if it had all been a feint; if it decided it simply didn't like us – I don't know. The head whipped round. The body coiled, then unleashed, flinging itself through the air like a javelin. The mouth went right over my head: a yawning mantrap ringed with rows and rows of pin-sharp teeth.

Fabio never stood a chance. A hundred and fifty kilos of snake travelling at warp ten knocked him flat on his back. That vast body wrapped him up in its coils and wrung him out like a tea towel. He opened his mouth to scream, but all the breath had been squeezed out of him. His eyes bulged; his shoulders writhed to get free.

The gaping mouth closed over his face, and I didn't have to look at him any more.

From the corner of my eye, I caught a movement. Something fast and violent heading towards me. I flinched back as it flew in front of my face, so close I swear I saw its orange eyes meet mine.

Another snake.

It flopped down and slithered away, gathering itself for another strike. In the corner, its mate seemed to have started swallowing Fabio's limp corpse. I saw black water lapping at the bottom of the hole in the floor, thought about diving for it. Not a good idea. I leaped for the side and tried to climb. Almost brought the whole mountain of wood on top of me.

The anaconda came at me again. I let go of the branch and dropped. A soup-plate-sized ring of teeth whistled past my ear. I fell to the floor.

The snake landed on top of me, a heavy weight that knocked the breath out of me. Moving already. It was like fighting Fabio again. Give it an inch, it would kill me. My only hope was to wrap myself round it and hug it for dear life, like a cowboy on a bronco. The stiff coils writhed against my chest; the snake bucked and rolled. I clung on.

Something stroked my back. Too late, I realised the snake had got its tail round me. The loop closed; immense muscles tightened against my chest.

This is how it feels to die. Strangely, mundanely, like running for a bus. Out of breath, knowing you've got to be there, knowing you'll never make it. The gap between hope and reality widening. Bright lights, big noise, and the smell of sulphur.

Then it was over. The pressure relaxed; I felt the weightless freedom of a soul without a body. I rose up, out of the snakepit and past the trees, through the canopy and into the wide open space beyond. The world spread out below me, a green ocean ringed with clouds. Just like the first time I saw it from the plane.

A face looked down at me from the clouds. I wondered if it was Jesus, and if he'd introduce me to Howie.

I flew away.

49

'Daddy?' Peggy's voice hits a spike of homesickness through my heart every time. 'When are you coming home?'

'I'm leaving tonight. I'll land in London tomorrow afternoon.'

'Did you catch a germ?'

'I'm all better now,' I promised.

'I got three stickers in school today.'

'Super. Well done.'

I closed my eyes and listened to her prattle on about her day. Then Cate came on the line.

'Are you still all right for cash?'

'Fine.' Landing in Puerto Tordoya with no possessions and no money hadn't been easy. Luckily I'd found a phone shop and managed to reverse the charges to Cate, who'd wired me enough cash for a hotel, a phone, clothes and a few other things I needed.

'I can send more.'

'I've got enough to get me to the airport. After that, it's an e-ticket, so as long as you're waiting at Heathrow . . .'

'We're both counting the hours. Peggy's made a banner for you.'

'I can't wait.'

I didn't have anything else to say. I hung on anyway, cherishing the silence.

'This must be costing a fortune,' said Cate. 'And Peggy has karate in a minute.'

I still didn't want to let her go. 'Listen. If anything happens to me before I get home . . .'

'*Happens to you?*' Cate gave a nervous laugh. 'You've done the dangerous bit. Business class all the way from here.'

'I love you.'

She sounded perplexed. 'I love you too.'

I turned off the phone and took out the battery. I crossed the dirt street. In daylight, Puerto Tordoya's hospital wasn't the nightmare I remembered when I brought Nolberto: just a clutch of breeze-block buildings with blue roofs, patients smoking on the verandas and chickens pecking the ground in between. I tried not to think about what I was about to do.

I'd been here every day since I came back: briefly as a

patient, afterwards as a visitor. It was a week since the helicopter had plucked me out of the jungle, into the waiting arms of the rescue crew. Low on fuel, they thought they were done; I was so far gone I nearly let them go. Raving, delirious, I'd made them go down and look for Drew. Fabio hadn't taken her far from the beach: a little way into the woods, where he'd hit her with the butt of the gun and left her to die. They found her unconscious, half drowned and bleeding from her head. I got off comparatively lightly.

When they got her to hospital, it turned out she had an infection. For three days, she was barely conscious. The doctors worried it could be malaria but there were moments, when the fever rose and everything she ate came up, when I wondered if it might be something worse. I pestered them to the point of hysteria about scrubbing up; I held her hand, and stared into her bloodshot eyes and trembled at the enormity of what I knew.

If you take this back to civilisation, it'll be World War Z.

I checked over my shoulder as I walked into the waiting room. I'd become paranoid. I hadn't seen Lorenzo since I got back, but I remembered what Tillman had said. *Rich gringo, family to think of. He can make you pay.* Apart from my daily trips to the hospital, and one to the market for supplies, I'd kept to my room. Even so – he was out there.

And who else? Sometimes, looking out of the window or crossing the street, I'd think I saw Tillman swaggering towards me. In the long hours sitting with Drew, my mind spun improbable scenarios: that he'd survived the falls, clung on to a log and gone downstream. Been picked up by a fisherman, or an illegal logger, nursed to health with rum, and hitched his way to Puerto Tordoya. If anyone could do it, he could.

I hadn't got used to the idea he wasn't coming back. None of them were.

The staff at the hospital knew me by now. They waved me through to Drew's room – a curtained-off corner of an overflowing ward. When I'd argued she should have a private room, to contain the infection, the doctors had looked at me as if I'd suggested parking her on the moon.

She was sitting up in bed in a hospital smock, reading the book I'd brought her. *Love in the Time of Cholera*. Her skin was pale, and a nasty bruise still inflamed her temple where she'd been hit, but she smiled when I poked my head in.

'Do I get to go home today?'

'Away from here, anyway. I got you these.'

I handed her a bag of clothes I'd bought from the market that morning. A T-shirt, a pair of cargo trousers and a set of underwear. I stood behind the curtain while she dressed. 'I had to guess at the sizes,' I mumbled. Everything she owned in Puerto Tordoya was in a stripy plastic bag next to the bed, a handful of things they'd found in her pockets. I'd insisted they burn everything else.

'Whatever happened to Nolberto?' she called through the curtain. 'Is he still here?'

'They transferred him to a military hospital in Lima. I tried to call, see how he was doing, but I couldn't get hold of him.'

'If he's still alive, he came out ahead.'

'Maybe.'

Drew stepped out. She'd lost more weight than I thought; the clothes were too baggy. She'd left her hair down to cover some of the bruises.

She saw the look on my face and gave me a chin-up smile.

'Is that a phone in your pants, or are you just happy to see me?'

I tapped my hip pocket. 'Would you believe it? Finally back in civilisation, and I forgot to charge the battery.'

'I need to call my mom, tell her I'm OK.'

'I'll plug it in at the hotel.' I grinned. 'I've booked us a room. Best place in town.'

A motorcycle taxi – a souped-up rickshaw – took us to the harbour. We squeezed together on the back seat and Drew held my hand. I wondered if she could feel it trembling.

'Everything you've done ... "Thank you" seems inadequate.'

On the windscreen, a plastic Virgin made eyes at me over the driver's shoulder. 'We got each other through.'

The taxi stopped outside the hostel, where Nolberto had brought me that jet-lagged day I landed. Just a month ago: it was like a different life. The hostel owner waved to us from her plastic chair. I couldn't tell if she recognised Drew, but I knew what she was thinking.

Drew looked up at the naked concrete, the peeling sign. 'I never thought I'd be happy to see this place again.'

The room wasn't much different to last time. Two beds pushed together to make one, under a ragged mosquito net. Harsh tropical light coming through the dirty gauze curtains.

'Best room in the house,' I joked. 'I even got us en suite.'

A toilet, a basin and a shower head were crammed into a corner, behind a short partition wall. No door or curtain.

'Don't tell your wife about this.' She saw me flinch at the mention of Cate. 'Sorry.'

'There's a lot of things my wife doesn't need to know,' I said, trying to make a joke of it. I plugged the phone into a power socket that hung off the wall like a dislocated eyeball. Nothing happened.

'Power's off.'

'They only run it between seven and ten,' Drew remembered. She threw herself on to the bed, arching her back. 'God, this feels good. If I never see another hammock again . . .'

She couldn't stay still. She swung her legs off the bed and

stood. She pulled the T-shirt over her head. Her hands moved to the fly of her trousers.

'I need a shower,' she said, and her voice was suddenly very different.

'Not much privacy, I'm afraid,' I said, ignoring the fact she was already almost topless.

Wild memories from Fabio's fever-dream potion flashed in front of my eyes. Drew took two steps towards me. Her fingers played with the buttons of my shirt.

'I was kind of hoping you could scrub my back.'

Our eyes met, and at last there was no ambiguity. No blurred lines; just a single, stark choice.

She'd already finished with my buttons. She bent her hands behind her back to unclasp her bra.

I'm not proud of my reaction. I didn't think of Cate, or what Peggy would say if she saw her daddy like this. None of that was real. I was back in the dream, an acid flashback of the best trip I'd ever had. All I could feel was how much I wanted her.

The bra dropped to the floor. Drew didn't take her eyes off me. She reached up and spread my shirt apart, back down my arms. Her gaze dropped to my throat.

I put my hand there and felt the cold black mineral of Anton's shark's tooth. It had stayed on ever since he gave it to me at the bottom of the cliff. *I make my own luck.* The day before he died.

She swayed, letting her breasts rub against my chest. She stretched up and gave me a long, penetrating kiss.

'Isn't this what you've been wanting since Mexico?'

I pushed her away from me. God it was hard.

'Get dressed.'

She stood there half naked, looking as if I'd slapped her in the face.

'Is it your wife? I didn't think . . .' She shrugged. 'I guess I misunderstood.'

'We need to talk.'

'I'm going to have that shower.' She tried to move past me. I blocked the way.

'Put your clothes on.'

I reached in my pocket and took out a small plastic bottle. She stopped. 'What's that?'

'You tell me.' I pointed to the bag with her things from the hospital, sitting on a plastic chair. 'I found it in there.'

'You went through my stuff?'

'I was looking for a phone number so I could call your parents.' I held up the bottle so she could see the label. 'Blackwater 102b Antiviral Medication.'

Her eyes flickered over it. Calculating.

'It belonged to Menendez,' she said. 'I found it in the cave.'

'Menendez's bottles were the *vaccine*.' I stared her down. She was almost naked, but my eyes didn't register that. 'This is antidote. Antidote to a vaccine. You know what that means?'

'I don't care.' She pulled on her trousers and the T-shirt. 'You want to get back to your wife and kid? Fine. Don't take it out on me.'

'You didn't meet Anton by accident. And you weren't working for an NGO. You were right: there was someone in our group cleaning up after Menendez. But it wasn't Zia, or Tillman, and it wasn't because there was anything wrong with the vaccine. It worked perfectly. *Didn't it?*'

'Listen to yourself. You're deranged.'

I saw her eyeing up the door. I leaned against it and folded my arms. I'd lost a lot of strength in the jungle, but I was still a head taller. She'd been lying in bed eating hospital food for a week.

'Menendez thought he was vaccinating Indians. Instead, he was killing them. A deadly virus you can put into food, and be long gone before it takes effect. Shame it had to be tested on the Indians, but no one's going to miss them, are they? Maybe no one'll notice. Uncontacted tribes, maybe they were never there in the first place.'

'I don't have to listen to this bullshit.'

'Who does that? What sort of sick person introduces a killer virus into the wild? Even the oil companies probably draw the line at that.'

Drew's composure was cracking. Her head twitched as she stared around the room: the window that wouldn't open, the door I'd blocked. I could feel the rage rising in her like a caged animal. I remembered the feel of the rifle in my hand, that day we shot the pigs, and I wished I had one now.

'I don't work for the oil company.'

'You're certainly not a missionary.' Looking at her now, all I could think of was the anaconda coiled in the pit. 'I had a lot of time to think while you were in hospital. My best guess, you work for the CIA, or someone like them. You used Menendez as a stooge to test your nasty new bioweapon, and when he didn't come back you piggybacked Anton to see what happened.'

Drew sat on the bed. I didn't delude myself that meant she was backing down.

'Meeting Anton was dumb luck, just the way I told you. I came out of the ministry and ran right into him.' She smoothed the bedsheet where it had got rumpled. 'For what it's worth, I liked him.'

'That's another thing.'

I reached in my pocket. Drew tensed, then relaxed when she saw what it was: a postage-stamp square of blue plastic. I held it up.

'I found this in your trousers. Right in the bottom of the pocket: it nearly went in the incinerator. It's the memory card from Menendez's camera.'

She pretended she didn't understand. 'I thought we lost it.'

'Anton kept it in his wallet.'

'He must have given it to me.'

'It was in his wallet when he went over the cliff. When you pushed him off.' I'd worked that out three days ago. It hadn't got any easier to stomach. 'Then you went down on the rope and stole his wallet. I suppose you were worried something in the photos might incriminate you. You used him.'

'*Used him?* This was his dream. He'd never have gotten his expedition off the ground without me. Howie, Fabio, Zia . . . You were the same. You were all in it for what you could get.'

'What I wanted didn't involve mass murder.'

An impasse. We stared each other down, two people who could hardly stand to look at each other. Drew scratched at a hole in the mosquito net.

'So why did you bring me here? Are you going to call the police? The newspapers? You think you can get some kind of revenge? *Justice?*'

The room was hot and airless; worse than the jungle. I stole a glance at the sink in the bathroom. I was dying for a glass of water, if I didn't think Drew might use the glass to cut my throat.

'I want to make a deal. My silence for my safety. Whoever you work for, if they're happy to wipe out whole tribes of Indians – not to mention Anton, Howie and everyone else – I don't suppose they'll have any qualms taking out a British doctor.'

Her lip curled. 'Who are you, Edward Snowden? You've got nothing.'

'I've got the blood sample I took from Howie, and the antiviral from your bottle. Sequence them, and I bet you'll find one matches the other, almost as if they were made for each other. You had the cure in your pocket the whole time, and you let him die like that.'

She actually looked bored. 'Are you expecting me to admit something?'

'I don't want to go into hiding in the Ecuadorean embassy, I don't want to be locked up in Guantanamo Bay, and I certainly don't want my family to die in a hit-and-run on a country lane one dark night.'

'Life's unpredictable.'

I could feel panic rising inside me. I had to get out of there. 'Do we have a deal?'

'Don't be ridiculous.'

I took two steps across the room and grabbed her shoulders. My thumbs dug into the soft hollows of her collarbone, and it would have been so easy to go for the throat.

'Tell whoever you work for to leave me alone. The samples and the antibodies are already in a parcel on their way to my solicitor, along with a copy of the photographs and a very long letter that explains everything. If anything happens to me – today, tomorrow, or in ten years' time – everything becomes public.'

'You think that's acceptable?'

'I'll find out.'

I held on a moment longer, inches from her face. Her kiss lingered on my mouth, a bitter taste I was desperate to wash out. I stared into her eyes, waiting for something. Remorse? Guilt? Regret? Anything.

Nothing. I let go, and pushed her back on the bed.

'I'm going home.'

I left her in the room and locked the door. I didn't think it would hold for two minutes, but at least it was a head start. I ran down the concrete stairs, past the woman in her plastic chair and out on to the riverfront. At the bottom of the bank, the brown river flowed by without a ripple.

A taxi was waiting, a big silver 4x4 sprayed with mud. I jumped in.

'*¿A dónde vas?*' said the driver.

'*Aeropuerto*,' I told him. 'Puerto Maldonado.' I wasn't staying in Puerto Tordoya one minute more. Drew must have friends. She wouldn't need longer than it took to get hold of a phone to contact them. We might have made a deal (or we might not), but I didn't imagine she'd honour it if she could avoid it.

The car took off with a spray of mud. Schoolgirls ran past on their way home, immaculate in their uniforms, white blouses and grey pinafores. The only clean thing in that whole dirty jungle.

I didn't look back.

Epilogue

Maybe you're wondering if it worked out for me. So am I.

Howie's blood sample, Drew's antiviral pills and the memory card are in a safety deposit box. Tomorrow, this narrative will go in there too. My solicitor has the key, and instructions to open it if anything happens to me or my family. I've done what I said. Every day – every van that parks outside our house, every night Cate's late back from work, every time school calls about Peggy – I wonder if they, whoever *they* are, will keep their side of the bargain. If we even have one.

Perhaps you're disappointed. You wanted me to be a hero, to show Paititi to the world and expose what Drew did, so Anton didn't die in vain.

I wanted to be the hero too. I'm sorry.

I thought life had short-changed me, that I deserved an adventure. The starring role. That's why I went to the jungle, and I can't complain: I got everything I wanted. River gorges, rope bridges ruined cities. I lost count of the number of times I felt I was living in a film. I faced death, for Christ's sake, and won. It didn't feel all that special.

Anton's ex-wife came to see me a few days ago. We'd been emailing for a couple of months; she'd got my address from Anton's account. I tried everything to put her off. I told her I couldn't afford the flight to San Diego; that I had nothing to add; that I hardly knew Anton beyond those few weeks together.

One morning I woke up to an email that said she'd bought a ticket and was coming the next weekend.

'I had to see you,' she told me, almost before she was inside the front door. 'You were with him at the end.'

She wasn't what I'd expected. Not a hippie chick or a surfer girl gone to seed. She was petite and self-contained, and looked as if she worked in a bank. She wore a lot of make-up. A gangly, long-haired boy trailed in behind her. I stared into his face, certain that Anton's strong personality must have left its mark. But he had his mother's eyes, and none of his father's energy.

I gave them tea. She perched on the edge of the sofa, holding the cup as if she didn't know what to do with it. The boy fiddled with his phone and looked embarrassed.

'His body . . . The insurance company aren't giving me any money.' She looked around the room, and I knew she was pricing up my life. Photos of us skiing or on beaches in Bali, the Maldives, South Africa and Mexico; the his'n'hers iPads; Cate's grand piano. I could see her weighing it against me. 'I thought maybe you could . . .'

'No amount of money will bring him back,' I said piously.

'I know. But if I only had something to bury . . .'

There were a lot of things I could have said to that. If I'd kept Fabio's video camera, I could have shown her what Anton's body would be by now.

'Anton died doing what he loved,' I told her firmly. 'He was a remarkable man. He's at peace.'

I sipped my tea, and wished she'd go away. The final, lingering guest at a party when you're desperate for bed.

'What was the last thing he said to you?' she asked.

I thought back. It must have been that night on the pyramid, relieving me from guard duty.

'He said, "No problem."'

She liked that. 'It sounds like Anton.'

TOM HARPER

'It does.'

Another silence. She'd come all that way: I wished I could do more, but I had nothing to say to her. Under my shirt, I could feel Anton's shark's tooth, hard and sharp against my throat. I knew I should take it off, maybe give it to the kid. She'd have appreciated that. But I needed all the luck I could get.

'Do you think it really exists?' she said at last. 'His lost city.'

I thought she might ask that. I had my answer ready.

'If we ever found it, it wouldn't be lost any more.'

After she'd left, with false promises we'd keep in touch, I poured myself a glass of wine and sat alone in the living room. It was going to rain. Outside the French windows, clouds gathered over London in an immense darkness. I stared at the room numbly, seeing it through her eyes. So privileged. So *comfortable*. The perfect life, Anton called it.

We live, as we die, alone.

And the man who wrote that was an optimist.

Afterword

The lost city of Paititi is real, as far as legends go. Andrea Lopez's story of his visit there was discovered in the Vatican archives a few years ago, though I invented the tale of Diego Alvarado. Huascar's golden chain, the golden sun from the high temple in Cuzco and the mummies of the fourteen Inca emperors are all treasures rumoured to be there. The petroglyphs in this book are based on the unexplained carvings at Palotoa Pusharo, which I visited. The guardian that Kel finds is similar to an intriguing rock structure discovered by Diego Cortijo in 2013.

Every year, expeditions go searching for Paititi in the unexplored regions of Peru and Bolivia; most of them come back. The expedition in this book, and the people who go on it, are entirely fictional. Any similarities to actual expeditions and explorers are entirely coincidental. And, frankly, worrying.

If you're going into the jungle, you have to know who to trust. Unlike Kel, I was exceptionally lucky with my travelling companions in the Peruvian Amazon. Fernando Rivera of EcoManu Peru was everything you could want in a guide: knowledgeable, reliable, resourceful and always good-humoured. The trip he organised took me to places I never imagined I'd see. Kevin Anderson battled wild Indians, ravenous jaguars, snakes, poisonous snails and a full suite of tropical diseases (mostly, it has to be said, in his imagination) to come with me. At time of writing, he's OK. Thanks also to Simon, Ray, Vicky, Callixto, Roberto, Moises and everyone else who drove, steered, pushed and fed us through the jungle. And special mention to Virginia, who loaned us her balsa raft when ours got washed away by the storm.

Back home, I'm very grateful to Carlos Remon for taking on the challenge of teaching me Spanish; to Dr Tim Thompson for advice on decomposing bodies; to Claire McGowan for telling me about Mexico; to Michael Ridpath for an aphorism about the jungle; and to the Fitzgerald Kay family, who won a character-naming auction in aid of Knavesmire School. In the wilder jungles of the manuscript, I was expertly guided by Oliver Johnson and Anne Perry, who carried a lot of the baggage. Kerry Hood made extraordinary things happen. My agent Jane Conway-Gordon frightened off predators.

There are several long-suffering wives in this story, letting their menfolk go off on dubious adventures in Peru. Mine is one of them. I'm grateful to her for indulging me; and to my children, who never let me forget how exciting this all is. As long as I'm home for bedtime.

THRILLINGLY GOOD BOOKS FROM CRIMINALLY GOOD WRITERS

CRIME FILES BRINGS YOU THE LATEST RELEASES FROM TOP CRIME AND THRILLER AUTHORS.

GN UP ONLINE FOR OUR MONTHLY NEWSLETTER AND BE THE FIRST TO KNOW ABOUT OUR COMPETITIONS, NEW BOOKS AND MORE.